SON OF THE DROWNED EMPIRE

FRANKIE DIANE MALLIS

SEVEN QUEENS PRESS

SON OF THE DROWNED EMPIRE

FRANKIE DIANE MALLIS

Cover Design by Stefanie Saw, Seventh Star Art

Undercover Design by Saint Jupiter

Character Art by Tony Viento

Map Art by K.C. Hayes

Hardcover ISBN: 978-1-957014-09-8

Paperback ISBN: 978-1-957014-10-4

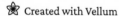 Created with Vellum

This one's for you, for when you had to save yourself.

DROWNED EMPIRE SERIES RECOMMENDED READING ORDER

1. Daughter of the Drowned Empire (Drowned Empire #1)
2. Guardian of the Drowned Empire (Drowned Empire #2)
3. Solstice of the Drowned Empire (Drowned Empire #0.5)
4. Lady of the Drowned Empire (Drowned Empire #3)
5. Son of the Drowned Empire (Drowned Empire #1.5)

CONTENT WARNING

Dear Reader, please be advised of the following topics before you begin:
- Narcissistic, psychological, and emotional abuse
- Domestic violence
- Depression
- Misogyny
- Violence
- Sexual coercion
- References to off-page rape
- Grooming of hero as a child/attempted CSA

SOLSTICE OF THE DROWNED EMPIRE

PREVIOUSLY

Lord Rhyan Hart, Heir Apparent to the Arkasva, High Lord of Glemaria, Imperator to the North has been forced to accompany his hateful, and abusive father on an official state visit to Bamaria, the summer he's nineteen.

After a miserable and lengthy journey filled with his father's abuse, to the southernmost part of the Empire, Rhyan comes face to face with Lady Lyriana Batavia, the third Heir to the Arkasva. Nine years earlier on his last and only other visit to her country when they were kids, she'd invited him into her library to read, and share cake. Though a small gesture for her, it left an impression on Rhyan who's lonely and abused. His impression of Lyr is only intensified as he takes her in now: grown up, intelligent, and breathtakingly beautiful.

Barely able to keep his eyes off her, Rhyan tries to get through the court proceedings without drawing attention to his attraction for Lyr. But his father quickly notices.

It is then, his father tells him he's considering a marriage contract between their countries, one that would force Lyr to marry their beastly warlord, Arkturion Kane. Rhyan's father has always hurt Rhyan, physically and emotionally. But since he secretly unbound Rhyan prior to his Revelation Ceremony, forcing Rhyan to hide a secret—he's vorakh, his abuse has expanded to others. And Rhyan suspects that he intends to make Lyr the latest pawn in his schemes to control him and his secret.

The only way Rhyan can keep Lyr safe from this fate is to pretend he doesn't care for her at all. And that means convincing Lyr as well.

Rhyan attends dinner at the fortress with Lyr, her two sisters, and her cousin Jules, along with the other Bamarian nobles—including Lord Tristan Grey. His plan to act like an asshole and turn Lyr away from him becomes more urgent as his father's counterpart in the Empire, Imperator Kormac, ruler of the southern countries, arrives at dinner. Rhyan's father has no jurisdiction in the South to force Lyr's father into a marriage contract, but Imperator Kormac does. Rhyan spends the dinner acting cold, and harsh toward Lyr and everyone else. But when the Imperator corners Jules, sexually harassing her, and no one dares to intervene against the powerful ruler, Rhyan steps between them. Still playing his role, he pretends he has his own ill intentions for Jules and manages to get her to safety away from the dinner and Imperator.

Hiding in his room, Jules thanks Rhyan for stepping in and asks if there's anything she can do to repay him. Knowing they both want to keep Lyr safe, but not yet able to trust Jules with his secrets, Rhyan asks her to pretend that something truly did happen between them. Jules seems suspicious of his request but agrees, and an unlikely alliance and friendship begins.

The following morning, Rhyan's father beats him for his

actions—angry he dared to come between an Imperator and his desire. Later that day, Rhyan's uncle Sean, an ex-pat from Glemaria who now resides in Bamaria with his fiancée, comes to visit and cheer him up.

They visit Gryphon Island, the beach which holds a giant gryphon statue Sean thought Rhyan would appreciate—knowing his love for the creatures.

But Rhyan's upset, wishing someone would say something about his abuse—or step in to help. Sean admits he knows what's going on, but he can't do anything as Rhyan's father has bound him from speaking. If Sean breaks the blood oath, he'll die, but he's trying to support Rhyan in any way he can.

Still angry, Rhyan pushes Sean—an action that throws him across the beach. Horrified and confused at his sudden burst of strength, Rhyan apologizes. His own power was magically bound by his father so he shouldn't have had the strength. He eyes the gryphon statue suspiciously, but the burst of strength does not come again. It's then that Rhyan notices two Afeya walking along the shore—one male, one female. The male Rhyan had seen once before—his first day in Bamaria—in the library with him, watching Lyriana.

Uneasy at the appearance of the immortals, Sean urges Rhyan to remember he's strong, and that he's not like his father. Maybe he can't control what happens to him, but he can control how he reacts and find his own strength.

A few weeks later, Bamaria is ready to celebrate the summer solstice. Jules has kept her word to Rhyan but has continually tried to coax him out of his shell to have fun. But Rhyan fears slipping. Every time he sees Lyr, he forgets how to act, so consumed with his feelings for her—feelings he both hopes and fears she reciprocates.

But the solstice celebration is interrupted by the reappearance of the Imperator, who has come to meet with Rhyan's father again. Suspecting that they're attempting to finalize the marriage contract, Rhyan attends the party.

While trying to avoid watching Lyr dance, and getting into a small fight with Lord Tristan who made it known he's aware of the torch Rhyan carries for her, he follows his father and Imperator Kormac into the woods.

But the two leaders disappear and Rhyan comes upon the Afeya once more. This time they're discussing their plans to lure Lyr into a dance, and a deal. Horrified, Rhyan rushes onto the dance floor, breaking all of his own rules, and asks Lyr to dance.

She's stunned, but agrees, and Rhyan takes her hand, a move which drives the Afeya away. As the song ends, his desire for Lyr is overwhelming, and he knows he can't stay with her for fear his father will notice.

Lyr isn't ready to leave his side. Not wanting to hurt her any more than he has all summer, he agrees to flee the dance floor with her. They end up deep in the woods, leaning against a sun tree, talking and growing closer. They kiss.

Rhyan's bodyguard, Bowen, interrupts, ordering Rhyan to see his father.

Rhyan awakes the following morning in a prison cell. His father is furious at him for his games. He knows his son is in love with Lyr, and he's more determined than ever to finalize the marriage contract. For the first time in his life, Rhyan fights back. He hits his father, surprised again at his strength.

Rhyan's father orders a mage to bind Rhyan again, this time with ropes Rhyan can see. Ropes that will torture him and remind him of his father's control.

With all the cruelty he's experienced, Rhyan can't understand why his father simply doesn't order a blood oath on him. Rhyan's bodyguard tells him his father would never put a blood oath on him, knowing Rhyan would break it and that it would kill him. And Rhyan's father wants him alive.

Rhyan realizes the one piece of leverage he has to protect Lyr, is to sacrifice himself and expose his secret vorakh to the Imperator. If Rhyan were to do so, he'd not only forfeit his life, but his father's as well.

Finally, Rhyan has his father's word that he'll end marriage negotiations. But he warns Rhyan he'll pay for interfering. He didn't want control of Lyr for Rhyan's sake, but because she has the potential to unleash more power and destruction than the Empire has ever seen.

Rhyan acts cold when he sees Lyr, letting her know that whatever existed between them, is now over. When Jules comes to Rhyan angry over breaking Lyr's heart, he admits his own is broken, too. Though he won't admit what he did, he lets Jules know Lyr is safe for now, and that he's returning home.

Jules admits she'll miss him, and that she grew to care for him as a friend. He feels the same, and says goodbye, never expecting to see her again. But Jules reminds him, "Anything is possible." And Rhyan leaves to return home, heartbroken, but with the smallest spark of hope.

THE GLEMARIAN COUNCIL

Arkasva, Devon Hart (also Imperator to the North)
    Master of the Horse, Draken Hart
    Arkturion, Kane Gaddayan
    Turion, Efraim Aravain
    Arkmage, Connal Hilson
    Master of Education, Breanna Shivan
    Master of Spies, Aevan Chandor
    Master of Finance, Blayne DeKassas
    Master of Law, Finn Teledor
    Naturion, Darragh Gaddayan
    Senator, Balyr Oryyan
    Master of Peace, Ronan DeTerria

LUMERIAN OCEAN

N

GLEM HARBOR

A'LYROTZ PRISON

THORNE FIELDS

CITY OF HARTON

ARAVIA

GLEMARIA

LUMERIAN OCEAN

N

LETHEA

ARAN

GRYPHON ISLAND

IA

MERIAN EMPIRE
ERIA NUTAVIA

THE FIRST SCROLL:

GLEMARIA

CHAPTER
ONE

(O*ne year after solstice)*

"Shhh," I whispered. "I've got you now. I've —*fuck!*"

The baby gryphon squawking like a maniac in my arms had been absolutely feral since I found him and had just attempted to bite a chunk out of my hand.

"Godsdamnit," I growled. "I'm trying to help you."

As a show of gratitude for saving his life, the little beast bit me again, this time drawing blood. Drops fell to my bedroom floor before I could stop them, and I shook my head. I was always cleaning up blood.

The gryphon's eyes snapped up to mine, pale silver and full of innocence and confusion. I sighed in defeat. His heart was beating too quickly against my palm, his tiny body shaking. He was scared. Hurt. Definitely hungry.

My own stomach grumbled.

I could relate.

Yelling at him obviously wasn't helping. So, I cradled the little beast against my chest, smoothing the back of his head,

1

and gently squeezing his neck where his baby furs shifted to feathers. "It's all right now," I soothed. My aura flared out, covering him in the cold his species preferred, winter cold, Glemarian cold, the cold that clung to my body at all times since my aura had been released.

His eyes closed, and with the tiniest pathetic squawk, he at last snuggled against me—at least, he snuggled as much as a gryphon could. I pulled him closer. "That's a good boy," I gritted through my teeth, the wounds on my palms smarting.

Shifting him so his baby legs were exposed, I was able to see his left back leg hadn't been merely twisted like I'd thought, but broken, explaining the ruckus outside my window. I'd spotted him immediately and without thinking made my way down the mountain's side, not expecting to fight for my life as I tried to save his.

Had he been right under my window, the rescue would have been simple—a quick opening of the glass panes and one grab, and it'd have been over. But he'd been quite a way below, stuck on a jut of Gryphon's Mount, lying helplessly with nowhere to go. Too young to fly, he should have had only three options: one, to fall to his death; two, to be scooped up by another gryphon, if one was willing to touch him; or, three, to starve until death claimed him.

The secret I carried, the ability I'd been forced to hide for over a year and a half, had made me his unlikely fourth option. I was vorakh, cursed with forbidden magic—traveling—the third and most feared of the three powers banned by the Lumerian Empire. This magic had allowed me to vanish from my bedroom and land on the side of the mountain beneath my Ka's fortress. The toes of my boots had desperately clung to the rock as I wrestled the terrified gryphon into my arms while my soturion cloak flapped wildly in the breeze.

I slipped and nearly fell to my death three times before I'd wrangled him out of his nook and reappeared with us both in my bedroom, my chest heaving from exertion. Bells had pounded into the cold morning sky, announcing the hour. It was the tail-end of summer, and we were still experiencing our warmest days of the year, but being this far north meant our mornings remained chilly—though not chilly enough to keep me from getting drenched during my rescue mission. My sweat had already turned cold against my forehead and neck.

Now, my own heart was hammering as the reality of what I'd done sank in. I'd broken *his* rules. I risked everything I'd sworn to protect—everything I fought for, suffered for— without even a second thought. All for one crying gryphon.

I squeezed my eyes shut, my stomach churning. *Fuck.* I'd been so good; I hadn't traveled for an entire month. It'd felt as if, after a year of forcing my will and tempering down my emotions, I'd finally gotten the power under control, and found the strength to suppress it. Gaining dominance over it, over my emotions, had been necessary, not just to avoid his wrath, but because he knew when I slipped. He always knew. And he always punished accordingly because if anyone else ever discovered the truth—if anyone else saw me vanish or suddenly appear—our lives were forfeit. Not just mine and his, but my mother's also. One slip, one mistake, and there'd be a one-way trip to Lethea for my Ka.

And one did not come back from Lethea.

I bit the inner corner of my cheek, as I perked up my ears for any shouts of my father's guards coming to drag me before him. Bowen, my personal escort and bodyguard, sometimes yelled my name to wake me, even on mornings I was permitted to sleep in. This had been one of those mornings. The Glemarian Academy was not yet in session. We were a week past Auriel's Feast Day. Tonight, we would celebrate the Oath

3

Ceremony, the forming of *kashonim* between apprentices and the newly made novice mages and soturi.

Technically, I'd been on break from classes for the past week. I was still required to train for the purposes of maintaining my strength and stamina, but I was free to appear in the Katurium whenever I felt like it. I could train as long as I pleased. I would lose this freedom in two days' time when the Academy's classes resumed, and I returned to my apprentice's brutal training regimen.

If Bowen had any idea that I'd spent part of my morning dangling from the side of the mountain after having used forbidden magic to get to it, I was fucked. He'd never admit it out loud, as he'd never be allowed to speak such things even if he wanted to, but Bowen knew my secret, too. No one could spend as many hours as he did guarding me and not know the truth about my vorakh. I had no doubt he'd reported me to my father each time he witnessed my body fade in and out of existence, confirming what my Imperator and my Arkasva already seemed to know.

The bells came to a crashing halt, a cool breeze singing in their absence. The wind carried the deep squawking growls of the fully grown gryphons soaring overhead.

The one in my arms whimpered as the clouds passed and the bright golden sun streamed through my window. And only then, safely removed from the shadows of the cliff and the danger of falling to our deaths, did I get a real look at what I'd risked my life for. There'd been a reason I'd seen him so easily from afar, a reason I'd launched into action, and a reason he'd been in danger.

My throat tightened. This was no Glemarian gryphon I held. His feathers were not made of the muted grays and browns of the creatures that filled our skies. They were not even the bronze or silver of the prized gryphons we'd bred and raised for centuries. This little one had feathers and fur made of the brightest, most fiery red.

Batavia red.

The thought came so suddenly I almost stumbled forward.

My stomach twisted, the backs of my eyes on fire, before I brushed all memories of *her* away. Her name in the back of my thoughts felt like a dream I could barely grasp, one I struggled to recall. And yet... she was a dream whose images had been burned into my mind. Branded onto my body. Imprinted onto my heart.

My soul.

Hazel eyes flecked with gold stared up at me beneath the golden leaves of the sun tree. The scent of vanilla musk in the air wrapped around my body, and the warm breeze of a summer night blew through my hair as her soft fingers tangled in my curls at the nape of my neck. Her gasp was a kiss against my lips, leaving shivers all over my body. My blood pumping...

I blinked back the image and shook off the sensation.

She was safe. That was all that mattered. She was safe because of me; I'd bargained with the only thing I had left in the fight—my secret. My shame. My silence. All I had possessed had been given freely in exchange for her freedom.

One year ago, I'd sworn to my father that if he touched her, if he set his sights on her again, I'd reveal our secret. I'd damn the whole Ka, my family, and even my mother. It had been the first battle against him I ever won, but the victory had cost me.

And just like that, there was a flash of black ropes tied around my hands and arms. Too tight, too hot. My skin burned and itched; my breath came short.

No. No.

I blinked, and the ropes vanished. My arms were clear, my hands unbound.

I took a deep breath. I was alone in my room holding the

gryphon. No ropes bound my body. There was nothing tied around me. There never would be again. As long as I stayed under his radar, as long as I kept our secret, I was safe. *She* was safe.

That was more than I could say for the little one in my arms, twitching in his sleep.

The red feathers and fur were not natural to Glemaria, nor any part of the Lumerian Empire.

I'd rescued an Afeyan gryphon.

I had been horrified when I'd realized a baby was trapped down there, but I hadn't stopped to think, to question *why?* Now I knew. It was his Afeyan coloring that damned him.

Gryphons were sacred in Glemaria. For centuries, they'd appeared on the sigil of Ka Hart: silver gryphon wings beneath a golden sun. We'd even named the Godsdamned mountain we were on after them. The beasts filled our skies, patrolled hourly for akadim, and transported us back and forth across the north. Severe fines were given to anyone found guilty of harm or cruelty to the animals. Worse punishments had been written into law for the purposeful or accidental killing of gryphons, but only if they were of the Lumerian breeds.

When Afeyan gryphons from the Night Lands crossed into our territory, they were to be shot down on sight. I'd only heard of it happening a dozen times in my life, though in the last year alone, that number had tripled. It was as if the Night Lands were testing our defenses, trying to see how hard they could push, how many of their brightly colored gryphons they could send through our skies before we'd retaliate or figure out what the hell their purpose was. Afeya were always up to something, and it was never good. I knew that well.

And here I was, harboring the enemy, saving his life.

Rescuing a hurt baby gryphon should have made me a hero in my father's court. Were I to be caught with this one, though... I looked down at him, his red feathers soft, his eyes so big, shiny, trusting. He was just a baby. I couldn't abandon him.

Whatever game the Afeya or Queen Ishtara were playing at, this creature was innocent.

I sucked on my bleeding finger and wrapped the gryphon more tightly in my cloak, hiding his body, drawing on my aura to keep him cold and quiet. Then, I headed toward my door. I still hadn't heard a word from behind it nor received any summons from my father. Possibly, I was in the clear. But still, my heart pounded and my body tensed. I was risking a lot. And for what?

I unbolted the lock and opened my bedroom door.

"Morning, your grace." Bowen was leaning against the wall opposite my room, his eyes half-open, not even looking at me.

I strode forward and slapped his shoulder with my free hand. "My enemies are truly trembling at my defenses."

He opened one eye all the way, a retort on the edge of his lips, before he shrugged, pushing his leathers back into place over his shoulder.

Bowen was more of a statement than a true protector when I was home. No enemy would dare attack me here—except for one, the one whom Bowen dared not stop. And because of that, he was often sleeping on the job, or not even paying attention at all. Except when he could get me in trouble.

"Katurium?" he asked, eyeing my armor.

I locked my elbow against my side, my green cloak concealing the gryphon. "No. I'm off to Artem's," I announced, knowing Bowen hated the stench of the stables more than anything. Hopefully, that would keep him from following too closely.

He cursed under his breath as I'd expected, and only as I

rounded the hall did I hear his footsteps pick up, echoing on the gray stone floor behind me.

The gryphon squeaked, suddenly alert, and I coughed loudly to cover up the sound before craning my head forward and cooing, "*Shhh, tovayah, tovayah.*"

He calmed and quieted, but if he made another sound, I was fucked. I picked up my speed, my pulse racing, both out of nerves at the thought of being caught and at the effort it took to not let my emotions take me away. I had to walk calmly but quickly; I could not allow my magic to interfere and transport me to my destination.

I'd become rather good at stopping my magic, but I could always slip without warning.

A few minutes later, I'd made my way outside, a practiced scowl on my face as I passed a line of my father's personal soturi. Their blank eyes seemed to glaze over me, I'd learned long ago not to drop my guard before them. They were obsessively, annoyingly aware of every move made by the Heir Apparent to the Arkasva and Imperator to the North. My father would have their heads if they fucked up.

Luckily, my habit of spending early mornings in the stables was well known, and it had been a long time since they'd really paid attention to my current route. Still, I held my breath, eyeing them as I passed, my scowl deepening. Handpicked by my father, every soturion standing before me was a right-shit asshole. Right-shit assholes forced to bow as I passed.

I pulled open the gates and was immediately blasted with the pungent scents of fresh gryphon-shit and hay. My little gryphon squawked to life, wings fluttering inside my cloak.

"Shhh!" I hissed. "Not yet."

I stepped forward into the stables, built like a giant arena. This was the training ground for gryphons, the place where they learned to transport us, to hunt what we sought, to follow our orders, and to remember their place.

Each stable was built with open walls that reached toward the domed ceiling; seven stories high. I greeted several of the stable hands, carefully making my way toward the stalls closest to Artem's office. He was occupied, dealing with a fully grown gryphon who'd been rather moody the past few weeks.

Before I could announce myself, Artem turned, having sensed me. He'd been doing that since I was a boy. "Good morning, Lord Rhyan, your grace."

His gruff voice rose above the chaos of the gryphon calls. He stepped back from his stall and slapped his thigh—his version of a bow since he had a bad back—then returned to his post. His gaze focused on the gryphon before him. "Down!" he yelled. "*Dorscha!*" The beast sat back on its giant haunches; its beak turned in submission. It received a nod from Artem, who tossed a steak into the air.

The gryphon's wings spread, its talons lifting from the ground as it flew up to catch its breakfast. With a surge of energy, its bronzed wings flapped, creating a gust of wind that pushed the hay across its stall out toward Artem. I'd seen this happen so many times, I was positive the scent of hay sticks and gryphon-shit had been permanently etched into Artem's body.

The gryphon growled as it came to a halt from a tug on its leg by the rope that kept it grounded. The baby squeaked in response, shaking and suddenly very awake and once more feral in my arms.

"Lord Rhyan." There was a warning note in Artem's voice as his eyes pierced me. Two fuzzy eyebrows turned down as he observed the rapid movements behind my cloak and the look of guilt across my face. "The fuck did you do now?"

I gave him a rather purposeful cough, my eyebrows

narrowed. To be fair, I had already broken two laws this morning, and I hadn't even had my coffee yet. But since I was the Heir Apparent, it wasn't Artem's job to question me.

"Your grace," he added through gritted teeth, nostrils flaring as his eyes darted back to the movement beneath my cloak.

"Please just..." I felt suddenly desperate. What if he refused me?

"Please what, your grace?" He rubbed some loose straws of hay that had stuck to his hands onto his pants.

"I didn't realize when I first found him, Artem. He's hurt." I moved toward the only closed space in the stables, Artem's office, jerking my chin for him to follow. He frowned but pulled a thick loop of keys from his belt and unlocked the door, ushering me inside.

With the door locked behind me, I opened my cloak to reveal the fiery red feathers of the gryphon, who was wide awake now and squawking angrily. One glance up at me though, his silver eyes watching me closely, and the gryphon softened.

Artem's eyes widened, first seeing the broken leg and then its coloring. "Auriel's bane, I..." He blew air through his lips, looking almost sick. "Where?"

"Right on my windowsill," I lied. "Leg's broken."

"I can see that." Artem was already reaching a hand out for the baby's leg, making a hushing sound as he grazed over the break. "Nasty fall. Assuming he hitched a ride with the mother who was shot down." He scooped the baby into his arms, his shoulders heaving with a tired sigh. The gryphon screeched in panic, a red wing reaching back for me. "I'll make it quick. Painless for the lad."

"No!" I pulled the gryphon back to my chest. His wings

10

fluttered rapidly against me, as he buried his head in my leathered armor. "Artem, the fuck! He's a baby."

"It's Afeyan."

"So? I came here for you to fix his leg."

Artem rolled his eyes. "Did you now? So, it could die with its leg in a cast?"

"So, you could help him," I snarled. The gryphon's agitation was growing. He seemed to be attempting to dig his way through my armor to crawl inside. I rubbed the back of his head, shifting my hold on his trembling body. One small talon wrapped around my finger.

"Oh, aye? And what then? I cast its leg, and it dies anyway once it's seen, and then I'm, what? Thrown into prison? Awaiting pardon from the Heir Apparent? You know your father's law. Afeyan gryphons are shot down on sight."

"Grown gryphons," I countered. That was exactly how the law had been stated. Nowhere did it say we were obligated to kill the Afeyan babies who entered Glemaria. It was a loophole I planned to exploit for all its worth.

Artem bit his lip, almost looking swayed. Then, he set his jaw. "Forget it. I'm not keeping this one alive and hidden just to kill it later when it's grown. We've enough to take care of here."

I was starting to feel hysterical. He was a fucking baby! He wasn't responsible for any of his homeland's crimes. He wasn't able to understand what was happening to him, too young to process his own pain. He was alone and injured, and no one else would protect him, something he seemed to realize with how tightly he was holding onto me.

We'd come a long way in our relationship since he'd bitten me.

"Lord Rhyan, your grace, I don't mean to insult you, but

you're too soft on helpless things," Artem growled, grabbing the gryphon from me again. "It's going to get you into trouble."

"Artem," I said, my voice full of the command of an Heir Apparent, of the Heir to the Imperator, the cold future ruler of Glemaria, which Artem Godsdamned well knew.

"Speak like that to me all you want, your grace. You think I forgot you outranked me before your balls dropped? It means gryphon-shit here." Artem rolled his eyes but rummaged through the drawers of his desk before pulling out a small broken gryphon harness. He unwound the worn leather from the buckle and slammed it on the table, shaking his head. "We both know what will happen if your father knows what we're up to."

I slowly processed his words and the appearance of the harness. "What *we're* up to?" I barely dared to breathe. "You'll help?"

Artem's face was scrunched in annoyance. "Aye. You're right about the law. You can't shoot a baby gryphon from the skies because a baby gryphon can't fly. But I'm not staking my life on some legal loophole. You hear me? It can stay until its leg is healed, until it can take its first flight. Not a minute longer. When that moment comes, you're going to set it free. If it makes its way back to those accursed Afeyan lands, so be it. If it's shot down, don't say I didn't warn you. And then we *never* speak of this again. Not if you want to come back here."

I nodded, the small knot in my stomach loosening. "Thank you, Artem. Truly."

"Oh, fuck off."

"I could have you punished for speaking to me like that," I said, trying to lighten the mood. I even narrowed my eyebrows in disapproval.

Artem smirked. "Believe me, Lord Rhyan, your presence is punishment enough." He rolled his eyes again, reaching for a glass vial on his work table. The gryphon was beginning to cry, a shaky, squeaking growl, his voice full of pain.

I moved to the other side of the table, holding the gryphon's head, his feathery fur soft in my hands, as I made shushing sounds. Artem tapped a few drops into his mouth. Instantly, his silver eyes widened. He looked ready to riot over whatever Artem had fed him, but then he fell silent, falling gently back asleep before offering one final trusting glance up at me. I smiled grimly before I pulled my hands away.

"Make yourself useful, at least," Artem said. "I have chores I can't get to now, thanks to some meddling pompous heir."

It was an empty request. I was here almost every morning before soturion training, helping Artem with his chores. Had been for years. When I was a boy, Lord Draken, my father's Second and Glemaria's Master of the Horse, had brought me to the stables with him for training. And then Artem took me under his wing as Lord Draken's duties pulled him away. It was one of the only places I could go where I could breathe, even with the stench of gryphon-shit surrounding me. I liked being around the beasts. I liked feeling as if I did some good in this Gods-forsaken world, something more than just being the Heir Apparent, something more than just being trained to become my father.

Before I could leave the office, there was a violent pounding on the door and a strangled yelp from outside. A fight was breaking out.

On instinct, I reached for my dagger.

"Stand down," Bowen yelled, his command carrying clearly through the door.

Artem was already moving: throwing the harness back in the drawer, covering the gryphon with a cloth, and stashing him behind the desk. The knock pounded again.

"Myself to fucking Moriel, your grace." Artem's already pale face turned white. "Were you seen?"

"I didn't think so." My fingers tightened around the hilt.

The shouts and stomps of more soturi echoed outside the office door.

"Open in the name of the Imperator." The yell came from another soturion, one I thought came from my father's escort, one of the assholes who'd watched me outside.

"Auriel's fucking balls," Artem growled as he unlocked and opened the door.

"I'm his grace's escort. I'll take him." Bowen, along with three soturi from my father's escort, crowded into Artem's office, where, despite Bowen's words, my father's soturi sprang into action.

One soturion turned his ire on Bowen, restraining him from moving forward and dragging him back out of Artem's office. The other two lurched toward me, grabbing my arms and forcing them behind my back, their fingers digging into my wrists.

I growled under my breath. Though these were the Soturi of Ka Hart, and all had sworn their lives, loyalty, and swords to my father, they were all the blood of Ka Gaddayan, the Ka of Arkturion Kane. And he was a monster.

"Soturion Baynan, what is the meaning of this? Answer me," I demanded.

Artem retreated to a back corner of his office, his eyebrows narrowing as he realized none of the soturi appeared to have come for him.

"Your father sent for you, Your Grace," snapped Baynan. He was a first cousin of Arkturion Kane, a fact that had made him far too bold for his own good. At some point, Ka Gaddayan had taken it upon themselves to take their posts a little more seriously than they ever had before. They were harsher with their judgments, quicker with their hits, and all seemed to worship the floor Kane stood upon. The more they worshipped him, the less respect they showed for me.

Bowen twisted in his restraint outside the door, his neck turning red. "Which is why I said I'd bring him," he shouted as he freed himself from the soturion holding him captive, another lesser noble related to Kane who fell face forward, his nose an inch from a fresh pile of gryphon-shit. Bowen rushed back into the office, reaching for his dagger. "I'm sworn to go by his side."

"Yes, but His Highness didn't tell you to bring him." Baynan tightened his grip on me, the shadow of a smile on his lips. He was loving this—overpowering me, overpowering my escort. "He told *me* to. Your oath holds no weight."

Bowen looked ready to riot. "My oath is everything!"

I flexed my fingers behind my back, grounding into my heels. Since my Birth Bind had been fully lifted, I'd grown stronger than anyone truly knew, than every soturion in my year, than half the anointed soturi picked exclusively for my father's guard. I could fight Baynan off me without breaking a sweat, and the asshole on my other side as well. I was powerful enough, but I wasn't fast enough to fight the next half dozen soturi armed and lined up outside the door—not without my vorakh.

My eyes narrowed on Baynan's hateful face. "He told you what?"

"To bring you to the Seating Room alone. Immediately."

"Did he also tell you to leave a scratch on his son?" I asked, my voice devoid of any accent. I'd slipped into the affect of the rich, spoiled, powerful Heir to the Arkasva and Imperator.

Baynan flinched. He realized the line he'd crossed, though this line had been blurring since I'd become a soturion. He'd seen my father strike me, bind me, humiliate me. They all had.

And as my father's punishments became more severe, as I'd become a target in the Katurium at his behest, his soturi had taken it as an allowance to be rougher with me, as if my father's mistreatment gave them permission to hurt me, too.

But it hadn't. My father didn't like his things to be touched. Not if he wasn't present to order the harm or do the harming himself. He always seemed torn between wanting to hurt me, and wanting me to be respected by others—it just depended on the current mood he was in, and which outcome better suited his ego.

"You'll be lashed if I find a single mark on His Grace," Bowen threatened. "We yield to the Imperator's command. You've made your summons. So, take your Godsdamned hand off him and let him step outside."

The soturi released me at once, but they each took a step closer, ensuring I didn't escape, at least, not in the traditional way.

I sucked in my breath, biting the inner corner of my cheek. I had to stay calm. To remain in control. To remain *here*.

Inhale. Exhale.

My father didn't know about the gryphon. He couldn't. The soturi would have grabbed Artem by now as well, and they hadn't. But I was sure I'd been caught anyway on another charge, on a far greater crime. He knew I'd used my vorakh. He knew I'd disobeyed him, let my emotions take over. And now I was going to pay.

CHAPTER

TWO

M y heart had risen to my throat by the time we
reached the Seating Room's thick stone doors.
Soturi in black leather and green cloaks lined the
hall, silver gryphon wings shining against their armor.
Bowen's heavy footsteps sounded behind me as my father's
soldiers came to a sudden halt. Though I'd technically been
unrestrained, the soturi walked so close to me that I was
sweating, overheated, and imprisoned by their nearness.

Arched windows lined the hall beyond it, and the sun
streamed in too brightly; the tops of the blades of each soturion's sword danced with flames.

The herald, an ancient, spindly man who'd stood guard
since my earliest memories nodded, bowing deeply before
opening the doors and announcing, "Lord Rhyan Hart, Heir
Apparent to the Arkasva, High Lord of Glemaria, Imperator to
the North."

I glanced back at Bowen. The flare of his nostrils, and a
slight nervous edge to his aura, were his only tells of his
unease. He lifted his chin and assumed a guarding stance, legs

apart and hand on the hilt of his sword, like the line of soturi beside him.

I was to go in on my own. Unprotected. Of course.

A gryphon with its wings outstretched had been carved into the wooden doors, and as the herald opened them, the gryphon split in half.

I stepped forward, steeling myself as the heavy doors closed behind me, their bolts thudding into place.

A sharp bite of cold rushed forward from my father's aura. His energy was so bitterly cold, it could stab as sharp as his blade. He sat on his golden Seat of Power, his golden laurel glowing beneath the fires. A starfire sword was strapped to his hip, the leather hilt gleaming. His dark beard was trimmed close, and he donned the leathers of a Glemarian soturion, but the golden-bordered black cloth slung across his shoulder marked him as something far more powerful and dangerous. He wasn't just my father or my Arkasva. He was my Imperator. Ruler of my country and every country north of the capital. Half of the fucking Empire.

Stomach clenching, I stepped forward, embarrassingly aware of the sound of my breathing, of my every footstep echoing into the emptiness of the room. I was sure he'd find fault with all of it.

How could I hunt akadim if I couldn't cross a room in silence? How hard was I actually training if I was this out of breath from a walk?

I willed myself to calm. I had to think clearly, to not give anything away.

Crackling torches hissed against the Seating Room's darkened interior. The room was stark, so plain it almost seemed like a space one would find in the center of town, built as a gathering place for commoners, rather than the room of the Court of Nobility in the Arkasva's fortress. The benches that created the aisle for me to walk through were plain and made of dark wood. Simple. Clean. Harsh. Green velvet tapestries embroidered with the silver sigil of Ka Hart, gryphon wings, and the sun, smothered the otherwise plain walls. The only ornate object within these walls was the golden Seat, the jewel upon which my father sat. Lest anyone dare look anywhere or at anyone else. When he was in the room, he was the center of the world.

My father's chill deepened as I reached the bottom of the dais. He was angry. Agitated. More so than usual.

I could never tell what it meant. For twenty years, I'd tried to understand, to do the right thing, to earn some kind of positive reaction from him, or, at least, avoid the negative ones. I never could. A minor infraction could have me suffer five lashes. An even smaller offense could land me ten. The punishment never fit the crime. My entire life, I'd received them, and they still didn't make sense to me. They just came. And came. All they had in common were their cruelty. Their harshness.

I hadn't seen my father this angry in months, not since I'd last worn the ropes. There was a reddening to his cheeks that made me feel sick. The color spread down his neck, and his chin twitched, as his eyes, dark and unfeeling, stared through me. Every step I took, I felt more ill and had more difficulty walking, as if he'd filled the room with a wind that was pushing me back.

Did he know what I'd done?

My heart was threatening to hammer through my chest, and I debated coming clean, apologizing in advance. But I didn't know if that would even help. If he was truly this angry at me, or if I was just the final straw in an otherwise tempestuous morning for him. Gods. I never knew.

He tapped his fingers against his thigh in impatience as I bowed formally.

"Took your time, Rhyan."

I stood tall, making sure to roll my shoulders back, to keep my chin lifted just the way he liked it. "Your Highness. How may I be of service?"

"Court is in session today," he said, his voice cold and clipped, devoid of any Glemarian accent. So many of the Council had altered their accents over the years, suppressing the natural Glemarian lilt, but he had never needed to suppress his because he had not been born with one. He was a foreigner, born in Hartavia. My mother was the true Glemarian, the true heir, the one who should have been sitting in the Seat. Every day, her accent reminded him of this fact, as did my own, much as I tried to hide it.

I took a deep breath, relaxing my hands as best I could at my sides, making sure I continued to affect the proper posture of an heir. Then, I sorted through his words. They were not what I'd expected. Not an insult, not a punishment, just a statement.

Court is in session today.

"Court is usually in session today, Your Highness," I said carefully.

"This is not the morning for your attitude. I needed to make sure you were prepared."

As if I ever wasn't. As if I hadn't spent my Godsdamned life trying to appease him, to do the right thing to avoid punishment.

Slowly though, I began to realize...he didn't know about this morning. For once, I'd gotten away with it. But only because something else was happening, something worse.

"Prepared for Court? The Court I attend every day?" I shook my head. "Why? Are we having guests?"

My mind instantly wandered to Emperor Theotis, and the southern Imperator, Avery Kormac, two of the most insufferable, hateful men of the Empire. They were the only men in all of Lumeria to rival or outrank my father's power and status. Was it actually possible his agitation had nothing to do with me? Was he so distracted that he truly didn't know I'd traveled or what I'd rescued?

"No guests," he said. "But some news has arrived. It will be publicly announced shortly."

My fingers clenched at my sides. "Correct me if I'm wrong, Your Highness, but news is announced every day."

He growled in annoyance, looking toward the ceiling. "How is it that I have the stupidest son in Lumeria?"

"You dragged me here for this?" I asked, my face heating. "To tell me today is like any other? To share an opinion of yours? One I know far too well?"

"Dragged you? An Imperator does not drag. He commands. And I had good reason." He leaned forward in his Seat, his head tilted to the side. "Tell me, Rhyan, what happens when you lose control of your emotions? When you can't handle your own little feelings?"

Tears welled behind my eyes like a trained response, and I didn't even know what was happening, or what news he could possibly be referring to. "I am doing all I can to control them." As he Godsdamned well knew.

"Forgive me if I don't trust you to stay in control with what I'm about to share with you. And as usual, it is my job, my responsibility, to protect you from yourself, from the wrath of the Empire." His nostrils flared with anger, "Ungrateful as you are."

"What news?" I asked. "What happened?" What made him doubt I'd keep control? I glanced around the room, so empty, so devoid of life. Had someone died? Mother? I tried to remember what mood he'd been in last night as the panic rose in me. No. She was okay, she had to be okay; my father was cruel and twisted, but I had to believe he wasn't this evil. And yet...

Fear rose like nahashim slipping through my skin.

Still, he was silent. Gods. What in Lumeria did it mean? The severity with which his guards had come for me, the unusually harsh bite of his aura...

"You're already fucking fading!" he snarled.

I looked down and saw my body blurring. I felt dizzy, light-headed; an invisible hook had stabbed its way into my stomach and was pulling me forward, threatening to take me away. I grounded my heels and took a deep breath, and my body came back into focus.

"Please. Just tell me this. Mother is..." I bit the inner corner of my cheek, "she's all right?"

"You forgot to say, Your Highness." He gripped the hilt of his sword, fingers dancing on a red stone embedded inside the leather.

I closed my eyes, praying for patience. He was just fucking with me, trying to get a rise, to force me to lose my temper so he could prove he was right—prove that I was weak and he was strong, prove that he had every reason to demand authority and remain in control of me.

"Your Highness," I said, using all the will I had left to keep my voice even.

He smirked. "Untense your jaw."

I forced my face into a neutral expression. My back was straight, my chin lifted, the perfect posturing of the Heir Apparent.

"She's fine," he said jovially as if I was farther than Lethea for having asked.

I unclenched my fists, my aura ready to explode. "Then, what is it?"

"Rhyan." His voice softened, and he shook his head, his

eyes sympathetic and crinkling at the corners. When he looked like that, almost vulnerable, I could swear I saw a hint of something else inside of him. Proof that he truly was my father, not the Imperator, not the Arkasva, but the man that shared my blood, the man that had once loved me.

If he ever did.

I hated myself for searching for such a thing. For still wanting. Needing. I knew better. Knew the truth. My heart didn't.

He shifted forward in his seat. "I know you had somewhat of an entanglement, to the point where I am not sure what this news will do to you."

Entanglement? I'd had no entanglements. Not for a year.

He continued, "I called you in here, as I said, to prepare." He snapped his fingers, and the back door opened behind him.

Arkmage Connal Hilsen appeared, his white robes and rainbow-colored leather belt a sharp contrast to the dreariness of the Seating Room. Connal had become the Arkmage of Glemaria on my nineteenth birthday. After I'd revealed my vorakh in a secret ceremony in my bedroom, Father had killed the old man who'd witnessed it. Connal had been anointed into his position as a replacement that very night. Since I'd officially been unbound, he had been the one my father most often called upon to put the binds back on me. To restrain me. To teach me. To humiliate me. To ensure that I didn't outrun the others on the track. That I didn't accidentally travel in our combat clinics, or in our habibellums.

He had no idea that the more he restrained me, the stronger I became.

I still hated every second of it. Still burned with fury. The ropes made me feel insane, made me want to crawl out of my skin. My power was like an itch beneath my muscle and bones, thrumming, pounding, making me too hot, making me feel the need to rip myself free of the confines of my body, to claw my limbs off and release the magic inside. The ropes were their own kind of hellish torture once the magic was unleashed.

If Arkmage Connal was here now...

"No!" I shouted. "I refuse."

"You refuse your Imperator? Your Arkasva?" my father asked. He turned to Connal, only in his late twenties, and still new to his position. He was weak, and completely obedient. "See how he still has no respect? Bind him."

My hands balled into fists. "Remember the last time?" I snarled.

Two months ago, Arkmage Connal raised his stave at me. I'd rushed forward so fast I'd knocked him off his feet. His back had slammed onto the floor, his head nearly cracking, the crystal atop his stave smashing to pieces. The rage had been mine. It had come from me, not my vorakh. It had been my speed. My strength. And had Connal not been so young and in good health, it might have killed him.

The newly replaced crystal on his stave now glowed a blindingly bright white.

"Rhyan, Rhyan," my father said gently, his face glowing from the crystal's light. "If you do not wish to cooperate with your sovereign freely, perhaps someone else can convince you." He snapped his fingers again, and once more, the door opened.

My mother was shoved inside the Seating Room.

"Shakina," he said coldly. "Talk sense into your son."

"Mother," I said, rushing toward her, but with one look from my father, I stopped in my tracks.

Her eyes were drooping, her long brown hair—always down, always covering something—curling down her back. She wore a silver diadem though she'd never rule. The golden sun shone in the center of her forehead, clustered between the silver gryphon wings that stretched back into her hair, but as she looked up at me, her face remained blank.

Her hands were clasped together beneath the flowing sleeves of her white dress and remained so even when she stepped onto the dais beside my father. A silver satin belt with green gryphon wings threaded into the material hung from her waist.

When I was still a boy, I used to be so intimidated standing up there with all the eyes of the Court on me. I was sure I'd do something wrong, make some mistake. I'd reach for my mother's hands, seeking them beneath her voluminous sleeves. She always squeezed my hands in return, her touch full of reassurance. When my father finally noticed, he ordered me to stand on the other side of the dais, alone.

"Rhyan," she said, her voice beautiful and lilting. She never hid her accent, her one small rebellion against him. "Your father has the right idea. Just listen to him."

He'd already hurt her today. I could tell. Her make-up was too bright, too heavy. Her shoulder was stiff.

"Do you plan to comply now?" he asked. "Or do I need to convince you further?" His eyes flickered as he reached for her. Rage surged through me as my mother flinched, pulling her hand away from his on instinct before forcing herself to relax and let my father take her hand. The small light of life in her eyes, her tiny resistance, was gone, and her gaze returned blank and lifeless.

"I can convince you myself...or I can have my guard." He gave my mother a pointed look.

Trying to calm myself, to catch my breath, I looked down, and my eyes fell on my bare hands and arms. I saw the ropes that might as well have already been in place. The image had my chest heaving, panic sputtering inside my belly. The need to be free, to run, to travel, was threatening to take me on the spot. I was almost nauseated with fear.

"For how long?" I asked, my voice rough, my accent heavy.

My father shook his head in disgust. "Try to ask me again, using actual words this time."

Inhale. Exhale.

"How long must I wear the bind, Your Highness?" I gritted through my teeth, my accent pushed down.

"Until I know you're under control." He jerked his chin at Connal.

With a sneer, the arkmage stepped forward, the crystal atop his stave glowing with fresh life. He uttered the incantation, those hateful words, as the black ropes sprang forth from his stave, glittering as they snaked across the room and grabbed hold of me. They coiled and tightened across my body, digging into my skin.

I stumbled back, unable to stop myself from retreating, from trying to escape. But it was no use. I was trapped.

All the strength inside of me vanished as the ropes dug into my flesh, burning me, weakening me. I bit my lip to keep from crying out. The sense of power I'd felt surge inside me was gone. And instead, a panicked, strangled sensation washed through me, and I lost my balance.

The glitter vanished, the ropes stilled and secured.

For two months, I'd been free. For two months, I'd avoided the itching, the burning, the feeling of losing my mind with my power trapped inside me, shaking, violent, desperate to get out.

I staggered backward, feeling the rope's effects, its weight, as my father casually dismissed the arkmage. The door closed behind him, leaving just the three of us.

"Well?" I asked. Tremors wracked their way down my limbs. "I'm as you wished. Share your news."

My father reached behind his sword and produced a scroll with a torn wax seal. It was red—Batavia red—a broken sigil of seraphim wings beneath a full moon.

Lyriana...

I stiffened.

Her name...there it was. Sacred, secret. And now it was in the front of my mind, the grip it had on my heart, tighter than ever.

"It appears that there was a commotion at the most recent Revelation Ceremony of Bamaria. One of the nobles unveiling their magic was discovered to have vorakh." My father's eyes scanned my body before his gaze landed on my face.

The tremors increased, my fingers tapping against my thighs. I knew two of the nobles who would have been in the ceremony, both of Ka Batavia, both deeply close to Lyriana.

"Who?" I asked carefully.

His eyes narrowed, and with a slight upturn to his lips, he said, "It was the niece of the Arkasva. The Lady Julianna Batavia."

Jules.

I stumbled again, a wave of dizziness washing over me as my stomach tightened. Swaying on the spot, my vision danced, going in and out of focus.

"Rhyan," my father warned. "Did you hear me?"

My eyes zeroed in on my father's sword, on the black leathered hilt, on the gemstone that had been embedded within it. It was red. Batavia red. All these years, I'd never noticed before.

Small details. Small details.

I gasped, feeling my chest tighten with panic. I couldn't breathe. I couldn't... *Gods, please... please.*

"Which... um... which vorakh?" I kept tapping my sides, trying to focus on the sensation of my fingers and legs and not the sinking doom in my heart.

"She was in possession of the first," my father continued, almost conspiratorially. "She had a fully violent vision in the temple, the entire Bamarian nobility witnessed. Imperator Kormac had her arrested on the spot. According to the reports, she was taken to Lethea the next day, escorted personally by him and the Bastardmaker."

Lethea. One did not return from Lethea.

There was a flash of gold in my mind. Golden seraphim wings designed to be a woman's arm cuff. I'd touched it last summer when reaching for her hand, had given it a squeeze as Imperator Kormac had arrived unexpectedly in Cresthaven on the night of the solstice celebration. Her sharp intake of breath, the fear she'd tried so hard to conceal in his presence, had haunted me for weeks. He'd hurt her before and had probably hurt her again, far worse now that she was under his power.

I caught the tips of my boots in my periphery. Black leather, scuff marks on the toe. A piece of hay from the gryphon stables stuck to the side.

Breathe.

"Remind me," my father said, "was this the one that you fucked last summer? Or not? I could never keep your ridiculous story straight."

I continued staring at my boots, willing every cell in my body to still, willing my heart to keep from pounding out of my chest, willing my eyes to keep from tearing.

Breathe. Breathe. Breathe.

"Well?" my father asked. "Was it?"

"Does it matter?" I asked. There'd never been anything between me and Jules, nothing more than an agreement. We let the nobility believe we'd slept together to protect Lyriana, to throw my father off my scent, away from my feelings for her. It hadn't worked. But then I'd found other ways to protect her.

Lyriana. Lyr... By the Gods. Was she all right?

"The...the other ladies of Ka Batavia... were they... are they...?" I was still finding it hard to find air.

Vorakh were arrested on-site and taken to Lethea. They were stripped. A process so painful and deadly it nearly always killed. But every noble I knew carried in their heart the fear of the fate of Ka Azria—the noble Ka which had kept their vorakh concealed. As a result, they no longer existed. The Emperor had ordered the execution of every last man, woman, and child from their Ka in Elyria.

The fear I felt for Jules, rising violently in my chest, was already battling the worry I felt for Lyriana having had to witness this. Or worse. The Imperator could easily have arrested her and her sisters, especially if they'd interfered. They'd been fiercely protective of each other, and based on what I'd seen, Imperator Kormac would have loved another excuse to steal more of Ka Batavia's power for himself. He would have relished any reason to station more of his soturi inside their country.

"The rest of Ka Batavia understood the unfortunate evil Lady Julianna possessed," my father said. "By all the reports, they stood back, remained still and dutiful to let the Imperator do his work."

I could barely process this—the horror Jules was experiencing, the helplessness, the idea that the people she most loved hadn't helped her but had stood back and watched. My eyes watered. "The report said they stood back?"

"Yes."

I tried to believe his words. To accept them, horrifying as they were. But I knew the stubbornness inside of Lyr. I knew the bond she had with Jules went deep. And I knew how easily she allowed her mask to slide in Court, to reveal her true feelings. The genuine smiles I'd captured all summer when she thought I hadn't been looking... so few nobles had them. Even fewer ever gave them.

"No one else was arrested? Arkasva Batavia still rules?"

"You're asking a lot of questions, Rhyan," my father warned. "Almost as if you care."

I stifled a growl. Of course, I cared. He knew I fucking cared. I'd bargained away all I had to him last summer because I cared so fucking much. It was the reason he had me in ropes in the first place. If I had more to give, more to bargain to keep her safe, I would have given that, too.

"Was anyone else arrested?" I asked again.

My father remained silent, drumming his fingers against the Seat.

I stepped forward. "Was anyone else—?"

"If you're asking about the fire-head—"

"Lady Lyriana."

"No. No one else was arrested. Lady Julianna's Ka did not act."

My eyes went to my mother, then back to my hands at my sides.

"Now, do well to calm yourself down," he said.

I forced myself to stare at my palms, not look back up. I couldn't bear to see my mother's sympathy, to look and face her for the hundredth time as she saw me in clear pain—saw, and did nothing.

"May I be excused now?" I asked. "Your Highness?"

"Do you understand what this means?" he asked.

I nodded. I knew perfectly fucking well. I had to play my part. I had to play it to perfection. When Court was in session and Jules's fate was announced, when she was ridiculed, when she was demonized for vorakh, when the name Batavia was uttered, I was to remain still, to remain cold. Indifferent. Heartless.

One misstep, one ounce of appearing sympathetic, and all eyes would fall on me. On my vorakh. On my curse.

And we would all be damned.

HOURS LATER, after the sun had set, I was alone in my room. The news had been met as expected, and I'd remained still. I'd refused to look at my best friends, even when Garrett's face had darkened as he heard, his blue eyes searching mine as I stood stoic on the dais beside my father. I felt his aura reaching out toward me, felt that he was far too aware and invested in what had happened, as if he'd suspected something, known something about me he shouldn't have.

I remained frozen and quiet afterward at the Oath Ceremony, not speaking, not commenting. Not taking part in the jokes going back and forth between Dario and Aiden. Not daring to breathe or make eye contact with Garrett who was watching me again as the soturi and mages formed their *kashonim,* entered their lineages, and swore their oaths. And when the celebration that always followed sprang to life in the fortress fields beyond Seathorne and my friends—already half-drunk and ready to let loose—insisted I come out and drink, I excused myself. I turned down request after request from my friends and other members of the nobility to join in. Then, I walked alone past the staring Council members and nobles.

I'd run back to my room the moment I'd been able to, Bowen on my heels. I couldn't bear to be around anyone. To celebrate. To act as if this had been some normal day, act as if my friend wasn't suffering, act like she wasn't scared, and alone. That she hadn't been given a death sentence.

Nor could I go on pretending that the girl I loved wasn't terrified and grieving.

Last summer I'd felt my heart breaking. Now that feeling was rushing back without abandon, leaving me lying in bed, clutching my chest in pain.

No one would come. No one would comfort me. Because no one could. No one knew. No one but Bowen, and my father.

And my mother.

We'd spoken about the events of last summer only once, on the night I'd returned.

"You've changed," she'd said, her Glemarian accent heavy, startling to hear after a summer away, especially when I'd spent that summer repressing my own. There had been a rising sadness in her eyes as she'd looked at me, a look I hadn't seen before on her. I'd been sure she'd already known my heart had been broken when she'd said, "Something about you, Rhyan. Something happened?" She'd looked to Bowen who retreated to stand guard outside the room then back to me, the question in her eyes.

I'd sworn that when I returned home, I'd forget it all. I made promises to the Gods that the moment I walked through the gates of Seathorne, I'd stop thinking about Lyriana, stop missing her, stop wanting her.

I had to talk myself out of seeking an Afeya to cut my binds. I'd been close—so close to losing control and traveling back to Lyr's fortress, so I could take her and press her against that tree one more time. I'd been consumed with desire, with thoughts of bringing her pink, pouty lips to mine and kissing her until I was breathless, until my heart pounded, until hers did, too.

I'd wanted nothing more than to hear her sighs, hear her say my name, to just hear what she was thinking. Even weeks later, I'd still been able to smell her, taste her, feel her, the heat of her... Gods. She'd consumed my every waking minute and flooded my dreams as I'd made my way home.

It had been driving me farther than Lethea. So, I'd decided when I returned to my life in the fortress, I wouldn't think. I wouldn't *feel*. I would return to who I'd been for years— someone without hope, without feeling. I'd bear my punishment, find a way to survive the ropes until the Revelation Ceremony, and close my heart back up again. The pain of the heartbreak... I never wanted to feel that again. So, I decided, I would keep my heart locked and sealed forever.

The whole journey home, I carried a golden sunleaf in my hand, plucked from the very sun tree I'd kissed her beneath. I slept with it in my fist every night and traced its veins with my fingers for the endless stretches of travel inside my father's litter. By the journey's end, it had become a crumpled mess of a thing, and I stuffed it into the bottom of my belt pouch, knowing it'd been a sign the dream had, at last, ended. It'd been time to extinguish the hope that'd been flickering in my heart, the fantasy that things had not been over between us, that somehow, someway, I'd find her again. That our story had been beginning, not ending.

It *had* ended. So, I decided I wouldn't think of what had happened, and wouldn't speak of it again.

But that night at my mother's urging, the whole story had poured out of me in a hurried rush of words. I couldn't talk fast enough, couldn't stay far enough ahead of my emotions, my mouth racing against my tears to tell the story before I crumpled against my rising sobs.

She stroked my hair like she had when I was a boy, as I confessed and waited for her to say something comforting, to ease my pain, to offer wisdom, to tell me some way I could repair the hole in my heart.

I waited for her to be my mother.

I used to sit with her for hours, listening to her stories, finding solace in them. Tales of great heroes of ancient Lumeria. Legends of the War of Light. Love stories from the Valya of Auriel and Asherah. She'd shared them with such excitement and passion, her Glemarian accent rolling and beautiful. They'd brought me peace. We used to visit the Temple of Wind together, just the two of us as Bowen stood guard, her eyes alight as she explained the pictures to me, describing their movement before my own magic allowed me to see for myself. For endless hours, she would effortlessly weave tales of hope, and of love.

But that part of my life was over. She'd long stopped telling me stories.

That night, she had no advice, no words of comfort, only a hushed, "My heart, I'm sorry." I'd lain in her lap and cried, and when I finished and sat back up, her gaze had been distant. She'd gotten up a minute later, leaving me broken and alone, my heart raw and open.

I hadn't been able to breathe when she walked away. I felt like I was going to die on the spot, like the pain vibrating from my broken heart would strangle me in my sleep. It had been too much, too raw, too fresh, and there'd been nothing I could do to ease the pain, to soothe myself, to forget Lyriana, to close the gaping wound in my chest left from wanting her.

That had been the last time I sought comfort from my mother.

By morning I sobered, my eyes puffy but dry. There had been a new wall around my heart, a new determination not to feel or remember, a new promise to banish the girl whose taste still lingered on my lips. I vowed to lock her in the darkest depths of my soul, to make my will stronger than my heart.

And then the letters arrived and split me wide open again.

That same feeling plagued me now. The feeling as if I couldn't breathe, as if I were drowning with emotion and nothing would save me. Were it not for the ropes cutting off my magic, I'd have faded, I'd have traveled to the woods by now, the distant wildlands of Glemaria, desperately trying to outrun my tears.

Without warning, my door swung open. Before I could yell at Bowen, my father strolled in.

"Unless you're here to remove my bind," I said dully, holding up my heavy hands, "get out."

"That's never been the way to get what you want." He closed the door behind him.

"I take it I'm to keep the bind on?" I sat on the edge of my bed, my hands lifeless in my lap, the black ropes crossing back and forth, cutting through my skin. All day I'd been resisting the urge to itch. And I Godsdamned wouldn't give in now—not in front of him.

He sat down beside me, his aura, for once, not too harsh, not too cold.

"You're missing the party," he said gently, his hand brushing against my face.

I flinched, my entire body tensed, prepared for a hit. But he only wiped away a tear rolling down my cheek.

He stared at the teardrop on his finger before wiping it against the pad of his thumb as if it'd been dirtied.

"I didn't come here to fight," he said, his voice still gentle. "Now tell me, why aren't you attending the party?"

I was still on edge. He could be his most dangerous when his voice softened, when the smallest hint of kindness shined through. These moods could end at any second, over any trigger.

He watched me expectantly as my stomach churned.

"You know I've never liked them," I said.

"All of the Glemarian nobility are there, all of your friends," he said, stroking his neatly trimmed beard.

I shrugged.

"So, you only attend parties on solstice? Or only when a certain *Lady Lyriana* is present?"

I closed my eyes, my nostrils flaring. By the Gods. Why were we still talking about her?

My father clicked his tongue. "I can't say I haven't minded your natural inclination to avoid people over the years. Gives you less opportunities to say the wrong thing, to threaten our Ka's great reputation."

"Great?" I sneered.

"I believe it's capable of greatness. After all, it has produced an Imperator. And... that Imperator produced you. We still don't know what you might achieve."

I turned my gaze toward the door.

My father clucked his tongue again, drawing my attention back. "I'm only trying to help you," he said, but there was a warning in his voice. He unsheathed his sword and held it up, examining the shine of the blade with slow twists and turns, letting the torchlight cast the steel in a fiery glow.

I knew that sword well. I'd been ordered to clean it a thousand times and nearly as often forced to endure its cuts and the brunt of its hilt. It had drawn a map of pain across my flesh over the years. But its blade had dulled. He relied more on his mind games now to rile me.

"You've never been the most social heir, but you at least had a presence in Court—remembered that it extends beyond meetings in the Seating Room. Remembered the duties of a *male* Heir to the Arkasva." He traced the ruby gem on his hilt before he lifted his gaze to me. "You used to have a regular number of girls brought to your bed."

I stiffened.

"I know it's hard for you," he said, his voice dripping with sympathy. "You pined long for the Batavia girl. But her Ka has been tainted with this news. She's not an option for you, for our future Arkasva. And certainly not if you're going to become the man that I always believed you could be."

He'd never believed in me. He'd spent my entire life making sure I knew. My fingers clenched at my sides.

"This self-inflicted celibacy, Rhyan, has too many at Court talking. Gossiping. That's a problem for me, and that makes it a problem for you. It ends tonight, along with this ridiculous rebellion."

The logs in my fireplace shifted as a pop of fire burst, the flames smoking toward us. "What rebellion?"

He tilted his head to the side. "I know you were trying to protect Lady Lyriana by forcing my hand last year. But there's nothing left to protect. And nothing left for you to do. Your little threats are null. What happened to Lady Julianna changed the game. It is possible for a vorakh to be exposed, for a noble to be arrested, and the ruling Ka to remain untouched."

His aura swelled, exploding across my room, snuffing out the flames of my fireplace, extinguishing every torchlight.

My body shook from the chill. The only way I'd been able to protect Lyr, to stop my father's negotiations for her marriage to Arkturion Kane, had been for me to threaten to reveal my vorakh. It had been all the leverage I had.

"You are done refusing me. Done with this attitude. Done with this ridiculous anti-social behavior, done spending your mornings covered in shit with the servants of the stables. And you are absolutely done keeping this bed empty. You're going to change your behavior—start acting like a proper Heir Apparent. And you will start tonight by attending this party. You're going to remind everyone of the presence of Ka Hart, and you're going to remember how it feels to get your dick wet. No one will wed their daughter to you if they don't believe you're capable of fucking her well enough to produce an heir."

I closed my eyes, trying to keep my hands calm in my lap, to not ball them into fists, to not lose control.

It had been more than a year. A year since I'd held a girl in my arms. Longer since I'd shared my bed with anyone. After holding Lyr, after kissing her, I hadn't desired anyone else, couldn't bring myself to even look at another, forget trying to...

I was still hers. Under the solstice sky, somewhere between the trusting look in her eyes, the swelling of love and hope in my heart, and the feel of her body against mine, I'd become lost. She had complete and total possession of me. I didn't want anyone else, couldn't imagine anyone else, and for the past year, there had been no one else. I hadn't wanted there to be. I wasn't sure I ever wanted there to be another again.

"This is your command, Your Highness?" I asked, my voice dry.

"Put your boots back on, get your ass outside, and remember how to be a man. And I *may* consider having Connal free you in the morning."

I could only seethe in response.

"Agree," he said. "Agree, or you'll watch as I find other ways to convince you. Nothing is holding me back now. You don't want to disappoint your mother, do you?"

Bastard.

"Fine," I snapped. "I'll attend. But you know as well as I that I can't promise anything further tonight, even if I wanted it."

"Look in the Godsdamned mirror. Remember the title I gave to you. You have no excuse to not be successful. Whether that be from your face, the diadem on your forehead, or any other means of coercion necessary, you make it happen."

I snarled. He was farther than Lethea if he thought I could do that.

My father shook his head, his dark eyebrows drawn together in a tight V. "Unless," his eyes dipped below my belt, "the rumors about you are true? The choice between a good fuck or the shackle of your ropes should be an easy decision for you. If you have half a brain." He stood and tossed a scroll and parchment onto my bed. The scroll was closed with a small plain purple seal, identical to the dozen others I'd cracked open this past year.

I bit my lip, trying not to scream.

"These arrived for you late this morning. Read if you must, then make your appearance. I was far too lenient with you this past year. Letting your attitude run wild. No more. You're not as strong as you think you are. Be smart about this, Rhyan, be smart for once in your Godsdamned life. Choose between the binds you hate or something sweeter, *warmer*. And I want you to remember, when you disappoint me, you're not hurting me. You're only hurting your mother."

I gritted my teeth.

"I know you don't want to hurt her." His voice was soothing, understanding. It made me want to scream. "So, do what you must to avoid that, hmmm? Consider carefully. I keep her around now only for you. But if you cannot do this one simple act, perhaps I'll find myself in need of a new Heir Apparent. And a new wife to make him with." He strode toward the door and left me alone with the scroll.

I was reaching for my dagger before I could think, my fingers tightening around the hilt until my knuckles were white, my muscles straining against the binds as I pulled my arm back and threw my blade, watching it slice into the door.

THREE

My vision swirled as I stumbled into the hallway of the Heir's private wing, the night's dying torches leaving dark shadows in my wake. My soturion cloak fell off my shoulders, and my hand braced against the wall before I crashed into it completely. My hands seemed to have doubled before my vision righted itself, and my head swam. A noble-woman from the party hung off my arm, giggling hysterically.

I started to laugh, too, watching her eyes light up. Watching Lady...um...Lady... I laughed harder. I definitely knew her name. I was sure of it. Or, at least, I was sure I had known it several hours ago. It started with an A.

Or was it a T?

My head was swimming. Too much mead. Too many hours at the party. Too many thoughts. Too many letters.

To my favorite friend in the north—also my only friend in the north (a fact that does not make you any less my favorite, by the way),

By the time you read this, most likely you'll be back to your rigorous soturion training. And I'll be dancing my heart out in the fields beyond Cresthaven, fresh off of having completed my Oath Ceremony, where I am sure I'll become part of the most amazing kashonim with an apprentice who absolutely adores me.

Slender hands pulled me from the wall.

"Oh, no," the noblewoman cooed, standing before me. "Your Grace, did you hurt your shoulder?" She stroked up the chest of my armor, flingers gliding across my collarbone. She had been wearing her hair down when I'd met her at the party, but after hours of drinking and dancing, she'd opted to pull her curls up into a ponytail. A fresh sheen of sweat on her face made her skin glow.

"Did I?" I asked. I hadn't felt anything. Then again, my hands were slightly numbed between the alcohol I'd consumed and the tightening weight of my ropes all evening. Twisting my neck, I caught Bowen following close behind, his face tight with suspicion.

Of course. Now he was worried about me. Now he was concerned.

"Your Grace?" he asked, his voice gruff.

"Yesssss?" I said, waving a hand expectantly.

"Lord Rhyan?" His voice lowered.

"Bowen, if you have a question, please ask it. I'm not a fucking—" I bit my lip, stopping before I said mind reader. Vorakh. I lifted my hand in annoyance. "Well?"

He took a tentative step forward, something vulnerable in his eyes. "Are you all right, Your Grace? If you'd like to lie down, I can escort the lady back to her—"

"You'll escort the lady nowhere," I snapped. "I'm her escort tonight." I waved my hand again, stepping protectively before her and only stumbling a little. "I'm escorting her to... escorting her to..." My mind went blank, but no matter. I was positively sure I had planned an excellent ending to my sentence.

"Your room," she finished, her voice breathy, mouth close to my ear as she wrapped her arms around me from behind.

"Yes!" I shouted. "To my room." To lie down...to lie...

"Your Grace," Bowen said, the look of concern in his eyes seemed to have grown; at least, I thought it had. "Call out my name if you need me."

The woman laughed, a seductive note in her voice.

"Believe me, Bowen. Your name won't be the one that's called out tonight." I winked.

But I truly hope that you actually took this week between Academy sessions to relax and do that thing you always swear you're going to do, though I know you're lying through your teeth—or ink, as it were. Rhyan, for the love of all the Gods, please, tell me you had fun. I know you're not a people person, and, yes, Glemarian parties are most likely somewhat boorish and cold, and, well, let's face it, they are missing me as a guest, but I imagine they are still a good time—a better time than classes at the Academy—and most importantly, you should be going to them. Promise me? Swear? At least show your face.

I reached for the doorknob to my bedroom, swallowing roughly as I saw the ropes, black, glittering, and harsh against my pale skin. With a grunt, I turned the knob only to find it locked.

"Bowen! My door!"

He coughed. "Perhaps if his grace cannot find his own bedroom door, then perhaps his grace is far too inebriated to be bringing ladies to it."

"I have found it! It's just locked."

Bowen sighed. "Your Grace may want to try opening his actual bedroom door. Which is *not* locked. It's also the next one over. This is the escort's suite."

I laughed. "Of course. Because I'm an escort."

Bowen glared. "I didn't know you had taken on such an esteemed position for Lady *Amalthea*."

I blinked. Lady Amalthea, right, that was her name. Lady Amalthea Oryyan, niece to the Glemarian Senator. Also, cousin to Thorin Oryyan. My pompous apprentice.

"You do not have to do this," Bowen said quietly.

"And what would you know?" I hissed. "You never do this!"

Bowen's nostrils flared, but he took a respectful step back.

"Come, Lord Rhyan." Amalthea took my hand in hers, squeezing my palm, and led me down the hall to my actual bedroom door. "Is it this one, Your Grace?" she crooned.

At the contact, my throat went dry. I needed water. "This one."

And have a glass of mead, come on, you know you want to.

As soon as you finish reading this letter—and take a moment to bask in the amazingness of knowing you have a friend like me who truly wants you to enjoy your life and be happy—write back and tell me some fun things you did. Regaling me with a funny party story would certainly fulfill my demands. Mainly because it would prove to me that you actually went to a party.

A loud cough pulled me back to the hallway outside my room. Bowen's eyes were boring into me.

I swore, pulled open the door, and stepped inside. Amalthea followed close behind, her skirts brushing against my boots, her flowery perfume sweeping through my nostrils and changing the scent of my bedroom.

And yes, I do actually enjoy your stories of Artem and caring for the gryphons. How dare you accuse me of not! I happen to be interested in a great many things. Speaking of which, I hope Dario, Aiden, and Garrett are all well.

Hours earlier, Dario's face had lit up brighter than the fireworks exploding in the night sky when I'd stepped onto the field. His dark curls had been braided back and threaded with tiny silver beads that glinted in the firelight. His arm had been around my shoulder instantly, his other hand shoving into mine a mug of mead, ice cold and spiced to perfection. Aiden and Garrett had cheered me on as I downed my cup. They cheered louder as I finished my second, screamed when I moved onto the third.

"Yes! Yes! Lord-Rhyan-fucking-Hart is back, my friends!" Dario had announced. "This man! This man is my best friend in the whole Godsdamned world!"

"And what are we?" yelled Aiden in mock anger.

"You're fuck off!" Dario had shouted. "Because Rhyan's out tonight! You know what that means! Party!" He held up his glass, urging more of the guests to join our circle. "Drink up! And keep your eyes on our Heir Apparent. No man is safe from his fists. No woman can resist this handsome face." He'd squeezed my chin and planted a sloppy kiss on my cheek before shoving me off and running at Aiden and Garrett, locking his arms around their necks. "Jealous? Want me to kiss you, too?"

Aiden and Garrett had shared one look before turning on Dario and wrestling him to the ground as everyone cheered.

"Relax!" I called to them, unable to help my own grin from spreading as the mead had warmed me from the inside.

Lady Kenna, a friend of ours for years, had raised her glass to me and smiled. Her aura was warm and glowing, as bright as the yellow dress adorning her. Kenna was beautiful and kind—even if she was the daughter of our arkturion. But before we'd been able to speak, another noble had wrapped her arm around her shoulder, giggling and pulling her away. She waved to me before vanishing into the shadows.

Someone had handed me another drink. And another.

At some point, Lady Amalthea stepped into our circle. Her

dark eyes found mine as she curled her finger around her hair. It had been red in the firelight. Fiery red.

Red...

Batavia red...

Flames crackled now from the torches in each corner of my room. Amalthea closed my door and slid the bolt into place. The lock dropped with a thud that echoed through the chambers. She leaned back against the frame, her chin tilted up, her back arched. The movement thrust her breasts forward until they were straining against her dress. The bodice was a traditional Glemarian green color, the neckline rising up to her collarbone, but the material was thin and... very tight.

I'll write you more soon. It's Auriel's Feast Day today, and I'm busy preparing for my Revelation Ceremony. Now, I know dresses aren't really your specialty, but trust me, the one I am wearing—it's gorgeous! The most amazing shade of purple, exactly what I wanted. I'll spare you the details of the many hours of shopping it took to find it. But I am so excited to show it off tonight. I mean, after the white robes come off and I have my stave in hand.

Feel free to include an extended paragraph on proper gryphon care in retribution for my tangent on dresses.

"Lord Rhyan," Amalthea said, crooking her finger, beckoning me forward.

"What?" I asked, realizing I somehow ended up on my bed. For just a second, I'd blacked out.

My heart pounded. I couldn't think straight at all. My room was spinning. I just wanted to lie down, to close my eyes.

Amalthea crossed the distance between us and stood before me, her dark eyes hooded with desire. She pushed my legs apart and stepped in between them, her hands on my shoulders. I caught another whiff of her perfume. Flowery. Pretty, but...

She leaned in, her mouth moving toward mine. Her lips were so close. So beautiful. So soft.

But wrong. Not the right shape. Not the shade of pink that haunted my dreams.

And her scent. That was wrong, too. Not sweet and musky. She wasn't vanilla or lemony. She wasn't...she wasn't her.

I turned my head, narrowly avoiding the kiss. Before she could feel rejected, I wrapped my arms around her waist and pulled her down into my lap.

"Hi," she said with a giggle, settling her weight on me.

"Hi," I said.

The backs of my eyes were burning. I didn't want this. I didn't want her.

No one will wed their daughter to you if they don't believe you're capable of fucking her.

Amalthea wiggled against me.

"Your Grace," she said sweetly, her fingers stroking up the back of my neck, causing tiny shivers to race down my spine.

My body responded, seemingly understanding what it was supposed to do even if my mind and heart were still grappling with it. I felt myself lengthen, strain against my tunic. The knowing smile on her face said she felt it, too.

"You," I sucked in my breath, "you can call me Rhyan in here."

"Rhyan," she whispered. "I've been wanting to taste your lips all night."

I fought the urge to be sick and the voices shouting in my mind that this wasn't right, that this wasn't *her*. I didn't care if this didn't happen for me again. Being alone was so much better than this painful squeezing around my heart and stomach. This feeling of wrongness. This feeling of anything and anyone that wasn't her, that wasn't Lyriana Batavia.

"Then, taste them," I said, my palm against her cheek, drawing her to me.

She is excited for tonight, too, of course. You haven't asked about her in a while, not directly, at least. But, well, I figured that I owe you an update. The plan we discussed last summer in Bamaria, it's in action. Your not-so-favorite lord, of the mixed colors of black and white, has finally made his romantic intentions known. She hasn't come to tell me yet, but I expect she will soon—they're together now. Officially.

I think this will be a good thing for her.

Could a heart shatter twice? Lyriana was with Lord-Tristan-fucking-Grey. His pompous ass was free to be with her, to talk to her, to hold her, to touch her, to kiss her, to... *Fuck.*

Jules had maintained Lyr's privacy in every letter she'd written me. She'd guarded her secrets fiercely. I never received details. They weren't mine to have nor mine to ask for. Not after the role I played. But she said enough. I could read between the lines. I knew after a small period of crying and hating me, she kissed someone else. And another someone else.

It stung every time. But I wanted the pain. I welcomed it. I wanted her to move on. Still, every time she moved farther away from me, I expected my heart to free itself from her hold. I expected my hope to die a little more. It never did.

Until tonight.

Amalthea's tongue licked the seam of my lips, and with a soft moan, my mouth opened to hers. One second, we were kissing, feverish with a hunger I hadn't known I possessed, a hunger that threatened to kill me if left unfed, a hunger I'd been dying from, that I'd been starving with for ages.

I still maintain what I said last summer—who I'd like to see her with. Who I'm rooting for. But for now, I want you to know that this is happening. Take care of yourself. Please?

I pulled Amalthea's hair free from its ties, my fingers tangling in her curls before sliding down her neck and shoulders. The color was no longer lit by firelight, no longer red.

Not Batavia red.

It never had been.

Amalthea pushed me back onto the bed, straddling my hips and grinding down against me. Her hips circled, and I shuddered beneath her, my mind wandering back to solstice, to Lyr dancing, her perfectly executed hip circles, the sinuously intoxicating way her body had moved, her hips snaking side to side, her curves giving shape to her white dress. Her skin had shone, warm, soft, and golden, and I'd touched her, my hands roaming up her stomach to—

I also gave her a hug from you. It's her birthday today—I'm not sure if you knew that. Don't worry, I didn't tell her it was from you. I give her so many hugs, she can't keep track. But I did. Be mad at me if you want.

Amalthea leaned forward, her breasts flattened against my armor, which she was now feverishly attempting to unbuckle as I rucked up the skirts of her dress, my fingers gliding across the bare skin of her legs.

As to your question from your last letter. I haven't seen any Afeya in Bamaria. Just one ambassador at Court, but he was only here for a day—met with Arkturion Aemon and left. He came from the Night Lands near you. I continue to keep my eye on her. I always do.

It's time now. I have to meet the rest of the Ka on the promenade.

Write back soon!

With love, from your wonderfully talented and amazing friend from the south, who is about to become a mage and wow everyone with her purple dress,

Jules

P.S. Yes! Anything is possible.

Maybe once upon a time, things had been possible, but I knew better. Possibility was just a poor man's version of hope, and nothing was more dangerous than that. Hope was a frail thing, and frail things didn't stand a chance under the weight of what this world had to offer. Under a world ruled by Imperators.

Amalthea moaned into my mouth, her hand pressing into the bed beside me. "What's this?" She'd picked up a small folded parchment with a broken wax seal, the imprint of a gryphon cracked in half.

I slid the letter from her fingers and thew it on the floor. "It's nothing."

With a smile, Amalthea brought her lips back to mine.

Your grace,

I'm sorry. Your father's men raided the stables after you left. It's gone. I had to get rid of it—couldn't keep it here. His Highness doesn't want you helping anymore. For your sake, and for mine, please, don't come back.

-Artem

The baby gryphon was dead. Of course, it was. Glemaria was the place where things went to die. The place where hope died. Everything I'd done today had been for nothing. Everything I'd done for the past year, for my whole fucking life, had been for nothing because everything I touched turned to shit.

They're together now. Officially.

Amalthea sat back, tugging off my boots.

It's gone. Please don't come back.

She finished unhooking my armor, pulled it off my shoulders.

It was the niece of the Arkasva...Imperator Kormac had her arrested on the spot.

The metallic sound of my belt unbuckling rang in my ears.

49

No one will wed their daughter to you if they don't believe you're capable of fucking her.

She loosened the leather of my belt, sliding it from beneath my waist, and tossed it and my dagger on the ground.

Anything is possible.

My tunic was tugged off, my torso exposed.

They're together now. Officially.

They're together now. They're together now...

All I could see was Lyriana last summer, offering Tristan her genuine beautiful smiles at dinner. All I could hear was Jules telling me how they'd been friends a long time, how he'd be a good match, and myself agreeing, asking Jules to encourage their courtship, to keep Lyr safe.

Amalthea dropped my tunic off the side of my bed. Sitting back up, she undulated over me as I grew harder beneath her. She slid the straps of her dress off her shoulders, tugging the material down until her pale breasts were revealed, her nipples pink and hard.

I stared, my heart beating fast, my head swimming.

"You can touch them," Amalthea said. "If you want."

They're together now. Officially.

I sat up with a growl, pulling her closer, one hand squeezing her ass, the other on her breast, something unleashing inside of me. I'd been so deprived. So, alone. So, fucking starved of any touch that wasn't cruel or harsh or hurtful. And Lyr had moved on. So, I had to move on.

Gods, she was warm, so soft. I'd forgotten, forgotten touches like this. Forgotten softness.

Her hand slipped beneath my short-pants, gripping me.

I tensed, panic suddenly tight in my belly, the sense of wrongness, a wave crashing over me. "Wait," I said.

She frowned.

"I don't... I don't have any protection," I said.

Amalthea's eyebrows lifted in surprise. "Someone as handsome as you?"

What are you thinking?

That handsome wasn't the right word for you. That you're so fucking beautiful, I can't walk away.

I don't want you to walk away.

I won't.

Stay.

I will.

The scent of Lyr felt fresh in my nose as if I'd traveled back in time, back to Bamaria, back to her arms. Vanilla. Musk. Lemon. The pistachio cookies I had that night, the spiced mead on my tongue, the warm Bamarian air hot on my arms and legs. The sense of home, of being safe. It was something I'd felt from being merely in her presence. Being near her.

They're together now...

I squeezed Amalthea's nipple between my fingers, my cock twitching as she arched against me.

"It's... It's been a while for me," I admitted.

I want to kiss you. Can I?

Yes.

Amalthea nodded, her lips lifting to a seductive grin. "I know. Don't worry. I'm prepared." She reached down, gripping my waistband. A log shifted in my fireplace, the flames hissing as wind blew at my window. A gryphon screeched in the distance.

My head was spinning. My heart thundering. I was lying back again on my bed as Amalthea freed my cock.

I couldn't breathe. I couldn't....

"Relax, Lord Rhyan." She worked the head, and my hips rose involuntarily. As I gripped my sheets with my fists, my eyes screwed shut. "I'm going to take such good care of you."

~

THE SUN STREAMED in through my windows. I groaned, opening my eyes. My head felt like it was going to split in two. I needed water. I needed... to puke. I sat up, only then realizing I was naked.

And I wasn't alone. Lady Amalthea's back was to me, the curve of her spine was bare against my sheets, my blanket falling off her hip. Flashes of the night returned to me as I raced for my bathing room.

Her mouth wrapping around me, sucking me in. Her sinking down on my length, rocking onto me. My fight to stay present, to remember who I was with, to forget whom I could never have, to banish the feeling that I'd never been enough for Lyriana and the doubt that I had ever meant anything to her in the first place. She hadn't fought for me. She'd let me go. She'd moved on.

She *had* to. I'd encouraged her to.

My stomach felt like it was being torn apart as I heaved, again and again. By the time I'd finished, my stomach was completely empty, my bed was as well.

I sat down at my reading desk and pulled out a parchment.

Dear Lady Lyriana, I wrote, my hand shaking.

I stared at her name, at my writing, my thoughts racing. I needed to write to her. To tell her I was sorry. To tell her about my friendship with Jules. To tell her everything. How I felt. What I'd done. Then, I crumpled the paper. What could I possibly say one year later? What right did I have to say anything to her at all? It wasn't my place. It was *his* now. And it was for the best. She was safer never hearing from me again.

I tore the parchment apart, threw the pieces into the fireplace, threw Jules's final message in there as well, and then the dozen that had come before it, watching them all catch flame, my stomach writhing and twisting in pain until nothing remained but burnt embers.

I would survive this. I would forget. I would be strong. My will would prevail. My will would be stronger than my heart.

I made a fist, pressing it to my chest before flattening my palm. Then, I reached under my mattress for the one final reminder of all I had lost. All I had once felt: the golden sun leaf.

It went into the flames, the gold swallowed by the red fire licking and spitting as it burned.

"Your Grace?" Bowen knocked on the door. "Is everything all right?"

I didn't respond. I tore off the sheets of my bed. They smelled like flowers. They smelled wrong. I threw them into the fire as well.

As the day was new and Lumerian gryphons filled the sky, their wings bronzed in the sunlight, I showered and pulled my tunic over my head, laced up my boots, strapped on my armor, and tightened the holsters for my dagger and sword at my waist.

I walked in silence to the Seating Room for Court. I stood tall on the dais. Lady Amalthea offered a lascivious smile as she took her seat in the back. Sweat beaded on the nape of my neck, my stomach twisting.

My father offered me one single nod of approval as my mother stared at the floor.

I'd done it. I kept her safe—just as I'd sworn I would. But I already knew, it wasn't over. It would never be over. None of this would.

I'd thought I was growing stronger. I thought I'd had leverage. Power. But I was wrong. Every step I took forward, he took something else away.

He'd threaten her again. He'd force new promises from me, tear out more pieces of my soul—take whatever I had left.

And I was resigned to my fate. Because I had no choice. Not if I wanted to keep my oath. Not if I wanted to protect my mother.

My heart pounded, and Lady Amalthea whispered to a friend. Another noblewoman smiled at me, her eyes snaking down my body, and I watched my father take notice.

And then another noblewoman did the same.

And somewhere between the daily proceedings, the monotony of nobles stepping forward to announce news, the hours passing by as I listened to commoners coming to make legal cases, it happened.

My will had prevailed.

My heart stopped thundering.

It simply stopped.

And I wasn't sure, if it would ever beat again.

THE SECOND SCROLL:

ALISSEDARI

FOUR

*(O*ne year later)

"Right there?" I gasped.

"Yes," Kenna breathed. "Yes... right... fuck." She tightened, clamping down around me with her release until I had no choice but to follow.

I groaned into her shoulder, pulling her closer against me. Her chest flattened against mine, and my fingers squeezed her ass as I pumped up into her one last time.

With a final moan, Kenna collapsed into my arms, her head on my shoulder, both our bodies covered in sweat.

Struggling to catch my breath, I gingerly slid myself out as I lifted her up and off my lap. I was already softening. She rolled contentedly beside me and stretched, arms over her head, her back arched like a cat's.

"Can I get you anything?" I asked, turning away. I slipped on a pair of short-pants before I took a long sip of water from a glass on my nightstand. I had a second glass prepared for her and held it out in offering.

"Thanks," she said with a satisfied sigh, taking a long sip before lying back.

I opened the curtains, letting in the morning sun, catching the tail end of a gryphon's wing as it soared past, its feathers gleaming with bronze and silver. Before I could sit back on the bed, there was a violent pounding on my door.

I squeezed my eyes shut in frustration. "Not now, Bowen!"

"Lord Dario demands your immediate attention, Your Grace," he said. "If you're... ready to receive guests."

"Rhyan!" Dario's voice boomed through the door. "Come on, man!"

I squinted at Kenna. "The hell's he doing awake?"

Lord Dario DeTerria, the son of Glemaria's Master of Peace Turion Ronan DeTerria, and my best friend, was many things. A morning person, Dario was not. After Kenna went on her way, I'd been planning to go to his apartment at the Soturion Academy and wake him myself. It was Auriel's Feast Day, so no training was scheduled in the Katurium, but as nobles and sons of the Glemarian Council, we were both still expected to appear in Court this morning, a responsibility we'd known since birth not to take lightly. Well, it was a responsibility I did not take lightly.

Somehow, said responsibility of keeping Dario on schedule had fallen on me during the past year of training. I discovered more mornings than not had required me going to Dario's bedroom and dragging him out to the arena. Sometimes I dressed him myself for training. Thanks to me, he had a perfectly pristine and unlashed back.

I hadn't been afforded the same courtesy, not by my father nor our arkturion.

There was another knock on my door.

Kenna shrugged. "Might as well let him in and see what he wants."

I eyed her naked body. "Did you want to get dressed first?"

She shrugged again with a sigh, twirling her light brown hair behind her shoulder. "Nothing he hasn't seen before." She sat up, reaching for her undergarments. "Let him in before he dies of impatience."

I waited for her to at least step into her shift, not wanting to give Bowen an eyeful, before I yelled back, "Fine!"

The door burst open, revealing a bright-eyed Dario, already dressed in his full soturion uniform. His black leathers were shined to perfection, his boots laced up to his knees. He wore his dark hair curled and half tied back with a leather strap—the style he'd adopted for training. Sauntering forward, Dario's hand jauntily played with the hilt of his sword, the edge of the blade turning to flame as he stepped into the sunlight.

"Morning. A good morning, I see." He lifted his eyebrows in appreciation at Kenna, who'd just covered her breasts. "My Lady Kenna."

"Lord Dario." She rolled her soft brown eyes, as she pulled her dress over her slim hips.

"You want me to help with the laces?" I asked, already moving for her, but Dario beat me to it.

"I got her." He winked, adjusting the position of Kenna's dress at her waist, straightening the fall of its folds. Gathering her hair off her back, Kenna stood still as Dario expertly threaded the ties of her bodice.

Kenna had been Dario's lover for a period of time. Their relationship had been like ours: not so much a passionate love affair but one of mutual convenience between friends.

In my case, it was a convenience that kept my father off my back. Kenna was the eldest daughter of Arkturion Kane, perhaps the only member of Ka Gaddayan to not have been born pure evil. Both our fathers wanted us together. Every father of a daughter who sat on the Glemarian Council or father who could consider himself part of the nobility wanted the same—for their daughter to be the future wife of the Arkasva. For them to be wed to me.

After I'd been through enough manipulations on their ends, some daughters attempting to force a betrothal with pregnancy scares (something I'd quickly put an end to with a rather expensive bit of magic) or feigning truly falling in love with me and claiming heartsickness, Kenna and I had fallen into bed together last spring. Partly out of loneliness, partly just to get our fathers off our backs. No engagement had been announced—something we both knew they would decide in the end. But at least for the moment, both rulers seemed pleased at our arrangement though the arkturion claimed in public that Kenna was a model of innocence and purity. As if it mattered. She and I had no true love for each other beyond that of friends, and I was positive that that was exactly how things would continue between us however long we kept this going for. Perhaps forever.

I was almost sure that the act of falling in love was one that was no longer a part of my future. I'd had my chance. I'd fallen. I'd lost her. Nearly lost myself. That was it. It was over, and it was never going to happen for me again. There'd be no one else for me. No one but her.

No new stirring in my heart. Only the strengthening of my will.

I cleared my head of *her* name, her scent, even the color red, pushing it all down as I'd done nearly every day for the last two years. It hurt too much to remember. And it wasn't fair to Kenna.

I tried to focus on the positive. It was a small comfort that if Kenna and I were forced to marry, at least we had an understanding. And a strong enough ability to communicate in bed —enough to take pleasure from each other. Although admittedly, it often felt more like we were *taking* from the other rather than sharing an experience together. But when Kenna was in my bed, for a few moments—or hours—I could forget everything else. I could let my mind retreat and let my body take over. Feel pleasure. Real pleasure. Something more than my hand. Something less complicated than my affairs with the other nobles at Court. Or the ones who'd visited from the other northern countries.

But after it was over, much as I liked and cared for her, I sometimes felt empty. In some ways, I'd been more intimate with Kenna than anyone else in my life, and in others, it still felt like she was a stranger. Like we were actors pretending to play these roles, and when the play ended and we rolled out of bed, I was left a hollow shell of a person, reminded of just how truly alone I was.

This morning, the hollowness was heavy, like a hole had been punctured through my dormant heart, leaving a gaping wound down to my belly.

Fully dressed, Kenna relaxed back onto my bed, carefully moving the blankets to cover the place where we'd, well, come together.

Dario leapt onto the bed without abandon, crawling over Kenna's outstretched body and patting the blanket beside him, signaling for me to join.

"Come on! Lie down," Dario demanded. "It's a holiday. Too early to be up."

I glared but joined them on the bed. "Then, what the hell are you doing here?"

Dario stretched, his arms snaking around my shoulders and Kenna's so we were forced to cuddle against him. "I may have been evicted from the bed of a not-so-friendly soturion. He was very *friendly* last night and extremely passionate about dick but woke up this morning with a newfound devotion to cunts. And cunts alone." He smirked. "Not that I have any objection to them." Dario winked at Kenna.

Kenna shook her head, her nose scrunched up as she laughed.

"And, so, you came all the way to the fortress to tell me?" I asked with a groan. "Why not just go home?"

"One, because for once, I'm not hungover, and I thought you'd be proud. Well, okay, I *was* hungover. Just a little. But I puked all over his door. Retribution! So now I feel fantastic. And two, because I needed to talk to you," Dario said, his voice turning uncharacteristically serious.

"You puked? That's my sign to go," Kenna said, extricating herself from Dario's arm. She sat up, leaning over him to squeeze my hand. "Thanks, Rhy."

I sat up as well, kissing her cheek. "Anytime."

Dario lifted his eyebrows, still lying between us, before pushing his cheek toward Kenna as she sat back. "What? No kiss for me?"

"Nope!"

"But I brushed my teeth," Dario protested.

Kenna ignored him as she hopped off the bed, slipping on her boots and grabbing her shawl from my floor. "Enjoy your serious conversation. I'm going to find breakfast."

I shifted out of bed as Kenna closed the door, cursing under my breath as I searched for pants. "Well?" I asked Dario, sliding a cleanish-looking pair over my legs. "What's going on?"

Dario frowned, turning on his side, his head resting on his hand. "Isn't sex supposed to put you in a good mood?"

"I am in a good mood," I barked.

"Yes, I can see that. I've never seen you happier. If you looked in the dictionary for the word 'happy,' you'd see the scribes have made a rather exquisite rendering of your face."

I glared.

"It's also a holiday," he said lightly.

"I'm thrilled," I said, my voice deadpan.

It wasn't just a holiday. It was the anniversary. Jules's arrest. And it was *her* birthday. I'd managed to go months without thinking about her, banishing her from my thoughts, washing away the memory of her face from my dreams as I woke. But as this date had crawled forward, I'd found myself weakening, my mind wandering to her again and again, my mood worsening as I forced myself to forget.

Two years. Two fucking years since I'd seen her, touched her, tasted her. I still remembered every detail, every sound, every scent. The kiss.... The Godsdamned kiss.

I'd fucked so many girls since then, spent more hours literally inside of Kenna than I'd ever spent alone in Lyriana's physical presence, but it didn't matter. Lyr had crawled under my skin. She was still haunting me. No matter what I did or whom I invited to my bed, her memory, her scent, her taste...it all refused to fade.

"What did you have to tell me?" I finally asked.

"We need to do something about Aiden and Garrett." Dario kicked off his boots and rolled onto his back, sinking deeper into my pillows.

"What do you mean? Are they fighting?"

"Worse. They're fucking. All the time. Rhyan, it's excessive, and this is me saying so. Not to mention they are not nearly as friendly as you are when I want to go back into my own Godsdamned apartment in the morning to rest. Well, except today." He waggled an eyebrow at me.

"Right, because most people don't like being interrupted mid-orgasm," I said pointedly.

"No shit. And for the record, I didn't interrupt. You and

Kenna were done—trust me, I know exactly what that sounds like. But Aiden and Garrett... they're never done!"

Dario and Garrett had been assigned together as roommates and shared an apartment at the Soturion Academy. I had my own down the hall as Heir Apparent. Not far from our building were the apartments for those in the Mage Academy where Aiden lived. However, the four of us had ended up drunk and passed out in Dario and Garrett's place almost every night since our novice training had begun.

Until Aiden and Garrett got together. Unlike Dario, they were extremely private and possessive of the other. As well as insatiable.

My chest panged. I'd known that feeling. Briefly. Since then, beyond showing my lovers basic care and respect, nothing felt sacred enough to want to protect or keep secret. They all seemed to have the same attitude toward me, like I was replaceable, simply a body with a part they needed, serving a momentary purpose. Their own hearts remained as closed off as mine.

If Kenna came to me tonight and confessed that she wanted to end things and return to Dario's bed, though I cared for her, I would let her go in an instant. I wanted her to be happy. I wasn't sure I actually cared whom that was with. I'd barely feel a thing if I lost her, and certainly not sadness. If anything, I'd feel disappointment that I'd need to find a new shield against my father.

Fuck, that was depressing.

I slipped a shirt over my head. "So, that's why you're here? Aiden and Garrett are enjoying their morning and left you out?"

"Look, I was all for two of my best friends falling in love and getting their dicks hard. But not when it's happening day and night in my apartment. Rhyan," he said dramatically, "we have no choice. We've got to break them up."

"Good luck with that," I muttered. Those two were so in love with each other, it was a miracle they came up for air long enough to even acknowledge our existence. And though their relationship was still fairly new, we all knew they'd been in love with each other for years. It had just taken them both ages to find the courage to admit it. "Give them some time. They'll cool off."

"And you know this how? You live in cool. You've never gotten this heated over a lover."

He didn't know. None of them did.

I wouldn't let our first kiss be in public.

"They will," I said. "Just give them a minute to enjoy themselves. It's new."

Dario shook his head.

"Anything else?" I asked.

"Why, you have somewhere more important to be? I thought I'd go to Court with you today."

"Of course, you did. Where else were you going to go?" I stifled a groan. "Let me shower first."

Dario grinned. "Go on. I'll have Bowen order breakfast."

The rest of the day was uneventful. There were private parties to celebrate the feast day, a festival in town in Auriel's honor, a morning session in Court, and then the Revelation Ceremony which, thank the Gods, was completed without anyone being arrested.

As each new mage or soturion stepped onto the dais to have their magic revealed, my mind wandered again and again back to *her*. To Lady Lyriana. To the temple in Bamaria where she'd be sitting at this very moment. Lady Morgana, her older sister, would be participating. Probably becoming a mage like all the other ladies of Ka Batavia.

The fact that I didn't have confirmation of this fact made my chest tighten. If Jules was... if she were...then I'd know every detail. I'd have received multiple letters about it, letters about her dress selection for the night...and some kind of update on Lyr and Lord-fucking-Grey.

I flexed my fingers at my sides. Those specific updates did come from time to time, but from Senator Oryyan. They were not detailed, merely notifications that the courtship and alliance between Ka Grey and Ka Batavia still stood, despite no official word of betrothal—nor had there been any word of Lady Meera or Morgana finding matches. Arkasva Batavia seemed to be actively rejecting all prospects on their behalf. My father's eyes always shot to me when the name Batavia was uttered, like he was testing me, taunting me. Then, he'd always follow with a pointed glance at my mother. I'd learned to keep a straight face, my aura under wraps, and my vorakh suppressed to the point of nonexistence. To keep him happy, keep protecting my mother.

To keep my heart from beating.

In all the updates we'd received the past year, no one ever spoke of Jules. It was as if she'd never existed.

As the Revelation Ceremony completed, I found myself out on the fields beyond Seathorne, sitting on the grass between Dario and Kenna, the three of us at least two mugs deep into our drinks. Drums beat into the night, and bonfires crackled around us. Musicians gathered in opposite corners of the party, their instruments battling for dominance as they each played a different song. Sitting in the middle of all the bands where we were, it all became some odd mix of noise that somehow worked together, though it was mostly just incredibly loud.

As expected, mages and soturi, drunk on their newfound power and wine, called on all the magic they could muster. Brawls were breaking out, untrained soturi testing their newfound abilities. Almost all of them ended up passed out on the ground while the mages released sparks into the sky, creating flashes of fireworks.

I was bored. I'd been to this party so many times before. It was always the same. The drinking. The fights. The false shows of power, the flirtations. I was a part of it all, and yet... not. I never felt like I truly belonged here—like I fit in. Everyone else was having fun. Enjoying themselves, celebrating.

And I wasn't.

A noblewoman walked past, the firelight adding a glow to her hair, transforming the light brown shade to a bright fiery red. I felt my throat constrict, some of my dinner rising. Lady Amalthea. She looked back at me, our eyes meeting. Just as easily, she looked away like I was nothing, no one, and continued walking.

Kenna's fingernails ran up my neck, tangling in the curls I needed to cut for the new year of training. "You want another drink, Rhy?"

Yes. No. I wanted everything and nothing all at once.

I wanted to *want*. But the hollowness didn't let me. I'd sworn my will would be stronger than my heart, and now it was, and it had become so fucking hard to face each day this way. I just couldn't...feel.

I shook my head and pulled Kenna onto my lap. She made a startled sound; I wasn't usually one for public displays of affection. But the hollowness inside me was so overwhelming today. Gods, I just wanted to feel something. Anything. Myself to Moriel, I was prepared to fuck her in the middle of the field, to let the entire Soturion Academy watch if it meant this emptiness would go away.

My mind wandered, unbidden, to the south. Was the same kind of party happening there right now? Was Lyr sitting in a

Bamarian field with Tristan, drinking and laughing? Was her hair up, was the night hot?

No, she wouldn't be sitting, she'd be dancing. Her hips would be shimmying in perfect rhythm to the music, golden-sandaled feet stomping against the drums, blue ribbons around her wrists and ankles. Next, she'd be retreating to the trees with Tristan like we once had, because he was allowed to be with her, to protect her, to touch her, to love her...

Kenna's lips crashed against mine; her fingers tangled in my hair. I opened her mouth to mine, sucking her tongue.

Her breath caught, and I pulled her closer, my body coming alive in all the ways my heart had been forbidden.

My hand rose up her waist, my fingers tickling the slight undercurve of her breast. "Let's go somewhere," I breathed.

"Real nice!" Dario said. "You know how rude this is to do in front of me and not invite me to join?"

Kenna pulled back and ran her palm across Dario's cheek. "Jealous?"

"Yes!" He pouted. "You know how lonely I am?"

"Dario," Kenna said, sliding out of my lap, "you're not even a full day out from your last tryst. I think you'll live." She turned back to me, her eyebrows lifted in question. *Where do you want to go?*

But the moment had passed.

Two people holding hands in the shadows beyond our bonfire were walking toward us. Within seconds, their tall, muscular bodies came into view. One was adorned in the green cloak of a soturion, the other in the traditional blue robes of a mage. Garrett and Aiden. Garrett brushed his free hand through his blond waves, a feature so oddly soft against the muscles he'd developed in training. He always looked so much younger than he was—until he was in the arena. I'd seen him annihilate his opponents in the habibellum, leaving unconscious bodies in a circle around him. Garrett had even been responsible for injuring a soturion of Ka Gaddayan to the point of him being forced to drop out. It was an encouraged normalcy in the Academy—but one he'd always felt guilty about.

Aiden leaned his head on Garrett's shoulder, and I watched, a feeling almost like longing moving through me, as they shared a quick brush of lips. Garrett pulled back smiling and lovingly kissed Aiden's nose. Big and gryphon-like, Aiden reminded me so much of the beasts in human form. He was strong like them, too, unusually strong for a mage. If his mind hadn't been so buried in scrolls, he'd have been a soturion to reckon with. As it was, he alone was the scholar, advancing even further in his High Lumerian studies than I had.

And I had advanced rather far.

Watching them now, I could so easily see that Aiden and Garrett looked right together. Happy. Whole. The opposite of everything I felt.

Dario downed the rest of his mug, slammed it on a rock beside me, and grabbed Kenna's, swallowing what remained of her drink in one gulp.

"Dario! I wasn't done with that."

He ignored her. He had a determined look on his face as he eyed Aiden and Garrett up and down. "Finally," he said, swaying before rising to his feet.

"Dario," Kenna warned, realizing his aim. "Be nice."

I stood, grabbing his arm. I knew what kind of mood he was in, and it wasn't going to end well for anyone in our circle. He wasn't just annoyed at Aiden and Garrett's relationship; he was annoyed with Garrett in general. Nobles sharing spaces didn't always work in everyone's favor. I'd seen them nearly come to blows over where Dario had left his boots at the end of the night.

Honestly, they should have never been put together. Dario's father was Master of the Peace, and Garrett, though not from a noble Ka, was the son of the official Turion of the Glemarian Council, Arkturion Kane's Second in command. Too much power had been crammed into too small a space.

"Hey," I said. "You're not going to start something right now just because you're bored and drunk."

"I resent that accusation, seeing as I'm neither. I'm sleep deprived and tired of being kicked out of my own apartment. Just want to set some boundaries. Have a conversation."

"Conversation? Come on, man, we both know what you're trying to do here, and you're too many cups in to not regret it. Wait until tomorrow." Dario pulled out of my hold and stomped forward. I groaned, looking back at Kenna. "Sorry."

She gave me a sympathetic smile but turned toward some of the other nobles sitting near us. She'd been friends with Dario since we were kids, and much as she adored him, she had little tolerance for his dramatics. At least, if he wasn't warming her bed.

"Happy fucking feast day!" Dario roared, throwing his arms around Aiden and Garrett. "My friends!"

Aiden looked Dario up and down, always the most serious of our group and also the one least likely to be drunk. He brushed his fingers through his dark auburn hair. "Dario, have you eaten anything tonight?"

"Not as much as you, apparently. What have you been snacking on? Some di—"

"Okay," I shouted, cutting him off.

Garrett offered me a weary look. He tended to have far less patience for Dario's antics than Aiden did. He tightened his hold on Aiden's hand, shifting his body protectively in front of him. "Dario, if you have a problem, just spit it out."

"I do have a problem!" he shouted.

Before he could rant any further, the bells rang, a sudden burst of sound drowning out the music and the conversations of everyone on the field.

I frowned. We were not near the calling of the hour.

A second later, a gale-force wind nearly blew me back, and I looked up to the night's sky just in time to see a gryphon swooping low across the fields. Debris from the party blew toward us, and everyone huddled together, squinting or shielding their faces.

The gryphon was chasing another, far smaller and quicker. An arrow from the larger gryphon's rider just missed the smaller gryphon's head, and with another display of fireworks, the sky lit up, revealing the color of the smaller one's wings. Not bronze, not gold. But bright orange. It was a gryphon of the Afeyan Lands.

The Afeyan gryphon soared upward, and I could make out the vague outline of another. The sky was too dark to reveal its color, but I knew in my gut it was also Afeyan.

Screams erupted on the field as the bells began to ring again, louder. The pattern was urgent, persistent, one I'd memorized as a boy and dreaded hearing every time it rang.

Akadim.

Ice-cold fear filled my body, rushing out through my limbs.

Immediately, Dario sobered, our group becoming still and silent as we counted the bells.

One. Two. Three. Four. Five.

Five akadim had breached the Glemarian border.

My hands felt cold, almost numb at my sides. I registered the distant screams now, the sounds of battle beyond the noise of the music and instruments sputtering to a halt. At the edge of the fields, approaching the crowd, a head was visible, several feet taller than everyone else's. It had a pale, grotesque face with bright red eyes. Demon eyes. A soul eater. An akadim.

Shit. Five akadim hadn't just breached the Glemarian border, they were all the way inside, and at least one had made its way to the fields, which meant the rest of them would be here soon. We had no time. We had to evacuate everyone we could, get them inside to safety, and take the akadim down. Now.

Soturi were everywhere, but too many of them were passed out and not only useless but in grave danger. Auriel's Feast Day made everyone sloppy; the idiocy of the after-party mixed with the complacency that we were still in summer, the season where akadim were least active. It had left us vulnerable. Weak.

Apprentice soturi, including Thorin, the soturion I'd been bound to through *kashonim*, were already screaming orders, ushering guests away from the threat, while others were brandishing their swords, preparing for an ambush.

I met Garrett's blazing blue gaze; the severity of the situation was already reflected in his face. My heart was pounding, the sudden need to escape awakening inside me. But this need was nothing against my need to fight, the instinct to protect my own, who were all over this field.

The chaos had already begun despite the soturi trying to maintain decorum. It looked like everyone who could run was running, and those who couldn't were being carried or dragged away by their friends.

"Aiden," Garrett mouthed, his face turning white.

"Kenna," I breathed, something twisting in my chest.

They were both mages, strong and fierce in their own ways but completely unable to fight akadim. The demons were impervious to Lumerian magic. With nothing more than their mage strength and staves for defense, they'd be dead in seconds.

Dario had sobered under the threat, but I knew with one

look at his balance that while he was able to think clearly and his own protective instincts had been activated, he had far too much alcohol in him to go up against an akadim. Not tonight. Not if he was going to live until tomorrow.

The first three rules of being a soturion raced through my mind—the way they always did when faced with danger.

One. Stop the threat.

Two. Become the weapon.

Three. Follow the chain of command.

We weren't anointed, weren't part of a legion. But the chain of command between us had always been understood.

As the Heir Apparent, and the Academy's best fighter—when it was a matter of life and death—they all bowed to my will without question.

"Dario," I ordered. "Kenna and Aiden. Get them out of here. Now!"

He didn't argue, only nodded solemnly, his hand pressed to his chest, two fists against his heart, and this hand flattened. "With my life," he swore. *"Me sha, me ka."*

Garrett's lips crashed against Aiden's, one quick kiss before they pulled back, holding each other's gazes. I turned toward Kenna, with a lingering look, my eyes unable to move from hers, from my friend, from someone beautiful, someone, I realized, I truly did care for.

Her large brown eyes found mine, my name on her lips. "Rhy," she mouthed.

I felt frozen to the spot—not wanting to move. Not wanting to look away from her. My pulse quickened.

I fought the urge to run to her side, to sweep her up in my arms and take her to safety myself. But that wasn't my job. Exhaling, I faced Garrett, who'd released Aiden to Dario's protection. Garrett's chest heaved, his eyes widening with fear, but I gripped his shoulder. He needed to be steady, to focus on the fight rather than his worry for Aiden's life. Dario was one of our strongest fighters, even drunk. He'd die before he let any harm come to Kenna or Aiden. I knew that without a doubt. I needed to remind Garrett of this as much as I needed to remind myself.

Garrett took an anchoring breath, his eyes tracking Aiden's retreat.

"Stop the threat," I said, tapping his leather armor.

"Stop the threat," Garrett repeated, his throat working as his expression slid into one of determination.

The akadim roared across the field, its steps making the ground shake. Mages, untrained novice soturi, and musicians —who'd all abandoned their instruments—ran in terror in a mob toward us, trying to escape.

Garrett and I sprang forward. Our boots raced across the field, our hands synching as we both reached for our swords in the same moment. I gave myself one second to worry, to look back and see Dario take Kenna's hand, surprised at the relief I felt in knowing she was with him and would be protected, as they, with Aiden, headed to safety through the crowds. I prayed to the Gods that the three friends I cared for most in this world, all of whom had become my family, would find shelter and safety tonight as I fought beside Garrett. And I prayed Garrett would be safe. I needed him as much as I needed the others.

My heart was suddenly shattering at the thought I might not see Kenna again.

I could almost feel her lips on mine, her breath against my skin, her reassuring warmth against my body.

No. No. I would see her again, hold her, kiss her. I had no time for any other thoughts. I would not die tonight.

Gazing ahead, my mind cleared. The sounds of horror around me hushed, all thoughts and memories gone. There was an enemy, and it was up to me to become the weapon of its destruction. To see it as nothing more than a rope I would tear apart.

I swerved in and out of the onslaught of the crowd, screaming for everyone to move as I ran faster, my breaths coming in rapid succession. Garrett was right at my side, and within a few more steps, the field had been cleared of partiers. Only the akadim remained ahead, and barely a dozen soturi had stayed. Most of those on the field who were sober were still trying to escort everyone else off though half a dozen soturi already lay knocked out on the ground before us—caught unawares or too drunk to fight back.

The akadim before us was a beast, standing at least twelve feet tall. Dingy scraps of clothing clung to its body, most ripped so thoroughly that I saw little reason for the material at all. Red veins cut angrily through its pale skin, extending to its clawed hands. An apprentice soturion raced forward, releasing a battle cry into the night, but with one swipe of the akadim's claws, he was thrown across the field. A bone-shattering crack echoed when he landed.

I tightened my grip, assessing the scene: the position of the monster, its focus, and the placement of every other soldier on the field. We had to be careful and not attack all at once, not unless we were organized—which we were definitely not.

No one was taking charge of the attack. Most of us had barely gone over battle formations. Sloppy formations against the strength of an akadim spelled death. I looked to Garrett. We'd practiced together, knew how to read each other's body language as easily as we spoke. But we needed to strike at the right moment, and not one second sooner. Akadim did not offer second chances.

Another soturion attacked in front of us, and then two more, but the akadim easily took down them all.

One of Dario's ex-lovers stepped forward, his sword raised, and I could see fear grip him as the akadim roared. Piss pooled between his legs, and he turned, running in cowardice into the trees.

The Academy did what it could to prepare us. The training was rigorous and brutal, sometimes cruel and unforgiving. Not everyone survived. But the truth was, nothing but facing one of these monsters could ever show a soturion what they were made of or how they'd react.

I'd seen over a dozen akadim since training had begun. I'd stopped nearly pissing myself after the third. My heart had stopped feeling like it was going to kill me with its pounding after the fifth. But I'd never seen one this big, this powerful. I didn't fault the soturi who were running; the desire to live felt far more present in me than it had in months, as did the awareness of my heart beating, and my lungs breathing. I felt suddenly so alive. And what shocked me most of all was simply this: I could feel.

Kenna's face flashed in my mind.

I blinked and refocused.

We needed to stop the threat. If one of us didn't take it down soon, it would plow through the Academy, and our lives would be forfeit either way.

The demon's muscles flexed as it extended its elongated arms, its claws out, eyes reddening, and sharpened teeth bared into a snarl that turned my stomach.

Another soturion charged forward, his sword out, glinting in the firelight. He was a member of Ka Gaddayan, one of Kenna's cousins. With a battle cry, he made one swipe at the akadim's arm, but its claws sliced through his shoulder. He stumbled back, blood gushing down toward his wrist as the akadim wrapped its hand around his waist. It picked him up and hurled him at two more soturi racing toward the fray.

With one maneuver, the demon had all three soturi in a pile on the field.

My eyes met Garrett's. We had to strike. Now. "Go right, I'll take its left."

Garrett nodded, and we raced forward.

Another two soturi charged at the akadim, trying to distract it, as a third appeared from behind. She jumped onto the beast's back, her arms wrapping around its neck. The akadim roared, reaching around and bringing her forward, its claws tightening around her waist as she released a blood-curdling scream right before her body went limp.

Garrett froze in his tracks and shook beside me. I grabbed his hand, sucking in a breath.

I'd expected the akadim to rip through her armor—to eat her soul, to do worse. But he left her—ignoring the prey. Like he was seeking out something else—something more.

I didn't want to know what.

Garrett's aura shook beside me.

"Stop the threat," I said quietly.

His throat bobbed, but a sudden fierceness washed over his expression as he steadied himself.

I dug my heels into the ground.

More bells rang, the continuation of the warning. Five akadim were still inside Glemaria. Our soturi were failing.

I tried to clear my mind of it all—where the others were, why this was happening, where my mother was, and if she was safe. If noble protocol had been properly followed. I was here, and I had a threat before me. Letting my mind wander now would spell death.

The bodies of our soturi, mangled and bloody with twisted and broken arms and legs, were piling up as the akadim raced away from us, attacking anyone in its path. Many of the soturi who weren't unconscious, who had turned around to fight or stayed concealed in the shadows, had begun openly retreating in fear.

Where were my father's men? There was no sign of the arkturion's legion or the elite members of the Master of the Peace. Both Kenna's and Dario's fathers should have rushed into battle, and ordered reinforcements. Even Garrett's father's forces were notably missing.

The few soturi who remained had encircled the akadim, attacking the way we'd been taught in a five. But each one failed as the monster tore through their cloaks and armor.

Soturion after soturion fell until I realized only Garrett and I still stood. The akadim had fought two dozen of our warriors in what had felt like seconds. Its red eyes landed on us as it kicked the fallen soturi out of its way and charged forward, not seeming to notice when it stepped through a fading bonfire.

This was it.

Garrett's jaw tightened, his neck stretching side to side before he charged forward, racing for the akadim. He leapt into the air, brandishing his sword and slicing his blade across the demon's arm. Blood spurted above its elbow as it roared. Garrett crashed down behind it, stumbling forward onto the grass before he regained his bearings. He turned instantly, racing back for the akadim, this time running past it while his blade cut through its thigh.

I started forward, my fingers tightening around the hilt of my sword. But my feet didn't move. I froze as a roar sounded behind me.

Two akadim were now on the field, and there was still no sign of my father's soturi. Not a single Glemarian legion.

I spun and charged at the new beast. My sword lifted, and with a leap, I soared past it, my blade slicing through its arm. But as my boots hit the ground, Garrett screamed, the sound so full of fear my heart stopped.

Turning at once, I found Garrett bleeding. His leathers had been ripped straight down the center. The akadim had torn through his armor and tunic to the point where the pieces hung limply off his shoulders.

Gashes across his chest and stomach were gushing with blood.

The akadim was going to eat his soul. It had unobstructed access to Garrett's heart, the place where his soul would leave his body. Garrett stumbled backwards, his grip on his sword too loose for him to fight back. The akadim advanced, but Garrett wasn't paying attention—he was staring ahead, at me.

Auriel's fucking bane. No. No. No.

"GARRETT!" I screamed, just as he yelled my name.

I barely had time to glance back and see my akadim reaching for my belly. The sound of its claws ripping through the topmost layer of my leather burned in my ears as I ran forward, barely avoiding being snatched.

Garrett seemed to have caught a second wind. He'd run from the akadim, which now pursued him; I'd never seen an akadim move so fast. But as the akadim made a move to grab him, Garrett suddenly turned around. He ran straight for it.

I held my breath. Garrett had to make the hit. His armor was gone, and it would be too easy for the akadim to take his soul. But he could do it, he could fucking do it. He had to.

His eyebrows furrowed as he slid under the beast, his sword slicing between its legs. The akadim fell to its knees as Garrett leapt to his feet, spinning and swinging his sword at the akadim's neck. His blade hit it again and again as the akadim screamed in agony—until it stopped, leaving behind a haunting silence. Garrett's blade sang as it swept across the beast's shoulders. Its head fell to the grass with a grotesque thud, rolling beside a fallen soturion.

My eyes widened in shock. He'd killed it. He'd really fucking done it.

But we weren't safe yet.

"Rhyan!" Garrett roared, racing for me, his sword still out. He'd retrieved his dagger from its sheath, both of his hands equipped with weapons, as a third roar erupted on the field.

Time seemed to slow down as I heard the yells of soturi in the distance and saw two akadim closing in on us. One akadim was dead, but it had been immediately replaced. And there were still two more out there doing Gods knew what. Garrett tripped, his blood loss starting to slow him down. One more hit, and he'd be dead. He was already exposed with his armor destroyed, and if I didn't get to him soon, he was going to die.

"Garrett!" I screamed. "To me!"

I ran, my arms pumping, faster than I ever had in my life until Garrett was within reach. If I could get him behind me, I could go for the two akadim until the soturi got here. They were getting closer and louder. We'd be okay. We'd have to be okay.

Then another akadim appeared from the shadows of the trees.

"FUCK!" Garrett yelled.

I felt like the wind had been knocked from my lungs. This new demon made the others look like children, and my heart stopped as I fell under its gaze. Its eyes ran down my body, and I knew in that moment death was on the horizon. This was maybe my last day, and Kenna was perhaps the last girl I'd kiss.

Though the sudden return of my heart beating was the most beautiful sound I'd ever heard, and the numbness I'd worn like armor was cracking, I knew I could still accept death in this moment. If I could save Garrett, then at least my death would be honorable, would mean something. If anyone deserved to live, if anyone had something to live for, it was him.

The new demon struck at me, too quickly for me to react, and I screamed as blood ran down my arms. I kept running, still reaching for Garrett.

"RHYAN!" he roared.

I sped faster, the breath of the demon hot on my neck, its claws slicing through the back of my armor, while another reached both of its giant clawed hands for Garrett.

We collided. The backs of my leathers started to tear, and before I could react, Garrett wrapped his arms around me.

The demons had us surrounded. Fuck. FUCK. We were dead.

Pain erupted in my belly in a sharp tugging sensation as my boots lifted off the ground. My heart lurched into my throat. But I wasn't in the grasp of the akadim.

The sounds of battle and the roar of the monsters vanished. The fields of Seathorne were gone, as were all of the fallen soturi and dead akadim. Disoriented and dizzy, my heels touched the ground with a heavy thud, and I slipped forward on slick river rocks.

No. No. No!

Fuck. Fuck! I'd traveled. I'd abandoned the fight. I'd abandoned my friend when he'd needed me most. I'd broken the first rule of being a soturion: *stop the threat.*

And worse... I'd been in charge. Garrett had been counting on me, had trusted me—and I'd...fuck!

The rush of the river beside me swelled in my ears, and I stumbled forward, trying to get my bearings, my boots still slipping. I had to go back. I had to travel to the fields. I had to save Garrett.

I closed my eyes, picturing the trees, imagining the exact

spot where Garrett stood, imagining the monsters, the blood, and the carnage.

"Rhyan?" Garrett asked, his voice shaking.

I opened my eyes. I was still by the river. And so was Garrett.

By the Gods. I'd brought him with me. He was safe. For a moment, relief coursed through my body. But it was quickly replaced with fear. And complete and utter dread. I'd just exposed my vorakh.

"Garrett?"

He was on the ground, bleeding, breathing unevenly, his face pale. I rushed before him, unsure what to do. His breaths were coming in loud, uneven huffs against the rushing river and the sound of gryphon wings soaring overhead.

His throat bobbed as he stared up at me in pure terror.

My entire body was shaking as my mind raced with excuses, lies, thoughts of taking him out to keep my secret. Thoughts of admitting everything to him and making him swear an oath to never speak of what he'd seen again. Threatening him to take this knowledge to his grave.

"Garrett," I said slowly, trying to keep my voice calm and even. "I... It's not..." I fumbled. What was there to say? Two and half years I'd carried this secret, this burden, and not once had I exposed myself like this. "It's not—"

"Rhyan, you can't tell anyone, not even Aiden. We can't burden him with this knowledge."

Watching Garrett get shakily to his feet made me realize I was trembling, too. It had been months since I'd last traveled. I hadn't since I'd started sleeping with Kenna and learned to fully shut off my emotions. Since my heart had gone hollow.

Garrett lost his balance, and I reached out my hand for him to take. He stared at it, and his face hardened as he made no move to touch me. I slowly withdrew, my heart sinking.

He didn't see me as me anymore. He saw my curse. He saw a monster.

"Garrett?" I tried again.

"I'm sorry, Rhyan," he said.

My breath caught in my throat. I waited for the damning words to come, for the look of disgust, of hate. I waited for him to break our bond of friendship and turn me in. My shoulders fell forward, my head down.

I'd failed him. Failed my mother. Myself. Glemaria.

"I... I didn't mean to do that," Garrett said slowly.

I snapped my gaze back up. "What?"

"I didn't mean to—fuck. I didn't mean to leave without stopping the threat. To dishonor you, but... myself to fucking Moriel. Rhyan, it was right there, about to grab you, and we were surrounded, and I was losing blood, and fuck. Fuck!" Now his own head fell forward in defeat, his aura releasing an agonized and painful flash of nerves. "I couldn't let them...let them get you. Or me. Because, if I became akadim... became akadim the way I am, with...you know what would happen. How dangerous I could become."

How dangerous I could become...

I stared at Garrett, my eyebrows lifting as the realization dawned on me. The usual exhaustion I felt each time I traveled wasn't present. It seemed impossible, and yet... The realization was slowly coming together in my mind. It wasn't me who'd traveled, wasn't me who'd used vorakh.

"You," I started. "Wait—Garrett. You mean...you..."

Garrett nodded. "I'm a vorakh."

CHAPTER
FIVE

I remembered in that moment the Oath Ceremony one year ago. We were in the Seating Room at Court, and we'd heard the announcement of Jules's arrest, the naming of her vorakh. Garrett's face had paled; he'd stared at me with what I'd thought was accusation in his eyes. I'd been trying so hard to keep it together, to remain neutral. I was desperate to not show how affected I was by the news of what had happened to Jules, and the way Garrett had watched me had left me so nervous. I'd been on edge the rest of the night, paranoid he knew my secret.

Terrified that if he did, he'd betray me. It would have been so easy. One word to his father, to Turion Efraim.

Now I understood. He'd looked like a ghost at the news of Jules's vorakh because he was vorakh, too.

And I understood the urgency with which he'd used it now. This was deeper than saving my life, deeper than saving his. It was about saving everyone else. Akadim were already the greatest threat we faced, with their strength and brutality, their lack of souls and a conscience. But an akadim who'd been vorakh when alive... one who could travel. They'd be a monster nearly impossible to stop.

Before me now, bleeding, pale, exhausted, his boots soaked with river water, Garrett fell to his knees, his arms outstretched, muscles tensed. "Aiden won't understand," he said sadly. He squeezed his eyes shut, holding open the pathetic remains of his armor and tunic. "Do it quickly, Rhyan. Just... do it."

"Do what?" I stepped forward. "Garrett, what the fuck? Stop holding your shirt open and let me help you up."

He snapped his gaze to me, his mouth open. "Rhyan, I'm—"

"You're vorakh," I said.

"Yes," he whispered, his voice frail and helpless.

With the sudden onset of emotions the night had awakened inside of me—the terror, the grief, the actual fucking longing—it all combined with the need to let Garrett know that he wasn't alone. Not the way I'd felt alone for so long.

Watching him carefully, I let go. I felt it happen. I *let* it happen.

My stomach tugged violently after going so long without using my vorakh, and my boots lifted from the rocks. My body vanished, and I reappeared a few yards back, my feet landing on the roots of a moon tree, the leaves glittering with silver.

Garrett's eyes widened.

"Me, too," I said, my heart pounding with an almost foreign intensity.

"By the Gods."

"By something," I said dully. If the Gods had done this to me, then, it was just another level of their cruelty I'd been destined to experience in this life.

My chest heaved, sudden exhaustion coming over me even though I'd only traveled a few yards. I was so out of practice.

Watching Garrett closely, I did it again, this time returning to the rocks, bracing myself so I wouldn't slip. Finally, he took my hand, and I pulled him to his feet. With our hands clasped together, our eyes met as our realizations truly sank in. We were both cursed, both hiding the same deadly secret. And now we had to decide what to do about it.

Garrett released my hand.

"How?" I asked. "How did you conceal it at the Revelation Ceremony?"

Garrett frowned; his eyes distant. "I didn't. It developed a few months after. The first time it happened, Gods, I was so pissed. Ended up in the woods, nearly falling into a pile of gryphon-shit. I tried to get back the same way I came, but I couldn't do it again and stumbled home before I passed out. Weeks went by, and it didn't happen again. I thought I'd imagined it or had been too wasted to really know if that was what had happened, thought maybe Dario was pranking me. Or I'd gotten fucked up over a shit batch of moonleaves. I was always too afraid to ask in case I was wrong. Then, it began to happen again, to take me away, over and over. It's been months, and I can barely control it most days. But Aiden... he grounds me. How did you hide it?"

"I was...um...unbound. Early."

Garrett's eyes widened. None of my friends knew that at my Revelation Ceremony, I had still been bound when I'd showed my first sign of strength. I'd had two bindings on me, and the arkmage had only removed the first. The second had been taken off so as not to interfere with the creation of my *kashonim* at the Oath Ceremony, but then my father had rebound me again and again until I had nearly complete control over my power. Until I couldn't *feel* anymore.

"Aiden doesn't know?" I asked.

Garrett's jaw tensed. "No. No one knows." His eyes fell on

his boots. "Gods, I love him. So, so much. He helps. But he doesn't know. He's such a stickler for the rules." He sucked on his lower lip, frowning. "I can't tell him."

I bit the inner corner of my cheek. Aiden loved Garrett fiercely. I tried to imagine a world in which he wouldn't protect him, wouldn't understand if he knew his secret. Then, I remembered the world we actually lived in. The one where Lyr had watched Jules be taken away. The one where no matter how much love Aiden held for Garrett, no matter how much he'd want to protect him, he might not be allowed to, not if he wanted to live. And I understood.

Garrett's eyes ran back and forth across my face. "Even if I thought with every bone of my body he'd understand," he shook his head, "I still couldn't do that to him. Force him to carry a secret like this, one that would endanger him."

I nodded. "I'd never endanger him either."

"And I can't risk my family." Garrett's voice cracked. "My father's position, our Ka, it's so new, so fragile. I couldn't do that to my mother, or my sister. Her future..."

Ka Aravain was not noble. Garrett's father had risen in the ranks due to his skill. But Efraim was the first member of Ka Aravain to earn a place on the Glemarian Council. It had allowed Garrett to attend school with me. To become my friend. And Aiden's, and Dario's.

His vorakh would ruin them. Ruin his sister's future— whether or not they escaped the Empire's scrutiny. They weren't nobles, but if his family was suspected of keeping his vorakh secret—they could still be killed. Ka Batavia as far as I knew was still an exception and not the rule—much as my father abused the knowledge of what had happened to manip- ulate me.

Garrett wrung his hands together. "Fuck."

"We're okay," I said. "We're alive. Neither of us are akadim.

Neither of us are going to become so." I was sure of that. We'd been cut, beaten. But they hadn't gotten to our souls. If they had gotten to those...sucked them out from our hearts to eat... we'd be turning forsaken. Half-alive. Half-dead, even if we were breathing. Even if our bodies were intact, our minds still working...the black mark would be spreading across our chests, waiting for the next nightfall when we'd become the monsters we feared.

Luckily, that wasn't happening. That would never, ever happen. Not as long as I could help it.

Garrett bit his lip, still looking unconvinced. "But...the vorakh?"

"We promise," I said. "Right here, right now. Neither of us will say a word."

"Swear," Garrett said.

I pressed my fist to my heart. "I swear. *Me sha, me ka.* I won't tell a soul."

Garrett shook his head. "No. The words of Ka Hart aren't enough. Not for this." He stilled; his eyes set on me. "We need a blood oath."

I balked. "A blood oath? Garrett, no. No." I couldn't imagine any circumstance where I'd expose Garrett or where he'd expose me. But blood oaths were dangerous. Breaking one meant death. And sometimes...sometimes secrets had a way of coming out, whether willingly or not.

"Not to keep this secret, not exactly," Garrett said, as if reading my mind. "One day I might—might need to tell Aiden. Might have to. I don't know. And you?" He shrugged. "Maybe you'll need to tell Kenna. But we both know we have a target on our backs the minute we fuck up. The minute we lose control and vanish. The minute we face akadim again. Just knowing what we know puts us at risk. So, we swear to protect each other from danger—

protect each other and protect our own. We protect our Kavim. And we protect Dario, Kenna, Aiden...no matter what."

A cold breeze left shivers on my skin.

My aura suddenly felt unfamiliar, overpowering me with its strength. My heart was pounding, my blood coursing through my veins. I was feeling more than I had in months. My emotions were overwhelming me. But right now, the main feeling was fear.

I clasped Garrett's shoulder. "You know I'd always protect you and yours. I protect my friends. Without question." I wanted to get back to the fields, to fight the akadim, to find Dario and Aiden, to see Kenna and hold her, to make sure everyone was safe. I didn't know how we were going to get back without being seen or revealing that at some point we'd abandoned the fight. And every inch of me was rebelling at the idea of the oath.

Blood oaths were my father's territory—his way of controlling everyone around him. Even Uncle Sean had fallen prey to them. When I'd seen him two summers ago, he hadn't been able to speak fully about my father's doings because of his oaths. An oath was also the reason why Bowen had never ratted me out for using vorakh to anyone but my father. And it was the one punishment, the one weapon of control, my father hadn't used on me.

For some reason, despite all of his abuse, all of the times I had disappointed him, all of the times he'd told me I was nothing, that I was no better than gryphon-shit—I knew this much —my father wanted me alive. Bowen had told me so.

"Garrett, listen to me. Please," I said. "I've never broken an oath before."

The wind blew, pushing his blond waves back, his eyes set with determination. He looked suddenly older than his years, his face haggard. "I know you haven't. That's how I know you won't break this one either."

I watched the blood still dripping down his stomach and chest, forming pools on his leather belt, his Valalumir stars shining and bloodied.

Garrett unsheathed his dagger.

It was the middle of the night, and we were all gathered in the Seating Room, tensed and silent save for the crackling torches spitting light across the aisles. Protocol demanded all nobility gather in Seathorne and stay there until the grounds were cleared. The threat had been stopped hours earlier that night, but we were still bound to the fortress and wide awake. And my father had decided to go ahead and call Court into session. Any other Arkasva would have waited for morning to assemble a Court after a night of horror, but not ours.

Mages were floating potent glasses of beer and wine to the gathered nobles. We'd suffered many attacks over the years. Akadim were nearly as native to the north as gryphons. But five akadim at once was a lot; coupled with the ongoing and increasing appearances of the Afeyan gryphons, all of the Glemarian nobility was on edge. Their auras flinging out across the Seating Room, crashing and bouncing off of the others, were making me nauseous.

But not as nauseous as I'd felt over the knowledge of what I'd done. What I'd promised. And what I'd endured afterward.

I stood tall on the dais, before the Court, trying desperately to maintain my posture, but the skin on my back still itched and burned like hell where Garrett had cut me. We'd tried to pick a spot on my body that wouldn't be noticeable, and considering how often I was lashed, no one would think twice if I had a raised scar there. Honestly, it was stranger to find unblemished skin on my back at this point, with my father and Arkturion Kane's penchant for torturing me.

My father had made sure I was no stranger to pain. It took a lot to rattle me. But something about the cut of Garrett's dagger for the blood oath had hurt far worse than I'd expected, worse even than what happened after. It'd been as if I were feeling not the sting of his blade as it sliced through me, but the weight of my oath.

I felt sweat pool at the nape of my neck, my hair beginning to curl more tightly. I lifted my chin and pushed my shoulders back, knowing all eyes were on me. I'd be punished accordingly if I failed for even a few seconds to appear in proper form as the upstanding and strong Heir Apparent before my people. On the opposite end of the dais, separated by the Seat of Power, stood my mother, her skin still pale from learning I'd fought and barely escaped the beasts.

My father's reaction to this news had been quite different than my mother's. He'd known I'd run from the fight—he just didn't know it had been against my will. Despite his taunts of my cowardice and stupidity, my failure to control my emotions, and the sheer force of his hits, I'd done nothing. I said nothing. I could not defend myself without giving up Garrett.

So, I'd been lashed—right on top of the blood oath that had still been smarting—three times. A new insult from my father had roared into my ears with each swing of his whip alongside reminders that he was doing this for my own good and I was lucky to be the one on the receiving end of this pain tonight, as opposed to my mother.

I was lucky he wasn't renouncing his claim on me, lucky he wasn't finding my mother's replacement.

I'd thrown up afterward, and now I had to stand tall as if everything was fine. As if I were a brave fucking hero.

I wasn't.

But, despite everything, Garrett was. He'd run right into danger when others had run in fear. And he'd killed an akadim, a feat that hadn't been accomplished by a novice in over a decade and before that, half a century.

Hours earlier, I'd been berated for that, too. How dare I humiliate my father by not killing one myself? How dare I let a friend, a lesser man who wasn't even noble—the mere son of the Turion—beat me to it? If any novice was going to be the one to break the record, it should have been me, the son of the Imperator, the son of the most powerful soturion in Glemaria.

But it hadn't been me because I was weak and embarrassing, I wasn't as strong as I thought I was. I wasn't trying as hard as I liked to believe. I'd been slacking, growing cocky and lazy, showing my true colors, proving I had no potential. I was a failure, an immature child, not a man, not a soturion. And once again, I'd brought shame to Ka Hart. Maybe I wasn't truly his son; maybe my mother had cheated on him. How else could the Imperator have birthed such a weakling, a creature with such strange green eyes?

Maybe my father should have accepted the truth—and finally free himself of the shame of us—end my mother's life right there on the spot. Now. Tonight.

The verbal assault was endless.

His escort watched, silent, and unmoving as he withdrew his sword. Bowen stood beside them, still, though his face had been contorted with fury, his eyes glancing worriedly between me and my mother.

Before my father could swing at her, I'd stepped between them, taking the hit and then another—the second one had been for interfering in his affairs.

Then, the lashings came.

No matter what my father said to me or how many times he grabbed my hair, ripping chunks of it out and spitting on my cheeks, I couldn't fight back. Not since Jules. Not since I no longer had any leverage to hold over him. With that knowledge, he was making up for the one year I'd found a small semblance of rebellion against him.

At least tonight it was me and not her. At least I'd saved my mother from him tonight. One fucking night.

I eyed Garrett in his seat several rows from the dais. He gave me a single, curt nod, a small acknowledgment of how everything between us had changed tonight, a look reinforcing that no matter what happened, neither of us would dare break the oath we'd sworn.

He had a black eye forming, a gruesome gash across his cheek. Deep, ugly scratches marred his neck between bruises. He'd covered the rest of his wounds in bandages and wore a freshly laundered tunic. Aiden was holding his hand in both of his. On the bench beside them was Dario, his arm around Kenna, his hand massaging her shoulder. She still looked shaken, but there was something else in her expression, something stubborn, like she was trying to find her courage.

Once my father entered and formally announced the threat was over, Garrett would be invited to stand, and he'd be named a hero before the entire Glemarian Court. Seeing Garrett honored instead of me—having to say the words himself—was going to leave my father in a horrid mood that I expected to last at least a month, if not longer. Tonight's torture session had been only the beginning.

Of the remaining four akadim who'd attacked, two had been dispatched by Arkturion Kane, which would no doubt leave him even cockier and crueler than usual when training began anew. The fourth akadim had been killed by Dario's father, Turion Ronan, and the fifth by another lesser soturion of Ka Gaddayan, another nephew of Arkturion Kane and one of Kenna's many cousins.

No deaths. No forsaken. Thank the Gods. It seemed to be the only thing keeping the nobility from rioting. Not having a single death was a miracle considering there had been five beasts. Not having a single death would have been a miracle with one akadim. But tonight had been strange. They hadn't been acting like normal akadim; they hadn't done anything I'd observed in the past, anything I'd been taught. Akadim were simple creatures. They wanted food, and they went for the food that was easiest to eat. They hunted whoever was in their path, but last night they'd bypassed so much prey...almost as if they had been on a mission. A mission to do what though? I had no fucking clue.

The only soturion they'd seemed determined to finish was Garrett.

And me.

But why? Why us? Why no one else? The question left a sinking feeling in my gut that I wasn't sure I wanted answers to.

Only one possibility came to mind. That Garrett and I were different. More powerful. We were vorakh... Had akadim learned to detect that? Fuck.

Lord Draken, my father's Second, stood in his full soturion armor before the golden Seat of Power, which was still empty of the Imperator. Every second my father made us wait for him, I could feel the auras of the nobility tensing, tightening, strangling me with their force. I was too tired, too beaten to block them out or push back. I focused on Lord Draken, who was giving a lascivious look to my mother. My nostrils flared. My father's Second possessed his exact likeness in almost every single way despite hailing from a different Kavim. Once he'd been kind. Once he'd taken me to the gryphon stables to learn to care for them, letting me trail him on his duties as Master of the Horse.

That ended years ago. Now he was just another copy of my father.

My father who was insisting on keeping us waiting for him to appear.

I shifted my weight between my feet—the pain and pressure of standing so still becoming unbearable. My skin itched, my legs ached, and my eyes were beginning to droop.

At last, the doors creaked open, and the Court members released a soft hush of breath as they stilled and turned their heads in respect.

"His Highness, Arkasva Devon Hart, High Lord of Glemaria, Imperator to the North."

Everyone shuffled their feet, bowing and curtseying as my father entered the room, bringing a darkly heavy auric power that seemed to snuff out all the others.

Lord Draken bowed low and retreated through the back doors while my father stepped up onto the dais and took his place, standing proudly before his Seat. The Court's forced adoration and his ability to command his audience left him pleased, but his chin twitched, revealing his simmering anger, snuffed beneath the surface of his being. It was a small movement I'd learned to watch for, one I knew to take as a warning.

"Be seated," he commanded. The room obeyed, save for me and my mother, expected always to stand at his side, along with the soturi. They remained at attention, their faces alert, their hands on the hilts of their swords, and their feet wide, ready to break into a fight at any moment.

My father's eyes narrowed in acknowledgment before he gave his full focus to his audience. "Thanks to the quick acting and powerful force of the Soturi of Ka Hart, Glemaria is safe.

The threat of the akadim tonight was stopped. And it was done so miraculously without a single death to our people."

The nobles cheered.

He continued, "I know how upsetting it can be to live through these experiences, but I want you all to know that it's going to take more than five pathetic akadim to defeat our soturi."

More cheers followed.

"Governed by my ruling and trained by Arkturion Kane Gaddayan and his Second, Turion Efraim Aravain we have once again proven that the strength of Glemaria, Ka Hart, and the Northern Lumerian Empire, should never be underestimated."

"What about the gryphon?" came a call from the back of the room.

My father froze, his aura snapping. "Shot down," he said. "As all of the Afeyan bastards have been."

Dario's father, Turion Ronan DeTerria, stood, his hair shorn severely short, the opposite of his son's dramatic styling. "Our soturi have been closely monitoring the concern of the Afeyan gryphons crossing our borders. There is no cause for concern. It has been dealt with." He offered a nod at my father, who only acknowledged Dario's father with a quick flick of his eyes in his direction.

"And an invitation to Her Royal Highness Queen Ishtara has been extended," my father said, his mouth smug as he absorbed his audience's reaction.

I narrowed my eyebrows. We never invited the Afeyan Queen to Glemaria. I was under the impression she wouldn't accept any form of invitation were it offered.

"I know what you are all thinking," my father continued, "but I have put together some happy news to ease the pain of what we experienced tonight. As you may know," he said coyly, "I have a rather special anniversary approaching. One I know you'll all be eager to celebrate." He stood, clearly loving the drama, his fingers stroking the ruby hilt of his sword, his hips pressed forward as he strutted to the end of the dais.

My mother sucked in a nervous breath beside me as a sense of foreboding ran down my spine.

"The week of my fiftieth birthday, and my twentieth year as your Arkasva and Imperator, will occur next month. And I thought, what better way to show you all how much I love being your leader and how grateful I am to our strong soturi for laying down their lives than to host a rather special event? One grand enough for even the Afeyan Queen to attend." He chuckled, as if she were ridiculous for not having attended any of our previous events. "It shall serve as the perfect moment to address the concerns we have with the Afeya's current activities."

My father paused, his aura crackling with energy, and the doors to the Seating Room opened. Artem walked inside, his piercing gaze on my father before his eyes flicked to me. He slapped his thigh in acknowledgment then attempted a more structured bow to my father.

"Arrangements have been in the works for some time, thanks to Lord Draken and our noble gryphon handlers." My father raised his hand in acknowledgment to Artem, whom he hadn't bothered to name. Soturi ushered him aside, and all eyes returned to the dais, as my father's chest puffed out. "Next month, beneath the full moon, I am proud to announce we'll be holding an *Alissedari*."

I tensed as an awed hush danced across the room. I'd only ever read about *Alissedari* in scrolls. It was an outdated form of entertainment considered rather barbaric by the current standards of the Empire. Many over the years had spoken out against this type of soturion tournament. It was fought for the pleasure of the Arkasva, based on the games fought in Lumeria

Matavia for the kings and queens of old. But there were two major distinctions about an *Alissedari* that separated it from other tournament games.

The first was that it was fought on the backs of gryphons. Not just a gryphon that you plucked from the stables or knew well; you had to go out into the wilds to find one, often traveling for hours deep into the untamed forests, the places where the gryphons flew without rules. There, you had to convince a gryphon to let you ride it and then have the strength to direct it into battle. Half of the tournament's players never even made it to the fight, as the *Alissedari* was often over by the time most soturi were able to mount and direct their gryphons. If there were even enough for each rider, forget there being enough willing to fly.

And second, the *Alissedari* only ended with one victor. To win the tournament, you had to either outlast the others in a show of stamina, become the last soturion riding their gryphon or, be the first to make a kill.

Soturi were precious to Glemaria—too many resources were thrown at their education and training to have them be killed so easily, and in a game no less, not when the threat of akadim continued to grow in the North. But every year in Academy classes—one was killed. Killed as a warning—as a reminder to the novices and apprentices of what was at stake —what happened if they did not train seriously, did not give the Academy their all.

Many soturi were injured, some to the point of dropping out, remaining maimed for life.

There was no doubt in my mind how the *Allissedari* would end.

With one kill. With the one kill allowed in the Academy.

One kill, and you won the *Alissedari*.

On receiving a single brutal look from my father, I already knew. I was to win. Or else.

It was the ultimate test, the ultimate show of strength for the Heir Apparent.

Perhaps I'll find myself in need of a new Heir Apparent. And a new wife to make him with...

My father's threat one year ago had been a constant shadow on my days. On my choices. On my every interaction with him.

I'd tried to get my mother out. Many times. I'd sworn I would. But I'd failed.

The best I could do was keep her safe—keep her alive. Keep her in her position of power.

But this... this felt like something else—something final in our unspoken agreement. I'd noticed a shift in my father's demeanor recently. And couldn't shake the feeling that this had all been planned for a long time, and that it was some kind of final test.

At the *Alissedari*, I was to bring my father honor.

Or...

I couldn't even imagine the thought. I brought my attention back to the crowd before me.

I suddenly understood why Artem had been ushered here in the middle of the night—he'd had the job of releasing the untrained gryphons into the wild and confirming enough of the creatures existed for there to be just too few for those who desired to participate.

I expected nearly everyone at the Academy would.

Glemaria would be chaos from this moment forward. Soturi from all over the North would come to see the *Alissedari*. And every soturion at the Academy and in the Soturi of Ka Hart would be throwing their sword into the arena.

Dario, Garrett, and I would have no choice. Three sons of

the Glemarian Council, three sons to men who held their positions of power through their show of strength.

My throat remained dry as my father began to announce the night's heroes. He called up Arkturion Kane, whose cold, cruel aura lashed out at me as he stepped up onto the dais. He was honored and revered, praised for his strength and for his killing of not one but two of the monsters. And then his nephew, Kenna's cousin, was called. Then, Dario's father. And finally, Garrett.

He moved slowly, more injured than he was letting on, more shaken and afraid by the night's events than he'd ever admit.

Our eyes met again; our promise reaffirmed as he stood on the dais with me. The sacred words we'd said earlier raced through my mind.

Ani dhara me sha el lyrotz.

I give you my oath in blood.

I will protect your life, and your Ka, from now until my last breath.

Me sha, me ka.

My back burned with fresh pain from the cut, as if remembering the words had sliced me open again. The longer I stood, the more I ached from my beating, and the more my soul hurt from my father's words as my palms itched with ropes that were no longer restricting me. But I could still feel them—I could always feel them.

The nobility cheered. Aiden was clapping harder than I'd ever seen, and Dario looked ready to cry, the fight he'd been in earlier with Garrett completely forgotten. Further back stood Garrett's mother, and his little sister Vanya, emotional, supportive, full of pride. They loved him so much, and showed it so easily in their faces. They still lacked the formal training of nobles, lacked the ability to withhold all show of emotion.

And then there was me... I just stood there, hardly cheering, barely able to smile.

Auriel's bane, I couldn't even be proud of Garrett, knowing all the ways this would be used against me. And maybe... maybe some deep secret part of me was bitter. He'd been the one to show weakness this time. Not me. He'd been the one to take me away. It was his fault I'd been robbed of my chance to prove myself.

After the heroes were acknowledged and seated, promises were made by my father that we were all once again safe. Court finally came to a close. Almost in time for breakfast.

Slowly, the room emptied until there remained only myself, my father, my mother, and my father's personal escort, a dozen of his most loyal and vile soturi, their backs against the walls of green tapestry. The same bastards who'd watched him brutalize me just before without so much as a flinch.

"If you embarrass me again," my father snarled, "if you run like a coward from this fight or you let some barely noble soturion beat you to it—" He grabbed my mother.

Bowen stiffened.

"Stop!" I yelled, as she cried out.

"Prove you are worthy of the name I gave you," he said, his voice low.

I blinked back the tears in my eyes, watching the soturi in my peripheral vision not moving, not reacting.

"Twenty years," he said. "Twenty years I've ruled. And what do I have to show for it?" He pushed my mother aside.

My heart jumped into my throat, but at least he didn't have his hands on her for the moment. Bowen held out an arm for my mother until she regained her composure.

"Rhyan," my father said, his voice now gentle and soft, full of love. He shook his head, his eyes drooping like he was speaking to a small child.

I felt my gut clench. The shifts in his demeanor never stopped leaving me feeling off-center, half-mad, and farther than Lethea.

He squeezed my shoulder. "You know what you must do. You know what is at stake if you fail. You will do whatever you must to win this tournament."

He thrust his arm around my mother's waist, and she offered me one sparing look, her eyes watery, before they headed for the Arkasva's exit.

I stood trying to catch my breath beside the Seat of Power, alone with a dozen soturi—soldiers loyal to my father and my father alone.

Gods. Nothing was enough. Nothing was ever fucking enough for him. Losing the girl I loved. Taking to bed every noble he wished me to. Remaining quiet when he hurt my mother, standing by his side for hours upon hours without complaint. Taking the brunt of his hits, his punches, his lashes in silence.

I'd given my life, my blood, my soul to Glemaria. To his rule.

And now...now he wanted me to do the unthinkable.

Win the *Alissedari*. Not just give my life in his service and honor—but take one. Kill.

Win.

Across the room, the doors to the hall remained open, and Garrett stood in the threshold. Our eyes met, my back burning still, as he gave me one final look.

CHAPTER
SIX

I punched the wall before I tore off my armor, throwing my weapons and clothes into the corner of my room, not bothering to hang the leathers over my dummy. Every muscle ached, and every inch of my skin either hurt, itched, or burned. I was so fucking exhausted. My father's words were pounding in my head.

Coward. Idiot. Weak. Failure. Embarrassment to the Ka.

I knew it wasn't true. I knew better than to listen to his words. Than to succumb to his insults. I'd told myself a thousand times. But somehow knowing this didn't alleviate the pain, didn't take away the feeling. Somehow tonight, I couldn't shake free of his grip, of his hatred.

His disappointment.

And now there were his new demands.

Win. Kill.

I'd kept my feelings buried for a year. And now...I couldn't gain control. Couldn't tamp them down.

A bath would have been nice. Or a shower. Something to

wash away this night, his touch. Something to soothe my nerves. To forget the task he'd set before me.

But I was too Godsdamned tired to move. And I didn't have it in me to call for a servant to arrange one. I didn't want to see the question in their eyes, nor could I bear the moment they understood what had happened, understood and continued to remain silent.

Down to my short-pants, I sat on the bed, reconsidering if I should at least call for some mead. Perhaps I could drink enough to black out. Not dream. Not think.

Not feel.

Auriel's bane. Something had shifted within me tonight, and it was overwhelming. I'd felt dead inside for so long. Every feeling seemed like too much.

There was a soft knock on my door.

"Come in," I called, my eyes closed, my elbows heavy on my knees as I winced. Whatever Bowen wanted, I didn't fucking care.

Instead of his voice, a soft, feminine one said, "I'm sorry it's so late...or early, I suppose."

I looked up immediately. "Kenna."

She wore a cream-colored shawl around her shoulders, her arms wrapped around herself, like she was cold despite the warmth of the summer night. Her brown hair was loose, falling past her shoulders. "I'm sorry, I just..." She shook her head, her bottom lip trembling. "I didn't want to be alone tonight."

I slid off the bed, crossing the room and wrapping her in my arms. "It's okay. You can always come here, you know that."

She nodded, letting her weight fall against me as her aura swept around me, cold and heavy. "I feel so stupid. I didn't even fight them. But, Rhy, I've never been so scared before. Learning about the akadim and hearing the stories about them, it's not the same as seeing them. Seeing them invade somewhere... somewhere you thought was your own. Somewhere you thought was safe. And knowing that your family, your friends, your..." Her eyes caught mine, her voice breaking. "The people you care about...knowing they were out there, too." She held me tighter.

It was almost a relief to feel her in my arms. It had been hours since we'd touched, since the danger had started. And it was a relief to be touched gently again—not with the intention to hurt me, kill me, or force an oath.

And...if I were being honest—I was relieved to touch someone in return in that way.

"It's okay. It's not stupid. It's a lot to take in." I stroked her hair, pushing it off her shoulder. "I've seen them. Many times. You never get used to it."

Her eyes searched mine as she absorbed the words, and then something shifted in her aura, some kind of uncertainty. "I know we don't really, usually..." She trailed off, pressing her cheek back against my chest. "But," she said, her voice unsure, "can I stay with you tonight?"

I squeezed my eyes shut. "Of course, you can." I wrapped my fingers around her hand, pulling back so I could turn and lead her to the bed.

But Kenna froze. "Rhy! Gods, your back."

I released her hand, turning abruptly on my heels to face her. "It's nothing," I said. I was suddenly hyper-aware of every cut, bruise, scrape, and scar that marred my flesh. Kenna had seen me naked more times than I could remember, but never like this, never when the wounds were this fresh, this raw, this new. I hadn't even bothered attempting to bandage them. What was the point? My soturion strength was already healing them. There'd just be more come tomorrow.

But underlying all of that was the one scar that burned far worse than the others. The one from Garrett.

I felt my heart thudding, trying to pound its way out of my chest. The cut on my back flamed to life as if warning me how close I was to breaking my oath.

Me sha, me ka...

Kenna stepped forward, her eyes raking over the cuts and scrapes across my chest.

I couldn't breathe. Couldn't believe I'd been this careless. This stupid.

But her eyes softened. Not with pity nor accusation, but fear. "That's what the akadim did to you?"

Tears welled in her eyes, and something unclenched inside me. She didn't know about the blood oath. About the vorakh. She didn't know what my father had done to me. Didn't understand the calculated pattern of cuts and bruises across my back. And she never would.

I nodded. "Shhhh." I wrapped her in my arms again. "Ken, I promise you, I'm all right. This is what soturi train for. I'll be okay, I swear." I tried to laugh. "Garrett looks even worse. And don't forget the hangover Dario will be nursing tomorrow."

She chuckled, still sniffling, and I kissed the top of her head.

She pulled back, just enough to run her fingers over my chest, her palm flattened against my heart. "And... you're... you're safe? Not going to turn into one?"

I shook my head. "No. See." I pulled her hand away, locking my fingers with hers. "No black mark. I'm not forsaken. Not going to turn akadim. I swear."

Kenna nodded.

"Come to the bed." I started pulling her back again, not wanting to give her a second look at my back, to ponder the questions I'd seen in all of my best friends' eyes for years—

questions that remained unasked. Questions I could never answer.

She frowned but with a faraway look in her brown eyes and let me lead her to sit on the edge of my mattress. I pulled back the covers for her then hesitated. Kenna never slept over. Nor did I stay overnight with her. My room was missing any sort of personal affects she might require or want to spend the night.

"Is there anything you need?" I asked. "For bed?"

Kenna shook her head, still watching my face carefully. "I'm fine. But what about you? Are you in pain?"

I was. I was in so much pain, I could barely hold it in. Auriel's bane, even my heart hurt. But I couldn't show it. I couldn't risk her mentioning anything of my extended injuries to Dario. I couldn't risk Garrett worrying I'd let Kenna in on our secret. I couldn't bear the looks in their eyes as they again revealed they suspected what was happening to me but, because of who I was, and because of who my father was, they wouldn't do or say a thing.

I cupped my hand around her slim neck and turned her to me, brushing my lips against hers. I kissed her gently at first, like always, allowing her to take the lead, to decide when to deepen the kiss and let it become something more.

Kenna crawled onto my lap, her legs wrapped around my waist, and with a moan, she pressed herself against me, a frenetic energy in her aura, like she was clinging to something —something to wash away the night's horror and fear.

She was already wet. I was sure of it even if I couldn't feel it through the fabric of the clothing between us. Her hands ran gently, down my back. I stifled a whine of pain. Rolling her hips into me, she kissed me again, her tongue stroking mine until she let out a small noise of frustration and pulled back.

I wasn't hard. Not even close. I hurt too much. I felt too defeated.

SON OF THE DROWNED EMPIRE

Kenna's cheeks were no longer red with arousal but embarrassment. "I shouldn't have. You're hurt. We don't... we don't have to. I swear I didn't come here for that. I came to sleep."

My eyes searched hers. And my father's words, his threats, his demands all pounded through my mind.

"We can do both," I growled, determined to not let any further weakness show. To prove I could do this. To prove I was strong, that my will was still stronger than my heart.

"Rhy," she gasped.

I tightened my grip on her waist, pressing her against me as I flipped her onto her back and rolled over her body. Her eyes widened in surprise at my sudden aggression, a question pulsing through her aura. I'd never taken her like this.

I'd almost always been the one on top with my past lovers, the one initiating the act, the one needing release to take the edge off a rough day and forget myself. But since my father had ordered me to fuck my way through the nobility and prove I was a man capable of bearing heirs, I'd been on the bottom. Every single time. I let them do what they wanted to me, take what they wanted. Even with Kenna, even when we rolled around the bed, shifting positions for hours, this was where I started. It just seemed easier that way. I could pretend I wasn't heartbroken or powerless. I could pretend I wasn't passive or disinterested. Pretend I simply preferred it like this.

I pressed myself between Kenna's thighs, forcing myself to be present. I pulled the hem of her dress up her smooth legs, higher and higher, until she was bare, and ran my fingers over her skin, feeling her warmth, her softness. Up and up my hand moved until it covered her breast; small and round, it fit perfectly into my palm. I squeezed, thumbing her peaked nipple as she writhed beneath me, a moan on her lips. Her fingers tangled in my hair, as I licked my way down her smooth belly, parting her thighs, sucking on her center as she whim-

FRANKIE DIANE MALLIS

pered, lifting and pressing herself against me. And there it was. I was hard.

Whether it was the adrenaline of the night kicking in, some animalistic instinct taking over me, or an actual spark rising between us, everything felt like it shifted in that moment. I wanted her. I craved her. I needed her like I never had before.

The cut on my back promised death, but here in Kenna's arms—between her legs and her mouth and her warmth—here was life. Just like earlier when I'd realized I'd wanted to live, I felt it again, that need to feel alive, to feel a connection.

I no longer *wanted* to want.

I wanted.

I hungered.

Heat rushed through me. "Gods, Kenna, the taste of you," I said, licking and sucking, needing to drink every last drop of her arousal.

I pulled her legs over my shoulders, pumping one finger into her and then another until she squirmed and cried out. Even as her legs shook, I didn't relent. I couldn't stop tasting her, sucking her, kissing her, as if my life depended on it.

She tensed again beneath me. I felt her pause and reach for my shoulders, drawing me up her body, her hand slipping beneath my short-pants, wrapping around me, stroking and teasing as I bucked against her, somehow growing harder.

There was an almost shy smile creeping across her lips before I kissed her again, rougher this time. The need that seemed to have been asleep for ages had awakened inside of me. I couldn't explain it. A moment ago, I'd been ready to pass out, not caring what happened. And now it felt like if I pressed myself close enough to her, I could live—I could find life. I could protect myself from the death that had surrounded me all evening, from the doom I felt around the secret I carried, from the oath I had to fulfill.

108

Whatever sensation had come alive inside me, she felt it, too. Her heels pressed into the bed as she rolled her hips to meet mine again and again. There'd never been this passion, this desperation, before between us.

We were frantic to come together as if we'd been waiting for this a long time, the two of us pulling her dress off completely. She reached for what remained of my clothes, sliding them down until I was able to kick them off around my ankles.

My breath came in shallow pants. The need to be inside her was overwhelming as she rubbed herself against me, coating me in her arousal.

"Is this okay?" I asked, suddenly unsure of myself. I normally took my time, and I never took this much control. I was rarely so full of need, so full of the desperation to fuck that we got here this quickly. I'd never once exhibited this much aggression. Not once had I wanted it this badly. Not since...

Kenna smiled, nodding breathlessly as I plunged inside her. My heart pounded. Our eyes locked, I held her gaze as I moved in and out at a brutal pace, she matched thrust for thrust, and our hands joined above her head. I'd seen Kenna come undone so many times, but every time it had happened, she had been over me, her face distant from mine or pressed against my chest or shoulder.

Her eyes always somewhere else. Looking away. Away from me.

Not tonight.

Tonight, her eyes bore into mine, holding my gaze, steady and unwavering and beautiful. When I came, I felt something come apart inside of me, a longing and a need that should have been sated but were only just beginning to awaken. Like a dream I'd just remembered.

She pulled my face to hers, kissing me and kissing me until

I slid out, still panting, and lay beside her. My eyes closed, an uneasy feeling snaking through my insides. The need, the want...they had been real. They had been so fucking real, so consuming, and now...now I didn't know.

Inside of Kenna, I could have sworn that something had sparked to life inside of me. Something I'd thought was gone. Hope.

But something was off. Something felt wrong.

Still trying to catch my breath, to temper the unruly beating of my heart, I pulled Kenna against me. She didn't push me away, and we fell asleep together for the first time, our arms and bodies entangled. I tried to take comfort in small victories. At least tonight, at least for a few moments, I hadn't hurt anymore. I could feel that, for once, my heart was alive, it was still beating. I could still feel something beyond pain. Something better. Something sweet. But it was something unbelievably dangerous.

∼

MY BOOTS SLID across the soft sand of the beach as the waves of the ocean rolled back and forth across the shore. The sun beat down, too hot, too bright, and I walked forward, catching sight of something shimmery in the water.

I had to get to it, retrieve it from the ocean's depths. Green light flashed, painfully bright, emerald... like my eyes. Then, the sand seemed to erupt like a small volcano until I could see golden leaves rising from beneath its surface.

The sun tree stood tall against the beach, having grown in impossible conditions, with impossible speed.

The waves crashed against the shore again and again, but their sound was gone, and instead, I heard only a light breeze, the rustling of leaves, and a familiar sigh.

Lyriana leaned back against the tree, looking up at me with her beautiful hazel eyes, her thick lashes painted black, and her lips that perfect shade of pink that was all her own. The golden light of the tree and sun shined down on her, turning her beautiful dark wavy hair to flaming red.

Batavia red.

I reached for a strand, rolled it around my finger, and waited for the fires to burn me, but her locks were soft and smooth. Cool to the touch.

"You left," she said, her voice distant and echoing across the waves.

My heart sank at her words. "I had to. To protect you."

She nodded, understanding. "You couldn't protect her." Sadness coated her voice.

"I miss her letters."

A tear rolled down her cheek. "I miss her."

I wiped it away with my finger, watching in fascination as the tear transformed into a seven-pointed star, golden and shimmery, almost blinding in its brightness until it vanished into nothing.

"You haven't visited my dreams in a long time," I said.

She gave me an accusatory look, her face suddenly full of a stubborn defiance I knew well. "That's because you tried to forget me."

"But I can't."

"Neither can I," she breathed.

My breath was heavy, like I couldn't get enough air. She smelled so sweet, like vanilla and lemon and something musky, something that was just... her. It was overwhelming me, drowning out the salt of the ocean. And my heart pounded. I had a distant memory of it beating, thundering in my chest. And thinking it was real. But it wasn't, it was shallow. It was nothing compared to this, to this feeling being before her. This was being alive. This was wanting.

"You feel so real," I said.

She smiled. "Because I am."

"It's your birthday."

She stared past me. "Not anymore. I stopped celebrating."

"Lyriana." I took her chin in my hand.

"It never stops," she said.

"What never stops?"

"You know."

I leaned forward, one hand against the tree, the other sliding to cup her cheek as I lowered my lips to hers.

I paused, just a breath away from her, waiting for permission.

Lyr nodded, and with a groan, I kissed her. She tasted so sweet, so familiar. I dipped my tongue into her mouth, needing more, needing to devour her until I understood the answer to some question I hadn't asked yet, but knew in my soul that I would.

Suddenly, the leaves of the tree crumpled and caught fire until even the roots were gone. Lyr stood several feet away from me, her bare feet in the water, the waves rushing forcefully against her ankles.

The water rose, rising to her calves and her knees, drenching and pulling down her white dress.

Panic thrashed through me. I ran forward, but I couldn't get anywhere; my feet kept stepping down in the same place. I pumped my arms at my side, running faster, faster, gasping for breath. But the water kept rising, higher and higher, and I couldn't get ahead. I couldn't move.

"Lyriana!" I screamed. "Lyr! You'll drown!"

"I know," she said calmly, the water now at her waist.

"Come out of the water!"

She shook her head. "I'm drowning."

Come on, come on, come on! Fuck!

If I ever needed my vorakh to work, it was now. But I couldn't travel. I couldn't move. I couldn't stop running in place. My feet were digging holes into the sand.

"Lyr!" I roared, desperate. "Swim!"

She remained still, the water now covering her breasts.

"LYR!"

Beside her, a man emerged from the water, his head turned away from me. His hair gleamed a rich brown in the sun, and he moved forward in the water, away from the shore, deeper and deeper, dragging Lyr with him.

"LYR!" I roared again, my heart shattering. "Lyr! No!"

The man turned to look at me, his eyes raking me up and down with disinterest. Lord Tristan Grey. He turned away again, pulling Lyr farther back, farther away from me, farther into the water.

"He's drowning me," she said, her voice still calm, serene.

The waters rushed over her head.

I jolted awake, my chest heaving, barely able to breathe. I was suffocating on the scents of vanilla, musk, and lemon. The way Lyriana had smelled two summers ago.

Kenna stirred beside me, as the visions of Lyr raced through my mind. The taste of her was on my lips, far more real and intense in my dream than Kenna's had been last night. My fear, lingering from the dream, was making me sick, drowning my body in a cold sweat.

Rushing to my bathing room, I squeezed my eyes shut, willing the images of Lyriana going beneath the waters to cleanse themselves from my mind.

Myself to Moriel. My dreams were often so hard to hang onto, filled with images I'd awake to, wishing to remember, desperate to keep, only to lose them the moment I sat up in bed.

So many had been filled with her—lost the instant my eyes opened.

But not this one. Gods, why? Why was this the one that would stay to haunt me?

I sank to my knees, my stomach twisting as I wretched. My face was covered in sweat, and I barely had the strength to wipe at my mouth before I sat back against the cold wall of my bathing room, trying to breathe and clear my mind.

He's drowning me.

The door creaked open, and Kenna stood before me, wrapped in my blanket.

"Rhy, are you okay?" she asked, crouching beside me.

I shook my head, turning away, not wanting her to see me like this—not wanting her to have to deal with me. It didn't matter how often we'd fucked or confided in each other or that we'd spent last night wrapped in each other's arms.

It wasn't until last night I'd felt true intimacy with Kenna, and now I understood why I'd been so hungry for her. I'd thought my will was stronger than my heart, but it wasn't. My emotions... they were back in full force. In every way. And as much as I knew now that something like love was growing between Kenna and me, it still wasn't enough. My heart was always going to belong to Lyriana. Was always going to beat for her. It was always going to hunger for her, no matter how deeply it opened to anyone else.

Kenna sat down beside me, holding open the blanket for me to move in toward her. I did and felt her arm wrap around me, warm and reassuring, but I couldn't face her, couldn't speak.

All I could see was Lyr. All I could feel was Lyr.

Lyriana.

Kenna took my chin in her hand, turning me to face her.

"Ken, I'm sorry," I said, my voice shaky. Everything between us felt like it was bursting inside my heart, and yet floating outside my body—too delicate and fragile to survive. I was terrified. Feeling was dangerous. Feeling for Kenna... Kenna who was already under my father's roof could be deadly —another toy for him to play with—to torture, to threaten.

"Rhy, it's okay. Whatever it is. I'm right here. I'm with you."

I rested my head on her shoulder, and her hand stroked my hair. I couldn't tell her. I didn't know how I could. She was there, and she was real, and I was raw with need and something like the beginnings of love for her.

But Lyriana was here, too, her ghost far too present, far too real for what she was, for what she'd been.

"You're okay," Kenna soothed. "I've got you."

I'm drowning.

A tear rolled down my cheek, and I squeezed my eyes shut, sinking into Kenna's touch.

Me, too. Me, too.

CHAPTER
SEVEN

T he night was nearly black. Fall had come with such a powerful force, it already felt like winter in Glemaria. Only four weeks remained for us to prepare for the *Alissedari.*

Tensions amongst the soturi at the Academy had intensified. Since the announcement of the tournament, most of my classmates had begun forming alliances and making secret deals to help bring certain soturi to the victor's mount while others seemed to be plotting who they could kill in order to win quickly. This was not the time to make enemies. Not when there'd been a pass offered to murder freely.

The thought of it made me sick. Even now in the night's habibellum, I could see the plotting, the pointing out of rivals turned bitter enemies. We already had too many factions. *Kashonim,* and small bands of soturi who warred with the group responsible for killing or maiming one of their own were beginning to stand out.

I'd always tried to stay out of the fights, to remain neutral.

But being the son of the Imperator, the Heir Apparent, and

being best friends with the son of Glemaria's Turion, and Master of the Peace... I was always a target. Always defending myself. Always had been.

And now... I had been tasked with winning. With making the kill. Unless someone else got to me first.

Garrett and Dario flanked me in the center of the arena. In the stands of the Katurium, all three of our apprentices were watching, their eyes trained on us. Somehow, we'd also ended up with a set of best friends as apprentices: Anil of Ka Vikken trained Dario; Garrett was with a distant cousin on my father's side, Carson Hart; and I had been bound into *kashonim* with Senator Balyr's son, Thorin Oryyan. Their friendship had allowed the three of us to frequently train together and form our own miniature legion of which I was in command. But it also meant that a dangerous alliance had already formed for the tournament—our apprentices against us. They knew our battle moves inside and out, and worse, they knew our weaknesses. For once, it wasn't the other novices I'd have to fear—but my own teachers who'd come for me—who'd have nothing to lose. Who could threaten not just me and my friends, but my mother if I failed.

"Thorin's in a mood," I said, holding up my arm. I blocked a hit from an opponent, some soturion from Ka Gaddayan that had been counting on his bulk alone to throw me off.

"The fuck cares?" said Dario, spinning on his heels. He barely avoided a hit, and as he turned, he punched his elbow back, taking out the same soturion from Ka Gaddayan that'd come for me. They never learned.

I tensed, seeing the space between Thorin's eyebrows crease. If I had to admit it, he was a good apprentice and taught me well. But he never budged a fucking inch, never gave me a break. As the son of the senator, he walked around the Katurium like he had something to prove. But since he wanted to win the *Alissedari*, he was going extra hard on me—not to prepare me, but to break me down. To take out his competition in advance.

I didn't think he'd have the guts to kill me.

But I wouldn't put much else past him.

"Dario," Garrett warned. "Your cousins are banning together."

"Shit."

Eyeing the oncoming group of DeTerria soturi, I brought my weight forward. They blamed Dario for breaking a popular cousin's leg. He'd broken it himself—with his own stupidity—but facts hadn't really mattered when they'd sworn their vendetta last spring.

"Fuck the defense," Dario said. "The hell are we guarding back here? Let's go."

Garrett's side-eye said all I needed to know. This was a bad idea. But if we didn't back up Dario, he'd go into the fray without us, and I'd be the one nursing his wounds all night.

We charged as all eleven of Dario's cousins closed their ranks, their black curls—the defining feature of the DeTerrias—blurring as they formed a single unit.

Dario released a battle cry as he surged forward, punching his first cousin right in the gut. He doubled over, groaning as he fell to the ground. Instantly, two more emerged from their unit and flanked Dario, grabbing his arms and pulling him back. Garrett ran to his defense, pulling the first soturion off then the second as another pair came to fight. This left the rest of his cousins with their attention on me.

Fucking perfect.

Thorin shouted something at me in that moment. I turned though I should have known better than to let him distract me.

It happened fast.

One soturion snuck behind, his hands pinning my wrists to

my back before I could react. I sucked in a breath, my whole body freezing with tension.

It's not a binding, not a binding. Just some idiots from Ka DeTerria who thought they could take me.

I could handle this. I wasn't bound. I was free. I was strong, and far more disciplined and trained than them. I inhaled through my nose, exhaled through my mouth.

They weren't binds. They were puny ropes. And I could tear through those.

Within seconds, I released my arms from their prison. They all froze, stunned at my show of strength. With a jerk back of my head, I took out the soturion who'd tried to hold me. One raced down the pathway that led to me, and I roared, running forward, grabbing his shoulders, and flinging him to the side. He knocked out another soturion, leaving four for me to take.

I steadied myself, prepared to hold my ground as they surrounded me.

One punched me from behind as another came at my left, leaving me winded. I'd be bruised, but it wasn't enough to take me down. With a swipe of my arm, I got the one at my side before I found myself face-first in the dirt. Fuck... I'd forgotten to protect my left. Seething as the sweat coating my forehead ran into my eyes, I kicked out, trapping my attacker's leg with mine. I had just enough strength to roll us over, and from there, I elbowed him in the nose.

Above the neck. I'd get a penalty. But I didn't care. I just wanted these fuckers off me.

Jumping back to my feet, I caught sight of Dario and Garrett relinquishing their opponents, but before they could come to my side, another band of soturi—this time from Ka Oryyan—flew at them.

I punched the soturion in front of me, three times in his stomach, my knuckles raw with the effort to push through his leathers. On my last punch, he wheezed and collapsed to his knees.

There were still two soturi of Ka DeTerria frothing at the mouth to hit me. I'd lost track by then of whether or not I'd already fought them. They kept reforming, and their matching curls made them impossible to tell apart.

"Come on, Hart," one taunted. "Why do you keep getting up? Heard you like it on your back."

My nostrils flared, and I ran. They charged at once, rushing too far out to my right and left sides for me to reach either. A second passed, and without warning, they both turned at a run, trapping me between them. Each took one of my arms, and before I could get my bearings, I was dragged back, away from Garrett and Dario. The chill of the silver habibellum ring was already at my back, the buzzing of its magic growing louder in warning as we approached.

Fuck. Fuck! They were going to slam me into it.

I dug my heels into the ground, my teeth grinding together. I had only just recovered from my father's last beating. With a grunt, I threw my weight forward, my arms pushing against them.

"Fuck!" yelled the one on my right.

I took that as a sign I was winning, beginning to overpower him. The freezing burn of the ring was nearly on me. I could feel its fiery ice. If they moved me another two inches, I was going to touch it.

Releasing another groan of pain, I put all I had into my arm muscles, feeling them nearly tear with the effort, but with seconds to spare, I pushed off the soturion on my right, freeing my right arm. I punched left, my fist slamming into the neck of the soturion on that side. There was a wheezing huff of breath as he fell, and I raced forward, wanting to get as far from the ring as possible. Garrett and Dario were surrounded. Again.

Before I could reach them, the time was called. Arkturion Kane yelled out, his voice enhanced by a sound spell from one of the Katurium mages. The rest of them circled the habibellum, their staves out as they removed the silver ring keeping the novice soturi captive.

Cheers erupted from the stands from all of the apprentices watching. I found Thorin; his mouth was tight, frowning.

If anything, I'd just shown him that I was, in fact, his fucking competition.

As Anil nudged him impatiently, I could tell our apprentices were planning to go drinking instead of sticking around to torture us. Thank the Gods.

The apprentices in the stands were cheering as they filed out. It had been a long week. Just as quickly, the field began to empty, the novices headed either for the baths or home. I started to move off the field with my friends when Arkturion Kane called out to me.

I bit the inside corner of my cheek.

"Your Grace. Stay," he ordered.

I turned to him and nodded once that I'd heard, willing my fingers not to tense.

"Want us to wait?" Garrett asked.

"No. Go on without me."

Dario's dark eyebrows narrowed. "The fuck for? You kicked ass tonight."

I shrugged. As if it mattered. If he'd been ordered to punish me by my father, I could have been the best one out there, and he'd still have found a reason to lash me, to tear me down.

"Not about Kenna?" Dario asked.

I shook my head and waved them off despite the sinking feeling that had begun forming in my gut.

Since that night, the night when our fucking had turned into something else and my heart had been cut open and left raw for both Kenna and Lyriana, our relationship had felt strained. We'd spent the following day stuck to each other's sides, holding hands, kissing, and falling back into bed, as if we were under some sort of spell and if we broke apart, it would end.

And then we did part, and I didn't know what to do. I had feelings for Kenna, and I thought she did for me, and that... that scared me more than the akadim attack had. Caring for Kenna made her vulnerable; it made her a potential plaything for my father to use against me, to control me with.

I knew it was cowardly, but I pretended that night never happened. That nothing had changed between us.

Every night afterward when she came to my room and I took her to my bed, it was like before. I was passive. Not present. Not holding her hands as I thrust into her, not holding her gaze as she found her release. My energy had gone into trying to reclose my heart.

She'd noticed. I'd seen the obvious confusion in her eyes. And I hated myself for it. I did want her. And I did care for her, more than I thought I'd been capable of, but caring or not caring, it didn't seem to matter. Kenna was leaving a hole in my heart, one only rivaled by the one left from Lyr.

The field nearly empty now, I walked before Kane. Instantly, the burning chill I feared from the rings began raining down on me, sputtering out from his aura. He was always so cold, so volatile, a mass of muscles and a cruel angular face made up of rectangles. His hair was the same shade of brown as Kenna's though noticeably streaked with slivers of gray. The similarities ended there. While Kenna was good and kind and, despite the issues we were having, a true friend, her father was nothing but a wretched killer, a cruel and vile excuse of a man.

"Arkturion," I said, standing before him.

"You've been requested to play ambassador tonight," he spat.

"*Play* ambassador?" I asked. "Correct me if I'm wrong, but don't we have actual ambassadors to fulfill such roles?"

He sneered. "Your father sent word. A foreign dignitary is arriving shortly. Apparently, you made an impression on him some years back. He personally requested your presence. So go bathe and redress in your armor. You'll be welcoming him to Bamaria in an hour's time at the Aravian border. A gryphon awaits you outside the Katurium to bring you to the meeting spot as soon as you're ready."

The skin of my right palm itched like crazy, and I rubbed it against my thigh as sweat beaded on my forehead.

"An impression?" I asked carefully.

I'm very impressed with you. You're far more mature for your age than any other boys in the Empire.

The itch intensified.

I swallowed, pushing out the memory. I was an adult now. I was strong. He couldn't hurt me again. But the idea of facing him, seeing him... I clasped my hands together, but the itch didn't stop.

"I'm not here to feed your ego," sneered Kane. "That's the message. Now go and get ready—sooner rather than later. Bowen's already been alerted. We have no reason to suspect danger, but Your Grace will be accompanied by a full escort, only proper for the Heir Apparent to the Arkasva and Imperator." He clapped his hip and dipped his head forward, the most minuscule of bows he could muster. "Your Grace."

I watched him leave the field, his red arkturion cloak muted as it flew behind him, then I went to shower and change.

Artem was waiting for me outside the Katurium along with my escort and a gryphon to ride. He slapped his thigh when he saw me but didn't speak, only tightened his hold on the gryphon's rope as the cold air blew against my cloak.

"This one's a year old," he said. "Fully able to carry you for this flight."

"So, a teenager?" I asked, my voice stiff. I'd never forgiven Artem for killing the baby gryphon, never gotten over the way he'd kicked me out of the stables.

I knew my father was responsible, but it didn't matter. I was pissed every time I had to see him. He'd been an ally, one of the few people in Glemaria who could offer me something else—offer me some solace. Peace. And he'd let it turn to gryphon-shit at the first test. Let my father condemn an innocent life.

"He's well trained," Artem continued. "Won't give you any trouble now." He stepped forward, placing the rope in my hand.

I flinched at the touch but wrapped the rope around my wrist before gripping the stirrups to climb onto the gryphon's back. His tail wagged behind him as he lay prone.

"Entering the *Alissedari*?" Artem asked as I found the seat. I tied down the rope, buckling myself in as I took hold of the reins.

"As if I have a choice," I said, staring ahead.

"The lot you lads will be picking from are all wild and untrained," Artem said. "Keep that in mind, aye. Attitudes on the bunch of them."

"As suspected," I said, pushing down my boots.

"Any gryphon can be used," Artem said. "None can be shot down once the *Alissedari* begins."

Like an innocent baby gryphon with red feathers? I turned back, eyeing Artem carefully. "Your point?"

"Just wanted to warn you. They're wild."

I stared ahead, biting the inside of my cheek.

Artem shook his head. "Safe flight, Your Grace."

I leaned forward, gripping the reins. *"Volara!"* I yelled.

My gryphon jumped up, leaned back on his haunches, and shot forward, his powerful legs running faster and faster, his muscles tensing beneath me until he leapt, my heart crashing into my throat as we were airborne. I leaned farther forward, keeping my head down, tightening my hold on the reins. Powerful gusts of wind pressed on either side of me as his wings flapped, bringing us above the trees until we were soaring. The temperature dropped, and I regretted not bringing gloves. But at the feeling of flying again, being so close to gryphons, the weight against my soul began to lighten. I'd missed this for the last year, and tried to soak it all in, even the bitter cold gusting in biting waves toward me. Staring ahead, I directed my gryphon through the night, rushing against the oncoming wind to Glemaria's southern border.

An hour later, I leaned back, ordering the gryphon to descend. He turned, his wings spread wide, feathers erect, as we glided forward, and then with a growl, he lowered his head, and we rushed to the forest floor of the Glemarian border. Gryphons went from flying to practically falling as if they were in a death race to touch grass.

Bearing my weight forward, my heels pressing against the stirrups of my harness, I rubbed the back of the gryphon's head, and he slowed his descent, just slightly. It was a trick I'd learned years ago from Artem. Three more gryphons swooped behind me, landing in formation. I gave the gryphon another pat on the head to thank him for the safe transport then waited for him to lie prone before I unbuckled myself and stepped out of the stirrups. Holding onto his rope, I slid to the ground.

"Your Grace," Bowen said, coming to stand beside me. He took the rope from me, tying it to the base of a pine.

The gryphon's dark eyes watched carefully, tracking the

rope around his leg to the tree. With a sigh, he sat back on his haunches.

A dozen of my father's sentries appeared behind me, all armored to perfection, their leathers tightened and polished. Someone raised a green flag with the sigil of Ka Hart.

I'd still received no word on whom I was to greet. Arkturion Kane had been given the message personally, and according to Bowen, he was "incredibly offended" I'd been requested as ambassador over him. He'd taken it as a direct insult to his Ka and his station.

That gave me some small hope it wasn't *him*, the senator from Hartavia. He was the only foreign dignitary to have ever called me impressive, but it had been years since I'd last had to see or endure his presence in my own country.

Fire burst as torches were lit to create an aisle from me to the border, and the wind carried the fresh scent of pine, so prevalent in the Glemarian woods, through the air. I breathed deeply, waiting for signs of our guest.

Several long moments passed, the torches crackling into the rapidly cooling night before the gryphons all at once began to move, their wings rustling against their sides, their beaks emitting small growls—not ones of annoyance or fear but of curiosity.

There was a sudden shift in the air, and I looked up to see small blue lights appearing and vanishing in the sky, casting a bluish glow atop the trees.

An ashvan horse was approaching. Within seconds, it was joined by others as the night sky was lit up by a dozen more of the lights.

I hadn't seen an ashvan in over two years. Not since Bamaria.

The lights began to lower, lighting up the hooved legs and then the bodies of the ashvan racing over the lights. An onyx horse appeared as the leader, and a horn blew as it touched the ground.

The rider dismounted so quickly, I could only see a flash of red, but it was a red I knew far too well. It was the red of an arkturion cloak wrapped around broad, muscular shoulders, heavily covered in golden armor. Above his shoulders was a head full of short, dark hair.

"Your Grace, Lord Rhyan Hart," he said, stepping forward, his voice deep and commanding. His hand rested casually on the hilt of his sword, and the golden Valalumir stars on the bottom of his leather belt straps glimmered as if in possession of their own source of light and power. He bowed as his remaining soturi dismounted and lifted a flag with a sigil that made my heart pang. Golden seraphim wings beneath a full silver moon flapped in the night's wind against a red—Batavia red—flag.

I stepped forward, my arms outstretched. "Welcome to Glemaria, Arkturion Aemon."

CHAPTER
EIGHT

"Your Grace, Lord Rhyan Hart, Heir Apparent to the Arkasva, High Lord of Glemaria, Imperator to the North," Arkturion Aemon said graciously. He spoke lightly, but his face was stern and tired. His aura was sweeping out, probing, and full of dark shadows. I'd never seen anyone with the power to darken the night, but Aemon was one of the most powerful soturi in Lumeria.

"You're quite some distance from the south of the Empire," I said, trying to remain calm, to keep my aura close to my body. But I was overwhelmed with thoughts of seeing her, of talking to her, of—Gods—just her. He'd been in her country. He'd seen her, spoken to her, breathed in the same air she had, seen the same sky, and drank from the same source of water.

But before me now was just Aemon and some of the Soturi of Ka Batavia accompanying him.

Still, I looked, my eyes straining in the dark across the border, for any hints of noble companions. None of the ladies of Ka Batavia were with him—they wouldn't have any reason to be here—but still, I stared beyond him, searching for more blue lights to appear in the sky. For a Bamarian seraphim to descend. For curvy legs wrapped in delicate golden sandals to emerge from a blue-jeweled carriage.

My heart sank though my mind had known the truth long before. She wasn't here. Heirs who were third in line to the Seat of Power didn't attend state visits. And that was for the best. She'd be in danger the moment her foot touched Glemarian soil.

Aemon laughed and took an exaggeratedly deep breath, inhaling the pine of our woods before tugging his red cloak closer across his shoulder. "I'm about as far north as I could go —at least if I want to avoid the Night Lands." He winked and stepped forward, bowing before me again. "Thank you, Your Grace, Lord Rhyan, for welcoming me. I received word that this was quite an unusual request."

I shrugged. "I believe Arkturion Kane was hoping to greet you personally. He is a great admirer of yours," I said cordially.

"And I of him."

Behind Aemon, several more soturi dismounted, wearing the golden armor of Ka Batavia, the shoulders sharpened into seraphim wings. Their cloaks were the traditional green all soturi wore, making them difficult to see until they came into the center of the torchlight. The cloaks were able to camou-flage the wearer when out in nature, but they were still a big step from true invisibility if one was paying attention. Allegedly, only Ka Shavo in Bamaria had true invisibility magic, though our Spymaster's glamour skills came close.

"I shall be very happy to speak to Arkturion Kane," Aemon continued. "It's been too long since our last meeting. But I must admit, I have come to Glemaria in order to speak with you."

I narrowed my gaze in confusion but quickly recovered and offered a perfect Heir Apparent smile. "I am honored. How may I serve you, Arkturion?"

His shadows stilled. "I heard word of the akadim attack here on Auriel's Feast Day. We all have." His voice lowered, growing more serious. "The reports we've been receiving these last several months have been, well, rather troubling, to say the least. Akadim numbers seem to be increasing rapidly. And perhaps of greatest concern to me and Bamaria, is that they are being reported more frequently down south. The North has held back the threat for far longer than my region, something I've always respected. But it has also suffered its losses, as has the South when the beasts make their way down in winter."

I nodded, unsure how this explained Aemon's interest in speaking to me. Akadim attacked all the time around here.

His eyebrow lifted in understanding as if he sensed my confusion. "I heard a rumor that you fought several of the akadim that night, and you not only lived to tell the tale but walked away almost completely unharmed."

My throat tightened. I'd been harmed. Just not by akadim.

"That sounds far more heroic than what I remember."

"More heroic than you might yet realize. Very few could escape an akadim that's intent on attacking them, and yet you did. That's why I requested to speak with you," Aemon continued. "I need to learn all I can and bring this back to those training in my own Soturion Academy. If the threat continues to spread south and as quickly as the numbers are suggesting, I want my soturi prepared."

I wanted that, too. I wanted Bamaria's soturi and the South to be ready; I wanted Lyr protected. "I would be honored to assist you. But I must admit, I didn't face the beasts for long. Arkturion Kane killed two that night, and he may be of greater assistance."

Aemon nodded dismissively. "An anointed soturion is expected to do so. And I know something of the strength your arkturion possesses. But he also has years of experience to inform him. If my Academy students were to be caught unawares as you were, if our borders, Gods forbid, were breached, I want to make sure my soturi, especially my novices and apprentices, are best able to survive. I, of course, can teach them all I know, but I believe there's a difference between hearing about survival from someone in your boat rather than someone who has sailed farther and maybe forgotten what it's like to be at the journey's start."

"That's wise of you," I said.

"You don't have to compliment me. It's logical. You did something great that night, whether you're aware of it or not, and I have questions."

I nodded.

"Now, I hear I've pulled you from a habibellum," he said.

"We were well finished by the time I was informed of your visit," I said carefully. "Either way, it is an honor to greet you."

His dark eyes flicked up and down, assessing me, something almost suspicious in his eyes. "A habibellum, after a full day of training, all before you came to the border by gryphon, and still, you aren't showing an ounce of fatigue."

I smiled. "Thank you. But it is all an act, I can assure you."

Aemon tilted his head to the side, his look casual, but his energy had darkened. "If you say so, but I knew when I last saw you in Bamaria you'd become a powerful soturion. You may be full of energy still, but I think I will have my soturi find their rooms at Seathorne before we speak further. It's been a long journey for them. And then, I would like to hear every detail of the attack when I'm fully awake."

Every detail. Including how I'd escaped and why I hadn't spoken a word about that night since.

"My friend, Soturion Garrett Aravain," I said quickly, "he should be there, too. He's another novice in my year, and he killed one of the five. Were it not for him, well..." I looked away.

"Ka Aravain?" he asked.

I detected a note of interest in his aura, but then it seemed to vanish. "Yes. His father is Turion Efraim."

Aemon's eyes flashed. "The son of Kane's Second? Bring him then. Tomorrow?"

"Yes. I will arrange that. He'd be honored to speak with you. He has long admired you."

"Well, I thank you for that. Are you also bound for Seathorne?" he asked.

"No." I lied. "Back to the Academy tonight."

"Good. Thank you again for the greeting."

"It was my pleasure," I said, glancing once more behind him, some part of me refusing to accept reality and stop looking for her.

Aemon bowed. "I nearly forgot. How long has it been, Your Grace, since your last stay in Bamaria?"

I stiffened, drawing my gaze back to Aemon's. "Two years, Arkturion."

"Too long." Aemon gestured to his soturi, patting the back of his ashvan. "Aditi, *tovayah, tovayah*," he said, before grabbing the reins and swinging himself back up onto her saddle.

Gods. I wanted to ask about Lyriana. If she was all right. If she was... happy. Her scent, her taste, the calm way she'd spoken as she'd drowned in my nightmares, it was all still haunting me a month later. But I couldn't think of what to reasonably say or ask, not without giving everything away. Forcing myself to let it go, I waved Aemon off, leaving him to his Glemarian escort. It had to be enough to know she was alive and safe. We'd have received word if it were otherwise.

The wind picked up, a cold rush blasting against my hair as

I retreated to my gryphon, stroking his head and ordering him back to the Academy as the ashvans' blue lights lit up the sky. I had to find Garrett.

∽

AN HOUR after Aemon's arrival, I was pounding on his and Dario's apartment door.

"Garrett!" I yelled. "It's me."

The door swung open, and I found Kenna standing on the threshold, Dario's arm around her. His black curls thrown into a haphazard bun on top of his head.

"Kenna?" I asked.

Dario lifted a dark eyebrow. "Why don't you come in, *Your Grace?*"

I narrowed my eyes. "What's going on?"

"What's going on?" he sneered. "What's going on is Kenna's father asked you and you alone to stay after training, then decided after said meeting to take his anger out on Kenna, and then you vanished for hours without word, and now you're here demanding entry into our home after midnight. Why don't you come in and tell *us* what's going on?"

I stepped inside and slammed the door behind me. "Nothing is going on."

Kenna's eyes darkened, her nostrils flaring in anger, and only then did I see the slight purple bruising in the shape of a hand around her neck.

I pushed Dario off her, wrapping my arms around her waist. "What happened? Did he touch you?" I asked, my voice low. I knew exactly what kind of man Kane was. I'd always suspected, but never seen the proof right in front of me. I'd deluded myself into thinking she was safe, that she wasn't suffering like the others he came across.

Kenna blinked several times, her shoulders rising and falling with heavy breaths before she pursed her lips together and held my gaze. Fury burned behind her eyes.

It was all the confirmation I needed. I tightened my hold on her. "Ken, I'm sorry."

"For the rest of the class!" Dario said. He gave me a pointed look and held up an icepack, one that was already half-warmed. Shaking his head in disgust, Dario pointed to the spot where it had been on Kenna.

I could almost read Dario's mind. *It's not always about you. I'm taking care of her, too.*

"Well?" he asked. "What business did you and our illustrious arkturion get into that left him in such a foul fucking mood?" He glared at Kenna's neck as if it were my fault she'd been hurt.

Maybe it was... My stomach sank.

Taking a deep breath, I said, "I was asked to greet Arkturion Aemon from Bamaria." I rubbed my hand up and down her back, gently pressing the icepack over her skin. She hissed at the sudden cold, her shoulder flinching before she relaxed in my arms.

"The Ready?" asked Dario.

I nodded.

"Why you?" Kenna asked. "Not that," she shook her head, "not that you don't deserve to be asked. But why wouldn't my father go to the border?" Her hands clenched at her sides. "Or Garrett's?"

I looked beyond her and found Garrett watching me carefully. He was sitting on the couch, his legs propped up on Aiden's lap, a mug of beer in his hand. There was an underlying tension brewing between the two of them, like they were trying to give Kenna some privacy, but I knew better. They were both incredibly invested in what was happening. And

Garrett, in particular, was trying to keep his emotions under control. His free hand grasped Aiden's. He looked like he was holding on for dear life. Only I knew the truth. He was. With his emotions heightened like this, he was close to traveling. Aiden was literally keeping him in place.

"Because," I said pointedly, "he came to learn more about the akadim attack last month. Specifically wanted to speak to me and Garrett about what it was like fighting and surviving as novices."

Garrett stiffened at this and sat up, swinging his legs to the floor. "He came to speak to us?"

"Yes," I said. "I wanted to let you know right away. He's planning to interview us tomorrow."

There was a flush to Garrett's aura, a nervous burst of energy and fear. I felt my back flare with heat, the mark of our blood oath suddenly alive and full of warning. For a month I'd kept his secret. For a month he'd kept mine.

Aiden took Garrett's hand into his lap. "Don't be nervous, it's an honor he wants to speak with you."

Garrett nodded slowly, still pale.

"No one cares about the origin of your Ka," Aiden said, taking his nerves to be about his status as a noble. "Your father's Second. And you're a hero."

"Some of us were saving lives in other ways," Dario said.

"Some of us were too drunk to do otherwise," Aiden quipped.

"And you could have done better, mage-boy!"

"Hey!" I released Kenna to step before Dario. "Relax! You did your part, too. And it was incredibly important. What's gotten into you tonight?"

"Nothing. Nothing I'm allowed to be let in on, at least." His aura flared, dark and shadowy. "Fuck this. I'm going to bed. And I'm sleeping in my room tonight." Dario glared at Aiden and Garrett over his shoulder before turning his ire on me and Kenna. "She was fine," he hissed. "She came to me, and I had it under control while you weren't here, while you were out pissing off arkturi."

"I didn't ask to be..." I exhaled sharply, not wanting to fight anymore. "Thank you," I said. "For taking care of her."

Dario sneered. "I didn't fucking do it for you."

"Dario. Rhy," Kenna said, moving between us. "Please. Don't."

"It's okay." I squeezed her hand before eyeing Dario. He got like this when he was drunk—belligerent, mean. But he seemed completely sober. We'd been fine earlier before I'd left to meet Aemon. I knew it wasn't jealousy. But something had pissed him off since I'd last seen him. "If you're mad at me, Dario, just spit it out."

"Maybe if you'd fucking let me in and help you, I would."

My throat went dry. "Help me with what?"

His eyes fell down my torso and rose back to my face. "You know Godsdamned well what."

My skin went cold. "Do I?" My voice shook. Was he finally going to say something, admit he knew what my father—his Arkasva, his Imperator—was doing to me? To my mother? I'd waited so fucking long for him to speak up. For him to push past my lies, to ask me what was wrong, to fight me for the truth—just one more fucking time. Gods, it had been years that I'd been his best friend, and still I was alone, waiting. Always waiting.

I glared at him when he didn't respond.

Come on, just ask. Just do it! Fucking do it! Tell me you know the truth. You see it. Feel it! Tell me our friendship is real. Tell me what exists between us is stronger than my father's rule.

But Dario remained silent.

And I knew then, I'd continue waiting. I wasn't just some

man, and neither was Dario. I was the Heir Apparent, and Dario's father was Master of Peace, our best friend the son of the Glemarian Turion, and my...lover...daughter of the arkturion. We were all destined to rule on the Glemarian Council in some capacity one day, and the idea of saying that the Arkasva and Imperator was a monster was treasonous and dangerous. Especially for every person in this room.

Garrett came between us, his hand on Dario's shoulder, a small shake of his head. Then, his eyes met mine, and my stomach dropped. I felt laid bare, and somehow completely invisible.

Dario's face fell, whatever courage he'd pooled together fading. "Just... keep icing her neck. And she'll need an icepack for her arm, too," he said with a cough and stepped back.

My eyes watered, but I blinked back the tears, looking past him to Garrett. "Meet me at sunrise. We'll go meet the arkturion together."

He nodded seriously, his eyes drooping before he sat back on the couch with an angry-looking Aiden.

Dario reached for his own mug of beer back on the coffee table. "Rhyan," he said quietly, almost apologetically, but then he shook his head, taking a long sip.

He only tipped back his drink, chugging the beer, his throat working until he slammed his mug on the coffee table, pulled the tie from his hair, and retreated to his room.

Garrett's gaze found mine again, and my hands trembled at my side, then I nodded, swallowing everything back.

I threaded my fingers through Kenna's, my thumb rubbing over her knuckles. "We'll go to my apartment. I'll take care of you."

Bowen and one of Kenna's escorts walked behind us to my front door. I'd spent so few nights here lately that the room was freezing. It had been ages since it had been heated, and that had been before the temperature drop. Kenna shivered.

"I'll start a fire," I said.

"No need." She'd already withdrawn her stave from her belt. Blue light flared at the tip seconds before my fireplace burst to life, and heat, gloriously warm and soothing, moved in waves across the room to reach us.

"Thanks." I unbuckled my armor, pulling the leathers from my chest and shoulders. "Can I see where you're hurt?"

Kenna looked away, replacing her stave in its scabbard and hugging her arms to her chest.

"It's okay." I coughed, imagining the roles were reversed, imagining that for once I'd been found bruised, for once, I was being cared for. That Dario had continued, that Garrett hadn't stopped him. What did I want to hear? What did I need to hear?

I stepped closer, and gently took her chin, turning her face toward me. "You didn't do anything wrong. He shouldn't have hurt you."

Her eyes reddened, flicking to me and away again. "I know." There was a bitter edge to her aura.

"Doesn't make it any easier knowing though," I said quietly.

"No."

"You're safe tonight. You're safe with me. Is it okay... I mean, can I take care of you?"

"Dario would have," she said, her voice defiant.

"You blame me?" I asked.

She was still for a long moment, the only sound in my apartment the fire crackling. Another sharp gust of wind blew against the windowpanes, rattling the curtains. It seemed enough to pull her out of her spell, and she turned. "I don't. I know who did this."

Her father. Arkturion Kane. Because I'd been asked to greet Aemon and not him. Fucking petty bastard. The backs of my eyes burned. Even when I did nothing, the people I most cared about were still hurt on my behalf.

I bit the inner corner of my cheek, trying to remain calm.

She was still holding herself, closed in.

"Kenna," I said, moving my palm down her arm. "I want to take care of you. But if you'd feel safer or better with Dario, it's okay. We can go back. I won't be upset. I swear. I just want you to feel better. Whatever it takes."

Biting her lip, she stepped toward me. "I know. I did want to go with you. Despite..." She waved her hand between us. "Well, I know our situation is," she laughed uneasily, "a situation. But you always make me feel safe. That's why I came to you. After the attack."

My eyes searched hers. "I screwed everything up that night. I'm sorry."

"No. You didn't. You just...confused me." She looked away.

"I got scared. I... I care about you. So much. I wasn't expecting to. And I can't tell you how important that is to me, or how scary it feels."

She shook her head, her eyebrows furrowed. "We don't need to discuss that now."

"Okay." I pushed her hair off her shoulder, taking a closer look at her neck. Clear outlines of thick fingermarks painted her otherwise pale skin. Kane had choked her. And Dario had mentioned her arm.

She followed my gaze down her elbow, which she was holding funny. "He's not touched me in a long while. Not since me and you. But he lost it tonight." She sniffled. "He looked possessed by Moriel."

"Can I take this off?" I asked, my finger slipping inside the collar of her dress. "So we can ice your arm?"

"I'll do it," she said, pulling her sleeve down her shoulder, rolling her gown to her waist. I tried to hide my gasp. The bruise was far worse than I'd thought. The fucker had to have squeezed her with a death grip. Soturi had the strength of five mages. Kenna hadn't stood a chance.

"Is there anywhere else he hurt you?" I tried to keep my voice even. To remain calm. But a fury was building inside me. I wanted to track down Kane and strangle him with my own two hands. And I wanted to smack Dario. He fucking knew there was more. And he knew about me. And still, he was saying nothing. Acting like a gryphon-shit asshole and leaving me to clean up all of our messes.

Kenna's eyes fell to her feet. "No."

"Ken, you can tell me."

"I know I can." Her voice rose. "But I don't want to."

I closed my eyes, understanding. I hadn't let her in that morning after my nightmare, or even that night with what had truly happened. A twisting in my gut reminded me that this was as close as we were ever going to be—as I was ever going to be with anyone for the rest of my life.

That didn't matter now. I just needed to make her feel better. To get her through this.

"Would a warm bath help?" I asked.

She nodded.

"I'll make it happen."

I had Bowen arrange transport for us to the Katurium where my escort team stood guard outside the bathing room as Kenna soaked. She let me climb into the pool with her, massage her shoulders, and wash her hair. We sat there a long while in the heat until she announced she was done and let me wrap her in a towel. I didn't say a word when I spotted the bruises on her backside, the ones she was unwilling to discuss. And then when she was warm and dry and her eyes finally drooping with sleep, we returned to my apartment to go to bed. This time, we didn't touch.

Instead, I lay awake, watching her breathe, unsure what to do. I'd found a way to protect Lyr. I knew what the cost would be to continue protecting my mother.

But I was lost with Kenna.

CHAPTER

NINE

The sun shone too brightly through the windows of Seathorne's breakfast hall. I sat at the long wooden table, my back stiff, across from my mother and father, their diadems shining. My own was a heavy weight against my temples. Garrett had joined us, along with his father, Turion Efraim. We were sandwiched in between Arkturion Kane and Arkturion Aemon. There were enough personal escorts between us all to form a private legion.

The soturi stood restlessly, lined up along the walls, in full armor that reflected the morning light. Golden armor—usually unseen in Seathorne broke up the wall of black leather. With the sun so bright, the starfire blades of each soturion's sword were alight with flame, the fires sparking from their holsters. The flames danced over the shadows on the wall, spreading across the green velvet tapestries.

Servants walked in and out, their staves pointed as they floated fresh mugs of steaming spiced coffee and beer. The air carried notes of cinnamon, cardamom, and ginger layered over the deeper scents of the savory breakfast cakes that were typical Glemarian fare. Plates of scrambled eggs, freshly harvested fruit, and smoked meats joined the mix, as well as anything else that was requested, all of which were delicately floated onto the table.

I could barely stomach anything in front of me. My body was at war between wanting to travel far away with Garrett, scream at my father, and tackle Kane for hurting Kenna. But I had to remain calm.

Garrett and I had already discussed in detail the story we'd have to tell. Once Garrett had made his kill, we had suddenly been surrounded by two more akadim. Fighting back-to-back, the akadim hadn't attempted to separate us but instead had fought each other for the chance to claim us both. We'd used the small moment of their turning on each other to escape from their reach. But before we could circle back and stop the threat, we'd seen the anointed soturi of Ka Hart finally approaching. We'd stayed back to give them a clear path to their target, not wanting to interrupt their formation, and once the threat had been stopped, we'd sought medical treatment.

We'd rehearsed this story a dozen times in my apartment, our voices hushed before the fire, while Kenna had remained fast asleep beneath my blankets. I'd sent for breakfast and fresh coffee to be delivered to her in my bed before I'd left with Garrett, and now we just had to recite the story back to Aemon and hopefully be done with this.

"You haven't had many akadim in the South, have you, Aemon?" Kane stabbed his fork through a sausage as he spoke, not looking up at the Bamarian arkturion.

"We've had our share," he said politely.

"And what's your kill record?" Kane asked.

A dark shadow swept through the room. Aemon's aura. He glared at Kane, his mouth tight with derision. "I imagine far less than yours. One must, of course, add in proximity to the threat as well as years lived."

Garrett coughed uncomfortably beside me. Aemon was decades younger than Kane. Even Efraim, Garrett's father, who usually remained neutral, smirked at this.

"I might ask you how many rebellions you've ended?" Aemon winked.

"Glemaria has no concern for such things since we have strong leadership already in place." Kane's eyes remained thin slits, and I saw an infuriatingly smug smile spread across my father's lips at the exchange.

"I simply want to be prepared for when the threat does rise," Aemon continued, his voice polite and proper, but that underlying anger was still filling the room.

"I imagine you'll be quite ready," my father said, his voice lightly teasing.

"Tell me," Kane grunted, "since you have so much experience with rebellions, how was it that you were so *ready* for Tarek's?"

Everyone knew the story of the rebellion that had almost unseated Lady Lyriana's father after he had taken the Seat of Power when Lyr had still been practically a baby. Tutors had explained it to me many times during my years of study as a boy. Arkasva Batavia's brother-in-law, Tarek, had believed the Seat was to pass from Lyr's mother to her sister, Lyr's aunt, Arianna. Tarek and his supporters had attacked Arkasva Batavia in the streets. But the Arkasva had survived. He walked with a limp that plagued him to this day because of it, a limp I'd observed myself. Aemon had quickly stopped the attack, earning him his infamous nickname the Ready, and a reputation amongst the soturi of the Empire that rivaled even Kane's—something both Kane and my father resented.

"It's almost like you knew in advance," Kane said conspiratorially. "To act that quickly, be that prepared."

Aemon's eyes flashed. "What exactly are you accusing me of? Performing my duties?"

Kane shrugged. "You came very far north to learn how to fight our demons. I'm simply asking how you fought yours."

Aemon took a long sip of coffee, his eyebrows furrowed. "I do my homework. I prepare for every possible attack and outcome. A dramatic shift in the line of succession was never going to occur smoothly. Not with how long-standing the tradition had been before Arkasva Harren. I knew I couldn't rely on established allies and enemies. I was right. And I will be just as prepared if your akadim threat decides to move from your lands to mine, which by all reports is exactly what's happening." He looked pointedly across the table at me. "The very reason why I'm here."

All eyes in the room turned to me and Garrett. His throat bobbed nervously, and I could feel his leg shaking beside my chair. He was a mess. He'd never been comfortable with nobles or the formalities of Court. Was always insecure about his Ka's origins. Add on his vorakh...

"One might ask," Aemon said, his gaze now intent on my father, "how the akadim in question got so far past your borders before the warning bells went off. I'd be curious to know what happened with your security protocols that night. How exactly did it come to the point that novice soturi were on the frontlines?"

Dark, cold energy swirled across the table, the hurricane of my father's aura. He was insulted and going to make sure everyone felt it.

I had to end this. I couldn't take much more of my father's anger even when, for once, it wasn't directed at me. And I knew Garrett couldn't stand the tension.

I sat forward, pushing my chair back. Its legs scraped roughly against the floor, and everyone's attention was on me again. "You've come a long way for answers, Arkturion. I think we should do the interview now."

My father's eyes narrowed, looking me up and down before he took a long sip from his mug. "You seem rushed, Rhyan. Did you have somewhere more important to be later? I can't imagine anything more honorable for you to do than to serve your Empire by relaying all you know to Arkturion Aemon. No one is asking you to lay down your life," he said, his voice dripping with condescension, "just have a conversation."

"I am trying to relay that very information by actually having that conversation now, Your Highness," I said.

"A shame," Kane said, glaring at me, "that you were too slow and weak to kill one yourself." His eyes flicked to my father, a challenge in his gaze.

Garrett's leg shook harder, and as I glanced down, his ankle began to fade. *Shit. Shit!* He was going to travel from nerves alone if we didn't get this over with soon. Garrett may have been the son of a turion, but his father didn't know about his vorakh and wasn't protecting Garrett's secret like mine was. And Garrett had had far less practice controlling it.

I straightened in my seat, sliding my foot across the floor to find Garrett's. His shaking increased, and I inched closer, placing my heel over his toe, trying to still him. To keep him here. Keep him grounded.

Garrett's father looked over, a note of worry in his light eyes, before he brushed back his hair—wavy and blonde like Garrett's—and resumed eating.

I glared at Kane, who seemed to be waiting for my response, as if not killing one of the deadliest monsters in Lumeria—one nearly impossible to kill without years of training—was something to be shamed for. As if beating your own daughter, humiliating her and, leaving marks across her backside because your ego was bruised by the Ready, wasn't the true crime. A flash of Kenna's injuries raced through my mind, and I exhaled sharply, hands fisted in my lap.

"Considering I select my fighting opponents to be only those who are my size or larger," I said pointedly, "by the Gods, I expect my kill record will be quite high. I mean, once I'm as old as you. Luckily for all of us, while Ka Hart's first legion, under your command, Arkturion, was nowhere to be found that night, Garrett here was present at the fight. Garrett did kill an akadim. He did what many of your best could not. And while we're on the subject, let's not forget the dozens of soturi who bravely ran into danger and fell fighting the beasts while your legion failed to answer the call. I was there, making sure the mages present were escorted to safety. And I stayed. I fought three akadim. Three. And I lived. So, we're happy to provide what information we can to Arkturion Aemon. But otherwise, we're both rather preoccupied with training for the *Alissedari* in our great Imperator's honor."

Kane's nostrils flared, his aura heating with irritation.

My father, on the other hand, despite my insolence, grinned at me like he'd just won some game. As if he'd wanted me to lose my temper. He leaned on his elbows over the table to speak with Aemon. "Arkturion, do the Heirs of Ka Batavia speak to their Council with such... fervor? The three young ladies?"

I stiffened. He knew what he was doing—dangling Lyriana in my face, trying to unsettle me.

Aemon laughed good-naturedly though I couldn't shake the intensely violent anger still burning under his energy. It was starting to nauseate me, all the intense auras pushing for power against each other, half of them directed at me. The room felt too small, suffocating.

"Of the three heirs, our poor High Lord is most likely to receive an attitude from his second daughter, Lady Morgana." Aemon smiled as he said her name. "She has quite the, shall we say, rebellious streak for one of her station. And since she celebrated her own Revelation Ceremony last month, she has become far more defiant...and powerful."

My father's eyes flashed to me and then back to Aemon. "And what about the youngest heir? Lady Lyriana Batavia? She made quite an impression the last time I visited. Is she as, let's say, *fiery*, as her hair turns in the sun?"

Kane leaned forward, suddenly looking interested, and my heart sank. Was it possible they were still plotting to have her married? Gods, no. She was with Lord Tristan. His stupid station, money, and Ka were all I was relying on to keep her out of my father's reach. But it had been one whole year that they'd been courting, and there was still no word of an engagement. And I had no one to explain why. My heart panged... Jules. She would have told me. She would have... Fuck. I missed her. I could have really used one of her letters these last few months. I just prayed the delay in Lyriana's engagement was for good reason.

"She is fiery, always was, but since you've seen her, she really has matured and become a model daughter of the Empire. Absolute perfection. I don't think she'd dare speak against her father out of turn."

Images of Lyr drowning in my nightmare flashed through my mind—the serene way she'd looked and spoken as her doom had swallowed her whole, the way she'd so casually named Tristan as the reason. The way she hadn't even tried to fight back.

"And what of her courtship?" my father pressed.

My mother touched his arm. "Devon," she chided lightly. "I thought we were discussing akadim."

"We are. But akadim are not simply isolated issues. Their presence can be influenced by all sorts of things. In the end, I think it all connects. It's all worth hearing, wouldn't you say, Rhyan? After all, knowing whom Arkasva Batavia's daughters will wed affects not only the politics of Bamaria, but all the Empire as well. Lady Lyriana's affairs are no exception, certainly not to me."

I stiffened in my seat. I was going to throttle him when I had the chance. Garrett was still shaking beside me. I sighed. I didn't think Garret or I could take much more of this.

"I would very much like to hear the accounts now," Aemon said.

My father lifted his hands as if in celebration. "Of course, of course. Go on, conduct your little interview."

Garrett took a deep breath at my side, his eyes flicking to his father, and then he stilled.

Aemon asked his first question.

CHAPTER
TEN

L ater that night, I found my way back to my apartment after hours of training with Garrett and Dario. My body ached, and I could barely move. We'd taken a single gryphon into the mountains and taken turns flying on its back for hours. There were a limited number of gryphons available for practice. Most were busy with their previously assigned posts—transporting, guarding—and those who'd been designated as part of the tournament were completely off-limits. Plus, the locations to reach them were too far to travel to each day. That left a very small supply of gryphons for soturi to use to prepare, even for sons of three of the most powerful men in Glemaria.

Luckily, Aiden was perhaps the most talented mage in the Academy—if not the entire Empire—in the magic of glamours. He was able to transform the appearance of anything he'd ever seen. Aiden even could—if he wanted to —change himself into our exact likenesses. It wasn't uncommon when he'd first mastered the spellwork, for me to sit down for lunch with Garrett and five minutes into the conversation discover it was actually Aiden in an enchantment.

Despite being rather on the quiet, and stoic side, when he was in his glamour, he did some of the most spot-on impressions I'd ever seen. He not only captured each person's appearance but their mannerisms, their speech patterns. And if I was being honest, he was rather funny, though he rarely let anyone know beyond those moments. If the day came that I truly did outlive my father and took the Seat of Power, Aiden would be my first choice for spymaster for this reason alone.

Tonight, his magic had allowed him to transform the local falcons circling overhead into gryphons. Garrett, Dario, and I had taken turns riding on the actual gryphon we shared, and then riding on the falcons in disguise. Flying on the falcons wasn't quite the same—they didn't move with a gryphon's speed or instincts. They also seemed completely befuddled for the first few hours on why their bodies had grown so large so quickly.

Still, it was helping all of us to become comfortable with combat in the air. And Garrett and Dario had desperately needed to clock more hours on gryphon-back before the tournament began. They had not had the same interest in the animals I'd had as a boy.

The day and night had been separated into training segments: one hour of mounting, jumping on and off our gryphons; one hour of flying, practicing soaring and directing; and one hour of descent, which was mainly me talking Garrett and Dario through the severely fast drops gryphons made and how to slow them. Unfortunately, they could only practice that on the real gryphon. The falcons in gryphon glamours didn't give a shit if you rubbed their head, nor did they descend as quickly as real gryphons did despite their additional weight.

We ended with several hours of fighting on gryphon-back

—sparring and attempting to knock each other off—with Aiden below prepared to slow our falls with his stave. Hitting the ground after tumbling off a gryphon from twenty feet in the air at a slow pace couldn't kill or break any bones. But I hit the ground enough times to know it still really fucking hurt.

So, when the night ended, and I'd successfully stumbled back to my room, I could barely feel my legs, and my arms ached so badly, I couldn't even lift my arms, forget removing my armor.

Bowen announced Kenna almost at once, and with a groan, I sat up, my stomach burning with muscles I was positive hadn't been there that morning.

"Hard ride?" she asked, her eyebrows lifted.

I winced. "You could say that." Managing to sit up all the way, I gestured for her to sit, stealthily trying to see her neck. It was still bruised, but like my mother had a thousand times before, she was doing her best to conceal the marks with her hair, wearing it long and over her shoulders. My fingers clenched at my sides, which triggered a spasm in my biceps.

Kenna sat next to me, her brown eyes searching mine, her lips pressed together with a look of defiance, as if daring me to mention what I'd seen last night or what had happened to her. Daring me to call her weak. I never would.

I knew now how strong she truly was—how much she carried inside. I could see it more clearly by the day.

"How are you feeling?" I asked anxiously.

She shrugged. "I'm fine."

"Today, was he—?"

Kenna glared. "I'm not discussing him." Her eyes flashed with heat. "You don't discuss yours."

My gaze fell to my lap. "No."

"I'm okay," she said, and again, I felt that separation

between us—that fissure that would never fully close, never allow us to connect.

The hollowness inside me grew, but there was nothing I could do tonight to ease the ache. I couldn't talk to Kenna. And I couldn't use my body to mask the pain, couldn't use hers to forget my own.

Silence fell between us before she asked, "Do you need any help with your armor?"

I started to shake my head, my own instinct to hide myself, to conceal my body and bruises and any tiny sign of weakness, rearing its head. Then I relaxed, forcibly untensing my fingers. "Actually, yes."

Kenna leaned over. She unbuckled and unhooked each piece, carefully, almost reverently, replacing all of my leathers on my dummy and setting my weapons on the table beside it. Then, she removed my clothes, her eyes constantly checking my face to see if I was okay, if I'd changed my mind, or if there was an article of clothing I didn't wish removed.

It occurred to me then, that I had forgotten what it was like for someone to check in with me. To ask for my consent. To ask first if it was all right. I was so used to being ordered around, bound, used, and hurt. My body not my own, feeling less and less mine, every time I was tied up. Not since I was a child alone with my mother had I been given a choice over my own person. The choice to say no, to decide if it was what I'd wanted. I hadn't received anything like this in so long. Not from my previous lovers. Not Amalthea. Not my father or his soturi.

My stomach turned with the realization, and my heart pounded with Kenna's gentleness. Until now, I hadn't known I was missing it.

The last touch that had been this soft on my skin, this consenting and admiring...

Is this all right?

It's more than all right. You feel so good.

I coughed, clearing my head of *her*, of the scent of lemon and vanilla, of visions of pink lips and golden skin wrapped up in Batavia red silks.

"Can we just sleep?" Kenna asked, already lying down beside me and drawing the covers up around us.

I suppressed a pained groan as I turned on my side to face her. "Of course, we can. We never have to do more than that."

Kenna rolled onto her back, staring up at the ceiling, chanting under her breath, the end of her stave lighting with blue as she removed all sources of light. Shadows filled my bedroom, and she dropped her stave on my night table. Only the fire roaring in my fireplace provided enough light to give me a faint outline of her profile.

"He was in a sour mood again," she said quietly, her voice confessional as if it were easier to speak the truth in the dark.

I rested my hand on her arm beneath the blanket, gently, not wanting to hurt her further and not having the strength to do much more.

"Did he do anything else?" I asked.

"No."

Her hand found mine, and our fingers clasped together. Her skin was cold, and I inched closer, pulling back my aura to allow only my body heat to reach her.

"Good."

"You said something to him?" she asked.

"As much as I could," I admitted. I should have said more. I wished I'd said more. Done more.

She released a heavy sigh. "You shouldn't have done that."

I stilled. "Did he hurt you for it?"

"No, he...." She swallowed. "No."

"He deserved it," I growled. "Deserves so much fucking worse."

I could feel her shaking her head against my pillow. "You're a good person, Rhy." Kenna's voice was low.

I shrugged, always uneasy when I heard this. I hadn't believed it for such a long time. Instead, I'd believed my father when he said I was terrible and unworthy. He'd said so enough times, I'd made it part of who I was. Pretended I'd chosen to be that way. Relished in it. I still found it difficult at times to remember it wasn't true, wasn't who I was anymore.

"You are," she said. "So good."

I bit the inside of my cheek. "So are you."

Kenna went quiet save for the even sounds of her breathing.

"Have you," I started, an idea taking root in my mind, "Ken, have you ever thought of leaving here? Leaving Glemaria? Leaving it all behind, your title, your station?"

Kenna's fingers twitched against mine. "All the time."

"Would you?" I asked.

"No," she said quickly, her voice sure.

"What if I went, too?"

Her hand stilled against mine; the steady sound of her breathing paused. Outside, the wind howled, loudly enough to drown out my breaths.

Kenna shifted beneath the blankets. "Are you asking me to run away with you?"

"Would you come with me?"

There was a long silence before Kenna said, "I'd want to."

"But you wouldn't?"

She let out a sharp exhale. "No. This is my home. What else is there for me beyond these borders?"

"I don't know. More?"

"More what?"

I swallowed, visions of hazel eyes staring up at me, clouding my mind, alongside golden, sun-kissed skin, hair that turned to fire in the sun, and delicate hands turning a scroll for hours on end beside half-eaten slices of lemon cake.

"Just more," I said, my voice hushed. Tears burned the corners of my eyes, and I was glad for the darkness Kenna had brought forth.

"Rhy," she said softly, "I don't need you to protect me."

"I know you don't. But what if I want to?"

She laughed, the sound empty and joyless. "You've always got to be protecting someone, don't you?" She squeezed my hand, her thumb rubbing my palm. "You can't save everyone, you know? It's not possible. Some of us... some of us don't want to be saved."

The backs of my eyes burned as I thought of my mother, of the hundreds of times I'd gone to her crying, begging, pleading on my knees for her to leave, to find a way out, to escape.

To save herself.

To save me.

"Sometimes," Kenna said quietly, "sometimes the ones you most want to protect, they are the very ones you can't—the ones who need to save themselves."

I bit my lip to keep from sobbing. She was right. And it was all so unfair. And I was running out of time. I hadn't been able to save Jules beyond a single season. I was no longer sure if I'd truly protected Lyriana two years later. And I was beginning to understand that I couldn't help Kenna.

In that moment I knew, deep in my soul, the days I had left were numbered. Soon, it would be too late to save my mother.

I didn't even know if I was capable of doing it. Of winning for her. Of killing.

If it would even matter. If my father was even going to honor his word in the end.

But it was all I could do. So, I would.

A tear finally escaped my eye, and then another.

And still, at the end of the day, after everything that had happened, no matter how much I wanted it, wished for it, needed it, felt like I couldn't breathe without it, there was no one. No one was coming to save me.

AEMON'S STAY in Glemaria was extended when my father invited him to attend the Alissedari. The Imperator could barely resist having two of the Empire's most esteemed arkturi present for his tournament, not to mention his birthday and anniversary.

Not only that, he was going to show off his restoration of the Gryphon Pits, the location of the *Alissedari*. The giant arena was located in the center of Glemaria, equidistant from all the wild locations and large enough to seat most of Glemaria and the northern nobles who'd travel here to watch. It had fallen into disrepair after so many years of disuse, and if my father wasn't bragging about his long and successful rule, he was bragging about the updates his mages were making to the Pits.

I almost wished Aemon would leave just to see the insult on my father's face.

I liked the Bamarian arkturion well enough. He was polite, and he was respectful in his interactions with my mother and my friends. But his continued presence was leaving me uneasy.

He seemed to be the sole reason Kenna's father remained in an extra shitty mood, taking his anger out on not only me during trainings and clinics but Kenna as well.

In the weeks leading up to the tournament's start, she'd come to my bed bruised again and again. Each time she'd remained stoic, refused to discuss what had happened, and only barely allowed me to give her the most minimal care.

And every time I saw Aemon, I saw his Bamarian armor, the golden seraphim wings cutting across his shoulders. When I saw the sigils of Ka Batavia flying in his path, the golden seraphim wings, the full silver moon on its red flag, I saw *her*. I felt her. I lost myself to her memory.

It was its own kind of torture, and all the while tensions were rising in the Academy every day. It hadn't mattered much when I'd begun my soturion training that I was Heir Apparent. I had a target on my back the first time I strapped on my armor, the moment I had my left wrist cut by Arkmage Connal and became a soturion, the moment I'd spoken the words at the Oath Ceremony, joining my bloodline and power to my *kashonim*.

My apprentice Thorin had made sure of that. Those from the noble families who wished to challenge my father had made sure of that. And those whom my father had forced me to become prey for when he'd bound and beaten me to the point where I'd been too weak to fight back—they'd made sure of that.

But I started to strengthen. I started to grow. I started to remember the power that had been buried deep within me, the one that had risen to the surface and allowed me to defeat my father in an old Bamarian prison, the one that existed even when my magic was cut off and I was tied down by ropes.

I'd called on it again and again until it hadn't mattered if I was bound or not—my strength, my skill as a soturion, was one to be reckoned with, even by the anointed soturi. I saw the outcome I wanted in my mind, I saw the ropes torn, and I fought, and I didn't stop until I won.

That made every moment of my life since the announcement of the *Alissedari* even more dangerous. Bowen had begun working overtime, actually doing his fucking job, but inside the Katurium, no escorts were allowed to protect soturi. This meant Dario and Garrett had taken to never leaving my side. Ever. Not even to piss. If one of us took a shit, we *all* took a shit.

Which, in its own strange way, was the kind of fierce protectiveness I'd dreamed of having with friends as a boy. But also, it was really fucking annoying.

The guidelines around injuries during combat clinics and habibellums had also gone lax.

While there were always a handful of soturi who were forced to drop out of the Academy from injuries each year, we'd lost a dozen novices and apprentices since my father's announcement alone.

Even Garrett's father, Efraim, who never encouraged unnecessary violence, had gotten bloodlust in his eyes at clinics. Fouls were no longer called out. And when the fights intensified, his aura flared with excitement, especially if Garrett was in the center of it—something that happened frequently, as he so often followed Dario into the middle of all of his ill-advised brawls.

In the week leading up to the tournament's start, Dario, Garrett, Aiden, and I had been spending every waking moment together inside the Katurium and out. Strategizing. Planning. Practicing. Kenna even began attending our training sessions and meetings, finding us with Aiden once their classes at the Mage Academy ended each day.

And all the while, the temperatures continued to drop, the early fall chill in the air already at a wintery blast that seemed to always be present in Glemaria with the small exception of a few measly months.

The weather mages called for snowfall. It would make the gryphons happy, but the idea of flying them and trying to fight soturi in blizzard-like conditions left me full of dread.

If the Gods had any mercy, they'd have held back the snow for at least one more week. But the Gods clearly had none. I woke the day before the tournament to a fresh coat of snow across my windowsill, the glass frosted, and snowflakes falling in thick, heavy clumps.

Outside, a gryphon squawked a trill of excitement as it soared past.

Kenna stirred from my bed; her eyes still full of sleep as she found me by the window. Stretching her arms overhead, she looked through the glass and frowned.

"I'll reinforce the enchantments over your gloves and armor."

I nodded. Inside the tournament we'd be bound by silver rings—both meant to keep us trapped inside, and keep mages and their magic out. Keep them from interfering. Any assistance I received had to happen in advance.

Kenna could ensure my armor and gloves repelled moisture, kept me dry if it continued to snow, and provide extra warmth before I entered the tournament, but she'd be unable to help me beyond that.

Aiden was adding an additional glamour to our cloaks, one that would help us further blend into the scenery around us. Lately, his spell work was so precise, that even staring right at Dario and Garrett before a moon tree, I could barely see their outlines if their hoods were up.

We were counting on this in the arena—on being too hard to be seen by our opponents, allowing us to strike quickly before they could anticipate or evade our hits.

A knock on my door turned my head. Before I could answer Bowen, the lock unclicked, and the door swung open.

"Bowen!" I yelled but froze as Arkturion Kane entered my bedroom instead. His muscled body like a dark shadow.

"Apologies, Your Grace," he sneered, "but I need Lady Kenna. Now!"

She was dressed in a nightgown, but the material was sheer enough to be worthless. I immediately stepped in front of her to block his view.

"You'll wait outside," I growled. "Let her dress first."

Behind me, Kenna had pulled the blankets up to her shoulders, her face pale as she leaned back, burrowing into my headboard as if she could get away from her father by disappearing into the bed.

"I'll wait right here," he said. "When I want my daughter to come, she comes. You're not her husband. You have no say."

"You think I care? I'll fight you," I said. "Arkturion or not."

His eyes slanted into thin, cold slits. "You'll lose."

Stepping forward, my hands curled into fists. "My father said the same thing."

Kane shook his head, his face full of derision. "Kenna! Get up." His face reddened. "You'll pay for this insolence."

"Father, please," she begged. "There's no need."

I looked past him to my opened door. Where the fuck was Bowen?

Then, right on cue, he stepped into the doorframe, his face sullen. He wasn't interfering. Wasn't even attempting to protect me. There was only one person he didn't interfere with. Only one.

"What does he want?" I snarled. "My father, what did he say?"

Kane's fist smashed into my skull. Once, then again. My head snapped back, as my vision went out of focus, everything a bright white, before shadows filled my eyes and pain exploded everywhere. Something had cracked. And my knees buckled.

"Rhyan!" Kenna screamed.

Forcing myself to stand back up, I faced Kane. My nose was bleeding, and I could barely see. I caught only a faint outline of Kane's hulking figure leaning over my bed, grabbing a protesting Kenna. She kicked and yelled as he pulled her from my blankets, hauling her in her sheer nightdress to his chest. A low growl, deep in his throat, left me covered in goosebumps.

Kenna's body went limp. Silent.

My stomach twisted. I was going to be sick. I'd never seen Kenna docile. Weak. Scared. Not like this.

Kane chuckled like this was all a game. Like he'd known that the small sound would win him the upper hand, force her to obey. What had he done to her to earn such an immediate reaction?

"You're going to be a good girl," he said.

Her chin shook then stilled as she stared up into her father's cruel eyes. My vision blurred again, my throat tight as I coughed up blood, feeling bile gather behind it. I sank back to my knees and tried to crawl forward, to fight past the blinding pain.

Bowen entered at last. His large hands wrapped around my arms and pulled me to sit up. The room spun, my head pounded, and I resisted the urge to punch Bowen, though in that moment I wasn't sure I had the capacity to hit him. I felt like Kane had punched my nose into my brain.

Slowly, Bowen's shadowy figure moved away from me, and I watched him bend over, retrieving Kenna's yellow dress and her shawl. "Her clothing, Arkturion."

Kane sneered, dragging Kenna to the door, everything on display. The fucking bastard was going to parade her basically naked through the halls of Seathorne.

"Colder than it looks out there," Bowen said. "Wouldn't want the lady to catch a chill." He held up Kenna's dress again. She was looking straight ahead, not at Bowen, not at Kane, not at me.

Kane stared down Bowen. The two men were silent, assessing the other, while Kenna stood frozen between them, a small tremor in her fingers.

At last, Kane grimaced and jerked his head at the clothes. "Cover yourself up," he spat in disgust, as if she'd tried to leave the room naked, as if he hadn't been the one to burst in here without permission.

Her eyes red, Kenna turned toward Bowen, who held her dress out for her to take, but Kane struck out at Bowen's arm before they could make the exchange, and the fabric dropped to the floor. Kane grunted as Kenna was forced to bend over and retrieve the items.

Bowen's back remained to me, as he was unwilling to turn it on Kane. But he did turn his head to my window, keeping his gaze averted from Kenna while she dressed in silence.

Kane offered his daughter no such decency. Nor did he offer to help as she struggled with the ties, her fingers trembling.

I tried to go forward, my entire body shaking with rage and the need to reach her, to scream. But I couldn't move. Everything throbbed, and every breath hurt worse than the last. I knew if I stood, I'd be on the floor in seconds, covered in vomit.

Fully dressed, her hair a mess and her skin flushed with embarrassment, Kenna stepped forward, and then she left with Kane.

"Your Grace." Bowen sounded worried for once, as he moved across my room.

"My father," I spat, recoiling from Bowen's touch. He'd crouched down on the floor, trying to steady me, to lift me into his arms. "He ordered this?"

Bowen's arms wrapped around my waist, and more gently

than I'd ever known him to be, he lifted me up and carried me to the bed.

"You already know," he said.

"Move!" I yelled and retched bile over the side of the bed. It made the ache in my skull double.

"Rhyan! The fuck!" Dario yelled.

I could hear my friend's boots stomping into the room, followed by two more sets, as my stomach twisted and blood spattered to my floor. My head spun, and I knew I was seconds from passing out.

"Oh, shit!" Dario stopped in his tracks.

"Bowen, what happened?" Garrett asked.

"Broken nose," he said. "Kane punched him."

"Fuck! Is that why Kenna looked so...?" Dario trailed off. "Shit."

"I can fix it," Aiden said, his voice far calmer than everyone else's. He looked like he'd been deep in thought, calculating his spellwork, his gaze hyper-focused on the injury to my face. "You'll be okay, Rhyan. Good as new. You'll never know."

I closed my eyes. Like I cared if my nose had a bump in it.

"Garrett, get some towels," Aiden ordered.

My bedroom door slammed shut.

Dario turned on Bowen. "Where the fuck were you? You're not supposed to let this shit happen to him. He's the Heir Apparent."

"I'm well aware. I was exactly where I was told to be," Bowen said curtly.

"Sit him up," Aiden said. "Gently."

I groaned, feeling like I was going to puke again—and actually puke this time.

"Is she...?" I tried to ask, but my voice was weak, shaking. "Is she okay?"

"She's with her father," Dario said. But the darkness in his voice said all it needed to. We knew she wasn't safe. None of our fathers were safe.

I felt weight beside me on the bed, the mattress shifting. Someone took hold of my ankles to hold me down, their calloused fingers against my skin, and I caught the vague outline of Aiden's beside me. His nose large and beaked like a gryphon's.

"I tried," I said, my chest heaving. "Tried to get to her."

"I know," Aiden said quietly. "We all know."

The tip of his stave rested on my forehead, and I tensed.

"Garrett, restrain his hands, too."

Firm hands clasped around my wrists, slightly smaller than the ones by my feet, and I tensed further.

It's just my friends... Not ropes. Not ropes. I'm free... not bound.

"Hey," Garrett said, "Rhyan, relax. Aiden's got you."

"You're going to be okay," Aiden said quickly. "We're all here with you. I'm going to fix this. Now close your eyes. Deep breath. This is going to hurt."

CHAPTER
ELEVEN

The moment Aiden's magic began to work through me, I passed out. When I woke, I was sprawled out across my bed. The barely there light from the window created shadows in a new location of my bedroom. My head still ached, but not as fiercely as before, and my face felt sore and puffy. I reached for my nose, tenderly checking that it was there and nose-sized.

"It's exactly as it was before," Aiden said.

I turned on my side, finding him sitting on a chair across from the bed.

He stood quickly, his hands out as if trying to calm a wild beast. "Easy. Slow. You're okay now, but you're going to feel, uh, delicate there for at least a day."

"Delicate?" Dario snorted.

I found him at the foot of my bed, his legs crossed before him, boots unlaced, elbows resting on his knees.

"Well, let's go, Your Grace. You heard the healer. Lay back down with your oh-so-*delicate* nose."

I tried to roll my eyes, but that was too painful. I settled for following orders and lying back on my pillow, noting Garrett in the opposite corner, a worried look in his eyes. His blonde hair was sticking up in all directions, like he'd been pulling at it with anxiety.

"Hmmm." Dario crawled toward me over the blankets until his knees straddled my hips as he bent his face toward mine.

"What are you doing?"

"Examining its delicateness up close." He grunted. "I don't know, Aiden. It's a little too..." Scrunching up his own nose, Dario sat back, careful to keep his weight off of me, and held his hands like a picture frame before his face. "Hmmm," he said again, his voice full of concern. "It's a little too delicate. You fucked up, man. I think you made him even more handsome."

"Fuck off," I said and closed my eyes. My vision was bleary, and I didn't want to admit it, but I was dizzy.

Dario laughed and climbed off of me.

"You do know that delicate was explaining how he would *feel*, not look," Aiden said pointedly.

"Please, for the love of all the Gods," Dario said. "Try and be fun."

"How many hours has it been?" I asked.

"Well, you missed breakfast and lunch and all chances of eating the very early dinner of a very elderly man." Dario gave me a death-stare that said he'd punch me if I moved. He reached forward and gently fluffed my pillow beneath my neck before pulling the blanket back around my waist. Another death-stare told me what would happen if I thanked him.

"So, a while, then," I said instead.

"How do you feel now?" Aiden asked, walking forward. He pushed Dario back to the edge of my bed and sat beside me, his palm over my forehead.

"Better than when you found me." My stomach sank as the

events from the morning came back to me. "Do we know anything? What happened to Kenna? Is she... is she all right?"

Dario shook his head. "We know nothing. The fuck happened before we got here?"

I sat back up, Aiden helping me get comfortable.

"We'd just woken up. Kane burst in here, demanding she come immediately in her nightdress. He refused to leave or give her any privacy. So, I threatened him. The bastard punched me. Twice. Bowen handed over her clothes. She got dressed. They left."

"Fuck," Dario said. He turned to Garrett. "You know anything?"

"My own illustrious father hasn't exactly been forthcoming lately. Or ever. All of his spare time has been spent focusing on the planning of the *Alissedari*. Like we are."

"I don't know anything either," Dario said, defeated.

Three fathers on the Council, three rulers of Glemaria, and none of us could help Kenna or would be privy to what had actually happened.

"Let's see if she comes to the welcome dinner," Aiden said. He moved off the bed and joined Garrett's side, their hands instantly together. He seemed to sink into him like they were actually one body that had been forcefully split apart and only achieved perfection when together. He smoothed Garrett's hair down, and the furrow between his brows unwrinkled.

"Shit, the dinner," I said. My father's pre-birthday and anniversary celebration. "When is that?"

"One hour," Garrett said.

I groaned. One hour. One hour before I had to be fully dressed as the Heir Apparent at the entry to Seathorne to welcome our special guest, Her Royal Highness Queen Ishtara of the Star Court, High Lady of the Night Lands.

"The eldest daughter of Glemaria's arkturion isn't going to

miss a dinner with the Afeyan Queen. Nor would she miss the first official festivities of the tournament and your father's birthday," Garrett said confidently.

"And if she isn't there?" I asked.

Dario's aura darkened, cold shadows spiking. "Then, we find out where she is."

"We don't have much time," Garrett said. "Not your fault, but we lost all of today for plotting and practicing tomorrow. We're not going to be able to make a final run-through of the Pits either. So, we need to prepare now as much as we can, finalize our strategy, and continue sticking together."

Dario clapped his hands. "Let's get our boy dressed."

"Can you stand?" Aiden asked under his breath. He still looked worried I had a head injury.

"I can," I said. Inside, my stomach was shredding itself into pieces. Something was wrong, and somehow, Kenna was at the center of it.

AN HOUR LATER, we were all dressed in our soturion-best. Our leathers freshly treated, Valalumir stars sharpened and shined at the edges of our belt straps. All of our swords were gleaming, and our cloaks had been freshly pressed. Except for Aiden, who'd opted for a new black jacket beneath his blue mage robes. While I'd been out, Aiden had taken over Kenna's job of ensuring my leathers, along with Dario's and Garrett's, were waterproof. He'd also worked over the glamour magic of our cloaks, heightening the camouflage one more time after he'd fixed my nose.

Bowen and two more escorts flanked me and my friends as we made our way to the front doors of Seathorne. The herald announced us each by name, and then we were all instructed to join the lineup, each of us standing with our familial Council members, shivering with cold from the opened doors. Everyone who was anyone in Glemarian nobility stood present except my father. He, of course, had to make a grand entrance. Only when I'd been directed to my place beside my mother, whom I'd anxiously looked over for any signs of bruising or new wounds, did I find Kenna.

She stood beside her father and the whole of Ka Gaddayan, her entire body stiff. She stared straight ahead, wearing a silk green dress with long sleeves. Sleeves that covered her wrists. My stomach turned. I'd never seen her wear this dress before—Kenna loved the color yellow. She'd filled her wardrobe with it. Her long brown hair was worn down her back as usual, but half of her locks had been braided into a crown that nearly lay across her forehead. Almost like a diadem.

"Ken," I hissed.

She sucked in a breath, her chest rising enough for me to know she'd heard me. But she didn't look my way.

Kane however, turned with a disgusting glare. His eyes flicked between me and my mother, and then he straightened his red cloak and black leathered armor, his attention back on the doors.

Lord Draken, who'd held his post as Second, suddenly departed.

"His Highness, Arkasva Devon Hart, High Lord of Glemaria, Imperator to the North," announced the herald.

We all turned, falling into low bows and curtsies for my father as he strutted into the hall, his version of a humble smile on his face, one hand on the hilt of his sword. Everything had been polished and shined to perfection: the red stone in the black leather hilt, the Valalumir stars at the bottom of his leather strapped belt, and the Laurel of the Arkasva, glittering with gold leaves atop his head. He was the picture of power, and his cold aura left shivers across my skin, as he took his place and signaled for all to rise.

My father was met with shouts of "Happy birthday, Imperator," and "Congratulations," and *"Tovayah maischa"* on his long and successful rule of Glemaria.

Then, everyone stilled, silent as explosions beyond the fortress stole our attention. With the doors opened and the curtains of the ceiling-high windows drawn back, we had a clear view of the night sky. It still snowed, and several snowflakes were blowing into the hall. Not a single star could be seen.

But at another explosion, the entire night sky lit up. A giant golden Valalumir star materialized and then split into a thousand smaller Valalumirs falling softly to the grounds.

It was just enough to light the snow-capped cliffs of the mountains beyond, the snow-topped pine trees. Small slivers of gold and silver peeked out from the leaves of the sun and moon trees. Beyond it all were two small fires. I frowned, watching the fires blaze and rise higher into the sky, undeterred by the snow.

The fires grew, moving closer and closer.

Wings. They were wings made of pure flame.

Agnavim. Fire birds. I'd never seen one before. They were survivors from the Drowning of ancient Lumeria, but they'd always been wild, refusing to be tamed by the Lumerians of the Empire. They resided in the Night Lands.

My breath hitched as the wings came closer, the flames forming a pattern like the feathers of a seraphim. Heat began to fill the hall, almost wiping out the chill of my father's aura. I could feel the warmth of the agnavim on my face, like that of a blistering hot day in Bamaria.

The bird's body seemed to be made of pure gold. On its

back was a silver carriage, round in shape with a pointed top. Silver stars spun in circles over the tip.

An Afeya appeared in the center of Seathorne's entryway.

For a moment, I wasn't sure if I looked at a male or a female. The Afeya had always been far more fluid in their expressions of gender. But as I took in the Afeya's clothing, I could see he inhabited a male body. Long limbs full of sinewy muscle were uncovered save for an ice-blue satin loincloth. His skin was also blue, with black whorls tattooed across every inch. A glittering diamond adorned the center of each whorl. His hair was long, obsidian, and hanging in silky strands down his back.

He bowed before the Council then slowly straightened, his neck snaking side to side, before he stepped forward with cat-like grace.

"We thank you, Your Highness, Arkasva Hart, High Lord of Glemaria, Imperator to the North, for your generous invitation."

I stilled, my heart pounding as his violet eyes found mine.

I'd seen this Afeya before, in Bamaria, over two years earlier. He'd been at the solstice celebration, about to go to Lyriana. I'd broken all my rules that night and rushed to her on the dance floor to get her away from him. And I'd asked Jules about him, time and time again. In one of her last letters to me, she'd said he'd met with Aemon.

I pulled my gaze from the Afeya to spy on the Bamarian arkturion, but he remained calm—at least, as calm as he usually appeared. He was always just slightly on edge, just slightly angry, with a far too inquisitive yet pained expression on his face. The Ready made no signs of surprise or horror at the Afeya, just offered a simple nod in recognition.

A bell-like laugh sounded in my head.

My gaze fell back on the Afeya. He was still watching me, amusement in his eyes, his lips quirking into a sly smile.

"I am Mercurial, First Messenger of Her Royal Highness, Queen Ishtara of the Star Court, High Lady of the Night Lands. May I present to the good Lumerians of Glemaria, my queen?"

He bowed low, his eyes on me still as his head dropped.

Mercurial. That was his name. What had he been doing in Bamaria? What had he wanted with Lyr?

Before I could think any further, he vanished.

There was an audible gasp at the blatant showing of a vorakh. Of my vorakh. Mine and Garrett's. Afeya were not held by the same rules as we were. They couldn't be.

I found Garrett, his face pale, his fingers fidgeting at his side as if trying desperately not to mess with his hair as he stood proudly beside his father, Turion Efraim, his mother, and his younger sister, Vanya, who held his hand and looked up at her brother adoringly.

My back burned, reminding me again of the oath I'd sworn. The secrets I kept. The protection I'd always give to my friend.

Then, the door filled again, this time with a female Afeya, her skin appearing to be covered in thousands of tiny diamonds. A silver dress cut a low V across her chest, and a crown of glittering silver stars floated above her head.

She cast her aura forward—something only Afeya could do—and Seathorne's hall filled with sparkling stars, too bright to look at directly. The flames of the agnavim puttered out, and darkness filled the sky.

"Welcome," my father said. "Welcome to Glemaria, Your Highness, Queen Ishtara."

CHAPTER

TWELVE

Queen Ishtara stepped forward, her movements swift, delicate, and entirely inhuman and un-Lumerian. Where Mercurial was cat-like with his facial expressions yet snake-like in the way he moved his neck and hips, the queen seemed to move too quickly and slowly at once, like she was not truly of this world. She seemed to turn her head the same way I'd observed the birds in Bamaria doing. It was like she was a seraphim trapped in a woman's body.

Twirling her wrists at her sides, she drew back her stars, and I tried to look at her directly, to see not just how she moved, but what she actually looked like. No matter how hard I focused, her features were impossible to grasp. No one part of her hair, her skin, or her clothing was without glitter or light.

"Shall we?" she asked, holding out her arm to my father. "I should like to attend dinner. It was not a long nor an arduous journey, as we have long been close neighbors." Her voice was unusual, melodic like a crystal: sharp, delicate, light, yet expansive. "But I would like to eat now. And my tongue has a taste for some wine." Her sparkling eyes flicked to me, and she blinked slowly.

My throat went dry.

"Hmmm," she purred, a sly smile spreading across her lips. "Or something sweeter. Something with honey."

Like mead? I thought.

She nodded.

Shit. I tried to empty my mind of thoughts. If Afeya had the ability to travel, they no doubt possessed the other vorakh as well—visions, mind-reading. I'd already had Afeya in my head before. I didn't want her in my mind. My memories.

"Of course," my father said, strolling through the aisle of standing nobles to reach her side. He took her arm in his, his smile widening. The Afeyan Queen never visited, barely deigned to treat with Lumerians, and now he had her in his country, in his fortress, and on his arm. He was going to be insufferable.

We all bowed again as he walked past, his soturi on high alert, everyone's swords out. She remained alone; I suspected she was accompanied by escorts, but I doubted we'd see them, not unless she wanted us to.

That also left me uneasy, as if there were ghosts flitting among us, ready to strike at any perceived threat to her name. Very little between the Lumerian Empire and the Afeyan Courts kept us from war. Our main compromise had been for Lumerians to occupy the lands that allowed us to mine starfire and for the Afeya to forge the steel into weapons.

I knew we traded. I knew they fed off of us, making deals with the desperate and the forsworn who'd lost their status to exile. We stayed away from their lands, from the places that still connected deeply to the Lumerian Ocean. We did not interfere with the strange magic of Lumeria Matavia that still ran through their veins. But despite all of my education, all my years of study, all of my time in Court, I understood very little about our treaty. And I didn't trust them one bit. My distrust had been drilled into me as a boy and reinforced as a man. I'd seen it with my own eyes in Bamaria. They had a plan.

But for tonight, I had to lay low. Not stir trouble, get in Kane's way, nor allow my father to lose his temper—not if I wanted to survive tomorrow.

And if possible, I needed to get to Kenna. To see if she was all right.

I walked to dinner beside my mother, her arm linked through mine. It was the rare opportunity where we could be together without my father's eyes. For once, everything between us felt unpressured, easy, like we were just mother and son, despite the occasion.

My mother looked up at me; I'd long outgrown her height. "You look handsome tonight, Rhyan," she said in her unapologetically thick Glemarian accent. She smiled one of her rare and beautiful smiles. Bowen moved beside us, and she offered her smile to him as well, before returning her gaze to me.

"Different?" I asked, wondering if perhaps Aiden had gone too far with his reconstructive glamour.

My mother's eyes searched mine, and she smiled wider. "More handsome than ever. But that's because of who you are inside, my heart. You know I'm proud of you, Rhyan. So proud of you. Who you are. Who I know you'll still become."

I pressed my lips together, nodding in acknowledgment. She was in a good mood for once, she seemed somehow free, relieved of my father. I didn't want to break the spell. But my throat was constricted, and tears were welling. I so infrequently heard this, heard her use the nickname she'd used for me when I was a boy, when we'd sit together for hours in the temple and she'd tell me stories. Every day she'd called me, "my heart." It hadn't been until I'd been seven years old that

I'd understood she meant *heart* and not Hart. She'd laughed so hard when she'd realized I'd thought she'd been calling me by the name of our Ka.

Since I'd stopped going to her—since the day I'd poured out my soul to her about Lyriana and she'd offered nothing— our interactions had been fewer. Now, I was sorry they had been. I didn't know it, but I'd been so angry with her. Blaming her. I'd needed her these last two years, and I suspected she'd needed me. Maybe she wasn't perfect. Maybe she hadn't protected me the way she should have. But maybe that had been impossible. Maybe she had protected me in the best way she'd known how, with the few resources that remained to her, just as I had tried to do for her. For everyone.

Sometimes the ones you most want to protect, they are the very ones you can't—the ones who need to save themselves. Kenna's hushed words in the dark raced through my mind. I didn't want to believe them. But maybe I had no other choice.

At least there was this—this moment. If all I got were these words from my mother tonight, a reminder that I was still "my heart" to her, I could accept it and take it for the blessing it was. I had so few.

"Be still," she said suddenly, her voice barely a whisper. Her hand reached down between us, slipping into the leather pouch on my waist.

It was subtle, but there was an additional weight at my hip. Without a word, she pulled her hand back to rest on my arm, looking proper and elegant, the wife-consort of the Imperator.

"What was that?" I asked.

"A gift," she said. "To help you tomorrow. To help you do what you must. You'll know what to do. Only open that with your friends. Do not speak a word about it to anyone else."

We paused outside the dining hall beside Arkturion Kane. My hands immediately tensed into fists.

"How's your nose, Your Grace?" he asked.

My mother's hand tightened on my arm, a light restraint. I knew then she knew what had happened in my bedroom that morning.

I readjusted my thumbs across my fingers, fists tightening, itching to repay him for the pain and for so much more, starting with what he'd done to Kenna. But not tonight.

I recomposed myself, forcibly relaxed my shoulders, and schooled my face to a neutral expression.

"My nose?" I laughed. "Since when did your arkturion duties give you leave to ponder the features of my face?"

"Looked better earlier," he snarled.

"I didn't realize it was my job to make my face so pleasing to you, Arkturion. Would you care to come to my room tomorrow morning and try again for the look you so desperately desire? We could play with another feature. Maybe change my hairstyle."

"Arkturion," my mother said sweetly, "I was just admiring your daughter's new dress. It's a beautiful shade of green. Very becoming on Lady Kenna."

Kane's eyes turned to slits, and then he walked inside the ballroom, breaking protocol by walking ahead of us.

My mother pulled me toward her. "Don't start," she chided. "You need your health for tomorrow."

Senator Oryyan entered the room along with Thorin, looking pompous as ever. His aura was one of pure violence. In fact, half the auras in the room were beginning to feel that way, feeding off everyone's bloodlust and excitement for the tournament.

But the violence in Thorin's aura felt more extreme. Ka Oryyan was vocal about their desire to rule. It was far more common in the North for power to swap amongst the Kavim, for the Kavim to go to war over the Seat of Power in each country. Maybe my father ruling for so long was actually something to celebrate.

"Watch out for Ka Oryyan. Thorin in particular," my mother said. "He gives me a bad feeling for tomorrow. Look out for his cousins, too."

I nodded. She often expressed tiny premonitions. They weren't visions, nothing that concrete, but her words sometimes made me wonder if she was something like a vorakh. It had always been believed to run in families though there'd never been definitive proof. If there were, far more than Ka Azria would have been wiped from Lumeria Nutavia by the Emperor.

"He wants to win," I said, glaring at Thorin.

"He can't," she said quietly.

"Because I have to."

"Not at the cost of losing yourself," she said, her tone suddenly serious.

"What about the cost of losing you?"

"You won't."

"But father..." I trailed off. She knew his command. And she knew the consequences that awaited her if I failed.

"Forget his demands," she said, her voice far graver than I'd ever heard. Her accent heavy.

"Mother," I said, desperately. "I can't."

"Rhyan, my heart, listen to me. If you hear nothing else, hear this. He may rule my country, he may rule over your life and mine. But he is not all-powerful. He does not rule over your heart, your mind, or your soul. Do you understand me?"

"But he threatened—"

"I know very well what he's threatened. And I am not concerned. I have endured it all. I know what it's cost you to protect me."

I bit my lip, not wanting to cry.

"I know you don't think I can protect you. But I can do this much. I can at least do what's right. Do not give in to his demands. Don't let him ruin the best parts of yourself—not for my sake. Swear to me."

"Please."

"Just survive tomorrow," she said. "Do that, and no more. Many will target you. But you're stronger than all of them. You have nothing to prove, nothing to win. Do not lose yourself for his vanity. Just survive. Live. But be careful." Her eyes flicked back to Thorin and then to me.

I understood her message, loud and clear. But I still didn't know what I was going to do. If I could live with the consequences of killing. If I could live with the consequences of not. Both options felt impossible.

"I'll be careful," I said, taking my seat.

We were at the head table along with Arkturion Kane and Arkmage Connal, my absolute favorite people, and, of course, my father and his guest of honor, Queen Ishtara. Though they'd been the ones to lead the procession to the ballroom for dinner, they were last to enter, once again prompting everyone to stand and bow or curtsey until they were both seated. My father looked overjoyed and clapped his hands, signaling everyone to sit and for the servants to enter. For once, his aura was light, drunk on the attention of his power play.

Soon bottles of wine and mead were freely flowing between the tables, plates of cheese were pausing before each guest, and bowls full of steaming bread and oils were making their way from the kitchen.

My mother leaned toward me, about to speak, but my father snapped his fingers, and her words were cut off by Bowen, now standing between our chairs.

"Your Grace, Lady Shakina," he said reverently, as if

standing there were the most natural thing in the world, and not a plot of my father's. "You look lovely tonight."

My mother nodded. "I thank you, soturion." Her eyes darted to me, apologetic. Guilty.

But she had nothing to apologize for in that moment. It was my father.

I bit the inside of my cheek. My fucking father. Our Gods-damned Imperator. Couldn't even allow us a moment of peace at dinner. Had to have Bowen interrupt.

I was forced to entertain several guests who walked to the table to pay their respects. Several dignitaries from the northern countries who'd flown in for the tournament. There was a faction from Hartavia that had me holding my breath.

But the senator wasn't present. Instead, my mother's sister, Lady Sheera and my Uncle Marcus approached, bowing and curtseying to my father. They both spent several moments with my mother, but upon some rather annoyed glances from their Imperator, they said their goodbyes, coming to my side.

"Ready for tomorrow?" Uncle Marcus asked.

"As ready as I can be," I said.

"To bring back the *Alissedari*." Aunt Sheera shook her head, clearly disgusted with the event. Her eyes flicked angrily from my father to her sister, before back to me. She looked so much like my mother, their hair the same exact shade of brown, their eyes were a match as well. Though Aunt Sheera's were sharper and more alert. I watched as my father looked up, sensing her distaste.

All at once Sheera's face changed, devoid of emotion, her opinion swallowed by the expectations of nobility. By the expectations of an Imperator. She rested her hand on my shoulder. "I hear you've become quite the warrior, Rhyan. Strong like your father," she said, nodding back in his direction.

He smiled at this; his face disgustingly smug.

"I've done my training," I said, knowing I couldn't contradict her compliments to my father, but unwilling to give him even an ounce of credit.

"Well, I certainly hope no gryphons are harmed tomorrow. Though I doubt that will be the case," Aunt Sheera said.

Uncle Marcus gave her a small nudge, and she straightened.

"Rhyan, if you should ever want to visit Hartavia again, our home is always open to you." Sheera's eyes glanced back to my mother, her sister, then to me. And with a quick curtsey and acknowledgment of the queen, she and my uncle excused themselves.

A light sparkled in my periphery and I felt the queen's eyes on me. Bowen shifted his weight, and my mother leaned forward, drawing her attention.

"Your Highness, we are honored to welcome you. I do hope you will enjoy your visit as well as the festivities for my husband," my mother said cordially.

She spoke in statements rather than questions, as questions could prompt the Afeya to answer, and answering had a price. A dangerous one.

"I shall try," the queen said, that crystal-like voice leaving shivers down my spine. "It has been ages since I visited Lumeria. Glemaria in particular. But I felt prompted to do so."

"You could not resist my invitation to such an auspicious event," my father said jovially. He lifted his glass to her.

The queen snapped her head toward him, the movement so birdlike I was startled to see her human features.

I expected her to respond to him—everyone always did, everyone always appeased him—but she only sneered and turned her head back to my mother.

The chill down my spine intensified. There was something

between the queen and my mother. Some mental conversation happening. I was sure of it.

I took her wrist in my hand.

She didn't notice nor break eye contact with the queen.

"Mother," I said, worried.

Still nothing.

What in fucking Lumeria?

I glared at the queen. "I would love to hear of your last visit to Glemaria, your highness," I said, trying to pull her attention away from my mother.

It didn't work. The queen still watched my mother in silent communication.

You'll get your turn. We are already aware of you. We have been for ages, the crystal-like voice rang inside my mind.

Then, Queen Ishtara looked to my father, raised her glass, and took a long sip of wine. "I said I shall try to enjoy myself. But I fear I am longing already for the Night Lands."

My father was no longer pleased. "You might give Glemaria a chance, Your Highness. I am sure they are no Night Lands. There are far less stars here than you're accustomed to. But we have many beautiful sights. And the Gryphon Pits restoration is magnificent. I am sure you will find tomorrow's tournament in honor of my birthday and anniversary as Arkasva to be quite the enjoyable spectacle."

"I have no doubt," she said icily. "That still does not mean any of this will appeal to me."

My father's aura flared. A biting blizzard. Freezing, all directed at me. He wasn't getting anywhere with Queen Ishtara, so, naturally, it had to be my fault. Like everything else was.

"And I shall tell you why," the Afeyan Queen continued.

Guests in the room began to shift uncomfortably in their

seats. Glasses clanged as they were set on the table, forks dropped, and plates pushed back.

"I am extremely concerned. And that is the reason for my visit. Did you really believe the birthday, the anniversary of an Arkasva, of an Imperator—a mere mortal who lives for a blink of my eye, who holds their position for a time that is even shorter—would be enough to draw me, a queen and high lady, from my lands? Did you believe you were important enough to summon one such as myself?"

I bit my cheek. If my father wasn't important enough to summon the queen, no one was.

"We would never presume to summon. We extended an invitation," my father gritted through his teeth.

"I've been reading context for centuries. It was a summons. But I have not answered it despite my presence here tonight. I came for another purpose. Your pride has made a grave error, Your Highness."

That was a threat. I glanced at my mother, but she seemed serene, at peace, as if she had no idea of the war that had just erupted at our table. Already, my father's soturi were on the move, their swords withdrawn, their fighting stances enacted.

Sweat beaded at my neck. We had a legion of soturi a foot away, but I didn't doubt the queen's ability to attack if that was her intention. And if she failed... I didn't even want to ponder the consequences of the Afeyan Courts' retaliation. No doubt all of the Night Lands would be at war with us.

My mother took my hand under the table, sandwiching it between hers. It was a steadying hold, one with a strength I hadn't seen from her in years. And I felt Bowen move in, somehow no longer between me and my mother, but standing guard as if he protected both of us. He was a shield, closing us in. A small look passed between them, and then at once, both of their gazes were on my father.

"I do assure you," my father said, aware all eyes were on our table and every second that passed, someone else understood the Afeyan Queen's disdain toward him, "I invited you here with honorable intentions. We are neighbors. We share a problem along our borders."

"Yes," she hissed. "We do! And do you know the difference between us? We offered a solution. You shot it down."

"We shot it down," my father said, careful to avoid phrasing a question, yet everyone could hear the uncertainty in his voice. "I am unaware of such a solution being offered in the first place, nor shot down."

The Afeyan Queen stood, pushing back her chair. My father's escorts inched closer, and her aura was flung out to every corner of the ballroom. Shadows darkened the space, and just as quickly, silver glittering stars appeared, spinning against the ceiling, faster and faster until I felt dizzy.

Bodies appeared, coming in and out of focus—Afeya of every skin color, size, and shape. Some had human faces, some had the faces of animals: deer, eagles, lions. I'd been right. She was extremely heavily guarded, and we didn't stand a chance.

Queen Ishtara snapped her fingers, and the bodies disappeared. "For some time now, the akadim in our region have been a growing concern of mine. Their numbers are greater. Their ability to organize increases. They are working together for the first time since the Drowning. They are not simply hunting easy prey. They are hunting for the best. They have plans. They have targets—Lumerians with power."

The akadim that night... Garrett and I had both seen the monsters pass by dozens of victims, of prey, of food. They had their goal in mind: Garrett and me. They were hunting vorakh.

It went against everything I'd learned, everything I'd seen before.

I felt Garrett's nerves across the room, his aura reaching out to me for reassurance. My back burned.

"We are aware of their growing numbers," my father said. "And we are concerned, as well. But they are not becoming smarter, nor more organized as far as I can see. Maybe that is what you think you have observed. But I have not. I have yet to see an akadim army that can rival my legions. Glemaria boasts some of the greatest akadim killers in Lumeria. My soturi only recently killed five. And we have more warriors coming into the world every day. There are no soturi better trained to hunt the beasts and squash their numbers than those here in this room."

"And yet, these efforts are no more effective at stopping the akadim than staves and crystals. Especially with faulty borders." Queen Ishtara's voice grew louder, sharper, more crystalline and intense as she swiveled her head, her sparkling eyes falling on each person in the room in that strange bird-like manner. "We have made true efforts. When we saw the rising population, we began to train our gryphons to hunt them down. Unlike you, we are civilized. We do not merely use the gryphons for transport of riders. Nor are they ridiculed and humiliated in your infantile tournaments and games. They are not insulted by fighting in *Alissedari*. For years now, we have been sending our gryphons to your lands to kill the beasts. And what you have done? Shot them down. Even the babies."

The red baby gryphon. The increase in the appearance of Afeyan gryphons. Gods. Right before the attack, we'd seen an orange one. Auriel's bane.

I didn't trust the Afeya. They were always up to something, plotting, trying to make a bargain. And her messenger and that strange female I'd seen in Bamaria, they were after Lyriana. But in this instance, because of what I'd seen, what I'd experienced, I believed Queen Ishtara. All along, they'd been helping us—helping fight the akadim—and we'd been spitting in their faces and killing innocent animals in the process.

Her soldiers flickered in and out again, their bodies visible for barely a second.

My mother slid her chair closer to me, her hands still holding mine. Bowen took a step back, offering us both some space. "Calm, my heart. You're safe," she said quietly. Her reassurance made me realize how tightly I was gripping her hand. I released my hold, but her words did little to calm the pounding of my heart.

"You, Your Highness," the queen chided, "you have missed the pattern. All to Glemaria's detriment."

"The pattern you speak of," my father said slowly, his hands straining at his side, desperately trying to appear calm and in control, "I am unaware of its meaning."

"And you shall remain so. As the High Lady of the Night Lands, I cannot interfere with these events directly—no more than I already have. As much power as I possess, I, too, am bound by the earthly laws of magic and the celestial oaths of the Gods. As well as their curse. I did what I could to mitigate the growth, the threat you so often say you wish to stop. You've undone our efforts. And far worse." She turned her head again, her gaze landing on the table where Garrett, his father, and Arkturion Aemon sat.

Aemon scowled, shadows filling his aura.

Queen Ishtara pulled back her lips in a sneer and snapped her head to my father. "You have allowed the enemy into your quarters. A day will come when you will regret that you did not act faster, that you did not stop the unleashing of more power and destruction than has been seen in the Empire since the Drowning."

My throat tightened, a memory surfacing.

You've made a huge mistake. That girl has the potential to unleash more power and destruction than anyone in the Empire ever has. You will rue the day we did not control it.

Those were the words my father had said to me in Bamaria right after I'd convinced him to stop negotiating for a marriage contract between Arkturion Kane and Lyriana. I'd never understood what he'd meant. I still didn't. But I didn't like how closely Queen Ishtara's words were to his nor the implication that Lyriana was somehow involved in our political plans and events and that, in the end, I hadn't actually saved her but left her more vulnerable.

Queen Ishtara's eyes fell on me, and she nodded.

Yes. We are quite aware of her, too. There are others you need to worry more about. But not yet.

She offered one more patronizing look to Aemon, and I wondered if she was warning him of the danger Lyriana could be in. Gods, I hoped so. And I hoped he listened, protected her.

The queen set down her glass, smiled at my mother, and fixed her sparkling Afeyan eyes on my father. "Happy birthday, Imperator. *Tovayah maischa* on your long rule." Queen Ishtara's words hung in the air, echoing through the room. Then, she vanished.

MY FATHER RUSHED us through the rest of the evening's ceremony, embarrassed, his ego hanging by a thread. He called the dinner to an abrupt halt the moment the final cup of wine was served—wanting to distance himself from his failure with the queen as quickly as possible.

We'd all been rushed onto the field in the center of the Katurium's arena. Thrown into line behind a bannerman for each of our Kavim. Dario was behind the largest line for Ka DeTerria. As the

SON OF THE DROWNED EMPIRE

ruling Ka, Ka Hart had been announced last which meant I'd been forced to stand in the dark of the arena's inner halls with Bowen breathing down my neck for over an hour. We lost Garrett early due to his Ka's status, and I'd ended up forced to bear Ka Oryyan and Thorin's glares at me as I waited. My mother's warning flashed in my mind again and again. When at last I could walk out into the arena, Arkturion Kane's voice boomed across the stadium.

"His Grace, Lord Rhyan Hart, Heir Apparent to the Arkasva, High Lord of Glemaria, Imperator to the North."

The crowd cheered as I walked into the field, turning in the center, looking back at all of the Glemarian nobility who'd come to see the spectacle. They filled the stadium seats in a way I hadn't seen before—not one inch of free space. Everyone was holding up sigil flags, waving them over their heads. Only my aunt and uncle from Hartavia, representing Ka Telor seemed displeased.

My heart hammered as I caught sight of my father in the stands, the Imperator's seating sectioned off and surrounded by his personal guards. His grip was tight on his sword, freed from the hilt, the point burrowing into the ground between his legs. A push of his anger made its way to the field, nearly knocking me back and adding to the already intense chill in the air.

My mother looked calm for once, and it left an uneasy feeling in my stomach. Her aura had diminished over the years, becoming something soft and submissive, a shadow against my father's anger and force. But just then, I could feel it almost reaching for me, calming the energy of his.

Arkturion Kane glared down at me from beside him. And sitting stiffly in the seat next to my mother was Kenna. Our eyes met, for the briefest moment, before she looked down in her lap, the braid in her hair gleaming beneath the flames.

My name was shouted again and again. And I watched nobles handing over gold and silver coins.

Bets had been placed.

I bowed as expected to my father, and walked solemnly to the pyre before me, the flames shifting color like the eternal flames of our temples. When it reached green, I pulled out the scroll I'd been handed, my name scrawled across. And then I tossed it into the fire, watching it spit and smoke, turning to nothing but ember.

"I, Lord Rhyan Hart, enter the Alissedari," I shouted, my voice rising through the Katurium, carried by a magic that seemed to emanate from the flames. Arkmage Connal stood on the other side, his mouth grim, and for a second, I felt the ropes, felt the binds snaking around me. The binds that were always too close, too present.

I swallowed, and continued. "I enter this tournament with honor, to bring glory to Ka Hart. I enter to celebrate the great ruling of my father, His Highness, Imperator Hart, Imperator to the North, High Lord of Glemaria. And I fight alongside my friends." I found Garrett and Dario standing beneath the sigils for Ka Aravain, and Ka DeTerria.

Then, I stepped back. Arkmage Connal tipped his stave forward, and a blast of glittering rope sprang forward.

I jumped back in terror—my stomach hooking as laughs sounded from my classmates.

It was a binding. But not the ropes I feared. This was simply a single silver cuff that wound itself smoothly around my wrist like a bracelet. Something to tie me to the tournament, to my promise to enter with honor. And it would be a way to find me if my gryphon didn't return to the Gryphon Pits.

I was now officially part of the *Alissedari,* whether I wanted to be or not. And I still didn't know how I'd proceed. If I could follow my father's orders, or risk my mother's request.

Then, I faced the rest of my opponents, all lined up and down the field, their eyes full of ire and violence.

Their auras were like a poisonous gas reaching for me. And with my mother's warning ringing through my thoughts, I realized that when the fights began... I might not have a choice.

Following the ceremony there had been another toast in my father's honor as well as a performance by water dancers, before every warrior wearing a silver band was sent home.

As far as I knew, the celebrations, and the attempts to soothe his ego, and praise him on the eve of his birthday would go on all night. They would continue until the festivities resumed in the morning, and last until everyone arrived at the Gryphon Pits. There I assumed further entertainment would be provided as the nobility awaited each gryphon rider to enter the arena. As they waited for death.

We'd crowded into Dario and Garrett's apartment with Aiden. I'd tried to get Kenna's attention to bring her with us, but she'd refused to look at me. Instead, she'd silently followed Arkturion Kane back to Seathorne.

"What the fuck happened back there?" Dario asked, as soon as we shut the door. "Do you think the queen was telling the truth?"

Aiden shook his head. "I'm not inclined to believe the word of an Afeyan. But I think it matters little, not as much as what happened with your father, Rhyan. This will put a strain on the relationship between our countries."

"Understatement," I muttered.

"We can't worry about that," Garrett said.

"Easy to say from the son of a turion," Dario snapped.

"Hey! My father's on the Council, too!"

"And mine's the fucking Arkasva," I said. "But Garrett's right. We need to worry about tomorrow."

There was a knock, and a small parchment was pressed beneath the door.

Aiden flicked his stave, floating the parchment to Garrett. It had been sealed with the symbol of a gryphon. It was from Artem, the seal identical to the one that'd been on his letter from a year ago.

"It's instructions," Garrett said, his eyes flicking across the parchment. "All who are entering the *Alissedari* are to be in their beds by one in the morning—dressed in their boots and armor and with their supplies ready to go."

"That's in a quarter of an hour," I said, biting my cheek.

"Why now?" Dario asked.

Aiden took the letter from Garrett, reading it over himself. "Probably to even the playing field. Have everyone stop plotting and planning at the same time." He frowned. "No guests allowed."

"Can you handle a night alone?" Dario teased, wrapping his arms around himself like a lover, his hands roving up and down his sides.

"Shut up," Garrett snapped, but he was already looking longingly at Aiden.

Aiden sucked in a breath. "Be safe tomorrow. I don't care if you win. You don't need to be the hero—just survive."

It was so like what my mother had said.

"I will, Ai," Garrett promised. "You've seen me on gryphon-back. Don't be worried."

Though Garrett was the warrior, Aiden pulled him onto his lap, his hands cupping his face for a kiss. Within seconds, Garrett's hands were tugging at Aiden's dark auburn locks, the passion between them as potent as ever.

Dario's eyebrows narrowed, and he released his arms as he watched me uneasily from across the room.

"One of us is going to die tomorrow," he said heavily.

"Dario!" I yelled. "Don't fucking say that."

Garrett broke his embrace from Aiden. "Seriously, man. What the fuck? No one's going to die tomorrow."

"You know it's true," Dario said. "You didn't feel the blood-lust back there? No one's going to wait this out. Half of the Academy's been thirsting to kill for weeks. It's going to be over quickly."

"That doesn't mean it's going to be one of us," I said, though some small part of me wondered—would things be easier if it were me? Simpler? Then, I wouldn't have to choose—wouldn't lose myself. Wouldn't have to take a life. No. I couldn't entertain those thoughts. It had been a long while since I had, and tonight was not the night to do so. Not when the part of me that had felt asleep for so long had awoken, had wanted to live. Not when I had an oath to fulfill. To protect my friends.

"It's not going to be any of us," Garrett said confidently.

Dario made a sound low in his throat. "I bet every other alliance of soturi is saying the same thing right now."

"One of those alliances is wrong," Aiden said quietly.

"But not us," Garrett said vehemently.

Aiden's throat bobbed. "No. Not us."

The tension between the four of us was suddenly too thick, too real. I needed to get out of there, to calm my mind and body, to find a way to rest. I had a sinking feeling that if we were wrong, it was going to be me. I could still feel Thorin's eyes on me. The mark his Ka had put on my back. My mother's warning.

I was always going to be the main target. I was the strongest soturion at combat clinics and habibellums, and everyone knew it. And I was the Heir Apparent. If one was going to prove themselves in the *Alissedari*, it wasn't going to be by killing the weakest soturion or going for the easiest kill. They'd target the most powerful. They'd target me.

Could I do it? If it came down to it–could I take a life? My stomach twisted at the thought just as it had every other time I'd considered it since my father's announcement.

I opened my belt pouch for my apartment key, and then I remembered my mother had put something in there. Fishing around, I felt the unfamiliar objects almost at once and closed my hand around them.

"What?" Dario asked, he'd been scrutinizing me since I'd opened it.

I opened my hand. My eyes widened as a gasp escaped my lips.

"Vadati stones!" Aiden said.

"Myself to Moriel." Garrett jumped up.

"There's three," Dario said. "How did you get those?"

I swallowed, not sure I could be beholden to one more forced oath or secret. Having these in my possession was illegal in every sense of the word. The fact that my mother had them was grounds for arrest if she were ever betrayed. Very limited numbers of the talking stones had survived the Drowning, and the possession and use of each stone was registered with the Empire and highly regulated. Except for these, which were unreported, handed down for generations in my mother's Ka as an heirloom.

"I have my ways," I said finally to my friends. "They're on loan. Just for tomorrow. For us."

Aiden shook his head. "They're illegal."

Dario grunted in annoyance. "Your point?"

"Aiden, I know," I said. "But we need them. We can use

them tomorrow—stay in contact through the tournament, warn each other of danger, have each other's backs."

Garrett grinned. "That's perfect."

"And illegal!" Aiden snapped.

Garrett frowned, his hand shifting uncomfortably over his belt.

"I'm sorry," Dario said, "so fucking what? Don't you want your friends and the great love of your life to have a way to call for help? To stay in contact?"

"I..." Aiden looked chagrinned. "I don't want anyone to get into trouble. The consequences could be far worse. And you're all more than capable warriors."

"Everyone's going to cheat tomorrow one way or another," I said. "This doesn't hurt anyone. It only helps us. And we won't get in trouble. We'll only use this for emergencies, if we're separated."

The tension in Aiden's aura finally dissipated, and he nodded in agreement.

"Good, then it's decided." I stepped forward, placing one stone in Dario's opened palm and the third in Garrett's. A moment of heavy silence passed between the four of us before Garrett handed his to Aiden.

Aiden frowned. "But I'm not in the tournament."

"No," Garrett said, "but before we enter the rings while we're out claiming our gryphons, if we run into trouble, we'll have you. The three of us are going to stick together. I'll share with Dario. We're already in the same apartment, we'll most likely go together."

Aiden's fingers closed and opened around the stone, like he was still unsure, and I thought of how worried Garrett was about him knowing his secret—*our* secret. Rules really meant something to him. And Garrett truly did respect that about him. But at last, Aiden nodded and secured the stone in his belt pocket, sweeping his blue mage robes over it.

I shared a quick look with Garrett as I placed mine back in my pouch. The bells began to ring. The day was over. I thought for a moment about telling them. Telling them the truth. I needed to win. I had to win. And I needed them to help me.

But I couldn't. Because I knew what it meant, knew what it would cost to ask them to support me in that. We all knew what we were getting into...but planning it in advance like this...planning to kill to win felt wrong on a level I couldn't even explain.

Just survive. That's what my mother had said.

"I need to go," I said. Luckily, I was already in my armor. I could fall into bed.

Aiden pulled Garrett back onto his lap, his fingers twisting in his blonde hair. They both seemed to gasp at once, their auras mingling, fusing together into something unique, something powerful. It was rare to see auras do that. Only when the connection was truly deep did auras join. Garrett pressed against Aiden, trying to hide a moan. I'd seen my friends kiss a hundred times now, but never like this, like it was their last.

Something heavy settled on my heart. My kiss with Lyr, it had been our first. Had it also been our last?

I stepped back, not wanting to intrude. "I'll see you in the morning."

"See you in the morning," Dario said, his pressed his fist to his heart. "We're going to get through tomorrow. All three of us."

"On my life," Garrett swore.

"*Me sha, me ka*," I said, feeling the weight of my words sink down on me.

A moment later, I was in my apartment, straightening my armor, securing my belt, my weapons, my gloves. The bells had just stopped ringing. Heart heavy, I lay down on my bed, positive I wasn't going to get even a full hour of sleep.

I closed my eyes, trying to catch my breath. At some point, I fell into a dreamless sleep. When I woke, it was daylight, but it felt like barely a moment had passed since I'd lain down. My door burst open.

I was on my feet in an instant, hand reaching for my blade, my eyes searching for Bowen's presence, but he was nowhere to be found.

Two dark figures crossed the room. I widened my stance, watching both, trying to decipher their identities, but they wore masks beneath their hooded cloaks.

I opened my mouth to call for Bowen, but the strangers were on me too fast for me to react. One hand held my sword, the other brandished my dagger.

A cloth covered my mouth, stifling my yell. Too late, I recognized the overly sharp scent.

My eyes began to close, my vision blurring as I was taken from my room.

CHAPTER

THIRTEEN

Groaning, I opened my eyes, moving my arm over my forehead to block out the light, it was pale but somehow still overwhelming. I caught sight of the silver band around my wrist.

Cold air blanketed my skin. My toes had numbed inside my boots, and a chilly, violent wind rushed over me. The tips of my fingers, exposed through my leather gloves, were nearly frozen. I was outside. And I was moving.

Something wet fell on my forehead. Snowflakes. Cruel laughter surrounded me.

"Shut the fuck up. You nearly rolled to your death before you woke." It was Garrett.

Squinting, I gingerly pushed myself into a seat. More snowflakes landed against my cloak.

"Finally joining us, Your Grace." That snide voice was Thorin's.

Opening my eyes all the way, revealed mountain cliffs. We were flying on some sort of raft. Leather bands crossed beneath my legs, tying us to the gryphon beneath. The *Alissedari* had started. My rude awakening hours earlier had been my transportation call, and now we were being dropped in one of three locations to retrieve our gryphons.

We could have simply been taken, awake, and undrugged. But something told me my father was delighting in how disorienting this was going to be for everyone. How it'd set everyone on edge, leaving them ready to attack.

I did a quick count and found nearly two dozen soturi surrounded me. Three more gryphons flew nearby, all carrying the same loads on their back.

I inched closer to Garrett, taking better stock of my opponents. Of course, Thorin was on mine and surrounded by his supporters, all members of Ka Oryyan, most of them accomplished apprentices, including his cousin, Sev. He'd been squirreling around Thorin last night, glaring at me. He'd hated me for years simply because I was a faster runner. I'd always ignored him before, but now he was so close, and acting too bold. And, to make things even more exciting, we were seated with several soturi of Ka DeTerria—Dario's cousins, who all violently detested us, mainly because Dario insisted on picking fights with them every chance he had, leaving us no choice but to back him up.

I searched for Dario's telltale curly hair, pulled back, and threaded with silver beads. He wasn't riding on our gryphon, but he didn't seem to be on any of the others.

"Dario?" I whispered to Garrett.

"They separated us," Garrett said quietly.

I stared over the horizon trying to figure out which of the three locations we were headed for, but all I could tell was that we were heading west, which, depending on how far we were from the Academy, could have meant any of the three wilds. The Gryphon Pits had been built in the north, in the center of Glemaria's mountain ranges. The wilds were all south.

"We can contact him when we drop down," I said. "Figure out where he is, fly together, guard each other's backs."

Garrett shook his head again, angling his hip toward me. "We can't," he said and pushed open his leather pouch.

My mother's vadati stone, clear and white, lay in the center.

"Aiden gave it back?" I asked, already annoyed.

"No." Garrett's voice darkened. "Dario and I switched before we fell asleep. He was nervous he'd lose it."

"Fuck!" I stared ahead. Dario alone without a way to reach us could be disastrous.

"He'll be okay. Here. You need to eat." Garrett shoved a small bag into my lap. I pulled it open to discover an assortment of nuts. Garrett was always good about keeping snacks on hand, and it was especially good now. Unless we took time to hunt or forage—I had a feeling this was going to be all I'd have to eat all day.

"Did you have enough?" I asked.

"Eat. Aiden packed enough nuts for three days."

Slowly, I began to chew, noting how glacially slow our gryphon was moving thanks to the immense amount of weight he carried.

"What time is it?" I asked Garrett.

"By my count of the last bells, just past noon."

I frowned. "Was anyone else out for this long?"

"No. But don't take it personal. No one else was punched twice in the face by the arkturion yesterday either."

I groaned at the canteen I'd packed, desperately wishing it was coffee instead of water.

"You're sure that's it?" I asked. I wasn't trying to be egotistical. I knew I'd been punched by the arkturion, full force. I knew how hurt I'd been yesterday. But I also knew my strength, my energy levels, my recovery time. I couldn't imagine any real reason why I'd have been out longer than everyone else, not unless my dosage had been heavier than the others.

Garrett shrugged, staring down at the silver band around his wrist.

The wind picked up in intensity, and my heart lodged into my throat as the gryphon dropped suddenly. It was time.

We'd come to the westernmost of the wilds, to the woodlands beneath the Allurian Pass—the tallest mountains in Glemaria. The Pass cut off the western border at the edge of the Empire, where the humans lived. I'd only been out here a few times, but by my guess, we were pretty close to both the human and Hartavian border.

We'd need to chart a journey going northeast to reach the Pits.

Garrett rolled his shoulders and stretched his neck side to side, a determined look on his face, as our gryphon's wings spread wider. The wind blew harder against us, the forest floor in sight. Around us were the sounds of over a dozen gryphons squawking and growling.

We reached for our swords, prepared to battle our way off the gryphon as it swooped below the treetops, taking us into the dark of the woods. The cliffs of the Allurian Pass were no longer visible.

The moment we touched down, a mage stepped out from behind the trees, his stave pointed at the rope around our gryphon's leg. The other gryphons in our cohort tapped down, and he repeated the same gesture before pointing his stave at his throat.

"Welcome to the first part of the *Alissedari*," he said, his voice amplified through the trees. Snow began to fall more forcefully, and the sky darkened. Gryphons snarled and growled beyond him, play wrestling and jumping onto each other, their

yells turning to squawks that drowned out the mage. He amplified his voice a second time. "We all fight in honor of His Highness, Imperator Hart, to celebrate his birthday today, and his
long and successful rule. May you find your own honor today."

I scowled as everyone cheered.

Then, he continued, "You all entered last night with your
oaths and your bindings. Now, the tournament truly begins
when I blow the horn. At that moment, you will find a gryphon
to ride. It is your job to claim your gryphon, to tame it enough
to let you ride it, to ensure another soturion doesn't take your
beast, and to have a sense of fucking direction and arrive at the
Gryphon Pits."

A few soturi snickered at this, but I was watching the
gryphons, counting the few present amongst the trees, and
looking for signs of others beyond the small clearing. A shadow
of a bronze tail swung in and out of view.

"Once you arrive at the Pits, you will enter the physical
bindings of the tournament, unable to leave until it ends. If
you fall from your gryphon, you lose it but remain in the tournament on foot. When victory is claimed, your wrist bindings
will vanish. There are not enough gryphons. More than half of
you will fail to compete today but you will remain bound to the
Alissedari."

Garrett flashed me a look, as several soturi shifted their
weight, their knuckles cracking in anticipation.

"When the horn blows, you will fight to claim and conquer
your ride. Fail and you're disqualified. No gryphon may carry
two riders to the Pits. Only one victor may win today. Good
luck."

Everyone got into position, either settling into low
crouches with one hand on the floor as they prepared to run or
standing tall, hands on their blades, ready to lunge.

The horn sounded.

Immediately, the soturi were pushing at each other, trying to knock down their fellow fighters as they scrambled off the gryphon's back. Though he was low, we still had a rather large jump. I locked eyes with Garrett as the DeTerria soturi banded together and Thorin gathered those loyal to him, including Sev.

Most of the soturi were heading for the sides, trying to descend down the gryphon's wings. But no one was heading for the tail.

I jerked my chin at it, and Garrett furrowed his eyebrows.

"Off the back," I said quickly.

"It's a bigger jump," he said. "We'll be behind everyone if we go off there."

"Not if we do it right," I said.

"You mean...?"

I gave a small nod. We could use our vorakh there to control the landing. It was a risk, but so was every other option.

I slipped my hood over my head. Garrett did the same. Our outlines blurred as the material settled around our faces, thanks to Aiden's glamour.

We took off, running for the edge and leaping. Halfway through the fall, I did it. I saw myself on the ground, my stomach tugged. My boots touched down, and Garrett was right beside me.

"Go!" I yelled, and we raced around the front of the gryphon, past the soturi still fighting their way down the wings.

Those from the other two gryphons had been faster getting off. Already, dozens of them were battling it out in the fields or running off into the trees, trying to track down the rogue creatures. At least three soturi already lay sprawled in the snow, knocked unconscious.

These gryphons were wild. Some had already decided they wanted nothing to do with the *Alissedari* and were flying off, cutting the already slim pickings down further.

A pissed-off gryphon, far too wild for a ride, threw his silvery wings out, knocking five soturi from Ka Oryyan to the ground.

One soturion from Ka DeTerria had managed to jump onto a gryphon's nearly black wings, but three others had jumped on with him, and all four were battling it out while the gryphon bucked, threatening to throw them off.

"We need to go deeper into the woods," I said. "We don't want any of these—they'll be too agitated. And I know there's more back there." The possibility of the gryphons refusing to let us ride or follow directions was a little too real—they were untrained, untested. Forcing a ride on a gryphon who didn't want you was one way to die.

Garrett and I moved behind a cluster of moon trees. Their leaves canopied together, leaving us in near darkness. We swerved through another growth, seeking out the place where I'd seen the tail. A low growl sounded from a few feet away, combined with the rustling leaves—a good sign. The ground was hard with cold as we ran, making it easier to hear our boots. I stopped, hoping not to give us away, and leaned back against a trunk, motioning for Garrett to follow.

Behind us came the sounds of soturi punching against leathered armor, blades clanging. A gryphon snarled. Someone screamed, and a gust of wind blew leaves and sticks in our direction as the shadow of gryphon wings rose over the trees.

More shouts filled the air, and another gryphon lifted off. The less gryphons available, the more desperate the soturi would become: the more violent. But what concerned me most were the ones who'd had the same idea as me. Sure enough, I could hear boots coming our way, crunching through fallen leaves.

Drawing my hood closer, I sprinted forward, Garrett on my heels. Someone screamed back in the clearing. I didn't have to look to know what sort of pain had caused a scream like that. He'd been bitten. And if he didn't get away fast, he'd be mauled.

I tried to clear my mind of the sound and all other thoughts but that of the task at hand. Garrett crept through a small opening. It led into a rounded clearing; two gryphons in its center, snapping at each other's necks, rearing back and pouncing. They both growled fiercely, clawing and wrestling, then shrieked with delight as fresh snow fell on their wings.

Motioning to Garrett, I stepped forward. "Shhhhh." I was loud enough to make my presence known, but quiet enough to show I didn't pose a threat. *"Tovayah."* I held up my hands, taking slow steps as the sounds of battle grew in the distance. More winged shadows filled the sky.

The gryphons immediately stopped fighting. One rolled onto his back, his gray wings flopping lazily on the field, sopping up the fallen snowflakes. His beak opened in question, his black eyes tracking us. But the other gryphon, majestic and bronzed, was on edge, snarling and snapping her beak, her tail frozen behind her.

"Easy," I said.

Garrett tiptoed beside me. "Good girl."

The bronze gryphon growled in response, her wings erect, feathers standing in irritation.

"Stand back," I said. "They're nervous with both of us approaching at once. You take the gray." That one at least seemed unthreatened, more curious.

"Got it," Garrett said, changing direction.

I inched closer, keeping my palms up, my fingers loose and unthreatening. "Good girl. *Tovayah. Tovayah,*" I said softly. Her hackles were raised, but her feathers were beginning to soften, and with another word of encouragement, she lowered her wings, stamping her talons as she tilted her head.

She didn't trust me. Not yet. She was still agitated by my presence. But she no longer feared me. It was a start.

I used the opportunity to check Garrett's progress. He was smiling, looking more easy-going than he had in days, giving his gryphon a belly rub. Figures. My gryphon looked over, too, her head snapping quickly at her companion. She growled low in her throat. Then, she looked back to me, an expression in her eyes that seemed to say, *Can you believe them?*

I almost laughed and was able to get close enough to press my palm to her beak. She lowered her head, letting me stroke up toward her eyes, the heel of my hand running through her soft mix of feathers and fur. Bits of silver and gold gleamed through the bronze, a happy purring in her throat. Looking me up and down, she lowered herself to her belly, allowing me to climb on her back.

"Garrett!" I hissed. He was still offering belly rubs, and his gryphon's legs were waggling in the air almost as much as his tail. "Let's go."

Sighing, Garrett stepped back. "*Volara?*" he asked then flapped his arms like wings.

After all the stress and tension of getting here, I couldn't help myself. I burst out laughing. "Auriel's fucking bane, Garrett! You don't have to mime it. The High Lumerian for 'fly' is more than enough."

Garrett scoffed. "Shut up. My gryphon likes it. Look, he's laughing."

In Garrett's defense, his gryphon's beak was wide open. I supposed if gryphons could laugh, this was it. But I was starting to notice how quiet it was beyond the clearing. We'd already lingered long enough.

Ears straining for any other hints of movement, I nodded. "How about we take your comedy show to the skies. Now?"

"Well, sure," he grunted. "I need a larger audience."

Luckily, his gryphon was already rolling onto his belly, subservient and ready for Garrett to climb on.

"Dorscha," I said, urging mine to lay down. Her eyes thinned into slits. I tried again, noting Garrett was nearly on his gryphon from my periphery. "Come on, don't make me look bad," I urged. *"Dorscha."*

Her legs bent, her head lowering, and suddenly her beak opened, and she released a shrieking growl into the clearing.

"Hey!" I said, stepping back as her feathers stood on end, her wings stiff and ready for battle.

"Hart!"

My stomach dropped, and I turned. Thorin stood behind me.

"You're too late. This one's mine." I backed up, closing in on my gryphon. She was clearly on edge, and I didn't need my pretentious asshole of an apprentice spooking her.

"Rhyan," Garrett said, a warning in his voice. "Rhyan!" he yelled.

Both of my arms were grabbed from behind. A soturion stood on either side of me, both apprentices from Ka Orryan. Of course, one was Thorin's cousin Sev, and the other, a non-noble who followed his every whim.

Two more came from behind the trees, rushing for Garrett, but his gryphon sprang into action, clawing the first in the face, his wings pushing aside the second.

I eyed my gryphon, trying to send calm waves of energy through my aura. She'd just warmed up to me and I didn't want to have to start over. And if she attacked them, she might accidentally maim me.

Thorin approached me, a victorious look in his eyes, his aura intensifying. My gryphon's wings flapped, as she stomped her talons again, this time in anger.

"I'm not afraid of you, Thorin." I tried to relax my arms against my captors. I waited for the right moment to fight. I wanted this to be over fast.

He sneered. "You should be."

My mother's warning returned to me. *Watch out for Thorin in particular. He gives me a bad feeling...*

Another step, and he was before me, his fists raised.

"Really?" I taunted. "You can only get a hit in when my arms are tied?"

"I'll get a hit in however I want. You're done."

"You're pathetic," I said.

"I don't think so. It's been ordered," Sev said gleefully.

"Ordered?" I asked without thinking. "Ordered by who?"

Thorin glared at Sev before turning his ire back on me. "Who do you think?" His fist thrust out, and I sank down to my knees, forcing the soturi holding me captive to fall with me.

They're just rope. They're nothing.

I sucked in a breath, using all I had to snap my arms from their hold. Freed, I punched right, snapping Sev's head to the side. Then, I spun back, kicking my other captor. Sev was recovering, but I grabbed his neck, slamming his face into the dirt. My elbow thrust back, knocking down the second soturion.

Jumping to my feet, I came face to face with Thorin, already preparing for another punch. I raised my arms, prepared to block. I knew his moves inside and out after two years of training. Whether he wanted to admit it or not, I was stronger. There was a reason he'd stuck his lackeys on me first. He wasn't strong enough to win fairly.

But he moved too fast for me to see, to process. He punched, and my head snapped back, my hood flying off. I screamed as his knuckles connected to my nose.

"Fuck!" I roared, seeing spots in my vision. I'd been slow. I was still healing from Kane's attack. Aiden had mended the bones, treated the swelling, but the internal healing couldn't be accelerated. Magic wasn't a true match for the power deep inside a soturion's body.

I stumbled, bumping into my gryphon, whose wings had tightened. With a snarled squawk, she pushed me forward.

I was dizzy, seeing double of everything.

Thorin punched me again. And again.

His hits were fast. Too fast, too strong, like they were powered by something unnatural.

Something I couldn't keep up with. It didn't make sense. Even injured, I knew I could take him. I knew I was stronger.

Then, it hit me. The asshole had called on *kashonim*. He was powered by our entire lineage going back to every soturion still alive, every soturion whose blood ran through our veins.

He'd chosen this moment to call on it to use it against me. This wasn't what we did—*kashonim* was meant for life and death scenarios. Not to attack our own.

"Rhyan!" Garrett screamed. He was on the back of his gryphon, both of the soturi who'd attacked him were unconscious. "Climb!"

My head rolled to the side before I realized what Garrett was saying. His gryphon was standing, and mine was on her belly, waiting.

Sev and Thorin's other lackey were stirring, their eyes fixed on my gryphon.

I ran, zigzagging in my unsteadiness, my head throbbing,

my nose probably broken again, but I was getting on that gryphon, and I was leaving Thorin and his idiot followers behind.

I reached for the bronze feathers, my fingers digging in until I found fur thick and long enough to hold onto. I pulled myself up and straddled her back.

Something grabbed hold of my boot, and with everything I had left, I kicked. Thorin stumbled.

"The fuck?" he said. He looked genuinely startled.

"Not even with *kashonim* could you take me," I growled, sick of everyone coming at me, always forgetting what I possessed on my own. Always trying to take it from me. Had I not been injured, I'd have taken him and his men down within seconds.

Thorin jumped to his feet, his legs moving so quickly that with enough power in his jump, he'd be up here with me. *Fucking kashonim.*

"*Volara!*" I roared. "*Volara! Vra! Vramahar!*"

My gryphon reared back, her beak open, her talons lifted as her back haunches sank into the earth.

Thorin jumped, his sword coming for me.

"*Mahara!*" I screamed.

Her front claws hit the grass, launching me forward. Blood dripped from my nose, and spots appeared in my vision while my face throbbed.

Thorin's blade swung behind me as we took off, my gryphon running through the edge of the clearing before her wings pulled back and her hind legs bent, and then we soared, flying higher and higher, swerving through the clusters of branches until we were above the trees.

Beside me, gray wings flapped.

Garrett yelled out, his aura full of enough adrenaline and excitement that it reached me.

My heart was still racing from Thorin's attack, my vision blurry after getting punched in the nose again. He'd had a sword ready. A sword and fucking *kashonim*. He hadn't just come to fight me or take my gryphon. He'd come to kill me.

I slid to the side, trying to get a better hold of the feathers, but I couldn't seem to grasp the right ones. My grip slackened, and a wave of dizziness descended over me. I couldn't find purchase, couldn't hold on. I was slipping as my gryphon angled up, flying higher and faster.

Something flashed in the distance. My gryphon screeched in fear, swerving before I could grab hold. Her entire body jerked.

"Garrett!" I screamed.

And then I fell.

CHAPTER
FOURTEEN

Treetops raced toward me. Blood rushed to my head, and my heart rose to my throat. My gryphon screeched from above, and before I could hit the branches, Garrett's arms wrapped around my waist, his fingers digging into my belly. His body hugged mine. One second, we were falling, the shadows of our gryphons flying past, the next, our boots were tapping down on the forest floor.

I stumbled, unable to catch my breath.

Garrett had saved me. Again. Using his vorakh. Again.

"Rhyan," he gasped, choking out a breath. "Okay?" Garrett swayed to the side and stumbled to a tree, his palm slamming against it for support.

I pressed my fingers against the side of my nose, gently testing. "Just dizzy. Getting nose-punched two days in a row like that isn't really good for my face." It wasn't broken, thank the Gods. But it hurt like fucking Moriel. I groaned, running my hands through my hair, breathing through the remaining pain in my head. "Garrett. You shouldn't have done that."

"What? Saved you?"

"Risked your life for mine."

His throat bobbed, his knuckles whitening as he pressed himself away from the tree. "The fuck you talking about? I had no choice."

I breathed in and out through my mouth, trying to calm my nerves. "Because of the blood oath?" I joked.

Frowning, Garrett clasped my shoulder. "No. Because you're my friend, you asshole."

My chest heaved, adrenaline still rushing through me.

"You would have done the same," he said, taking stock of our surroundings. We were deep in the darkest part of the woods, in Gods-knew-where Glemaria.

Wings blew a forceful breeze through the leaves, forcing snow from the treetops to blast at me.

"Of course, I would have done the same," I said a moment later, turning to see Garrett petting the gray gryphon. "Otherwise, your little blood oath would have murdered me."

Garrett stiffened, dark and regretful shadows shading his aura. "I'm sorry," he said. "I... I got scared that night. So fucking scared. I wanted to protect so many people. Protect myself."

"I know," I said gently.

"Shit. Rhyan, I've wanted to talk to you about that. Apologize." He stared down and kicked a rock. Looking back up, his gaze settled on mine. "I should have never made you swear. You've been protecting me this whole time, carrying your own burdens, your own secrets and promise, and... I'm sorry."

He'd owed me that apology—I hadn't realized just how much until he'd said it. He never should have sworn a blood oath with me nor forced the consequences onto either of us. But I understood the fear, the desperation behind it. My mind had gone there, too, that night.

A sharp breeze rustled through the moon trees canopying

us, as fresh snow began to fall. "Well, as long as we have each other's backs," I said, "we'll be okay."

Our gryphons growled in annoyance as they settled down on the forest floor. The gray gryphon looked curiously at Garrett as if questioning where he'd gone. But the bronze gryphon, she was pissed. I could see it in her eyes. Stomping her back paws against the ground, she was letting me know that she took my falling off her mid-flight as a personal insult.

I would have managed to stay on if she hadn't allowed the light to spook her.

The gray gryphon rolled aside, attempting to lure mine back into a wrestling match. Garrett tightened his belt buckle, adjusting his weapons. "First, we've got to get out of here." He exhaled sharply, still catching his breath, but some of his color seemed to be returning.

I looked up at the trees, trying to find some slivers of light, but the day had grown so overcast with snow, I could barely see a thing. I pulled back up my hood.

"Wait a minute. Catch your breath."

He sank against the tree. "You think Dario's okay?" he asked anxiously.

I frowned, wishing he'd taken the vadati stone instead of Garrett so we could know for sure. But said, "I do. As long as he's sober."

"He is."

I tightened my gloves, reclasping the wrists. "Then, I'm not worried."

"Maybe we can check in with Aiden," Garrett said, fishing through his pouch. "Get a feel for what's happening. See if Dario's back."

I nodded. "You know how to use it?"

"Speak his name into the stone?" He held the clear white crystal in his palm, rolling it back and forth.

"It'll turn blue when it connects."

Garrett focused on the vadati. "Aiden," he said, his voice breathless, excited, like he'd been dying to say his name, to speak to him this whole time.

Mist swirled, cloudy but white.

Garrett frowned.

"Give it a second," I said. "He's not supposed to have it, he might not be able to answer right away."

I remembered these stones from when I was a boy. I'd call my mother on them while playing hide and seek in the fortress. She always gave me clues to her location that were far too easy to solve. I'd thought I was so smart at the time for figuring them out and sneaking up on her, but she'd wanted me to find her. I learned years later. We'd played when my father was in his worst moods, when his aura was thundering like a storm through Seathorne.

One day while I'd been hiding, I'd called her and watched the stone mist and cloud again and again. She hadn't answered. My father had found her. He'd abruptly ended the game.

I stopped playing hide and seek after that.

In the darkness of the forest floor now, a blue spark glowed, filling Garrett's palm. The light illuminated his face.

"Garrett?" Aiden's voice was urgent. "Are you all right? Are you hurt?"

"We're fine," he said, a smile spreading across his face. Even his eyes seemed to smile at Aiden's voice.

"Are you sure? You sound winded."

"I am," he said uneasily. "But I'm okay. It's just me and Rhyan right now. We were... unseated from our gryphons. Haven't seen Dario yet. He went to another location. Is anyone at the Pits?"

"Shit. Wait, you were unseated?"

"We're fine. We'll be flying in a minute. Have you seen Dario?"

There was a long pause before Aiden said, "No. Not yet. But your father has been making announcements. We're expecting the tournament portion of the *Alissedari* to begin within the hour. Scouts reported two dozen gryphons with riders on the way."

"Two dozen," I said. "That's such a low number."

"There were three dozen reported originally, but a handful flew into Hartavia instead. And some grounded to get rid of their riders. A few soturi were thrown. Medic gryphons are supposed to be rounding up the injured."

"Okay, just checking in," Garrett said. "We'll see you soon."

"Be careful," Aiden said. "I love you."

"I love you," Garrett said, his aura flaring around him with a burst of warmth.

I folded my arms across my chest, not wanting to intrude on the moment between them. Somehow, they always seemed to be in their own little world.

Garrett looked up at me with a sheepish grin and coughed.

I stepped back, signaling it was okay. My heart panged. What I would do to have someone on the other end of that stone that made me feel the way Garrett looked in that moment.

"Is Rhyan okay?" The vadati shone with a fresh blue glow as Aiden spoke through the stone. "How's his head?"

Garrett lifted an eyebrow.

I felt like shit. It was the reason we'd lost our gryphons. But I didn't want to worry Aiden, not when there was nothing he could do to help us at this point.

"I'm fine," I called. "Just feeling *delicate*."

Aiden snorted, then his voice lowered, "See you both soon. Call again if you need anything."

"We will," Garrett said.

The stone went white.

"Here." Garrett handed it back to me. His aura still felt warm, elated after having talked to Aiden. "I don't need it now. I'm with you."

I slid it into my pouch with the other. "Let's get out of here." I stared down my gryphon, hoping she wasn't going to give me this attitude the whole way. I stepped forward, motioning for her to lay down.

Her knees bent and then straightened, her eyes alert, her tail still.

The gray gryphon growled low in his throat, stepping back from Garrett. He went preternaturally still beside mine. For a moment, they appeared frozen as statues.

Then, without warning, they both took to the trees, their tails vanishing through the canopy of leaves.

"The fuck?" Garrett said. "Get back here!"

Sticks cracked behind us, and the ground shook with heavy footsteps. A snarl released into the air.

I froze, my body filling with tension. The air was freezing already. But there seemed to be another source of cold now, creeping through the forest.

Garrett inched closer to me. "More gryphons?" he whispered.

The heaviness of the steps felt familiar. It could be the gait of a gryphon—older and meaner than the ones we'd found. Gryphons were territorial and fought for dominance over anything they'd claimed as theirs. But they weren't afraid of each other, and the way our gryphons had left so suddenly— they'd been scared.

There wasn't much in Glemaria that could scare a gryphon.

A hawk flying above the trees circled overhead then took off, his wings flapping furiously before stilling for him to soar.

The forest had fallen silent. There were no birds, no insects, no movement. No sound. Only Garrett's and my breath.

I strained my ears, trying not to breathe.

Another branch snapped. The ground continued to shake as the cold intensified.

I peered closer at the trees, realizing the shape of the leaves had shifted. Glemarian moon and sun trees had a very distinct shape, one that started to shift by the Hartavian border. My heart sank. The western borders were weak and suspectable to akadim attacks, as they liked to travel through the human lands to reach us.

The snarl became a growl. Two growls.

Garrett's face paled.

His hand slid down to his sword, fingers tightening around the hilt of his blade. I mirrored him, and we stepped closer, our backs were touching. The metal of our starfire steel blades sounded as we withdrew our weapons, but the starfire remained silver. There wasn't a single flame in the darkness to light the sword.

The akadim stepped into view. I reached for my dagger, a blade in each hand, as my throat tightened.

Garrett's back was still to mine, which meant only one thing. There were two akadim.

No bells had rung. We'd have heard them by now, loud and clear.

Again, akadim had gotten past our defenses, taken us by surprise. And if we didn't kill them, if we didn't ring the alarm, there was no telling what damage they'd do.

"Do you think," Garrett asked under his breath, "do you think they... they came for us?"

For vorakh. They'd hunted us last time.

My throat went dry. "It doesn't matter if they came for us," I whispered. "You know what to do."

"Stop the threat," Garrett said, though it sounded like a question.

I swallowed. "Stop the threat."

The akadim before me was female, well over ten feet, with white-blonde hair braided with sticks and leaves. Scraps of dingy clothing barely concealed her body. Red stretchmarks ran across her pale skin. Her eyes blazed red, and long sharp teeth jutted out of her mouth. Behind me came a roar, and Garrett's elbow bounced against mine.

"Become the weapon," I said. The second rule of being a soturion.

"Any commands?" Garrett's voice shook.

The third rule of being a soturion.

"Kill it," I snarled.

Garrett launched himself forward. His battle cry raged behind me as I took off, blades up.

I still wasn't fully recovered from Thorin's hits. A burst of fear rose up inside of me, and I used it to travel, unleashing my vorakh. But I landed too far off to the side to hit her directly. Still, I was fast, and I took off, sword ready.

I caught her off guard, and my blade sliced through her arm. She snarled. I'd given her a small cut, not enough to hurt her or slow her down. Instead, she seemed to grow angrier. Her claws swiped out at me, reaching for my face. I dodged and leaned back, focusing on her other side.

Behind me, Garrett swore.

I vanished, my stomach tugging, my boots hitting the ground, and with a grunt, I slashed my blades across her arms.

She released a jarring screech of pain, her spiked nails nearly piercing through my armor.

My boots barely seemed to touch the ground as I ran. I was just beyond her reach when I heard a ripping sound behind me. Garrett hollered in pain, the sound unlike anything I'd ever heard before.

I jumped without thinking, traveling just beyond the akadim's claws as I yelled, "Garrett!"

He was lying flat on his back, his akadim crouching over him, claws spreading his leathers, trying to clear the way to his chest—to his heart. He was going to eat Garrett's soul.

I was gone without thinking. Stomach tugging again, I traveled behind his back. With a roar, I launched myself on the akadim, my sword lifted.

Garrett screamed, his elbows barely visible in my periphery, as he struggled to free himself. I zeroed in on my target—the akadim's neck—and thrust my dagger into his back, using it for leverage to pull myself up to the monster's shoulders. But he remained crouched over Garrett, his mouth making a sickening sucking sound, like he was preparing to feed. My thighs tightened around him. I lifted my sword with both hands and, with a battle cry, plunged it down his neck. The blade sank in.

The monster froze and shook, claws scratching at his back to get to me. One sliced my boots, the other cut my thigh.

I started to pull the sword back and forth. I'd saw off his fucking head if I had to.

The beast rushed backward to squash me against a tree, still fighting even with his neck severed. With a grunt, I pulled my sword all the way out and retrieved my dagger. Feeling the trunk rush against me, I squeezed my eyes shut, the hook in my stomach pulling me.

My boots touched the ground behind Garrett, who looked remarkably recovered. He jumped to his feet, wide-eyed, his mouth hanging open. There was a gash on his forehead, but his leathers were in place, and his hands full of weapons.

Before I could attack, Garrett rushed forward, death in his eyes. He leapt at the last second, his body vanishing then reappearing, flying past the akadim's shoulder. Garrett unleashed his sword, finishing what I'd started. The akadim's head severed from his neck in a swift, fluid sweep of Garrett's sword.

A crude, wet thud sounded as the akadim's head hit the ground.

My eyes met the female akadim's. She hadn't helped her companion but seemed to be waiting for us to finish with him so she could attack. I stepped protectively in front of Garrett, whose knees had given out. His sword fell to the ground, as he retched on the forest floor.

The akadim launched her body forward, her eyes wild, her teeth bared.

I held up my sword, but she was faster, grabbing the steel. I pulled back the hilt, slicing her hand open, but she didn't care. She kept holding the blade, bleeding, and letting the steel tear her apart. The sound of her skin ripping mixed with her screech of pain, but she still held fast.

I gritted my teeth, digging my heels into the ground, gripping harder, my muscles burning. I almost had the blade free when she pulled the sword with renewed force, dragging me forward. She roared, the scent of death on her breath before she released her grip and pushed the blade back to me.

The hilt punched into my stomach, knocking the air from my lungs. I wheezed, gasping, trying desperately to breathe as my knees hit the ground.

Laughing, the akadim stepped over my prone body. Garrett was behind me, but he still seemed to be in shock. I couldn't get up, couldn't breathe, couldn't move. I was seeing stars everywhere I looked. I needed to stand, to travel, to at least roll away. I needed Garrett to act, but we were both weakened and stunned, and she was too strong and too close. And I realized with horror that she was in Glemaria, in our country, and we were the only two souls who knew. It would be hours before anyone found us.

We'd be akadim by nightfall, too close to our loved ones, able to travel, able to kill.

"Garrett," I wheezed, but barely any sound came out. I didn't even have the strength to turn around and find him.

"Mine," she growled, her tongue lolling out to lick her fangs.

"Gods!" I tried to yell, but my voice was still gone, my breath still too far away.

She lifted her hand, bleeding and destroyed, but her claws remained sharp, some inhumanly evil power keeping up her strength.

I sank back, trying to crawl, to roll, to travel, to do anything to get away from her, but I couldn't move. I was stronger than this. I fucking knew I was. She was a rope, just a fucking rope. But I'd been caught off-guard, twice, brutally attacked in the same place, twice—almost like it had been coordinated. The idea seemed preposterous, and yet every event that had happened today was pointing closer and closer to that reality.

Sev had said something had been ordered. Thorin had confirmed it. But what?

A violent shriek cut across the forest.

One second, her claw was about to strike, and the next, a gryphon flew out from behind me and Garrett, throwing her to the ground.

The akadim roared as she was forced onto her back. She clawed at the animal and kicked, but it was no use. The gryphon dragged her deep into the shadows of the trees. With a shriek that ended in a low, violent growl, its talons pierced her chest, its hind paws crushing her thighs as its beak attacked her face.

My breath returned, and I rushed to my feet, turning to see

Garrett standing frozen, his face still pale, his hand clutching his chest.

I scanned him quickly to see if there were any tears, anything out of place, but he seemed to be covered, his leathers buckled.

"Garrett," I said, reaching for his shoulder, squeezing. "You're all right?"

His eyes were glued to the gryphon ahead of us, unblinking, unmoving. A shudder ran through his body as the akadim screamed.

The gryphon screeched, its call echoing as it battled, wings lifted in the dark.

Then, from the shadows of the trees, two more gryphons stepped forward. One gray, one bronze.

"Garrett!" I yelled. "Talk to me. Are you okay?"

He stared down, his eyes on his hand and chest. Blood dripped from his forehead. He wiped it away then looked back up at me, staring for a long moment, his eyes distant, before he said, "Yes."

"Go," I said, urging him forward. He still seemed stunned as he stepped toward his gryphon, crawling onto its back like he'd never seen the animal before.

I turned, ready to jump onto mine as the akadim's screams came to an abrupt stop. The akadim's leg twitched once, twice, and then she was no more. And then the gryphon turned to face me.

Large familiar silver eyes stared from the shadows. My heart stopped. The gryphon stepped forward and spread its wings, covered in bright, fiery red feathers.

"By the Gods," I muttered, stepping forward.

The red gryphon trotted to me with a slight limp, an injury I knew he had incurred as a baby when he'd fallen outside my window. He kneeled before me, and his head pushed into my chest. I gasped, touching the space between his eyes, and one talon reached for my arm, and wrapped around me. The last time, it had only fit around my finger.

The baby gryphon had lived. Artem had lied to me.

The night I had met Aemon, Artem said no gryphons could be shot down. It must have been his way to tell me the truth, that all gryphons were safe, even mine. At least today.

"Rhyan!" Garrett yelled. "We need to go! Now!"

The bronze gryphon stalked behind me, pushing her beak against my hand, and the red gryphon stepped back into the shadows.

Another growl sounded, a deadly threat teasing its way through the breeze. I climbed on.

We couldn't wait any longer. We had to get to the Gryphon Pits. We had to warn everyone.

Red feathers soared into the sky above and vanished.

I leaned forward as my gryphon raced past the dead akadim. She leapt as her wings spread, and we were off. There was no sign of the akadim below—nor the red Afeyan in the sky.

FIFTEEN

Garrett and I flew in silence, both in shock. I thought of calling Aiden over the woodlands, but after I asked Garrett what he thought and he shook his head in response, I knew I couldn't. It had been risky enough calling him once, and even if we did pass on the warning, who could he get to in time? How could he explain what he knew without revealing we'd broken the law?

And we were so out in the wilds. I had no idea where the soturi were posted—most were camouflaged. We could lose time searching for someone to raise the alarm. Heading to the Gryphon Pits was the fastest, most efficient way to let the soturi know about the threat.

The threat I prayed was over.

The idea that I might have left too soon was twisting my stomach, but I knew Garrett hadn't been able to take much more, and we couldn't allow ourselves to be turned. At least we'd left two akadim dead.

My mind kept turning, insisting I'd made the right choice, and then falling into doubt all over again. I just knew this: the red gryphon was still there, and he was more than capable of taking on another beast. Far more than Garrett and I were.

I urged the bronze gryphon to fly faster. Beside me, Garrett grimaced. Something darkened in his aura, spilling across the sky. He shouted to speed up, and upon his command, the gryphon's wings flapped, emitting powerful gusts of snow-dusted wind into my face.

I kept my ears open as we flew, anxiously listening for the sound of warning bells. I wasn't sure if I truly wanted to hear them or not. Hearing them meant more akadim were in Glemaria, but it also meant our security measures were in place, that we were attempting to protect our own people, that someone knew, that something was being done.

Through the shrieks of the wind, the only bells that rang, in the end, were the ones calling out the time. We'd be at the Pits within the hour by my calculations. The woods below had long grown sparse, leading into some of the smaller towns and villages. We'd have a short window to fight in the *Alissedari* before the sky went completely dark, barely hours before sunset, but not much.

Occasionally, I called out to Garrett. He was uncharacteristically silent, staring ahead, no longer playing with the gray gryphon. He barely offered him a pat on the head when he followed directions. Gryphons, while fully capable of having and expressing emotions, did not pout, yet somehow, Garrett had found one who did.

As we soared over another cluster of sun trees, their golden leaves muted beneath the overcast sky, I spotted the Pits on the horizon. The structure grew taller as we approached, and I tried to remain calm as I took in its size—larger than the Katurium, larger even than Seathorne. I tightened my grip.

The Gryphon Pits had been modeled after our Katurium. It was a large, round building with an open center that held a soturi's training arena. Seats along the sides rose to the top of the open structure. Every country had a similar school, but ours was the largest, the most prestigious, and the only true place to become a soturion in the North, especially for nobility. Its reputation and size only had one competitor: the Soturion Academy in Bamaria.

Pale gray stone built on the top of a hill had formed a round fortress. Glittering silver ropes crisscrossed over the top, giving the illusion of the arena being a closed building with a round dome.

My throat tightened at the sight. I'd known what we were getting into—what we'd been forced into—but seeing it so close, knowing we could be trapped, knowing it was just for my father's ego, just another symbol of his cruelty, just another excuse for violence, as if our world needed more, left me enraged. Violence was literally breaking through our borders, going unchecked, unwatched, and it was up to the novices, to me and Garrett, to defend our home while everyone in true power was drinking in the Godsdamned waste-of-resources Pits.

Still, no bells had rung. I prayed it was because the threat truly had been stopped, but I no longer trusted in our defenses.

The sky darkened as more snow fell, and a wave of panic blew toward me. It felt like Garrett's aura, but it was weak. Gryphons shrieked and growled; more riders entering the tournament had begun to catch up. Ahead, circling the Pits, were dozens more riders.

Garrett flew beside me, having paled even more since I'd last seen him.

"You okay?" I yelled, my voice barely audible against the wind.

Garrett nodded, his eyes still ahead. I directed my gryphon closer, the tips of her bronze wings nearly brushing those of his. Garrett was starting to worry me. There was a kind of desperation and longing in his eyes. And something else. He was upset. He'd been attacked brutally by akadim twice now. He'd killed akadim twice now.

I imagined that as much as we honored and celebrated the killing in Glemaria—the act still took a toll. I couldn't imagine the act of taking a life not leaving a mark, even if that life had already been stolen by monsters.

"You sure?" I yelled. "Are you sick?"

Garrett shook his head again, still staring at the Pits.

I waved at the guards ahead on gryphon-back and began stroking my gryphon's head—she was so prickly, I didn't know if she'd perceive the gryphons before us as a threat. I needed her to slow down enough that I could talk to them, tell them what happened, and get some scouts out to the borders.

But as we entered their space, I realized my mistake. The riders that flew out to meet us weren't soturi at all. They were mages, and they'd already placed a protection dome around us —one that kept us from backing out. We'd unknowingly entered a binding.

"Hey!" I shouted. "Akadim! Akadim at the Hartavian border! We need soturi out there now."

The moment the words left my mouth, they died in the wind. There was too much noise, too many gryphons, too much chaos for the mages to hear or focus on anything other than entering another contestant into the game; following my father's orders.

I urged the bronze gryphon closer to the mage before me, but his gryphon's wings were flapping too roughly to get as near as I needed. I called again, louder this time. Nothing.

I turned to Garrett. "Tell them!"

His eyes darkened. "I can't." His voice had weakened considerably.

"Are you sure you're not hurt?"

He shook his head again, that same desperate longing in his eyes, his focus fully on the Pits.

"AKADIM!" I roared back at the mage.

Instead of heeding my warning, the mage yelled out, his voice amplified, "Lord Rhyan Hart, Heir Apparent to the Arkasva, High Lord of Glemaria, Imperator to the North, enters the *Alissedari*. Bronze gryphon."

A riot of shouts and cheers sounded from the Pits in response.

Silver bindings escaped his stave, rushing at my gryphon, who squawked in fear, just before the rope tied itself around her ankle.

"NO!" I screamed, the binding around my wrist heated. I tried to steer my gryphon up, away from the Pits, but we were already being dragged forward, forced through the domed rings and into the fight. "There was akadim!" I shouted desperately, my voice pleading.

My warning fell on unhearing ears.

Another mage performed the same binding on Garrett. "Soturion Garrett of Ka Aravain enters the *Alissedari*. Gray gryphon."

My gryphon flapped her wings, angling her body backward, and nearly bucking me off as she attempted to escape the rope. But it was useless. Magically powered in this situation to resist her strength, the rope pulled, and we were sucked toward the dome of the Pits within seconds.

My ears burst from the sound of cheers; the audience filling the stadium had to boast at least two thousand.

I'd grown almost numb to the cold. I'd been outside the entire day. But the sudden heat of the tournament's bindings crashed against my body with such force, I was stunned for a moment, barely able to move. Sweat beaded the nape of my neck, and my skin itched and burned until I made it through. My ears popped.

A spiraling doom burrowed its way deep inside my belly. We were inside the *Alissedari* now, no way to warn the others or escape.

Not until it ended.

Not until someone died.

I could see Garrett's face register the same realization as his gryphon fought his bindings, kicking his legs, desperately trying to fly back toward freedom. Instead, he crashed against the burning cold of the silver rings.

Garrett ducked low, but it wasn't enough. He shouted in pain, grimacing and laying his face against the gryphon's back.

I kept steady, waiting for Garrett to descend.

"Find Dario!" I yelled once we were at the same height. I thought it'd be easier to talk in here, but it was even harder. The wind was gone, but now we were surrounded by the sounds of thousands of Glemarians shouting. My ears hurt. Aiden may have kept our armor and cloaks from absorbing moisture, but we'd been wholly unprepared for the noise.

I wasn't sure if Garrett heard me or not, but he immediately directed his gryphon down, flying toward the outer rings, as close to the seats as he could manage without actually crashing into the wall that magically separated us from the audience.

I craned my head, trying to catch my bearings. Below me, a tawny-colored gryphon was being chased by three more. I wasn't sure the gryphon had a rider, but then a head full of dark curls with silver beads appeared, his hood blowing back.

"Dario!" I yelled.

My gryphon dove, swooping in and out of fights and swerving around another gryphon flying straight for us. I tucked myself against her neck and directed her to the left then to the right, narrowly missing a black-feathered beast.

"Dorscha!" I ordered. We were so close to reaching Dario.

Without warning, my gryphon swerved and growled, the sound vibrating furiously through her body as we came face to face with a pale white gryphon carrying a soturion from Ka Oryyan.

I withdrew my sword, recognizing Thorin's cousin, Sev. He was charging forward, flying swiftly toward me, blade flashing.

I leaned forward just as we passed. Our swords clanged, the metal singing above the din of noise.

We both turned at once, my gryphon's wings pulling back as we soared, swords repositioned. This time, I wasn't aiming for a hit. This time, I'd unseat the bastard. For good.

Cheers erupted below, and in the distance, I could hear announcements, someone calling out the names of those warriors in battle.

"Lord Rhyan Hart, Heir Apparent..."

I loosened my grip, my muscles tensing as I recalled my years of training, allowed my sword to be an extension of my arm, and moved to make the hit I needed.

A countdown started in my head, the fight before me becoming clear. *Three...two...one...*

Our gryphons passed, wing tips touching, and I struck, catching Sev's leathers hard enough to push him back. He hadn't engaged his core, I could tell the second we made contact. Sev fell backward and rolled off, hands barely catching onto the edge of a wing.

He'd been cocky, unprepared to exert more than his magic stores. Just like earlier. He fell lower, sliding down the wings, until he dangled only by one hand. He screamed in horror.

I yelled out for his gryphon to descend. Either he hadn't practiced his High Lumerian enough to recite the command himself, or he was too terrified of the fall. I tried once more, urging my own gryphon down as an example. But Sev fell, and despite my dislike for him, my throat tightened with fear.

The audience screamed as he dropped, but the floor was soft. He landed on his knees and rolled over.

I exhaled sharply, relieved.

Only one death was allowed. I should have known it would come from something far more sinister than a soturion being knocked off his gryphon.

No longer facing an immediate threat, I tried to take stock of the tournament around me. There had to be at least two dozen gryphons and more battles happening below me. On the ground, Sev had his sword out and was still fighting. He was limping a little on his left leg but clearly had enough strength in him to attack an apprentice.

Looking up, I saw two more gryphons fly through the bindings, screeching and struggling against the ropes that pulled down their legs.

"Soturion Sev Orryan is gryphon-less. Now fighting on the ground."

The gryphon Sev had fallen from was soaring upward, the silver rope around his leg torn. There was a flash of white light —an opening in the dome that he flew through. The second his tail passed, the hole knit itself closed, and the silver hummed with its warded magic, reigniting its defenses.

Two more gryphons flew before me, nearly crashing into us. One soturion lifted up from his seat, kneeling before standing. He eyed his opponent's gryphon and, with a shout, jumped from his gryphon's back. His blade was drawn, and I held my breath, terrified he'd go for the kill as he landed. His opponent seemed to suspect the same thing, and rather than fight back, he rolled off the gryphon, falling to the ground. He landed on top of another soturion.

I directed my gryphon to fly around the stadium. I needed to catch my breath, and I couldn't see amongst the chaos of wings and blades where Dario or Garrett had gone. I chanced a look at the audience filling the seats. Most were a blur of faces, black leathered armor, green cloaks, and blue robes. But I spotted my father, sitting proudly as he watched the senseless fighting and carnage—all in his honor. Like last night, he was completely surrounded by his personal guard.

My mother sat beside him, her face strained. Our eyes caught and I saw the sigil for Ka Gaddayan one row behind, but I wasn't fast enough to find Kenna.

Just as I passed the section of seats, I found the Ready. Aemon's eyes were dark and stormy as he watched me pass.

Coming round the opposite side of the arena, I found Aiden. But he didn't see me; his eyes were fixed ahead, no doubt on Garrett. I turned, following his gaze, and sure enough, there he was, his gray gryphon swooping down, his sword out as he knocked out another soturion.

I screamed his name, flying toward him.

In the opposite direction was Dario, at last. He roared in delight at seeing us, his eyes lighting up, but then three riders swooped down on him.

Dario was quick, leaning forward and head-butting his first opponent hard enough to knock him unconscious.

Garrett turned, coming to Dario's aid. Another rider soared past, his sword pointed right for me. I was ready. Our swords met, once, twice, and then with a third thrust, I knocked the blade from his hand. He reached for the spare on his back. I didn't wait. I flung my sword out against his leathers, blunt side smacking into his unprotected stomach. I didn't cut him but hit hard enough that he fell back, his second sword dropping to the ground. Cursing, he took off to retrieve it.

I locked eyes with Garrett, and stilled, my stomach churning. His eyes were different—distant, dark. Something had been off about him since the forest, since the akadim attack. His aura had darkened... weakened. Even his gray gryphon looked agitated with him.

Garrett wobbled, his head lolling side to side, and then he fell headfirst from his seat.

I screamed, ordering my gryphon to move. She followed the command at once, her head diving down, and we descended in pursuit of Garrett. His name was called out by an announcer, and from the corner of my eye, I spotted his gryphon bursting through the bounds of the Pits, free of the tournament.

I urged on my gryphon, my vision blurring with sweat. My arm straining, I leaned forward and grabbed hold of him, pulling him into my lap as we careened to the ground.

I squeezed my eyes shut, sure we were about to crash, then tightened my grip on both my gryphon and Garrett as we suddenly rushed up.

My chest heaved as we evened our pace, flying around the arena once more. Garrett shifted to a riding position next to me.

"Rhyan?" His voice was weak.

I reached for his shoulder, squeezing gently. "What happened? What's wrong?"

His face fell. Tears streamed down his cheeks.

I'd known Garrett for years, seen him through so much, yet not once had I ever seen him shed a single tear, much less cry.

"Garrett?" I steered my gryphon to fly over a battle between two riders, and then we angled down again, narrowly missing a tawny gryphon flying toward us.

He let out a pained sob. "I'm sorry. I... I—" He sobbed again. "I should have said something. Hours ago. But I wasn't —sure. Didn't want to believe, didn't want it to be true.

Convinced myself I was okay. It didn't happen like I thought. Like we'd studied."

"What?" I searched his eyes, dark, shadowed. And something like fear twisted inside of me, my veins filling with ice. Those weren't Garrett's eyes. Surely that was just a trick of the light, of the *Alissedari*. "What didn't happen?" My fingers tightened on his armor. An itch began to spread across my back where the blood oath had been carved into my flesh.

Another gryphon growled, coming at us, and I didn't hesitate. I thrust my sword out with a yell, cutting right through the soturion's arm. He screamed in pain, blood falling onto his gryphon's wings before it screeched and turned.

I turned back to Garrett.

"I always thought it happened right away, you know?" He was practically babbling, his voice shaking. "When there wasn't—wasn't a black mark, I put my armor back, buckled it all up before..." his fingers tensed, clawing at his chest, "...before you saw. But I could feel it. Feel it happening. Feel part of my soul leaving me. Not leaving. Fuck. Not leaving. Eaten."

Eaten? My eyes widened, my throat constricting. "No. No." I shook my head. "Garrett, no. That's not how it works."

"It is. At least, this time it is." His hands trembled as he reached for the buckles on his shoulders.

All day, Garrett's aura had darkened, felt foreign, unfamiliar. I'd thought he was tired. I'd thought it was the distance. I'd thought it was the chaos of the tournament. Even the silver binds around our wrists could have dulled his aura, but that hadn't been the reason. Because this wasn't him, wasn't how his energy felt. Because right now... I felt nothing.

Garrett had no aura.

Nothing was coming from him. And his eyes—by the Gods. It shouldn't have been possible. They were black, and somehow, they were getting darker, unnaturally shadowed.

His shoulders shook, fingers trembling as he pulled back his leathers just enough for me to see his tunic had been ripped to shreds. His jaw tightened, his eyes on me, as he pushed the pieces aside.

A black mark had formed over his heart, and it was growing right before my eyes, spreading to his collarbone, neck, and shoulders.

Suddenly I was seeing what I hadn't allowed myself to see back in the forest: Garrett on the ground, the akadim over him, his leathers open. His shrieks of pain...

"No! NO!" I roared.

Garrett put his leathers back together, methodically, lifelessly, like he was preparing for a battle—one he found boring, one he fought every day. He laughed, the sound joyless, filled with horror. "I should have known. I wasn't going to be lucky twice."

"It was never about luck!" I snarled. "You killed the akadim before because of your strength, and you killed that second bastard today because you're fucking strong. You hear me? You didn't survive once because of luck. You survived then and you will survive now because of you. Are you listening? You're going to be okay. Just hang on. I'm going to get you to help."

He was fine. He was going to be fine. He *had* to be fine.

"How? We're trapped here until the game ends."

Something hardened in my heart, in my soul. That sense of doom I'd felt before grew. My father had warned me. I was supposed to win. I was always going to be the one—even if I couldn't have imagined it. Thorin had come at me with the intent of great harm. As had Sev. They'd been brutal. They had permission. And so did I. Today was always going to end with death.

I'd been fooling myself for weeks. Pretending I'd had a

choice. But like the rest of my life, it had been an illusion–a dream.

Imperators did not offer choices. They commanded and we were helpless but to submit to their will.

I knew what I needed to do.

"Then, we end it," I snarled. "We end the game now."

I didn't recognize my voice or the words coming from my mouth. I'd never killed before. Not a person, not even an akadim. I'd only half-killed the one who had done this to Garrett. But I would change that now. I'd do it if it meant saving my friend. If someone had to die, then let it be so Garrett could live and not to satisfy my father's ego.

I scanned the gryphons that remained, the soturi still fighting on their backs, the ones battling on the ground.

I could jump. Take out my sword, let Garrett stay safely on the bronze gryphon.

"Just wait here," I said. "I'm going to do this for you. You're going to be okay. We're going to get you help." I knew dozens of soturi who'd survived akadim attacks. Garrett would survive.

But a small voice warned... they survived with their souls. No black marks.

"No," Garrett said. "Don't. Please."

Tears were burning behind my eyes. "Garrett, I have to do this." I turned away, prepared to jump, to make my first kill. "It's the only way."

He grabbed my arm, and pulled me back, his fist unnaturally strong around me.

"No, it's not." He sniffled. "It's not a way at all. Rhyan, you're not a killer. And I can't die knowing I made you one."

I shook my head. "I would do this for you, I swear."

He sighed, the sound heavy, defeated. "I can feel it. It's too late for me." Garrett pulled on his blonde hair. "I feel it happening. You know there's no cure. No help for me now. I've been lying to myself and to you. But the truth is... the truth... I've been forsaken for hours."

The blood oath on my back was heating. Burning. Warning me. I was in danger, I was close to violating the oath, to breaking my promise, to not just losing Garrett but suffering the consequences, the punishment that would come from failing to protect him.

"It's not too late. You're still you. You're still in there."

"I'm not going to be me for much longer." His throat bobbed. "Please. My father's out there, watching. My mother. Vanya. The shame... the shame of having a family member turn akadim—you know the taint that will have on our Ka. And I don't... I don't want them to see me turn. Don't let them. Don't let them see me become a monster."

"You won't. It's day. It's not possible."

"Night's nearly here. It's okay. I've had hours to process this. To decide. Just... please. Don't let this hurt them anymore than it already will. And don't let me...don't let me hurt them. You promised. Promised to protect me, to protect mine."

I cried out in pain. The scar on my back was growing hotter.

"End it," Garrett said calmly. "It's easier this way. Here, now. I can't... can't take much more. And if I have to see them, say goodbye... I don't think I can."

"NO!" The scar burned even hotter. Sweat was pouring down my tunic, rising up my neck.

"Please, Rhyan," he said, his voice growing weaker. "You swore."

"Swore to protect you!"

"This... protects me."

I shook my head.

He reached for my hand. "You have to win, don't you? He's going to punish you if you don't."

I shook my head. "I don't care. It doesn't matter."

"Yes, it does. I'm sorry... I should have spoken up a long time ago. I shouldn't have been silent. I should have... I should have protected you better than I did. And I never should have made you swear that oath to protect me...not when I didn't do the same for you. But now you must. And now... This is how you protect me. Let me die as myself. While I'm still me. While I still feel. While I still..." his bottom lip trembled, "...while I still love. End the tournament. Win. Stay safe from your father. Warn the others. Protect Aiden. For me."

"Garrett!"

"You feel it, don't you? The blood oath. I can see it in your face. The pain will stop. For both of us. I'm sorry."

A rider charged forward, his gryphon small, its wings bronzed with snowy tips. I pushed Garrett down, reaching for my sword, and I struck with the intent to kill. My back burned hotter than before, the pain so bad, I dropped my arm and ducked, just missing the rider's blade.

Slowly, I turned to Garrett and held my sword to his neck, angling it just so, as if I would kill him.

And he was right. It worked. The pain vanished.

I pulled my blade back. The heat started again.

Gods. This couldn't be happening. This couldn't be how I protected him. But letting him die as Garrett, not letting him become akadim, that was my duty now.

The announcer called my name. From his vantage point, it looked like I was in a duel with Garrett.

He reached weakly for my shoulder. "Stop the threat," he whispered.

"Stop the threat," I said, my vision blurring. I bit the inside of my cheek. "How?" I asked. "How do I...?" Gods. How was I supposed to kill my friend?

Garrett tilted his head to the side, exposing his neck.

A memory flashed through my mind. We were sixteen, studying in Seathorne's library. Garrett had just been allowed to start studying with the nobles thanks to his father's position as turion.

"*Best way to die?*" *Dario asked, as Garrett sat down.*

"*Not dying,*" *I said, kicking Dario's foot.*

"*Not dying isn't an option. You have to die. Best way to go?*" *he asked again, his eyes brimming with mischief.*

Garrett shifted in his seat, pushing back his blonde waves. Aiden looked up, watching him intently.

"*I'm going to assume old age isn't an option?*" *Garrett tapped his finger against his chin.*

"*Nope,*" *Dario said.* "*You're going to be killed before old age can get you. Best way to go?*"

Garrett's eyebrows narrowed like he was taking the question seriously. A moment passed before he said, "*Quickly.*"

I laughed, and a librarian walking by with a stack of scrolls in her arms shushed me.

"*Fall from a mountain?*" *Dario asked.*

"*That's not exactly quick,*" *Aiden said.*

"*It is when you hit the ground,*" *Dario said.*

"*I don't like the idea of falling. And I don't want to bleed out. Head chopping can be fast but risky. I'd rather not see it coming,*" *Garrett said thoughtfully. He paused for another moment, running his fingers through his hair and down to his shoulder.* "*Neck snap,*" *he said definitively.*

"*Perfect,*" *Dario said.* "*That's what I'll use for my paper.*"

"*You just had me ponder my death for your homework!*" *Garrett yelled.*

I knew what to do.

I reached for his neck, positioned my hands just so—just as I'd seen demonstrated in class. Just as I'd practiced a hundred times on a dummy in the Katurium.

"Tell me when," I said.

Garrett seemed to relax. A small flare of energy came from him like he was at peace, like this was right. I felt it, too, even though I shouldn't have. Everything about this was wrong.

"Will you tell Aiden that I'm sorry? And tell him, tell him I love him. Tell him I said, *Mekara. Mekara*, Aiden."

My heart is yours. Garrett wanted to tell Aiden that he was his soulmate.

I was going to be sick.

"Tell him, too, that I want him—need him to be happy. Make him swear. Move on, find happiness in this life. Tell my family the same."

My hands shook. I was disgusted with myself. This couldn't be right. There had to be another way. And yet, I knew in my heart that there wasn't. The black mark had seeped past Garrett's armor to his neck, shadows were forming under his eyes, and his skin was turning white.

"I'm sorry, Rhyan," he said. "Sorry, I made you swear. Sorry, you had to be the one to do this."

"Me, too."

"But I'm glad it's you. Wouldn't trust anyone else."

I bit my lip, knowing he meant that as a compliment, but it didn't feel like one.

"You're a good friend, Rhyan. Know that. You're blameless. Nothing to forgive. Your oath is fulfilled."

I nodded, trying to think of what to say. What words could be meaningful now, what words could possibly matter?

In the end, there were no words. Nothing was going to be right in this moment, no matter what I said, no matter what I did. There was only one thing I could do: protect my friend.

Fulfill my oath. Let Garrett remain Garrett. Keep him from suffering more. Keep his family from that same fate. Not allow him to become a monster.

Stop the threat.

"Me sha, me ka," I whispered.

"On my life." Garrett smiled at me, his lips shaking. His eyes locked with mine and he nodded. He was ready.

I tightened my hold, his body went limp in my arms, a willing participant even if his chest was rising and falling with rapid breaths, as if his lungs knew they were about to run out of air. Our eyes met, and then his gaze went to the stands, seeking out Aiden.

My heart constricted. I couldn't do it.

Gods! Fuck!

As if by some other force, my hands moved. His eyes widened. The sound of the crack broke through every other sound of the arena. Louder than the growls of the gryphons. The shouts of the riders. The roar of the audience. The clang of metal on metal on metal.

All I could hear was one single sound. The sound of Garrett's life ending. In my hands. My bare hands.

His eyes closed, his head rolling to the side.

A scream from the audience rose above the din, replacing the sound of the crack in my ears that had splintered my heart. It was a scream of pain and anguish.

I thought it was me at first, that I was screaming, but I wasn't. It was Aiden. Aiden crying out. Aiden shouting because his soul had been cleaved in half.

And so had mine.

Garrett was gone.

CHAPTER
SIXTEEN

T he silver band around my wrist snapped open. Magic buzzed against my skin, flaring with heat, and the rope vanished. The *Alissedari* was over.

I stared at the exposed skin, the place where I'd been tethered to the arena, to my fate, to Garrett. I tightened my hold on him and caught sight of his uncuffed wrist. It looked so exposed and empty. The ghost of his bracelet had left behind the smallest shimmer.

A fog descended over me, slowing time, and yet, everything was happening around me all at once, too quickly. The fog grew thicker, heavier, drowning me. The silver ropes imprisoning the riders in the tournament faded, and the domed ceiling opened, revealing a black sky. Torches flamed to life around the Pit's upper level, brightening the arena, signaling the end of the show for the audience, and I saw just how close Garrett truly had been to transforming from forsaken to akadim. I saw the black mark rising against his collarbone and the way his skin had paled unnaturally.

Every voice and sound came from far away yet was too close, too loud. Clear. A blur. A dream. A nightmare.

Aiden's scream.

The announcement that the *Alissedari* had ended.

My name. My title. The announcement that I'd won.

The shuffling of coins by gamblers whose bets were honored.

Drinks poured. Drinks spilled.

Cheers. Hisses of disgust.

Aiden's screams sliced through my soul. Garrett's family and Ka were crying out. Garrett's baby sister was sobbing. His mother was shrieking. I could hear it all. I could feel it all. Their anguish, their heartbreak.

My own heart was breaking in half. The beats slowing. Stopping. Just like they had before.

And there was Dario. Dario's fury, his anguish, was like a pyre swallowing me whole.

There were so many screams. But none louder, none more gut-wrenching or painful, than the scream in my heart. In my soul.

My gryphon sank to the ground, and I held even tighter onto Garrett. Now was not the time to grieve. Now was not the time to cry or panic. The sky was too dark, the sun too low. We were out of time. He would transform—it would be soon. It couldn't be out here, in front of his family, in front of Aiden.

He was gone. Dead. But his body remained in danger, and I still had to protect him. Still had one more task at hand. I could feel it in the dulled pain of my blood oath. It still sliced through my flesh, burned against my spine.

I couldn't breathe. It was too much. Too heavy. Too real. I could feel the panic washing over me, drowning me, sinking me. Feel the grief, the horror.

No. Not yet, it couldn't come yet, not until Garrett was safe —his body kept away, kept from becoming a monster.

I opened my mouth. I knew what I had to say, but I couldn't get the words out. I couldn't speak. It was like my nightmares when I couldn't move, but this was worse.

It was too much for me. Garrett had had no idea when he'd made me swear just how much he was asking of me, just how far this oath would have me go.

I was too weak for this. I didn't want to be here anymore. I didn't want this to be real. I didn't want this to be on me.

I looked down at Garrett, at my arms still holding him, and I began to fade. My stomach was twisting and turning, my vision was blurring, and my arms vanished and reappeared. My stomach tugged forward with a violent lurch.

I was going to travel.

My hand faded next, my body pulsing in and out of existence, here and not, here and not.

"Bind him," my father ordered.

I craned my neck back. Dario ran with fire in his eyes, his sword pointed at my heart. Turion Efraim, Garrett's father, raced toward me, his aura blazing with shock, with despair. Soturi raced for me in practiced formation, their daggers lifted. Arkturion Kane was among them, and Aiden was pushing through to the arena, his stave out, his mouth open. They were all coming for me.

My father's mages were faster. Black glittering ropes unwound from their staves like snakes. A blast of white light rose from the ground, circling me, and forming a protective dome. A prison. I let go of Garrett as the ropes wound and slithered through the arena.

Now, I thought. I had to go now.

But I couldn't. The ropes burned across my skin and my leathers, and bound my hands to my sides.

No. No. No.

Garrett rolled down the bronze gryphon's wing, his eyes closed like he was sleeping. It made him look younger. It made him look alive.

But he wasn't. He was forsaken. He was... Gods. He was going to change. Even now the black mark could be seen.

I reached for him, struggling against my bindings. Lifting him into my arms, I stood.

"Akadim!" I shouted, but the sound was lost to the chaos.

Arkturion Aemon joined the chaos on the field, his black shadows storming across the arena. He was blocking the soturi coming for me. Dario stared at Garrett's lifeless body, his aura reaching out, pulsing, pounding like he was trying to breathe life back into his friend. He grabbed Aiden, who'd just rushed the field, holding him back, pushing his stave up to the sky as magic shot out. I could feel it—Aiden's blind hatred, the force of his magic and will—seconds away from obliterating me.

He could do it. I'd welcome it. But I just had to do one more thing. One more thing to protect my friend.

"Akadim," I said again. "Akadim."

The ropes burned against me, warmer, tighter. It was too much. Garrett started to fall from my arms.

My eyes closed.

I WOKE IN THE DARK, my entire body aching and sore. My skin itched, and my throat felt like it was coated in sand. I groaned, rolling over in the bed, and nearly rolled onto the floor. I gripped the edge, forcing myself to lay back.

I lay on a cot in Glemaria's prison, Ha'Lyrotz. I recognized the gray walls, the familiar stench. I should have known the feel of the cot at once.

I tried to sit up, but something was holding me down. The ropes that bound me were dark, crisscrossing cruelly over my body.

A blue light flared to life in the hall outside the cell, casting an eerie light into my room. A vadati stone.

Bowen stood guard, one hand on his blade, his armor fully strapped into place. "He's awake, Your Highness."

Something was mumbled in response. The blue faded to white, then nothing. Darkness returned.

"Bowen," I called, but my voice was still weak, scratchy, quiet. "Bowen."

He stepped toward the bars, his hulking frame blocking the thin light from the hall. "Your Grace," he said, his voice curt. "You're awake."

"Where's Garrett?"

He pursed his lips together, his forehead furrowed, his eyes searching mine in concern. "Dead, Your Grace."

"I know that! But his body!" I shouted desperately. "Where is he? What happened?"

"Entombed in the Temple of the Wind. His funeral is set for tomorrow."

"Is he akadim?" I asked.

"Your Grace?" Bowen's voice shook, and he looked at me like I was farther than Lethea.

"Is he akadim?" I stood from the cot, my head pounding. My entire face hurt, and it felt like every inch of my body had been punched.

"You've been unconscious a full day," Bowen said gently. "You were injured. Do you not remember what happened?"

"I remember too Godsdamn well what happened!"

"Do you remember winning the *Alissedari*?"

"Winning," I spat, stepping to meet him at the bars. "I won nothing. Bowen, listen to me. Please. We were attacked after we found our gryphons. At least three akadim made their way into Glemaria. Unchecked. We—Garrett—killed one. A gryphon came to our aid. Killed another. It went after the third beast when we escaped. We raced back to warn everyone. The bells hadn't rung. They'd slipped past our defenses. We tried to warn the guards here, but no one listened. The binding of the tournament pulled us in too quickly. And I didn't know...didn't know that Garrett's soul...he was... he had a black mark, he was going to turn. So, I had to... I had to..." My voice broke, my accent so heavy, I could barely understand myself. Fuck. How was I going to get through this?

"Lord Rhyan, I understand that he was your friend, and you may regret—"

"Regret!" I snarled. "Of course, I fucking regret it. He was my best friend! You think I killed him on purpose—to win? You think I fucking care about that? I'm not making this up to excuse what happened. It *is* what happened. And we could all be in grave danger because of it. Now tell me! His body. Has anyone seen it?"

"Your Grace, Soturion Garrett remains entombed until his funeral."

I slammed the bars. "We have to check. You can't let his family see. And we can't... can't let him out. Not until we're sure he's...he's not a threat."

"He's not a threat," Bowen said carefully. "He died in the tournament, Your Grace."

"He died forsaken! You know what that means!"

Bowen was still, watching me carefully, not speaking.

"You don't believe me?" I yelled. "All these years, Bowen, have I ever been a liar? Confused? Delusional?"

He still looked uncertain, his eyes flicking down the hall before returning to me. A door opened and closed, echoing in the distance.

"Bowen!" I yelled.

"Soturion Garrett is dead, Your Grace," he said again, but he looked pained saying it. As if he was being forced to.

And I understood all too well. He was under the compulsion of his blood oath.

"Bowen, please, tell me." *You know!* I begged internally. *I know you know.*

"Your father wants to speak with you." He stepped back from the bars, turning and bowing low.

My father's boots echoed across the floor, the familiar heavy sound of his gait like a drum in my ears. "Bowen." He nodded curtly on arriving in front of my cell. "Leave us."

"Your Highness." Bowen bowed once more, but his eyes flicked toward me. He frowned, his eyes darting to my father, one hand fisted as he stood tall. Then, he released his fingers, his hand limp at his side as he walked away. Like he always did.

"Thought you could sleep your way out of this one?" my father said, his voice cold.

"I thought nothing." My fingers squeezed the bars, my knuckles white. "Where's Garrett's body?"

"Garrett Aravain?" he asked, something dangerous in his tone. "Garrett Aravain!"

"Where is his body?"

"You!" His aura blasted forward, filling my cell with the full force of his power.

I released the bars, too weak to hold onto them.

"You!" he shouted again.

I stumbled backward, the backs of my knees hitting the cot before I fell back.

"You had to fuck everything up. Killing the son of my turion! The fuck's wrong with you?"

I scrambled to sit back up and rose to my feet, my entire

body trembling with rage. "You wanted me to win. I did what you told me to do."

"Win? Win? You foolish idiot. Of course, I wanted you to win! What son of the Imperator does not win an *Alissedari*? Except for my son! My idiot offspring. I knew you'd fuck it up. Just like you always do. I arranged everything for you, laid out exactly what to do, and still! Why do you think you were surrounded by Ka Oryyan and Ka DeTerria? Brought to the Allurian Pass, the one place I knew you'd recognize? Even paired with your Godsdamned best friend? All you had to do was kill anyone other than the son of a Council member. But you couldn't even do that right." His neck was turning red, his nostrils flaring.

I flinched, my stomach turning.

"Why else do you think Thorin Oryyan attacked you so freely? Attacked an Heir Apparent when he's the mere son of the senator? I fed you the one to kill. Set his Ka on you to ensure you'd harden yourself up enough for it, stop being so Godsdamned soft. But no! You killed Garrett!" He slammed the bars, leaving them vibrating with his violence. "You weren't supposed to kill the boy the whole country knew as your friend! The one they all hailed as a hero since he killed the akadim!"

My knees gave out as I sat back on the cot. "Who then? Who was I supposed to kill?"

"Anyone else! I'd particularly hoped it would be Thorin's sniveling little cousin, Sev. You've seen him at the Academy. Poor marks. Poor skills. Barely tolerated by his family, let alone strangers. You think politics weren't at play in that arena? It's a wonder he's survived the training this long. Sev's death would have been a mercy." He sneered. "There's nothing worse than a weak member in a powerful Ka."

I bit the inside of my cheek. He wasn't talking about Sev.

"I even convinced your mother to warn you!"

My heart sank. I'd thought she'd sensed something intuitively, but she'd just been a pawn in his schemes. Like always.

"Thorin was given false hope, prepped to attack you. To make you move, make you act."

Anger boiled inside me. Thorin's attack had knocked me off my gryphon. Thorin's attack had exposed us to akadim. Thorin's attack had caused Garrett to...to...

My father slammed the bars again, his aura roiling with anger. "You saw how that bitch queen acted toward me. You knew what was at stake! If not Sev, then anyone else! Anyone whose father did not serve on my Council. How dare you win like this? How dare you ruin my celebration with your stupidity? How dare you taint my legacy with your idiotic actions."

"How dare *you*?" I was back on my feet before I realized I'd moved, rushing for the bars, my anger carrying me forward. "How dare you force such a vile event on your people? How dare you ignore the warnings of akadim. We were breached on Auriel's Feast Day. And your soturi that you claim to be so strong were too late to stop them from getting to the fields of your own Godsdamned fortress. Your soturi weren't there to stop them from posing a threat to your mages, to your novices, the people you're supposed to protect! And then weeks later, three more akadim entered. And no one fucking knew! Where are they now?" I stilled. "Where's Garrett's body?"

My father stepped back and laughed. "Akadim? There are no akadim in Glemaria."

There were no akadim in Glemaria? Just like the sleeves my mother wore were for fashion! Just like I hadn't been illegally unbound before the Revelation Ceremony! Just like my father was a native of Glemaria without an accent!

My breath was heavy, my chest heaving with the truth I bore. "I had no choice but to kill Garrett. His soul was eaten. He was forsaken when I killed him. And if you don't take the proper precautions, you're going to open the tomb and unleash another akadim into the country."

"You're farther than Lethea, Rhyan," he said, his voice dangerously quiet.

My entire body tensed, on high alert.

"No such things have occurred," he said, false concern dripping from his words. "There were no akadim. In your desperation to win, you turned against one of your oldest friends. You murdered the son of my turion."

"Stop," I shouted. "Stop trying to fuck with my head! I know what happened!"

"Do you now?" he asked, his voice so calm, so confident in his lie.

My whole life he'd done this, made me doubt myself, forget the facts I'd been sure of. I couldn't let him do this to me, not now. I could still see Garrett's face in my mind—still see his black mark, remember the way his aura had weakened. I'd had no choice.

"Fuck your gryphon-shit lies! None of that is true. And you Godsdamned well know it. Are you really going to leave your Council members exposed? Garrett's family? You don't know what you're doing if you don't listen to me!"

He smoothed down his beard, his fingers stroking his chin. "Here is what I do know. I know that my country needs to be kept in check, and sometimes that means doing things that appear unseemly—like allowing an akadim attack from time to time. Creating just enough fear to keep my people in line and under control. How else do you think we keep the peace amongst so many warring Kavim laying claims to my Seat? Our Ka remains on top and unquestioned because of what I do. And you remain safe and pampered alongside your mother for the same reason. Do you think I don't know everything happening before me? I knew the gryphons were sent by the Afeya. I knew our people would never accept their aid, and would see me as weak if I did—so I refused. I know what Garrett became. And now, I know this. You are my greatest liability. My greatest weakness. Half of the country is calling for your head. They're naming you forsworn in the streets, condemning you as an oath-breaker. Turion Efraim wants your head on a stake. You should be grateful that I'm keeping you here. I put you in Ha'Lyrotz to save your Godsdamned life."

A lump formed in my throat. I was going to be sick. I'd suspected he'd known about the akadim, thought maybe he was letting the attacks happen, letting our people suffer on purpose, but it was one thing to think it and another to hear him confirm the truth in plain words.

I'd always known who my father was, how he was with me, how he was with my mother. Why had I never suspected that this was how he was with the entire country? With the whole fucking North?

I sucked in a breath, my heart thundering. "Why admit it to me now? If I'm such an idiot, such an untrustworthy, stupid liability, why tell me?"

"So you understand. Your part in this isn't over yet. I said you'd save your mother if you won." He scoffed. "You only put her in more danger. I'm going to leave you here until this political fallout cools down. You will be Godsdamned grateful that this is all I'm doing to you. And then, by the Gods, you will pay the debt that is owed. You are going to make this right."

"Make it right?" Nothing was going to make this right. Only the truth. But it wouldn't bring back Garrett. "How?" My hands fisted.

"When it is time, I will send for you. If you value your life, you'll do exactly as I say. And you will never again mention Garrett turning into an akadim. It's been handled." He turned on his heels, his black and gold cloak swinging behind him. "Bowen! Back to your post." But he was already marching away from me. A moment later, the hall door slammed shut.

Bowen was still, standing in position across the hall from my cell, his breathing unusually heavy.

I retreated and sank back onto the cot, my head in my hands. "How? How will they have a funeral for him like this?" One look at his body, stretched and clawed, and they'd all know.

"They will have a funeral in the way they are always conducted," Bowen said.

"That's not possible," I said, practically spitting between each word, "when his body is a demon's."

"Isn't it?" he asked.

I looked up.

Bowen drummed his fingers along his dagger and glanced down the darkened hallway, then back to my cell, his gaze focused on the small window above my head. "I heard Aiden is a master of glamour," he said nonchalantly.

"Don't fucking talk about him!" I spat.

"The best the Mage Academy has seen in years. Decades, even." He paused, his eyes meeting mine, and his hand stilled. "He was invited to study under Lord Aevan Chandor, wasn't he? Received private lessons."

I glared.

Aevan Chandor was my father's Master of Spies. Aiden was a master of glamour partly from his own skill, partly because he'd learned from the best.

A glamour...

Bowen seemed to see the realization in my eyes as it happened, and he nodded. He was telling me what he could, what was allowed within the confines of his blood oath. There would be a funeral, and everyone—Garrett's Ka, his parents, his sister Vanya, Dario, and Aiden—would all see the version of his body my father wanted them to see. They would have no idea I'd killed Garrett to try and save him from a worse fate, to fulfill my oath. They would mourn him, but they wouldn't know he had been a hero again. No one would know how brave he'd been until the end.

And no one...no one would mourn me. I'd stay here. Hated. Forsworn. A monster in their eyes. I'd never be absolved because my father would rather appear strong than admit weakness, even if it cost me my life. It was better to have a son as a murderer, than admit he'd let akadim inside.

I lay down on the cot, my back itching. The scar still burned, which meant some part of Garrett still lived. And despite everything, despite how hopeless it all was, I still had to find a way to protect him.

CHAPTER
SEVENTEEN

The day of Garrett's funeral passed. And then the next day. And then the next. I was left alone. No visitors. No contact with the outside world. I was watched only by Bowen, alone in my grief. The bindings remained on me, tight and impossible to forget. They kept my skin too warm, kept me from sleeping, kept me from escaping.

By the third day of my imprisonment in Ha'Lyrotz, I'd stopped begging Bowen for news. I'd stopped asking for any hint of what had happened, how Aiden was doing, or Dario, or Kenna, or my mother. His lips always tightened at the last request, but he gave me nothing.

I could no longer feel anything. Not in my heart and barely on my body. I'd grown numb.

When a week had passed, I heard the doors down the hall open and the sound of at least a dozen soturi marching toward my cell. I sat up on my cot, my fingers scratching at the rough sheets beneath me. The sound of the boots echoed against the walls, the soturi's steps in perfect formation.

"You've been requested in the Seating Room, Your Grace," Bowen said quietly.

I stood up, my ankles shaky and my knees weak after days of hardly standing. Bowen unlocked the cell door, and I stepped forward.

Immediately, I was surrounded. There was soturi to my left, my right, before me, and behind me. As if I could escape in these ropes. As if I had the strength to fight back. I began the march, walking outside for the first time in a week in the cold dark of night, from Ha'Lyrotz back to Seathorne.

It seemed like an eternity had passed before we stood outside of the doors of the Seating Room, and I listened for the millionth time as they creaked open. The wooden gryphon carved across their expanse split in half, the wood groaning as the herald announced my presence. On the opposite end of the room, my father sat on his golden throne, his fingers drumming impatiently against his thigh. The golden border of his Imperator robes gleamed as brightly as the golden laurel that sat atop his head. My mother stood still beside him, her hands clasped before her, her voluminous sleeves falling to her knees.

I paused at the threshold. Bowen placed his hand on my shoulder. It was a reassuring touch, so unusual from him and so surprising I looked back. But his gaze wasn't on me, it was ahead. He squeezed and released his hold, and then I was alone, hearing the doors close behind me with a deafening thud.

I shivered, moving slowly, finding it difficult to keep my usual pace. The binds felt heavier and heavier as I moved through the empty room. No guards. No soturi.

Bracing myself for his ire, for his aura, I bowed as much as I could when I reached the edge of the dais. "Your Highness."

"Rhyan," my father said, his voice gentle.

"You sent for me?" I asked, my voice shaking with fear. My

heart pounded thunderously as I stood and focused my gaze. I grimaced as I rolled my shoulders back; even now, the practices drilled into me were trying to make their way through.

"The time has come. I managed to bring some order back to the Council. Remind them of their duties. Keep them from coming for your head."

"Shall I assume your methods of persuasion did not involve the truth of what actually happened to Garrett?" I seethed.

"Rhyan, it's time you learned that there has never been any other truth beyond what I've told you."

"The akadim," I snarled, feeling a sliver of my own aura escaping my binds.

"There were no akadim," he said, a note of finality in his voice.

I bit my lip to keep from shouting.

His eyes narrowed. "Luckily, the tides have turned in your favor. Thanks to my great efforts on your behalf." He waved his hand in the air dismissively, crossing one leg over the other. "Garrett was weak. He was jealous. He was never as good as you, not noble. He had everything to prove—a reputation to uphold after that one lucky akadim attack. Everyone knew you were the strongest, the most noble, the Heir Apparent." His nostrils flared. "He tried to fight you—he dared to threaten you on your gryphon after he lost his own. It didn't matter that you had lowered yourself, degraded yourself to befriend him. You merely defended your honor in the tournament. That is what I've told everyone. That's what everyone believes."

Tears rolled down my cheek. The disgrace, the dishonor to Garrett, to his life, his memory. He'd been so strong. He'd killed not just one but two akadim all before he was a soturion apprentice, and no one would ever know.

Not unless I found a way to reveal the truth.

"Ka Aravain?" I asked. "They've accepted this... this story?"

"Ka Aravain took decades to climb the steps to status, but they've only come far enough to merely sit amongst the nobility. To claim a seat that they're hardly holding onto."

I squeezed my eyes shut. They had no choice but to remain silent and swallow his lies, just to keep their position.

"My friends will never believe that. They knew Garrett. He had nothing to prove to them. Or to me. I don't know what they're thinking now, but they're going to figure it out. They'll know the truth."

"Just like they figured out your secret? Your vorakh? What about all your scars? Your bruises? They've showered with you at the Academy, have they not? Bathed with you? I've never heard word of them thinking or asking where the additional bruises you earned came from."

"I..."

"Did you really believe they valued your friendship over their own status and livelihoods? Did you truly think you were worthy of them risking everything?"

My whole face felt hot.

"And what about you?" he taunted. "Did you ever confide in them? Did you ever trust your best friends with your secret? Despite your promises to me, I know all about your childish defiance. But you didn't. All these years, you kept your mouth shut. Why? Because you knew they wouldn't accept you. You knew you weren't worth protecting." He reached into his pocket and produced three small vadati stones. They were clear and scuffed, rolling over in his palm.

My mother stiffened.

"They were using these during the *Alissedari*. Items like these," he turned them over in his hand, examining them, "they're rare, precious." He looked up at me. "And illegal. The status of each vadati stone is carefully regulated by the Empire. And with the rise of the threat of akadim, these should be turned over at once. Handed directly to Emperor Theotis. The consequences for having been in possession of them, for having kept them, used them, would be quite severe." He threw the stones at my feet.

"Devon!" my mother cried out, breaking the silence she always held when she stood at his side.

I bent down, quickly picking them up and stuffing them into my belt pouch. I couldn't listen to him, his lies, his manipulation. My friends would protect me. I had to believe that. And yet, the doubts were always present, always creeping in.

How many times had I sworn they'd finally ask me about my bruises enough that I'd answer, break down and tell them the truth? But they hadn't. Even if I could ignore my father now, he'd still won. With these vadati stones, he had complete control over Aiden. And with his father's position on the council, he had control of Dario.

"So what?" I asked. "What now? You got what you wanted. I won your little tournament. And now everyone is falling in line with your story." I held up my hands to showcase the black ropes crisscrossing against my skin that kept my power inside. "What more do you fucking want? You want me to parade around Glemaria? Fly into each town on a gryphon with a fucking victory flag?"

"Rhyan," he said softly, and his face was transformed by the expression I always looked for, wanted, needed—something akin to fatherly concern. Then it was gone, and his eyes narrowed into slits. "You forget that all I've done is to protect Glemaria, to protect the reputation of our Ka. But I can see now... you're too wild. Too disobedient. Too foolish for your own good. And for mine. I am a busy man. I can't spend all my time convincing the Council of Glemaria that you aren't its greatest fuck up over and over again. It ends now. I should have ended it a long time ago."

"Devon." My mother stepped before him. There was a sudden and unusual blast of power from her aura, like a bright, warm light that filled the room. "He's your son."

"Then he should have known better." He withdrew his sword, the red stone in the hilt catching the light of the fire before small flames danced across the starfire blade.

"Devon! Stop!"

"Shakina, sit down. Now."

Our eyes met, and I nodded, a barely there shift of my chin, trying to communicate everything I needed. For her to sit. For her to listen. For her not to get hurt—not again, not on my behalf, not when I was trying to protect her. Not when there was nothing she could do to help me.

"Kneel," he commanded.

"Devon!" my mother screamed.

"Mother, please!" I begged, falling to my knees. "It's okay. It's okay." My heart was pounding, alive... alive. The desire to live, it was there, despite everything. Despite how alone I was. Despite the fact that everything I'd touched had turned to shit, that everything in my life was completely fucked.

"Don't hurt him!" she pleaded. "Please! Devon, stop! I've never asked you for anything. All of these years. Do this one thing for me."

"Our boy's had far worse, haven't you now?" He stood over me, holding the blade I'd cleaned and sharpened myself so many times over the years. "We're done. No more surprises. No more games. You're going to swear your oath to me now."

I blinked, realizing he wasn't going to kill me. My heart seemed to pound harder in response as I asked, "Swear what?"

"To obey."

I looked up at him. Hadn't I done every fucking thing he wanted? I'd even kept his abuse secret all these years out of some fucked-up loyalty to him and our Ka.

"I have obeyed," I seethed.

"Not enough. I want your oath. To follow every command. Without question."

"Why now?" He could have asked for this years ago—demanded it, forced it—but he never had because I was a liability. He knew I'd inevitably break my oath to him, because he knew I would become forsworn and our Ka's hold on the Seat of Power would be in danger.

"You will swear that you will obey everything I tell you. No more objections. No more opinions. No more questions. What I want, I will get from now on."

I wanted to live, but not at this price. The cost was too high, it would take too much of my soul. "You'll never get that oath from me."

"I think I will," he said, reaching for my mother.

It happened so fast, his hand behind her neck, the blade sliding across her collarbone.

I was on my feet in an instant, running for her.

The back door opened, revealing the Arkmage. Connal stepped forward, the crystal atop his stave alight. The flash nearly blinded me, and I crashed to my knees, my head pushed back by the force of his magic.

My father pressed the blade into my mother's neck, drawing blood, as Connal stalked toward me, the light blinding.

"Rhyan, you will swear your full and complete obedience to me. You will give me your oath in blood."

"No!" I shouted, my hand slamming into the floor, my muscles straining as I tried to crawl forward, to reach my mother, to escape from Connal's power.

But then I sat back—not on my own. Connal was controlling me, moving my body like a puppet. It was worse than the ropes, the feeling of having no autonomy, no agency, no power, no strength.

I was brought to my feet, and as I opened my mouth to yell, I found my lips sealed shut.

Blood trickled down my mother's neck, and the doors opened. Twelve members of my father's personal guard marched inside. Bowen still stood outside, his aura nearly across the Seating Room. And then the doors closed.

My father pulled the blade back and handed off my mother to two of his guards: Soturion Baynan Gaddayan and another asshole related to Kane. They pulled her arms behind her back.

NO! STOP! DON'T HURT HER! I yelled. But no one could hear me. My mouth didn't move. I couldn't make a sound no matter how hard I tried. The shouts only echoed in my head, useless. Sweat was rolling down my forehead, my nose. My arms burned as I fought against Connal's hold.

Leave her alone! I tried again. But nothing. My chest hurt. I couldn't breathe. My fingers were numb as I kept fighting.

Then, my father stood over me, his blade poised above my head. A drop of my mother's blood fell onto my cheek. I couldn't flinch. I was frozen, forced to feel the blood drip down my face.

"Lord Rhyan Hart, my son, your Heir Apparent," he said, addressing his guard, "has agreed to submit himself fully to my will. To the will and the good of Glemaria. He is ready to give me his oath in blood. You will all witness."

I didn't stop fighting. I kept trying to move, to escape. I felt a pop in my shoulders, a painful ache in my back, then something like a release.

My arm broke free of Connal's hold, and my wrist snapped forward. The light on his stave weakened. I had only seconds to act. If I could break free of his will, maybe I could break my other binds, too.

"That's not possible." My father's face was red.

He'd said the same thing when I fought back in the Bamarian prison, when I overpowered him then.

"Now!" my father said, but there was a hint of worry in his voice.

My arm lifted, and I was rising to my feet. Connal grimaced. My muscles burned.

I'd sworn my will was stronger than my heart. Now I was going to prove it was stronger than my body, stronger than mage magic, stronger than my father.

My teeth clenched, and I took a step forward, every muscle in my body screaming in agony.

My father's eyes widened. There was a slight jerk of his chin, and I felt the nervous vibration of his aura. Biting down on my cheek, I drew blood as I focused on my power, the one that I'd developed, the one he couldn't touch. That couldn't be bound with magic. I was beating him, and he was too slow to hide his fear of me.

But then his mask was back up, tighter than ever, his unease swallowed by shadows swirling around his aura, darkening the room. "Swear yourself to me now," he said.

The word "no" was on the tip of my tongue, so close to being uttered, the sound almost there. Gods, I was close—so close to breaking free. To ripping through these binds. To tearing these ropes apart.

His fingers pressed into my arm, as his sword pressed against my face. I stilled, my stomach twisting. The steel was hot, warmed for the oath, for the magic to unleash itself, to bind itself and curse me. My father clicked his tongue, the gesture subtle but victorious.

My heart sank. Even though I'd moved against my binds, even though I'd shown strength that should have been impossible, it wasn't enough. Wasn't fucking enough. I was still no match for the magic's full force, not while also bound.

My chest was seizing, and my father's eyes lit up as if he'd seen the defeat in mine.

I opened my mouth, but I hadn't wanted it to. Connal's magic was in control again, but I forced it shut. Maybe I was fucked, but I wouldn't give them this. Even if I didn't survive, I would die as myself. I would never swear to him. I would never submit. If I gave him my oath, I gave him my soul. And maybe it was already torn apart from Garrett. Already half-dead. But it was all I had. I would not give him what remained.

My father lifted his blade. Drops of blood slid to its hilt. I caught my father's eyes with a desperate plea of mercy. One final appeal from a son to his father.

It didn't matter. The steel rose above my head. His mouth was set with a grim determination, and a wild, vindictive madness danced in his aura, and his eyes.

"Now, you'll never forget your promise to me. You won't be able to forget your oath or manipulate your way out. Every time you touch your face, every time you look in the mirror at your Godsdamned reflection, every time you feel the sting of the diadem against your scar, you'll remember where your allegiance lies."

"NO!" my mother screamed.

The blade lowered.

I jerked my head, closing my eyes as pain erupted through my skull. My eye was on fire, and I felt warm, thick blood dripping down my cheek.

The pain was almost unbearable. I couldn't see past the blood, the heat. My left eye wouldn't open; my forehead was on fire.

"*Ani dhara me sha el lyrotz.*" My voice, but not my voice, echoed in my ears. My accent, my essence, everything that made me *me*, was gone. Through every syllable of the ancient High Lumerian forced from my lips, my mother screamed.

I give you my oath in blood.

I fell to the ground. I couldn't see, couldn't think, couldn't feel past the pain in my forehead.

Some of the soturi laughed, and a sudden release of my muscles left me sprawled on the floor before my father's boots. Connal's magic released me. It was done. I'd sworn the oath. And if I broke it...I'd die.

My heart thundered, and I struggled to balance back on my knees, to fight every ache and pain as I rose to my feet.

"Shall we put it to the test?" my father asked. "Connal, bring her in."

I frowned. My mother was already in the room. Connal nodded with a sinister turn of his lips as he pointed his stave at the back door. Blue light flashed.

Chest heaving, I tried desperately to wipe the blood from my face, but my heart sank before I could see past the shadows. I already knew. I'd known the moment my heart had beat for her, the moment I'd decided I'd wanted to live, to feel again. I'd always known she'd be in danger. I'd always known it'd be my fault.

Kenna was ushered through the door.

"Rhy!" she cried out, a look of anguish on her face that vanished almost instantly. Her eyebrows furrowed, her lips thinned, and her face turned stoic as my father wrapped his arm around her, his leathers crushing the satin of her green dress. He took her hand in his, forcing her arm to tremble, her skin to go white.

He looked down at her, and she glared in return, but he leaned closer, whispering in her ear. Kenna's arm stilled, and a small smile appeared on her face.

I bit back a sob. I knew better, knew he was crushing her

266

fingers. He'd done that to my mother's hands too many times to count.

"Lord Rhyan has sworn his oath to his Imperator. I know how close you once were. I thought you'd like to be the first to see how devoted he is to our Ka and Glemaria."

Kenna's nostrils flared before her smile widened. "How... fortunate," she said, her words stilted.

My father pushed her forward, right into my line of vision, showing me exactly where he was twisting her arm. "Kneel," he ordered. His hand turned, and red splotches ran toward her elbow.

Kenna cried out, quickly trying to cover the sound with a laugh.

I wanted to scream. Garrett had died just so my father could maintain this vile balance of fear and control in this country.

It didn't matter that I'd sworn the blood oath. It wouldn't matter if I obeyed his commands to perfection. Kenna was never going to be safe. My mother was never going to be safe. Nor was anyone else whom I loved, who dared get close to me, befriend me, or care for me. I couldn't risk one more person being hurt because of me.

"Kneel!" he said again, his voice cutting like glass.

Right then and there, I made my choice.

I was forsworn.

I took a deep breath, my last one like this—free, alive—and I ran. I brandished my sword, fingers sinking into the hilt like my hand and blade were one. My forehead burned as I pointed the tip at my father's belly, right where his leather was weak, right where I could stab in and up to pierce his blackened heart.

His soturi all moved at once, screaming, their swords singing as they were thrust forward one by one. We were surrounded. A dozen blades pointed at my neck but they all came to a halt from a single jerk of my father's head.

"No," he ordered. "He's mine." He tossed Kenna to the side, and she stumbled toward his Seat, grabbing the armrests for support. My Imperator held up his sword, his mouth tightening as he stared at me.

"Rhyan," my mother yelled. "My heart! Your oath!"

I didn't listen to her. I couldn't. It was the only way. While I lived, everyone would suffer. Our swords clashed, the metallic ringing echoing through the room. Again, he struck, and I deflected. I hit and struck, pulled back and thrust, just before he caught the blade, forcing me to the side.

I recentered, leg forward, the sword an extension of my arm. I thrust and made my hit.

My father stumbled back. Quickly, I attacked again, my arm swinging above my shoulders, my vision still blurred with blood, my head on fire. I couldn't see out of my left eye. The oath was like a living flame burrowing into my skull, burning me from the inside out, taking its debt, the blood and life it was owed.

I didn't care.

Let the Godsdamned oath kill me. Let my father's blade swing true. Let it finally end. If I died now, then I'd take him with me.

He could see it, the farther-than-Lethea look in my eyes, the fire in my soul that said I had nothing left to lose. Nothing left to protect. I'd risked it all before and won. I'd done it when it was all I had to save Lyriana, and I was betting now on doing it again, on sacrificing everything.

But he wasn't.

It happened fast. The order was given, and a light flashed before me, white, consuming. I couldn't see out of my right eye now either. I couldn't move.

Connal's magic had snaked around my body once more.

I stumbled backward, my sword too heavy, slipping from my hand under Connal's sway. His eyes were alight and slit like those of a snake, a cruel imitation of my father.

My hand shook, my fingers shivering before I reclaimed my grip.

Connal's mouth fell open, shock momentarily breaking his grip on his spell.

I sneered. Even tied up, even bound, he could not hold me. Not for this.

With a cry, I thrust my blade over my head and raced forward, but the weight of it was too much. My arm spasmed and the sword fell. Its metallic clang was like a death drum as it hit the floor.

I cracked my knuckles, balled my hands into fists, still determined. I continued racing for my father, pushing through every restraint, every bind.

I didn't slow down. I raised my hands. I would choke him. I would snap his neck. I would end him. Even with a sword in my belly, even bleeding and dying, wherever my soul was going next, he was coming with me; I would drag him along. Down to hell if I had to.

My father's eyes locked with mine, and he thrust, the blade aimed perfectly for my belly. I tensed, prepared to take the death blow, but it didn't come. My father's gaze fell from mine.

A shadow had moved between us, small and quick like a wraith.

"Shakina!" he roared.

"NO!" I cried, realizing far too late.

My mother stood between us, her body where mine was meant to be. The blade with my name on it, my death blow, had pierced her body.

She stumbled forward into my arms.

"Mom!" I clutched her arms, trying to hold her upright. Blood flowed from her stomach, dripping down her white dress.

She stared into my eyes and nodded, like this was right, like this had been her plan. "I'm sorry," she said. "For... not protecting you."

"It's okay," I cried. "It's okay." My throat constricted, and I clutched her tighter, trying to drag her away, praying, praying, praying that she was all right, that we could fix this, that it could be me with the blade through my belly because I was forsworn, I had broken my oath, and I was meant to die.

Not her! Gods! Fuck!

I started pleading. To Auriel. To Asherah. To anyone who would listen. Please. Let me trade with her. Let me be the one. Let me do at least one thing right in my life.

But the Gods had never listened to me. Nor had they ever been kind.

There was a grunt, and the blade was removed. Steel and starfire and blood all flashed across my line of sight.

"Hold on," I begged. "Just..."

There was something like relief in her eyes. "Tell him it was right," she gasped.

"Tell who it was right? What does that mean?" I asked desperately, trying to make sense of it, to keep her awake, to keep her here.

"He'll know... he knows." Blood spilled from her lips. She was bleeding out, dying. "It's okay," she said, as if to herself.

Her legs gave out first, and her body sank to the floor. I dropped to my knees to stop the bleeding.

"My heart," she whispered. One hand curled up, and her fingers caressed my cheek. "No oath. Just promise. Survive. Just survive..." She went still. Her arm fell limp. "My love," she said. But she wasn't looking at me. Her gaze had grown distant and I felt the last whisper of her aura brush past me, and then I couldn't feel her at all.

No. No. No.

"Murderer!" my father screamed, his blade coming down on my head again.

I couldn't move. I was frozen. Holding onto her. Trying to turn back time to her being alive and breathing, and here.

A fresh gush of blood poured down my face. The blood oath reopened. The cut was so deep, I could feel it pushing through to the bone, scarring me, branding me. If I lived, I'd be disfigured.

"Now the outside matches what's within." He laughed, the sound was cruel and devoid of joy. "You are no longer Lord Rhyan Hart. I revoke your title. I name you forsworn and an enemy of Glemaria. I name you mother-killer and cut you from your *kashonim*."

I was vaguely aware of Connal pointing his stave, of a sudden sharp snap inside my body, the cutting of my oath. My *kashonim* was gone.

My father's voice rose. "You no longer have the power of your lineage to draw from. You no longer have the right to be a soturion in Glemaria. And for your crimes, you will die in Ha'Lyrotz." He turned to his soturi, his twelve most trusted guards. "You all witnessed. You will all swear to what you saw. Testify to this monstrosity, this spawn who killed the wife of your Arkasva, your Imperator."

Through the haze and the blood rushing into my eyes, I saw Kenna. Alone. Forgotten in the chaos. She'd been stepping slowly away, inching toward the back of the room to the door that led to the servant's hallway. In all the violence, no one noticed.

Our eyes met at the threshold. She pressed one hand to her heart, a wavering look in her eyes.

I nodded, hoping she understood.

Tears fell down her cheeks as she clutched the door frame.

Go, I mouthed.

Her lips thinned, and she vanished, the door closing behind her.

At least I had saved one person.

I looked back at my mother's body. And felt what remained of me tear itself apart. The pieces shattered, falling inside of me.

I closed my eyes, finally letting the pain consume me. I wasn't sure in the end what took me—the excruciating agony of my injuries or the churning tide of my grief.

All I knew was I couldn't hold on. My eyes were closing, and some part of me hoped they'd never open again.

THE THIRD SCROLL:

FORSWORN

CHAPTER
EIGHTEEN

I think time passed. I wasn't sure. In the darkness of my prison cell, my eyes had eventually opened again. Traitors.

At least... one eye had. My left had been bandaged shut and greased with sunleaf paste. Stitches ran from my forehead to my cheek, which gradually became full of stubble. I didn't know who'd healed me or why they had. I'd broken a blood oath. I was supposed to die.

But I had lived. And she had died. And my body was covered in bandages.

I knew she'd been buried. I knew there'd been a service. I knew he'd already selected a new wife. Once the official period of mourning ended, he would remarry, and I would rot down here. I was finally how my father wanted me: powerless, useless, under his complete and utter control. Oath or no oath, it didn't matter in the end. He'd won.

Bowen watched over me. That first night, when I'd opened only my right eye, he'd cried. I'd never seen him do that before.

He'd turned away from me, weeping, his aura so full of soul-crushing grief I thought I'd die from feeling it.

Then, he stopped. His aura had stilled. He'd gone silent and begun staring past me, toward the window, to the moon. At night, his reddened eyes reflected its glow. He didn't speak to me, or acknowledge my presence. Sometimes he walked off, his gait determined as if he were possessed. I could hear him pacing the halls before he returned, silent, his lips pressed together.

My tunic grew too big for me. I didn't have the strength to take it off nor to bathe when they brought the tub of cold water to my cell. Everything felt like too much. I resigned myself.

Until the day Bowen spoke for the first time. "Your Grace," he said.

I was not *Your Grace* anymore. I was not *Lord Rhyan* either. I was forsworn. An enemy. Exiled from my Ka and station even if I wasn't yet exiled from my country.

I shook my head—the most exercise I'd had in days. "Just Rhyan," I mumbled.

Bowen sucked in a breath. "You have a visitor."

My heart sank, my one eye closing. The left still remained concealed behind a bandage, though the stitches had been taken out. I'd been told I was perfectly capable of seeing out of that eye, but I didn't feel like I could. In fact, I couldn't feel that part of my face at all, so I'd left the bandage on.

"A visitor?" I rasped, dread coursing through my veins. There was no one in Glemaria who wanted to visit me. There was no one in Glemaria allowed.

Which meant it was him.

I rolled onto my side, facing the wall, and drew my knees into my chest. There was a soft thud on the cell bars, someone resting their hand. I was going to be sick. I didn't want to see him. I didn't want to see anyone.

But then I didn't feel his aura, and it wasn't his voice that spoke. It was soft and feminine and warm: "Rhy."

Kenna.

CHAPTER
NINETEEN

I rolled over on my cot. Kenna stood in the shadows before my cell, her hair shining and polished, her body sheathed in a Glemarian green dress.

Bowen bowed quickly. "I'll give you both some privacy. I'll be just down the hall until you're ready." He bowed again, holding Kenna's gaze for a long moment, something unspoken passing between them. "Lady Kenna."

She nodded, watching him retreat. Only when he was gone did she turn back to me, her expression hardened. "Rhy." Both hands gripped the bars. "Rhy." She took in my weakened body, the bandage over my eye.

I exhaled a sharp breath, pressing my hand to my face to cover the wound, hide the evidence. Not that it mattered. I squeezed my eyes shut. I barely had the strength to see her. She wasn't supposed to come see me. I didn't want to be seen, didn't want to be pitied. I didn't want her here to see how pathetic I'd become. And if she was here, then she was still under my father's rule, and still within reach of her own father's cruelty.

"I thought you'd escaped," I said weakly, my voice dull.

A long moment passed. The only sounds beyond the night's snowy gusts of wind were her uneven breaths. I opened my eyes and watched her.

"I couldn't." The moonlight cast a faint glow on the braid wrapped around her head and disappeared into the gleaming locks that fell past her shoulders. She wore a headband of silver wings behind the braid. "This is my home. I'm not running away."

"You did tell me that before," I said, shifting.

A sob burst from her. "Your eye."

I rolled back on my cot, staring up at the ceiling, my teeth grinding. "It will heal. I don't know how. The last healer who checked it said I should have lost it completely. I should be blind from the injuries around it."

"The Gods protected you."

"Protected me? Fuck the Gods." My hands clenched at my sides. "They didn't protect me. All they saved was my eye."

She sniffled. "And you."

I softened. And Kenna.

"Will it scar?" she asked.

"Yes."

"I'm sorry."

"Don't be," I said bitterly. "Not like anyone ever has to see it."

She didn't respond. She grew so quiet, I thought she had left. More guilt crept through me.

I sat up. "Before the *Alissedari,* when your father took you..." I stopped. I wanted to ask what happened. If she was okay. But she was here. And that seemed like enough. If she told me more, and there was nothing I could do about it...it would only hurt worse. "You're okay?"

"I'm okay," she said uneasily.

"Well thank you for coming to see me."

"I'm not leaving so quickly. I came here for you. I needed to...to see you. See that you're all right."

Do I look fucking alright? I wanted to scream. Gods, the outside really did match the inside now.

"Dario and Aiden are safe. They're—"

"Good," I said, cutting her off. I didn't want to know more, didn't know if I could handle knowing more—if they hated me, if they forgave me. Safe was more than I could ask for. More than Garrett had received. More than my mother.

"Are you able to stand?" she asked.

"Yes."

"Will you?"

I closed my eyes again. "Why? So, I can come admire the view?" I snarled.

"Please? Please just, I had to... had to do some negotiating to get this meeting with you."

Only that could have gotten me up, gotten me to stand and approach the bars.

"Negotiating? My right eye immediately began to scan her body—searching for injuries. "What do you mean?"

She shifted her weight, and her body turning in the moonlight revealed the fresh bruises on her neck. I stepped closer. The second I was within reach her hand pushed through the bars and took hold of mine.

Tears fell immediately. This was my first touch in days that wasn't from a healer, wasn't from someone paid to methodically treat a wound I'd never truly heal from.

"I'm sorry, Kenna," I sobbed. "Did they hurt you?"

"They... um." She swallowed roughly. "They want me to write a statement. I'm to proclaim to the whole Council that I witnessed everything. And that you're guilty of murder. But I can't... I just... I know what happened. I know the truth. Know you're innocent." She made a strangled sound. "Even if I hadn't been there, I'd know the truth, know you'd never be capable of anything like that."

"Why not? I killed Garrett."

"No."

"Yes. You were there for that, too, you saw me."

"Stop! Stop trying to turn me against you, to convince me you're evil. It won't work. I know you. I know who you are, and I know you only did what you had to. I know Garrett... I know he...know he was turning."

"You saw?" I asked, something desperate in my voice.

"I..." She shifted again, uncomfortable. "I was told."

No one was supposed to know. My father didn't want anyone to know.

"Was anyone else told? His family? Aiden?"

She shook her head. "It's all a secret at Court."

I let out a shaky breath. It would always remain secret, and now her knowing that would only put her in more danger.

"Write the statement." My voice broke. "Name me forsworn. Denounce me, say I'm a murderer. Just do it. Promise me. Swear."

There was a stubborn look in her eyes. "You're not though."

"It doesn't matter. If it will keep you safe, then you must."

"I can't. It's not right."

"Nothing is. But they're only going to come after you more. Hurt you. Let me do this for you. Please. Please. I lost Garrett. I lost my..." I trailed off. I couldn't say out loud that my mother was gone. "I've lost everything. And if this is all it takes to let me protect you, then please, let me. Write the statement. Tell the Council what I did, tell them whatever they want to hear. Make me a monster."

She sniffled. "I came here because I wanted to protect you. And yet you're still..." She squeezed her eyes shut.

My heart pounded, as something I'd thought was dead came alive inside of me. It was the will not just to live but to protect my friends. I needed to protect them more than I needed to breathe. She'd said before I always needed someone to protect and I couldn't save everyone. Now I knew she was right. Maybe I couldn't do more for her—couldn't get her out of Glemaria, couldn't guarantee she'd be free from physical harm or save her from my father or hers—but I could do this. With my last bit of will, I would do this.

Another tear rolled down her cheek, and I reached forward to brush it away.

"It's okay," I said. "Kenna, it's all right. Just listen to me. I know this is your home, I know you want to stay. Do not under any circumstances let them hurt you for this. Nothing is going to change my father's mind or his lies. Nothing is going to undo this. He knows Godsdamned well what he did, and so do all twelve of his guards. So does that spineless arkmage. If you need to say that I did it, then say it. Say I'm a monster. Say I was..." I swallowed, my throat tightening. "Say I was a violent," tears blurred my vision, "a violent lover. That I was cruel to you. That I happily killed Garrett." My hands trembled, and she took them between hers. "Say I was jealous he'd killed an akadim before me. Say I was in a rage over what I'd done that caused me to kill my mother, too. Say anything," I whispered, "just keep yourself safe. Don't be a martyr for me."

"But you're innocent."

"And you know it. That's enough. Now swear. Swear to me you'll do this. Denounce me. Have Dario and Aiden confirm your story—whatever it takes." I took hold of her hands, my grip tightening. "I need to know you're okay. I... I can't live with myself if you're hurt by this, too."

Tears ran down her face as she shook her head.

"Kenna, swear!"

She was crying now, but with a nod, she pressed her fist to her heart, and her eyes closed.

"*Me sha, me ka.* I swear."

I exhaled, my head falling against the bars, shoulders slumping with exhaustion. "Thank you."

There was another stretch of silence during which I felt the cool metal slowly warm against my head.

"Rhyan?"

I took a deep breath, pulling my head up.

"I love you," she said.

I tried to take in those words, to let them be a comfort. To pretend they were true. But I knew otherwise. I knew how it had always been between us.

"No, you don't," I whispered.

Her fingers ran over mine, and I found myself leaning back into her touch, her softness, her warmth, needing it far more than I wanted to admit.

"Yes, I do," she said. "I love you. In my way."

I knew what she meant. It wasn't about sharing a bed. It never had been. We'd been something more than friends. We'd been a solace for each other, a small light in the darkest corners of Glemaria, a shield against our fathers' expectations and manipulations. Against their cruelty. We'd been a soft place for each other in a world that was harsh and unfair. A temporary bandage for our hurts. But that was all. And that was enough.

"I love you, too, Kenna."

She smiled through her tears. "I know."

At least there was this. At least we understood each other. At least one person was alive who knew me, who knew the truth. At least there was one person who loved me anyway.

She pulled my knuckles to her lips, pressing a kiss to them through the bars. There was a rise in tension from her, a burst of nerves and sadness rippling through her aura. It was a good-bye. I could feel it in my bones—my time with Kenna running out, slipping away forever. She was already pulling her hand back with another glance down the hall. The faint echo of boots marching in the distance sounded.

"Do you know something?" I asked, gripping her fingers between mine.

Kenna tensed; her expression startled.

"You reminded me of hope," I said. "Reminded me it exists. I hadn't felt that in a long time. Not since..." Not since I'd stood under the golden leaves of a Bamarian sun tree two summers ago.

"Give it time. You will feel hope again." She set her jaw, and for a moment, I saw her as I'd known her long before all of this had happened: brave and headstrong, always keeping step with me and Dario and Garrett without missing a beat. She was the girl who decided something was true and made it so through her sheer force of will. She was the girl who'd been through more than I knew and yet was standing here, stubborn as ever, determined for things to be right.

My mouth twisted into a joyless smile. Kenna was fierce, but there was no strength of will, no amount of stubbornness or determination, that could change things now.

"I don't think so," I said honestly.

"Trust me," she said, a forceful, commanding tone in her voice.

I nodded, not believing her. But if my agreement was what she needed from me, if it gave her peace, I'd give it.

"Rhy. I have to go." Her voice broke, and she glanced again down the hall to Bowen before she turned back to face me. "I'm not sure... I don't know if I'm ever going to see you again."

Our gazes locked, and I let myself see her. Her kindness. Her beauty. Her bravery. Her love. She'd been a good friend, more than she knew. She deserved so much more than what I could give her, than what I had given her. Her coming to see me like this was one more kindness I could never repay.

"Kenna, wait, do one more favor for me, will you?"

"Anything."

"Promise me that when you walk out of here, when this is all over, promise me you'll find someone to love. Someone who loves you back. Loves you the way you deserve. Because if I know anything, you of all people deserve a great love."

Something softened in her expression as she watched me carefully. "Only if you make the same promise back to me."

I couldn't help but laugh. "Kind of hard to court someone when this is what I'm working with." I gestured to the dirty cell behind me. And yet... my heart thumped, remembering a very different prison. A different punishment. A different type of desperate hope.

Kenna's eyes remained serious, like she was trying to convey something bigger than her words. "Promise. Promise you will love. Promise you'll live. Not just survive, but live."

I gripped the bars to keep from stumbling back. My mother's final words. I wasn't sure I could keep that promise to my mother, and now Kenna was asking for more, for the impossible.

The clock tower began to ring, the bells booming through my cell.

Bowen came back into view. Kenna stepped back from the bars. "Remember who you are," she said. "This," she gestured to the left side of my face, to my scar, still fresh and red and angry beneath the bandage, "this only changes you if you let it."

I nodded, biting the inner corner of my cheek. Then, I watched Bowen take Kenna's hand, offering one small squeeze before he released her.

Only then did I see what had truly happened. She'd handed him a key.

"Goodbye," she said, her eyes lingering on me before she raced away.

I watched until her figure faded into the shadows, until she was gone.

The sound of metal scraping against itself turned my attention back to Bowen. He'd inserted the key Kenna had given him into the lock and was opening my cell door.

"Bowen? What are you—What are you doing?"

The bells stopped ringing.

His lips turn up into a rare smile. "Breaking you out of prison."

CHAPTER
TWENTY

"What? Bowen, what is this?" I stepped back. "I put one foot outside, and you pull me back in? Run to tell my father so he can humiliate me. Put me in tighter chains?"

"I expect he'll receive word," he said roughly. "But it won't be from me."

"Right. Because twenty-one years of experience says otherwise."

Bowen frowned. "This time's different."

"Shut the door, Bowen. Return the key."

"Your Grace?"

"I said shut the fucking door." I retreated and sat back on the cot. Hadn't I already given everything? My pride, my secrets. I'd tried to give my life. And my father always remained one step ahead, pushing me and back taking more. Not this time. "I'm not escaping. There's no escaping. You're farther than Lethea if you think I can!"

He grimaced, his hand flying to his left wrist. "Maybe I am! Maybe I also know we can do this. You have a window of

SON OF THE DROWNED EMPIRE

opportunity, Rhyan, and it's right now. The guards are changing. Soturi are on the move, heading to their new posts. It's the
final hour of shift and the darkest time of night—when they're
most tired, most likely to make a mistake, miss something they
weren't supposed to see. I've been planning, preparing, far
longer than you know. And it's now. We need to use this
chance. You might not get another." He jerked his chin at the
hall. "Come! Your chances to escape thin every second we
wait."

"They thinned the moment I was named forsworn."

"They are thinning right now!" Bowen roared, glancing
anxiously down the hall the same way Kenna had. He'd never
yelled at me before. Never lost his temper. He was gruff and
grouchy and dismissive, but he'd never been angry with me. I
looked up into his wide eyes, and found a surprising desperation in them.

"If you had a whole plan, why not say anything before?" I
demanded. "For weeks you've been silent."

"Because I couldn't. He's been checking your fucking aura.
I couldn't tell you. Couldn't risk a shift in your emotions. The
smallest bit of hope inside of you, and he'd have known. Just
trust me. It's all set. Now come on."

I hadn't seen my father since it happened. He hadn't
visited, but I'd sensed his presence. It sounded just like something he would do.

"Bowen?" I asked, barely daring to believe him. "You're
serious?"

"Yes." He squeezed his wrist like it was hurting him then
straightened, one hand on the hilt of his blade.

I thought of when I'd asked Kenna to run away with me. I'd
understood her objections. Much as I hated it, this was my
home. Maybe not anymore. But nowhere else was either. It was
one thing to be the runaway son of the Imperator, the rogue

Heir Apparent gallivanting through the Empire, and quite another to be forsworn, accused of murdering the wife of the Imperator, accused of murdering his own mother. There was nowhere in this world for me. Nowhere I could go.

My hands opened and closed helplessly at my sides, my fingers numb from the ropes.

"Even if I escape, I'll have nothing. He'll track me, you know he will. If not through you, through one of his other spies. Someone else he pays off, someone else whose oath he'll demand, who's loyal to him. He'll find a way. He always does. He owns the North. He'll punish me. Punish everyone I care about. Punish everyone who... who's left." I punched my hand. "Haven't I done enough? Haven't I hurt enough people? If I leave, it'll only make things worse."

"Then, don't let him bring you back!" he hissed. "Rhyan! You're acting like this prison and these last few weeks are all you have, all you are. That's gryphon-shit. You know it's gryphon-shit. You're more than this. So much more. I wouldn't be here now, risking everything, risking my Godsdamned life, if I didn't believe in you. Believe you were capable of escaping, of evading his reach. I wouldn't be doing this if I didn't think you were fucking worth it. If I didn't know with all I am that you're stronger than this. Stronger than he is."

My breath came heavily. Bowen had just said more to me in the last minute than he had in a month. All these years, he'd never shown this level of concern, of care. He'd always just done his job. Barely guarded me, then reported to my father.

"Rhyan, I'm taking you out of here whether you like it or not. I made promises, too. Swore my own oaths. And I intend to keep them." He was across the cell in seconds, easily overpowering me in my state, as he brought me to my feet and pushed me against the wall.

"What!" I struggled against him as he reached behind his

back and produced a fresh soturion cloak, which he immediately began wrapping around me. I stilled.

"It's been extensively glamoured," he said. "You'll go nearly unseen, even indoors if you keep the hood up."

I stared down, seeing my body fading in and out of the shadows, almost like it did when I was losing control of my emotions, starting to travel. A second later, he switched out my prison shoes for my soturion boots. My heart pounded, my mind too stunned to object or move.

"Now do I need to carry you," he snarled, "or is Lady Kenna's final gift going to be wasted?"

"She glamoured this?" I asked. Kenna's talents were immense, but I'd never seen this level of spellwork. Except from... from Aiden.

"She paid for it. Heavily. This is Aevan's work."

My father's spymaster. I tried to quiet the part of my soul that knew Kenna asking Aiden for help hadn't been an option. Tried to tell myself it didn't matter.

Bowen pulled up his hood, newly enhanced as well. But I was frozen, still disbelieving this was happening. Still waiting for the trick to be revealed, for my father to be at the end of the hall laughing cruelly.

"Myself to Moriel!" he growled. "Are you really going to make me carry you?" He extended his hand. "Trust me."

I took his hand, and we kept walking, moving down the hall. I felt the unusual sensation of burning in my calves. So many days without exercise, cut off from my power and my strength, had left me winded.

There was a small noise behind us, and I turned just as Bowen's hand clamped down on my mouth. A door had opened at the opposite end of the hall, and a small flare of torchlight poured through the threshold.

"Aye, Soturion Bowen?"

"Aye," he called back, his fingers digging into my cheek. My bandage dislodged.

"Taking final shift?"

"Aye!" Bowen yelled.

"Any trouble?"

"No."

"Aye." The door closed.

Bowen shoved me into a darkened corner, his eyebrows narrowed into a tight V before he released my mouth. "We need to reach the next rest point."

He urged me forward, taking me farther down the hall before shoving me inside a small alcove. Another hallway jutted forth; thin torches lined the wall, and prisoners shouted in the cells along it. Two soturi marched back and forth. Bowen pressed his back to the stone, watching as the soturi turned, changing direction. They began marching away from us.

I gritted my teeth, trying to control my breathing. The moment the soturi were out of sight, we moved again, crossing the hall and winding down another just before two more soturi arrived at their stations. Bowen jerked his chin toward a door. A closet.

I moved inside, breathing heavily, my arms folded across my chest.

"You still don't trust me?" he asked.

I glared, the bandage covering my eye starting to fall off my face. "You betrayed me before," I said. "Turning me in. Getting me into trouble. Don't think I didn't know. I always knew that you knew. Knew that I was... I was vorakh." I gasped at my own words. Panic fluttered in my stomach after all these years of never saying it out loud, of keeping the secret. But what was the point of hiding it now?

Bowen uncuffed the leather around his left wrist, then shoved it under the faint light above us. I ripped the bandage off my eye and blinked rapidly. The whole left half of my face felt stiff as I peered closer at Bowen's arm. There were two thin scars, the traditional ones soturi wore.

The first was the cut he'd received when he was nineteen at his Revelation Ceremony, promising to become a soturion. The second came from the forming of his *kashonim*.

I frowned.

"There are four scars," he said, bringing his wrist closer to my face. "Here. And... here." His finger traced two invisible lines.

"I don't see any—" My eyes widened. Beside the two thin ones, another was forming, red slowly seeping to reveal a raised scar. "Gods, Bowen, is that...?"

"My blood oath to your father." He sucked in a pained breath. "It's been burning since I opened your cell."

"You said there were four. What's the other one?" As soon as the question left my lips, a single bell cut through the air, calling the quarter past the hour.

"We need to move," he said, replacing his cuff. He grabbed me by the collar, pushed us out of the closet and down the hall, and rounded another corner.

We walked silently through one door and then another. Bowen paused, still holding my collar, and we stood pressed against the wall, barely breathing as another soturion passed by. My father's prisons were an endless maze, but Bowen never faltered. He seemed to have the schedule and pattern of every single soturion completely memorized. Was this what he'd been doing when he left me alone?

"Faster," he muttered, steering us further into the shadows. We stopped in front of another closet door before he unlocked it. As it opened, the footsteps of a patrolling guard sounded in the hallway. Without warning, I was pushed into the closet, and the door was slammed in my face.

"You were relieved, Bowen?" The muffled voice of the soturion came through the door. I did my best to still my labored breathing.

"Need a small break," he said. "Oskar's on post. All quiet. The little lord's asleep."

"Not lord anymore," he laughed.

"No," Bowen said. "Not anymore."

"New one on the way, I expect. Already fu—"

"Well, that's expected. I'm beat," Bowen said pointedly. "We'll talk later."

"Aye," said the soturion.

A minute later, my door creaked open, and he slipped inside.

"There," Bowen muttered, pointing to a bag stashed in the corner. "Your weapons. Your armor, it's all here."

I reached for the rough cloth, nearly dropping the whole thing as I pulled it against my chest.

"Why?" I whispered. "Why break your oath for me?" Giving me the cloak, knowing the schedules, having my things waiting for me...this was more than just Kenna's last gift. It was his as well. "It'll kill you."

Bowen pushed past me in the closet, saying nothing. He reached up and knocked each corner of the back wall. Wood creaked, slowly swinging away from us. A secret door. After shoving me through it, Bowen sealed the opening behind him. His aura was growing in intensity with his nerves, but there was also an odd kind of peace in it.

He grabbed my bag and tore it open. My armor was shoved over my head and my belt tightened around my waist before he slid swords and daggers into the sheaths at my hip. Another sword was strapped onto my back, and another.

"I swore a blood oath to your father, but he never knew that I swore another," he said, strapping the leather across my chest. "I can't show you. It won't appear because the one who made it...she's gone." His eyes reddened, and he waved his wrist at me again. "But I can still feel it. Feel her touch."

Tell him it's right.

"My mother?" I asked, my heart pounding with a truth I'd taken too long to put together.

A tear slipped down his cheek. "Yes."

I sucked in a breath. "She said to tell him—"

"To tell me it was right," he finished. "I heard." He opened a pocket on his belt and removed a vadati stone. It was small, far smaller than the ones issued to the rest of my father's guard and Council. It was rough and scratched and a perfect match for the three my mother had gifted me. "I..." He swallowed roughly. "I heard everything. Knew everything. I always did. I know exactly what he did to her," he seethed, "what he said to you. And I know," his voice cracked, "what she said to me."

"What was right?" I asked, trying desperately not to hear my mother's anguished cry in my arms.

He stared at the ground. "Saving your life. Giving her life for yours."

"My father's killing blow—she came between us," I said. "It was supposed to be me."

"No," he said fiercely. "No, it wasn't. I didn't want it to be her, but it shouldn't have been you, either. Rhyan, your father set you up. I told you before that he'd never force you into a blood oath, that he was afraid of you breaking it and dying. He found the workaround. Had Connal force the words out of your mouth. I know you have the evidence on your face, but it wasn't a true blood oath. It didn't have the same power. You have to say the words on your own."

My father would have known that—would have counted on it. Gods. "He wasn't going to kill me for breaking the oath?"

"I don't know. But at some point, he will try. Every day you stay here, he comes closer to giving into the urge."

A rock fell from the ceiling. Boots marched overhead, and Bowen pressed his finger to his mouth. The sounds faded, and he led me ahead, stopping in a stairwell.

"He'd been planning your mother's death for some time. He's had plans to marry another, one he thinks will bring him greater power. More authority. He was waiting for the opportune moment."

My mind reeled, trying to put the pieces together, to solve the puzzle Bowen had figured out long ago. "I...I don't understand. Why now?"

"He needed a problem to fix. Needed her death to bring the country together instead of tearing it apart. It would only work if he had the right person to blame. The right person to control."

We reached the end of the stairwell and turned left, moving into a stairwell that smelled of earth and cold. I shivered.

"You," Bowen said. "It was you."

Of course, it was me.

My entire face felt hot as a new wave of sadness crashed down on me. "So, it's my fault, my fault she's dead."

"No."

"Yes, it is. He *should* hurt me more. He should—" I turned back. What in Lumeria was I doing?

"NO!" Bowen said. His eyes widened, as he listened for sounds of soturi nearby. "Rhyan, you're not thinking clearly. Your mother knew she'd only have one chance to protect you. She'd been unable to for years and blamed herself. She got her chance. She died doing what she wanted, loving you, protecting you. He was going to kill her anyway. She always knew that."

"It doesn't fucking matter now." Only it did matter. It all mattered. Because I was crying. My throat tightened, and I turned from Bowen, staring at the wall.

"I haven't always been the best protector, I haven't always kept you safe. And I am truly sorry."

"None of this is right. Why would my mother say that?" I asked.

"You told me in Bamaria," he said slowly, "I was the shittiest guard that ever existed."

"I remember," I said, my voice dull. I'd just kissed Lyriana, just come alive for what felt like the first time in my life. Then, I'd been knocked out. I'd woken the next morning in the Bamarian prison with Bowen watching over me. And Bowen had been the one to put me there.

"You also told me my life was meaningless." He shrugged. "It may not be an important one. But it's not meaningless. Not to me."

I turned and met his gaze.

He urged me forward, and I took another step, then another, making my way to the next landing.

Bowen followed me, his body tensed. A soturion walked just outside the door, his steps hurried and purposeful, on his way to his posting. When the sound faded, Bowen continued, "Your father forced me to swear to always obey him. I couldn't refuse a direct order. If he told me to report seeing you travel, I had to. If I tried to lie, my scar burned. Or worse. So, I stopped looking at you. I stopped listening. Found every loophole I could." He closed his eyes, his face screwed up in pain. "Not to save myself. But because I swore my first oath to your mother. To protect you."

Her final words, *I love you.* I had sensed they weren't for me, that she wasn't speaking to me. I stared at Bowen. "You loved her," I said. It wasn't a question. It was a thousand tiny moments coming together at once. All the looks he'd given her over the years. The way he'd turned his back whenever I'd found myself in trouble. The way he'd never seemed interested in taking lovers, in finding a wife. The tears he'd shed the first night I was imprisoned.

His throat worked, his eyes blinking rapidly before he exhaled. "With all my heart. With every breath. I loved every moment of hers I was allowed. I've spent the last two decades toeing the line between their oaths. Upholding both as best I could. Now, I only intend to honor one."

"But you'll die," I said. Blood oaths always took their price. The magic found a way—even with me. Even if the words had been forced from my mouth, the magic had found a way. It just hadn't been my life that was the debt.

"Your mother said it was right, and I agree with her. I will happily honor your mother's last wish. It's the right thing to do."

"Bowen... don't be a martyr over a promise."

"That's not what this is. When are you going to hear me? You're more than just a promise. Your father's evil, a tyrant. But if anyone in this Gods-forsaken world has the power, has the strength to bring him down—it's you, Rhyan."

"Me?" I laughed, gesturing at my weakened state.

I was barely standing up straight, barely able to hold the weight of my armor and weapons. Weeks ago, my sword had been an extension of my arm, wielded as easily as I moved my fingers, and now I barely had the energy to hold it up.

"Yes, you. This, right here, right now, this isn't who you are. This is temporary. You're going to find your strength again, and you're going to become even stronger. I make few promises, but I promise this. You won't feel this powerless forever." His jaw worked. "And you won't always feel this sad."

I shook my head.

"Everything that happened with your mother, with Garrett, it's not because you're weak. Everything happened because he fears you. He always has. Since Bamaria, he's lived in terror of your power. He bound you twice, left you weakened in prison, stuck his mage on you and surrounded himself with twelve guards, and still... still! With all of that against you, you still nearly brought him down. What happened that night was inevitable. He was dangling the idea of saving her to manipulate you. It was never going to happen. She knew the truth, had known for some time. So had I. And in her capacity, she was protecting you, all the way until the end."

I stared down at my hands.

Bowen sighed, placing the vadati stone in my palm. "She had the other. She'd given it to me before... before they were married." He closed my fingers around it. "Here. This completes your set."

I'd have four. But this was more than just a means of communication. It was a love token, sacred between them in a way I didn't think I'd ever understand. I couldn't take it.

"She gave it to you," I said. "You should keep it."

He pressed it to his heart. "Thank you." His voice shook. "Do me a favor and remember what she told you."

"Survive. Just survive." I swallowed a sob.

I was forsworn. I'd be in exile. I might not find shelter. I might never find comfort or return here again.

Bowen nodded. "Just keep going. Keep running. Do whatever you must. But get out of Glemaria. Get beyond his reach. Even if you're scared. Even when you doubt yourself. Do it for her." He turned and led me to the top of the stairs.

We came to a window three stories from the ground. He offered a nod before kicking a stone in the wall. It fell forward, silent as he caught it in his hands and carefully laid it aside. He sucked in a breath, pain pinching between his eyebrows.

"Fuck." He undid his cuff and tossed it to the ground. The scar was redder than before. "I don't have much time." He reached through the hole he'd created, producing yards upon yards of thick, woven rope, the kind we used to tie down the gryphons. "This is our only way out, the only place that has any sort of blind spot for his soturi."

I watched nervously as Bowen secured the rope to a hook opposite the window. I was no stranger to heights or climbing, but I could feel the stark difference of having scaled heights before, knowing my vorakh was supporting me, versus now. My vorakh was cut off, and I was at the weakest I'd been in years.

"You've got this."

I almost laughed. I was not used to Bowen being reassuring. How much of our interactions my entire life had been an act on his part—an act so he could keep protecting me?

"You go first," he said. "You run into trouble, I'll catch up to you. But you won't."

He was right. My arms burned, and sweat ran down the nape of my neck into my two sets of cloaks, but we made it to the bottom without issue.

Bowen led me forward, around the corner, and we continued unseen. A crack of lightning lit up the field surrounding the outer gates of Ha'Lyrotz, and thunder clapped across the sky. Despite the snow we'd been having, rain began to pour violently. It blew out the torches of every soturion on guard, leaving us in near darkness save for the moon.

Another bolt of lightning hit. As the field came to life with light, so did the appearance of our unseen enemies. A dozen soturi stood in formation before us, their swords drawn, their bodies guarding the sole exit. A bell began to ring.

"Prisoner escaped!" came a yell.

"Fuck," Bowen breathed. We'd both ducked behind a wall,

Bowen's chest rising and falling with rapid breaths. "Someone must have doubled back to your cell hall." He pressed his fingers to the bridge of his nose.

"What now?" I asked, peering over the ledge.

Bowen sighed and shifted on his heels, looking over the wall before crouching back down beside me. "Unless a mage magically appears to remove your binds, we have no choice but to go through those gates." His eyes met mine. "Now we fight our way out."

TWENTY-ONE

"I can fight," I said, rain streaming down my face. I'd already reached for my sword, my body remembering how to prepare for battle. Even weakened, I felt a sudden strength in my fingers. Adrenaline was already kicking in like it did at habibellums. "I'm ready."

Bowen pressed his palm to my wrist. "No," he said. "I swore an oath to protect you. And I didn't come this close to fulfilling it to fail now. I've seen you hurt too many times. I won't see it happen again. Not on my watch. In a minute, I'll go out and draw their attention. You stay back, stay hidden, no matter what happens, no matter what you hear. Wait for the gates to clear. They won't see you in the dark, not when they're coming after me. That should give you enough time to run. Clear the gate and head straight for the woods beyond the wall."

"But there's already a dozen soturi looking for me. More are on the way."

He blinked rapidly before his expression stilled. "Aye, there are." He took my hand. "But I swear on your mother, they won't find you. Not while I still draw breath."

"Bowen, please," I said. "Let me help." I felt like I was meeting him for the first time after twenty-one years. I'd spent my life resenting this man, thinking the worst of him, believing his sole loyalty had been to my father, that he'd hardly cared for me, that he'd repeatedly betrayed me. I couldn't have been more wrong about him. This whole other life, this whole other relationship between us was suddenly filling in the gaps of my knowledge; a whole new reality was coming to life. I was finally seeing Bowen for who he was, and I wasn't ready to say goodbye. Not yet. Not when I'd just found him.

He guided my sword back to its sheath.

"Turn around," I begged. "Go back to your post. Claim I fought you. You don't have to do this, you can live. I'll run. I'm fast, I have the cloak."

But as I spoke, more soturi were marching past the wall, their boots splashing in the rain as they joined the others at the gate.

"Find him!" came a roar.

"Third rule of being a soturion?" Bowen asked.

I frowned. "Bowen."

"Answer the question. Third rule?"

My throat tightened. "Follow the chain of command."

"Right. And I'm in command now. Once you reach the pinewoods, you need to head west, right to the clearing of moon trees. You know the one, about a half mile in. Keep your hood up, don't stop until you reach it. Artem's waiting for you there. He'll help you cross the border."

Alarm bells were ringing, and the energy between us shifted. We were out of time.

"Don't you worry." Bowen squeezed my hand, and I wasn't sure anymore if he was reassuring me or himself.

I squeezed in return. The soturi were closing in on us.

Light shined on his face. The guards had scrambled to replace their torches with crystals.

"Rhyan. I want you to know. It's been an honor being your guard. I wish I could have done things differently for you. But I can go in peace, knowing I did what I could." He smiled. "I've always thought that if I hadn't been born to this station, if your father hadn't set his eyes on the Seat, I would have been proud to call you my son." He stood. "The moment the gate clears, run!"

"Bowen!" I cried.

But he'd already leapt over the wall, his swords withdrawn, steel shining beneath the crystals. "This is right," he said. My mother's final words. He turned back to me, eyes shining. "It was never about breaking an oath. It was about keeping one." Then he ran.

"Soturion Bowen," came a yell. "Surrender! Now!"

"You want me!" he roared. "Fight me!"

"Where is the prisoner?"

"Cowards!" he roared.

I watched in horror as he reached the center of the field. The soturi raced toward him as his body came into full view beneath the lights.

The first soturion reached him. Their swords met, and with a violent clash, Bowen knocked him back, pushing him into another guard.

His other sword was already battling the soldier on his right, and again Bowen defeated his opponent. He kicked the third soturion, knocking him onto his back, and spun, elbowing the next in the face. He roared, stabbing the next through his armor. The soturion fell instantly, and those who remained at the wall sprang into action.

Bowen was winning, but I knew he couldn't keep up this

energy, not when the soturi kept coming, kept attacking from all sides.

The sword in his left hand fell, and Bowen was punched in the face. He stumbled back but recovered quickly, lifting the sword in his right hand overhead. He lunged forward, taking out two soturi. But as he reached for his dagger, another came from behind him.

I threw my hand on my mouth to cover my cry as the blade ran through Bowen's stomach.

Suddenly there was a blue light in his hand, casting a halo over his body. "SHAKINA!" he yelled out, something like joy and relief in his voice.

I ran—for once away from a fight instead of into it.

As I made my way through the gates, miraculously unseen, I could have sworn I heard Bowen laugh before one final clash of metal.

Then, I heard nothing more.

I kept running, flitting through the pine trees that surrounded the prison, away from Seathorne, from my home, from everything I'd known and held precious, deeper into the woods, heading west. I kept running without stopping, just as Bowen had said to. The trees lightened, the pine giving way to silver-leaved moon trees. I could see the clearing up ahead, the grass glowing with silver.

A gruff voice yelled out, "Your Grace."

I slammed my hands against a tree, catching my breath. Sweat was pouring down my neck. "Artem?"

"Aye, lad, it's me." He stepped forward carrying a lit crystal in his palm for light. "Reckon I don't need to bow down to you anymore."

"I wouldn't say you ever did bow to me." I slapped my knee, imitating the gesture he'd used all these years to greet me. "This doesn't count."

"Yeah, well, no one asked ye." He glared. "You're all right now?"

I threw my arms around him, breathing out a sigh of relief. He smelled exactly as he had the last time I'd been in the stables, like hay and gryphon shit. I'd never been happier to smell it.

Thin, wiry-muscled arms tightened around me, and his palm clapped the back of my head before he pushed me back. "What'd I tell you about being too soft?" he scolded. His eyes searched mine. "Bowen?"

I bit the inside of my cheek, trying to hold back the tears, and shook my head.

Artem swallowed, wrinkling his nose. With a cough, he said, "What the lad wanted. Come on, then." He moved ahead of me, gesturing for me to follow. We walked quickly in silence, staying close to the trees until Artem turned and stepped out into a clearing. Moon trees grew in a perfect circle against the pines, their silver leaves glittering and full of light that reflected and expanded the faint glow of the moon. Lying in the center of the clearing was the bronze gryphon I'd ridden into the tournament.

The moment she lay eyes on me, she stood at attention and shook her head as if to admonish me. There was a definite attitude in the turn of her beak as she stomped her clawed front legs.

Artem nodded appreciatively. "She likes you."

The gryphon growled in annoyance.

Artem was already in motion, checking her saddle despite me having ridden her into the tournament saddleless. I stepped closer and realized the saddle was holding several bags.

"Provisions for you," Artem said. "Listen to me. You'll need shelter first. Aye? And another Arkasva to vouch for you. It's the

304

only way to get protection against your father. Swear to someone. It's that or...hiding out west in the human lands. But I don't think you're cut out for that. No gryphons out that way. Think where you have connections. Friends. Family. Get them to put you up."

Already, my mind was working. I had family all over the North, family that was directly related to my father or had proven time and time again that their allegiance lay with him. The ones whom I suspected of not being unconditionally loyal had all been paid off or forced into blood oaths. Not one would offer me shelter, would even consider it.

But on my mother's side, I had a cousin in Payunmar, a respected mage, only a few years older than me. He was an option but barely noble, his family small. I wasn't sure I trusted they had the ability to protect me or that my presence wouldn't put them in danger.

There was Sean. Sean was in Bamaria.

The realization left both an ache and lightness in my chest. A flash of hazel eyes and thick black lashes beneath a sun tree came and went in my mind. I could almost feel the warm breeze against my skin, smell the salty ocean air, feel her.

But Bamaria was on the other side of the Empire, and I was still bound. There was no way I could cross all of Lumeria without getting hurt, or worse, caught.

Aunt Sheera and Uncle Marcus were the closest, and they'd clearly been displeased with my father's actions before the *Alissedari*. They were my best bet. But that meant I needed to go to Hartavia. And *he* was there. The senator. The idea of being in the same country as him made my stomach twist.

But my aunt and uncle would be there, and once I was strong enough, once I had freed myself from these ropes one last time, then I would head south.

"There's food in the packs for you. Blankets, some gear. Extra knives. You know what to do."

"Thank you, Artem." I gripped his arm. "The red? I'm sorry I doubted you."

Artem's mouth tightened. "Said I'd help, didn't I?"

"You did. I'm sorry."

He rolled his eyes. "Just do this old man a favor and don't get caught, aye? I've enough work to do without some Heir Apparent causing trouble for me," he joked, but his voice broke, and his eyes were wet. Shaking his head as if he could deny the emotion in his voice, Artem stepped aside. "One hug was enough. Now get on her. Get out. And stay alive."

I nodded one last time, resisting the urge to reach for him. My heart thumped with fear that he'd be in trouble for this, that he'd lose his life like Bowen had, but I knew Artem wouldn't want me to be afraid for him, and every second I stood here, my escape window shrank. We'd already lost enough time, and the alarms were going off. My father would be after me any minute now, combing the country to find me.

I rubbed my palm over the bronze gryphon's beak, stroking between her eyes. They closed, as she made a low purring sound in her throat. I climbed up her back, settled my boots into the stirrups, and belted myself into the saddle, my chest tightening. "*Volara!*" I yelled.

She reared back, emitting a squawk that burst through the clearing and ended in a loud, resounding growl. The rain continued to pour down, and I tightened my grip on her reins, as her front claws touched the ground, launching me forward. I leaned in, my face nearly against her feathers as she raced toward the trees, her wings tucked back. With another resounding squawk, we lifted, soaring above the forest.

I tried to catch my breath as I looked back. The rain had knocked out the torches across Gryphon's Mount, but I could still make out the faint outline of Seathorne. Of my home. My last view of it...

When we'd flown far enough, the outline fading into shadow, the rain shifted to snow, then stopped altogether. I tightened my belt at my waist and lay my cheek against the gryphon's feathers, watching the dark shadows of my country pass me by. I recognized the landmarks beneath me, the flames on the mountaintops marking the miles, providing light to the soturi on guard. They would soon be looking for me if they weren't already.

We were nearly at the border. I sat back up, thinking about the last time I'd been there. It had been over two months ago, but it seemed like a lifetime. In that life, I was still Heir Apparent. Still Lord Rhyan Hart, riding out to greet The Ready. Aemon.

I hadn't heard any word of the Bamarian arkturion since I'd entered the tournament. But he'd been there in the Gryphon Pits, watching. He'd seen me kill Garrett. He'd heard the jeers of the crowd. Had he also been in Glemaria while I'd been held in my father's prisons? Had he heard what had happened to my mother, what I'd been accused of?

The idea of Bamaria suddenly seemed impossible. Even if Sean vouched for me, even if Arkasva Batavia had been friendly to me two years earlier, he wouldn't offer me sanctuary if Aemon believed me dangerous. Being forsworn was enough reason for me to be turned away, but if I were accused of murder, too?

I thought of the bruises on Kenna's neck and what she'd had to negotiate to see me. Of Bowen, the sword slicing open his belly. Of Artem saving the red gryphon. So many people had risked their lives to get me out of Glemaria, but none of it mattered if I had no Godsdamned place to escape to.

Ahead was Aravia. There were some solid cave systems that

could offer me shelter. Dario, Aiden, and I had camped there one summer before Garrett had fully integrated into our circle. But I couldn't live my days out in a cave, certainly not one that close to Glemaria.

Fuck. I knew where I had to go first. But Hartavia didn't feel any safer than my father's prisons.

I'm very impressed with you. You're far more mature for your age than any other boys in the Empire.

I resisted the urge to scratch the itch running up and down my palm. It would be different this time. I was stronger than him. I wasn't going to let some pervert senator ruin my chances of survival, my ability to uphold my mother's final wish, or Bowen's sacrifice.

Even as I decided that, I could feel the gryphon shift her flight pattern, a nervous, unsettled energy in her wings. I wasn't sure if she'd picked up on my distress or if something else had scared her.

I tensed, sitting all the way up, scanning the horizon. Night's darkness still blanketed the land, but a shout below had me on high alert. We were crossing over the border.

I leaned forward, burrowing into my cloak.

Something whooshed past my head, nearly slicing through my ear. An arrow. And attached to it, a rope. The exact rope used to tie down gryphons.

Another arrow flew at us, and then another.

"Mahara!" I commanded, urging my gryphon faster.

She uttered a terrified screech.

I leaned over, looking down past her wing. She hadn't been injured, but one of the arrows had made its mark. The ropes had no special magic associated with them—not like I'd believed they had as a kid—but mages spelled them to self-tie around a gryphon's leg if they needed to be brought down.

I caught sight of the rope knotting, the arrow falling away.

My stomach burst into my throat, my heart thundering as we dropped several feet at once.

My gryphon growled in distress, her wings flapping in desperation, trying to escape as I rubbed her head, trying to calm her, to slow her.

My efforts were pointless.

The wind pushed against my face and cloak, ripping it off my head as the rope tightened and we plummeted to the ground. My hand shook, my breath seized, and my stomach twisted as I imagined being somewhere else. Anywhere else.

The tug against my stomach came, almost nauseating with its violence, but it wasn't enough to free me. I was still bound, still unable to touch my vorakh.

Within seconds, we hit the ground. The gryphon's legs sprawled unceremoniously out to the sides, her tail thumping in agitation. And without warning, I was thrown from her back, my shoulder hitting the fields first.

Ignoring the pain, I rolled over, jumping to my feet, dizzy for only a moment. Just as I recovered, two soturi came up behind me, grabbing hold of my arms, twisting them behind my back, angled and tightly enough to break them. Sweat beaded my head, as I was brought before a tall soturion with short dark hair.

He stepped forward into the faint torchlight, and I paled.

Ronan DeTerria, my father's Master of the Peace and Dario's father, stared down at me, his dagger pointed at my neck.

CHAPTER
TWENTY-TWO

"What was the plan, you foolish idiot?" Ronan asked. "Always knew you'd be nothing but trouble." He jerked his chin at the guards on either side of me, two distant cousins of Ka DeTerria. One had the traditional black curls, the other was bald with a jagged scar on his neck. "Fucking Bowen. Can't trust anyone." He stretched his neck then removed a vadati from his belt, eyeing me up and down with a look of disgust on his face. "Devon," he said.

"Ronan," my father's voice barked through the stone, now brightly lit with blue. "Find him?"

I could feel his anger even now, and my entire body was shaking.

"We've apprehended him, Your Highness," Ronan said. "Found him trying to cross the border on gryphon-back."

"Myself to Moriel. Bring him to me immediately," my father yelled. "Call off the search. Tell everyone it was a mistake and he's with me."

"At once, Your Highness."

"Rhyan!" he roared, the vadati pulsing with his voice. "You

listen to me. Enough of these games. Time to stop acting like a pathetic child and face what you've done like a man. You think you can just take a life and not suffer the consequences? Now you have people dying for you—for you! For no fucking reason. We're losing soturi because you can't accept reality. If you think you've been punished before, you have no idea what's coming."

Survive. Just survive.

I closed my eyes. I had only one chance to fight back. It had to be here, on the ground. If I was brought back to Seathorne, if I was brought back to my father, that was it. I'd never have another chance. And Bowen would have wasted his.

I wiggled my fingers, flexing my arms, testing, straining, resisting their hold.

The vadati stone's light faded, and I was hauled before Ronan.

And then... Garrett's voice was in my head, clear as it had been when he'd been alive.

Stop the threat, he said, just like always.

Maybe it was my imagination, maybe I was so desperate for help I'd hallucinated, but I felt it—my strength, my power. This wasn't *kashonim.* My lineage had been cut. But I could swear Garrett's energy was here, helping me. Like there was some final link between us, some connection allowing me to draw strength from him, to draw hope. The scar on my back was suddenly alive, burning the way it had when our blood oath had been first forged.

I fisted my hands, lifted onto my toes, and slammed down, sliding out from their hold. I rolled forward, jumped to my feet, and unsheathed my blades.

All three soturi ran for me, and in the distance, I could see another.

"Rhyan!" Ronan roared.

The black-haired soturion was before me, his eyes dark and spelling death. I didn't wait, didn't think. I struck with my sword, pushing it through his belly.

He fell immediately, a stunned, blank look in his eyes.

Some part of my mind was going into shock. I knew where I'd struck him, knew the blow would kill him before he got help. I'd just killed one of Dario's cousins. Now I was the killer my father had claimed me to be.

But it was his life or mine.

My sword met the neck-scarred soturion's blade just as Ronan grabbed me from behind. I stabbed backward with my dagger. He groaned in pain. I pulled out the dagger and slammed my head back into his just as I brought my sword forward again.

The steel sang as it met my opponent's, hard enough to force him back.

Ronan released his hold on me. I lunged forward. I knew I had one more chance with the stunned soturion. They'd underestimated me, heard I was weak, heard I was bound, felt my lack of strength when they'd grabbed me.

Now, they were suffering for it.

"Take him down," Ronan ordered.

Another lunge, a step. The scarred soturion reached behind his back, withdrawing his second blade. I could see death in his eyes. I didn't wait—I jumped, knocking him to his back.

"Forsworn bastard!" he growled, knocking the sword from my hand. He flipped me onto my back. My lungs wheezed as his hand tightened around my neck. I reached for his, my fingers pressing into his scar. He hissed in pain before he drew his dagger over my heart. "Got you." He drew the point up and pressed the tip of the blade against the base of my throat.

"Enough," Ronan said. He stepped forward. I was out of time.

I glanced beside us. With the right stretch, I could reach my sword. I grimaced, my muscles burning as I reached. My fingers wrapped around the hilt. With a grunt, my breathing thinning, I lifted the sword, angled the blade, and brought it down on the soturion on top of me.

"No!" Ronan said.

"I've got hi—" The soturion's eyes widened, and his hold on me tightened.

I gasped, unable to breathe, my strength fading.

Then, I pulled the sword up, but I was too weak to hold it above my head. I threw my arm out to the side, and with everything I had left, I plunged it into him.

I turned my head away just as the blood spilled from his mouth, and I pushed him off me.

Ronan was roaring at me, flinging himself onto my body. The air again went out of my lungs in a whoosh as his knee dug into my stomach. One hand trapped my arm against the cold ground. My heart began to pound, not with fear or guilt but with another sensation I knew far too well.

His aura was wild, erupting around me, full of malice and violence. There was something there I hadn't seen before, hadn't noticed all these years, something that I should have recognized. Ronan possessed the kind of anger and hatred I'd only ever felt from my father, the hurricane of vitriol that only came when he was mad at me, when he wanted to hurt me, when he was hurting her.

In all of our years of friendship, I'd never seen a bruise on Dario. He'd hinted at knowing what my father did to me but had never said anything about my scars. He always had the right salve to help them fade. And Dario's anger from the night Kenna had been hurt; he'd come so close to asking me again. Just before I'd left, he'd sat down, said my name... like he'd wanted to tell me something, reveal something.

All of Dario's drinking, his volatile moods, the way he fought... I was seeing it differently now, seeing the shadow of my father's reflection in Ronan.

He dug his knee into my belly as he choked me with his hand.

There were shouts in the distance. More soturi were on their way. They'd be here in minutes.

I could feel the scream in my chest, desperate to explode. Stars played at the edge of my vision. I couldn't breathe. I'd be unconscious soon and brought before my father.

The blood oath felt like fire on my back. I focused all my strength on the arm he had pinned and shoved. Caught off guard, he loosened his grip, just for a moment.

It was all I needed. I freed my hand, reached for his neck, and dug my fingers in. He jerked against me. But then he wrapped both hands around my throat.

I flailed and kicked.

Then, a monstrous growl curled against the wind.

Ronan froze, looking up.

I felt a shadow looming behind me. My heart stilled. Akadim?

With a grimace, Ronan eyed the creature. My gryphon was on the ground behind us, agitated. Her wings fluttered, and her squawk sounded desperate.

Something flew at Ronan, too fast for me to see. One second, he was cutting off my air, and the next, he was on his back. A trail of blood ran down my torso.

My lungs filled and I gasped, coughing as the crushing pain began to fade. I sat up slowly, still dizzy from the lack of air. My knees wobbled, and Ronan screamed in pain as I rose to my feet.

When I looked closer, I realized it wasn't akadim attacking. It was the red gryphon.

He turned, his red wings fluttering, as he leapt from Ronan. Ronan had been mauled, but he was still moving.

The rest of my father's men were approaching. If Ronan died, it was on me, just like the deaths of the other two soturi.

The Afeyan gryphon bounded forward. He'd grown even bigger since I'd seen him weeks earlier. Artem would be proud.

He reached my side and lay on his belly. He wore no saddle, no strap. It would be up to me to hold on. I climbed up, hearing Ronan's faint yell.

The gryphon sprang to his feet, not waiting for me to adjust. He tore past the border, running faster than any other gryphon I'd trained with. We were in the air in seconds.

The first arrow whooshed by, missing us completely. The next two grazed dangerously close to my leg.

"Mahara!" I yelled.

Another arrow shot past us, another just an inch from the gryphon's front paw. The next arrow hit.

"NO!" I screamed as the rope unfurled and began tying itself around the gryphon's front leg.

I tried to reach forward, to untie it, but it was too far from me, and without a harness, I'd fall.

The rope went taut, and my gryphon screeched in annoyance. His entire body jerked back, and we dropped several feet in altitude as I screamed, "No! No!"

The gryphon's feathers were standing on end, his wings spread wide. We dipped, tilting to the side, and I barely held on, preparing to fall.

But the gryphon righted itself, soaring higher and higher. I looked down. The rope around his leg was torn.

This gryphon hadn't been raised like the others. He hadn't been taught to fear the rope. He hadn't been taught that the rope was stronger. He was stronger, and he knew it.

So was I. I'd escaped Glemaria. I'd escaped my father. Now

I was going to face my past. It was the only way I could have a future.

I steered to the west, my stomach rolling. It was time. I was going to survive.

"To Hartavia," I called, just as the sun began to rise.

CHAPTER

TWENTY-THREE

I was nine. I remembered clearly. The senator from Hartavia had come to visit. He'd been so kind, always had something for me when he saw me, tiny gryphon figurines made of stone that I'd proudly displayed above my headboard. I'd been excited every day to wake up and see him, had looked forward to talking to him.

Bowen had hated him. He'd growled every word he'd spoken to the man, and had always been urging me to do something else, go somewhere different. He'd made a hundred suggestions of things I could do instead of whatever activity the senator had suggested. His hatred had only made me like the senator more. Bowen had been a bother and no protection against my worst enemy: my father.

When the senator had announced he'd invited a singer to perform at Seathorne, I'd been thrilled. She'd sung stories of the Wars of Light, which I'd been obsessed with. I'd read scrolls from the library about the war, visited the temple, and listened to my mother retell the stories while she'd pointed out their paintings on the walls.

Even as a small child, I'd been expected to be at Court every day, but I'd always been told I didn't understand what was happening or that I was a nuisance or in the way of the proceedings. Not the senator. He'd told me how bright I was, how smart.

And he'd told me I was handsome.

I'm very impressed with you. You're far more mature for your age than any other boys in the Empire. It's only fitting that you attend this concert. I don't think the others would appreciate it. They're not like you. They're not as smart. Not as special.

I hadn't had any friends at the time. I wasn't yet being tutored with the other nobles. I'd only seen Aiden and Dario from a distance. Garrett hadn't yet been allowed in Seathorne.

My mother hadn't wanted me to go that night, but my father had said I could. He'd looked right at Bowen and told him to take the night off while I attended. After all, he'd said, what harm could come to me with such an esteemed member of the Hartavian Council as my companion? Bowen had looked ready to riot, and my mother had been furious—I understood why now.

At the time, I'd felt victorious. I'd finally gotten something I'd wanted, and I'd thought I was getting some kind of revenge on Bowen, getting back at him for not liking one of the only people I could have called a friend.

I'd had no idea what would happen as I entered the concert hall...

I stood now at the edge of Blackthorn, Hartavia's fortress, my palm itching fiercely. A sharp gust of wind blew. Winter had nearly reached Hartavia. It had been a week since I'd flown from Glemaria. A week of hiding, camping in a cave, and the Afeyan gryphon my only source of warmth. I'd been on edge, barely sleeping, barely thinking about what had happened, what I'd done. I had killed two men. And gravely injured a third.

I just kept remembering one fact. I had to survive. So, I did. Every day I went out and scouted the grounds, keeping my cloak on as I walked through the woods and ventured in the evenings to the nearby villages. I'd looked for my father's men, and, more than anything, I'd looked for the courage to do this.

Tear the rope apart.

My first thought was to go to my aunt and uncle's and throw myself at their mercy. But the Soturi of Ka Hart had expected that and searched their manor on four different occasions, tearing their home apart while I watched, hidden in the woods.

I was almost ready to abandon the plan. To head to my cousin's in Payunmar. But I'd seen my aunt's distaste for my father's rule. She was potentially my strongest ally—the most likely to believe my story. And she was most likely the one who could convince others of the same.

When my father's soturi retreated, leaving Hartavia, I remained hidden an extra day. I knew some had been left behind, that his spies were watching my aunt's home.

Which meant going directly to her would never be an option—not with an order of protection from the Arkasva. I only had one shot at requesting sanctuary. I had to go to him directly, and no one could know before I made my appearance.

The red gryphon nuzzled my hand, the one that'd been itching, the one the senator had taken...the one he'd placed on his...

The itch faded as I wiped the sweat from my palm against my riding pants. Exhaling, I stepped out of the shadows and emerged from my hiding place amongst the bushes. I'd been in the woods beyond the capital, keeping to the shadows of the fortress walls.

Two soturi stood before the black gate, their green hoods up, their eyes staring past me. They couldn't see me, not with my cloak as glamoured as it was, not when I had the trees behind me to add to the camouflage.

I took a deep breath and removed my hood.

The soturi's eyes immediately widened.

"Hold!" the first yelled. Their armor was similar to ours, made of black leather. The cuts were different, the pieces braided together, allowing for more movement but also more opportunities to be pierced by an opponent's blade. "State your name and your business."

I'd practiced what I'd say for the past hour. "I'm the nephew of Lady Sheera and Lord Marcus, of Ka Telor. I seek an audience with Arkasva Taria."

The second soturion stepped forward, his blade drawn, his blonde beard cut close to his chin. My heart sank as his gaze went immediately to my left eye, to the scar running from my forehead to cheek. I still hadn't seen it, hadn't had access to a mirror—much less the courage to look in one—but I could feel it.

I kept my chin up, willing my body to still, for my noble posturing to carry some weight, but I barely felt like myself. My cloak was roughened, my boots needed to be polished, I'd grown a beard, and my hair was in desperate need of a cut. I felt like a fraud of my former self.

"What happened to your face?" he asked, raising an eyebrow.

I shrugged, praying I'd masked the sound of my heart drumming. "Got cut."

His nostrils flared. He was clearly dissatisfied with my answer as his eyes ran down my uniform, my black leathers and the sigil of Ka Hart—gryphon wings and the sun—

stitched across my torso. "Lady Sheera, eh? Glemarian armor. That makes you the son of Lady Shakina."

"Yes," I said.

"That also makes you the son of Imperator Hart?" asked the first, sounding almost afraid.

"Yes," I said again. "I came to seek assistance from Arkasva Taria."

"Imperator Hart has been looking for you. He's named you forsworn," he said.

"He has," I said evenly, my heart thundering. I was terrified I'd waited too long to approach the High Lord. But if I'd come sooner, I'd have been dragged back. "I believe the Imperator is mistaken."

The two soturi stared at each other with disbelief in their eyes before they turned back to me, each one gripping their sword a little tighter.

I doubted my decision again. Maybe I'd waited too long—maybe I should have risked coming sooner. I'd expected word had been sent to the Arkasva of my crimes long before I escaped. Maybe I shouldn't have come here at all.

Straightening, I said, "I came to request temporary sanctuary as is my right. No harm may fall on me while I make my request. I ask for nothing more, only to be brought before Arkasva Taria and to summon my aunt and uncle so they might vouch for me."

"Bring him in," said the first, announcing my presence into his vadati. "Weapons?"

I bit my lip, not liking to be separated from them, but I'd known this was coming. I removed my dagger from my belt, unsheathed my swords, and removed the straps across my back.

The gates opened, and five soturi stepped through. I braced myself, knowing they were about to tie me up again, and held my hands out in front of me, compliant. I bit down on my cheek as they tied the rope in a knot, and then I was led forward, down the waterway to the front doors of Blackthorn.

The halls were full of nobility. All of them paused their gossiping to gawk as I was hauled forward, bound like a prisoner. Some pointed, and others whispered. The words *mother-killer* and *eye* were uttered over and over again. I felt my face heat and stared ahead, trying not to hear their voices, wishing desperately I could free my hands, cover my face with my cloak, and hide.

But this was part of it. I needed them to see what he had done to me, see his cruelty. My father controlled what everyone saw, but he couldn't control this—the mess he'd made of my face. Letting them see what he had done to me, his anger, his loss of control, was important.

He hadn't expected me to be scarred. He didn't like visible evidence to remind him of what he'd done. There was a reason my mother always covered up, a reason the ropes he chose to bind me in were invisible to everyone else.

Even my scar had been meant to go unseen—it was a blood oath. A blood oath he'd planned to go beneath my diadem. He hadn't counted on my breaking it, on it being real enough to scar me. But it had, and he'd missed his mark. Now, I needed it to earn the sympathy of Hartavia, enough that they'd hear me out and, at least for a little while, offer me protection.

We came at last before the doors to the Seating Room. A golden sun and silver moon were painted across the center and covered in a mosaic. Shining pieces of gold and silver configured in a braid-like design swirled behind the sun and moon.

The herald was a young mage, perhaps fresh from the Academy and just starting his post. He looked barely older than me and lacked the ability to hide his thoughts as he gawked openly at my eye.

I pressed my lips together, forcing myself to take a deep breath.

"Your... your name?"

"Lord Rhyan Hart—" I froze. "Just Rhyan Hart. Soturion."

The soldier leading my escort leaned forward. "This was the Imperator's son. Former heir. Forsworn."

Recognition flashed in the herald's eyes, and he turned, suddenly appearing confident and official as he shouted, "The former Heir Apparent of Glemaria, Rhyan of Ka Hart, recently named forsworn by our Imperator."

My fingers rose to my palm and itched before I stilled my hands. *Lord* wasn't my title anymore. I was no longer a lord, the Heir Apparent, much less an heir... I was no longer even of Glemaria. I was exiled.

I was ushered into the room's center to another room filled with chatter and laughter and hissing whispers, which, upon my arrival, fell to a sudden silence that left me dizzy. A few nobles I passed looked away in embarrassment as they saw my face and the state of my hair and clothes, but most nobles treated me with open stares and looks of horror at my scar.

The whispers turned into cries of *forsworn* and *killer*. My eyes started to close, as flutters of panic rose inside of me. My scar felt like a flame drawing everyone's attention to my face. It wasn't earning me sympathy, only disgust, and they weren't even trying to hide it. I knew my father's men had been here, that Hartavia submitted to my father's rule, but I hadn't expected public opinion of me to be this low this quickly. I hadn't expected for them to view me as the monster my father claimed me to be.

The soturi who was pulling me along down the center aisle finally tied my rope to a post in the floor just before the raised dais of the Arkasva's Seat of Power. I'd seen that pole before on previous visits to the Court, but I'd never seen its use. I felt like a caged animal to be used for entertainment.

Arkasva Taria was a middle-aged man, completely bald and unassuming-looking with a blonde beard. His wife, Lady Estraya, stood beside him. She was far younger and wore her blonde hair in long twisted braids that reached her waist. Their two daughters, both in their early teens, stood by her side, their hair braided in a similar style.

I felt a pang in my chest. I hadn't been allowed to stand beside my mother on the dais like that. Not for years.

There was a loud cough, and I looked up at a glaring High Lord. Arkasva Taria's aura trickled toward me, full of annoyance. Shit. I'd broken protocol, having forgotten to bow.

Quickly, I folded forward, waiting a few extra seconds to remedy my mistake. As I stood, I held out my hands in supplication.

"You're some distance from Glemaria," he said.

"Yes, Your Grace, I am. And I thank you for the audience, and your generous hospitality. I came here to—"

"To lie?" he asked.

The room burst into laughter.

"Your Grace," I said, "I merely seek sanctuary. I've always known you to value justice and honesty. You've always honored the truth, and since I have my aunt and uncle—"

"I gave you the courtesy of coming to see me," he said, "but I have no intention of dealing with you despite what your aunt or uncle might say."

"Please, if I could share my story. I don't ask for anything in return. No soturi, no money. Just sanctuary and immunity from my father...only for as long as you please."

"We did hear a story from your father, His Highness, Imperator Hart. You killed your mother. We are in the midst of grieving her death. Your aunt is grieving her sister."

"As am I," I said, voice hoarse.

"And your role in her passing?"

I sucked in a breath, the backs of my eyes burning. "I loved my mother. Dearly. I would never—"

"Your father has said otherwise," Arkasva Taria said.

My chest heaved. "I fear that I have a different story from my father."

"Your father is the Imperator to the North. His word is sacred. To say he is a liar is treason. A crime I do not intend to commit. I suppose you're already forsworn, what more can you risk?"

"I just... I never got to tell my side of the story."

He waved in dismissal. "Your side? I am sure you believe your side has merit. I am less inclined to share your belief."

"If I could just—"

"We shall play a game, you and I," he said. "A game of good faith. I shall assume that you will say the Imperator is a liar. Dangerous for you to suggest, but I will entertain the hypothetical for a moment. Say he is? Why should we believe you when we also have the sworn word and testimony of his twelve guards."

"His guards have no choice but to be loyal to him."

Arkasva Taria nodded. "Perhaps. We also have eyewitness testimony of Glemaria's arkmage, a man full of honor. He has also named you guilty. Is that not enough for me to know who speaks the truth? This now makes fourteen men who were witnesses to your crime—who swear you're a murderer."

"My father is a powerful man. Many fear him," I said carefully. "Many agree to say what he wants to hear."

"I understand," Arkasva Taria said. "As I said, I am playing a hypothetical game. I will entertain this one step further. Twelve guards, one arkmage, and an Imperator is quite a lot.

But in determining your guilt, I shall take this one step further. Do you agree?"

I already knew I was walking into a trap. But I nodded. "Yes, Your Grace."

"Let's say we can cast doubt on your father, on your arkmage, on these twelve noble soturi of Glemaria." Arkasva Taria emphasized each word to an almost comic degree. The nobles beside me began to laugh, tittering quietly into their hands. "We can pretend that they all felt obliged to lie on behalf of your father. It would certainly add credibility to your claim."

It was my whole fucking claim.

"But there is one person whom I believe should have been at your side, who should have defended you, particularly if they were a witness and also," he paused, "your soon-to-be betrothed."

"Betrothed?" I asked, and my heart sank.

"We were all sent a witness account of Lady Kenna Gaddayan, eldest daughter of Arkturion Kane Gaddayan, Warlord of Glemaria." I squeezed my eyes shut as Arkasva Taria unrolled a parchment. "She said she came into the Seating Room, worried about your violence. She said that not only did you kill your own mother a short time after killing one of your best friends, but you always had trouble controlling your anger, and often fell into fits of rage. Rages that were so violent, your father had to have you bound for your own protection. Like an animal. According to her, even your friends feared you. And after seeing what happened to Soturion Garrett, I can see why. She said in her testimony you frequently left her bruised after... intimate activities. She claimed on multiple occasions to wake in your bed with bruising around her neck and arms. Even her," he paused, barely concealing a chuckle, "backside."

My fingers clenched. Her fucking father had pressured her to write those details. I had asked Kenna to lie and call me a violent lover. To denounce me. I'd begged her to. But those injuries had been real, and private, and pained her.

And this Godsdamned bastard was laughing, making a mockery of her abuse.

"Lady Kenna claimed she had intended to wait for marriage for such...intimacies. But you, as the Heir Apparent, wouldn't wait." He curled his lips in disgust. "I will spare my nobility the rest of the gruesome details. But I must say I am not surprised. I had heard many stories of your...unnatural proclivities."

"My what?" I snarled.

"You don't know what I speak of? Your offenses have gone beyond Glemaria. Do you truly claim to have no knowledge of these stories?" he asked, tilting his head to the side. He was speaking to me like I was a child.

"I do not." I had a sinking feeling in my stomach.

"A shame, since as you said, I value justice and the truth. But I am afraid I cannot take you at your word after I heard enough tales of your whoring. It seems that you not only tried to control Lady Kenna by abusing her body in the vilest of ways, but wanted to secure the power of Glemaria's warlord by wedding his daughter, attempting to turn her against your Imperator. I heard that you slept your way through the Glemarian nobility, attempting to do the same, to secure power from each lover, from their Ka, much as you once attempted to gain the most protected secrets of the Hartavian Council by propositioning our own Senator Dorjan."

I bit my lip, hearing the name. "I never—he—" Then, I saw him, his rat-like face, his black greasy hair. His eyes were wide as he stared at me in alarm, his aura vibrating with some feigned mix of fear and disgust.

What do you know about sex, Rhyan?

Oh, I...um, well...

Have you ever touched a man?

I couldn't breathe. I couldn't... I was nine, and I was help-less, and I knew I'd made a terrible mistake and it was all my fault and I was completely on my own, and no one, not my mother, not Bowen, not anyone could save me. I'd wanted to be here, I had chosen to be here, I had fought my way here, and now I was trapped, and powerless, and it was my fault, and I deserved it...

I squeezed my eyes shut, trying to regain my focus, to take back the narrative, to get what I had come here for.

But I couldn't because Dorjan was speaking now, and his voice was the same as it had been all those years ago, the voice that had haunted my nightmares as a child, and my skin was crawling in disgust and fury, and my hand was itching as he said something about me propositioning him and using my body to gain protection in Hartavia. That I'd been like this for years, always using my body to earn secrets, to try and turn anyone I could from any Ka against the Imperator. That my lovers in Glemaria had gone as far as to confide in him of my violence.

The lies spewing from his mouth were endless. And Dorjan, the middle-aged rat sitting in his seat of honor as the senator, his neck collared in gold, actually had the audacity to look scared of me.

A low growl erupted from my throat. He fucking should be. I could see now that if I were at full strength—perhaps even in my current state—I could fight him. I could smash in his skull before he knew what was happening. And I'd fucking enjoy doing it. I'd relish taking his life. I'd already taken others. This one I would not regret.

But it was too late. I couldn't touch him now. The damage

had been done. In the eyes of the Hartavian Council, I was the liar. The killer. The whore.

Dizziness washed over me. Because I'd done it again. Chosen wrong again, and walked into a situation I shouldn't have. No one was coming to save me. No one could. There was no one left.

I could barely hear the words coming from the senator, the Arkasva, and the nobility that surrounded me. I was in a foggy haze of panic and anger.

Then, the words came bursting through the fog, loud and clear.

"Whore."

"Whore!"

"Betrayer."

"Forsworn."

I took a step back, and the rope tightened at my wrists. "I apologize for taking your time," I said, my accent thick and heavy. "I came here for sanctuary, with no harm intended to you nor anyone of Hartavia. I hope you will honor the old ways of the North and allow a stranger who entered the land for sanctuary, a stranger who has not been convicted of a crime against Hartavia, to leave freely. As is the custom."

"Just as you honored your friendship in the *Alissedari* with your friend Garrett?" Arkasva Taria crossed one leg over the other, his fingers walking up the armrest of his Seat as if he were deep in thought. "And what do you think the Imperator will say if we simply let his wife's murderer walk freely?"

"I..." My mind was whirring now, trying to keep up, to keep me safe. There were rules. I could be caught by my father in Hartavia. I could be brought back to Glemaria in chains by his soturi. But I was legally permitted to ask for protection and to be unharmed during that period.

Arkasva Taria remained silent, allowing his Court to again erupt, louder this time.

"Whore!"

"Murderer!"

"Forsworn!"

"He's a monster."

"Looks like one, too."

The auras of everyone in the room were intensifying as their anger grew. I contemplated fighting my way out, but even unbound, I couldn't fight this many soturi or face off against Hartavia's mages. And my weapons...they were all outside.

There wasn't going to be a Kenna, or a Bowen, or an Artem here to help me escape. I wouldn't be lucky a second time.

"Your Grace!" Aunt Sheera shouted; her voice magically amplified to rise above the yells. "Pardon, Your Grace."

Everyone turned, and I craned my neck to look back. I hadn't seen her when I'd walked in, I'd been so distracted.

Arkasva Taria stood. "Quiet, quiet. Lady Sheera, you may speak."

She stepped forward. I could see the sorrow in her eyes, feel her grief. Gods, please... please let her know. Let her see the truth. She made no indication either way. She stepped forward.

"Your Grace, I will vouch for my nephew long enough for him to have free passage to leave Hartavia at once. Let him go, and let him have until nightfall. I do not wish to go against the wishes of Imperator Hart. My home has been disturbed enough this past week while I still grieve my sister. I do not know the truth of the matter, but in all the years Imperator Hart has been my brother-in-law, I know that he believes and respects the laws and traditions of the North. Rhyan sought sanctuary for crimes committed in another country and nothing more. He is unarmed. He has been fairly denied. I have no personal knowledge of these stains you've assigned his character. As his aunt, I ask that you allow him to leave in the same manner in which he came. To honor the rules of sanctuary. And to honor my late sister. Should he be found within our borders after sunset or should he break honor in Hartavia in any way, break any rules, cause any harm, then we shall administer justice."

"Sympathizer!" came a yell.

Uncle Marcus stood. "Hush! My wife merely follows the law. As do I! As I believe all good Hartavians do. Imperator Hart originally hails from Hartavia, does he not? The laws keep us together. He has the right to ask. If he commits an offense here, then and only then will we remind him of the justice and honor we carry in Hartavia." He bowed to Arkasva Taria. "Your Grace."

I looked back to the High Lord. His eyes were still thin. I could almost see his mind turning, deciding what move would earn him more favor with his Court. Releasing me, the son of the Imperator and the murderer of his wife, certainly sent a bold message. So did arresting me on his behalf, as if he were the Imperator's servant.

"Rhyan Hart, formerly Lord and Heir Apparent to the Arkasva, High Lord of Glemaria, Imperator to the North, your request for sanctuary has been denied. We will not interfere with Glemarian justice. However, we will not shield you either. I suggest you take your leave of Blackthorn and take it quickly. By nightfall, this promise ends."

Senator Dorjan's eyes found mine, a rat-like sneer to his lips.

Do you want to know what it feels like? It's all right...

I turned in a blind rage. I was free to go, but that didn't mean the humiliation was over.

The shouts and accusations picked up again, and the soturi of Ka Taria threatened to hunt me after dark.

I grabbed my weapons at the gate, sheathing and armoring myself in a blind panic before I pushed my cloak over my head and ran.

My legs burned, running far slower than I needed them to while my arms ached. My vision was blurry as I found the Afeyan gryphon again and climbed on his back.

We flew non-stop the rest of the day, the insults and jeers of the Hartavian Court racing through my mind. I kept pressing the gryphon onward until night fell and I was too tired to go on.

We'd reached Aravia in the middle of the night, not far from the coast. We were as far east from Hartavia as we could be but too close to Glemaria for my liking. I knew I needed to find shelter; akadim were often reported here, so a cave seemed like my safest option.

We searched for about an hour, my sword drawn. The final promise to my mother was the only thing that kept me going until, at last, I found a cave. I led the gryphon inside and managed to drag enough loose sticks and bramble together for a fire. Inside the cave was a small pool, not warmed, but clear and clean.

I leaned over it, brushing my hand in as the fires reflected in its ripples. When the water stilled, I had my first glimpse of my face since that night.

Now the outside matches what's within.

He's a monster. Look at him.

Half of my face was covered by the red scar. I was mangled from forehead to cheek.

There was no way to not see it, no way to hide it. Every time I saw my reflection, every time anyone saw me, they'd see what I truly was. I'd never escape the reminder of my failure, of the fact that I was an oath-breaker, forsworn. Even if I hadn't been the one to stab the blade, I knew the truth. I'd killed my mother. I'd killed Garrett. It was my fault Bowen wasn't here. It was my fault the soturi at the border were dead, that Dario's father had been mauled.

And for what? All those deaths. All those lives lost. To save this? To save me? To save a monster who managed to get everyone he'd ever cared about hurt in some way?

I was a fool to think leaving Glemaria meant leaving my father behind. I knew now there was no escape. No matter where I went, he would follow. He'd either send his men, or his lies. They were one and the same at this point. My life was in his control. The only choice I could make was to go where he couldn't hurt anyone else. Not on my behalf. I had to disappear. For good.

I smashed my fist into the water, blurring the image, then crawled back to the fire, and closed my eyes.

CHAPTER
TWENTY-FOUR

ime passed. When I arrived in the cave the first night, the moon was gone, the sky pure black, save the stars. Each night afterward, I peered out and watched the moon grow, become fuller and fuller until it reached its peak. Then, I watched it wane back to nothing. I marked a line on the cave wall when one month had come and gone.

∾

ANOTHER MONTH WENT BY. Some forsworn came by the cave. Three men from Sindhuvine. Two soturi. One mage. I was too weak to fight them off. I made it out with only the weapons on my back. I also snagged a loaf of bread they'd stolen from the village. The gryphon flew me to the next location. It's another cave.

∾

THE MOON WAXED. The moon waned. I lived to see another month. I had three sightings of my father's soturi. They didn't see me. I've stopped sleeping. Too many nightmares. I've barely eaten—only enough to stay alive. I've wanted nothing. But I've continued to exist because I'd promised I would. Because I was too cowardly to do otherwise.

I'VE STOPPED LOOKING at the moon.

ONE DAY I saw an Afeyan in the village. I was sure she'd come from the Star Court; her skin was purple, and small golden stars glittered across her flesh, exposed despite the chill in the air. I watched in the shadows as she moved about the village, searching for prey. I wasn't the only forsworn hiding out there. The cave systems on the Aravian borders of Cretanya and Damara meant quite a few of us had come seeking shelter. Only the strongest held their spaces and kept their supplies. I'd kept mine and slowly gathered more. I'd made a nest that allowed me to fall asleep after I'd spent hours training.

When the Afeyan approached me, she knew right away who I was. She asked if I wished to be reinstated. I didn't respond. She then asked if I wished for my binds to be removed. I said I'd pay a mage the normal fee when I came upon some money. Then, she asked if I wanted to know who I was. I said I knew. She tilted her head, looking at me as if I hadn't heard her question. At my refusal to make any sort of deal with her or fall prey to asking a question, she held out her hand for the gryphon. The traitor went right to her.

"You know he doesn't belong out here, he's too wild. He deserves to be in his home, in the Night Lands."

"I know," I said. I blinked back tears, surprised I had any left to cry. I'd known deep down this day had been coming. Gryphons couldn't be pets, and the Afeya belong in the Afeyan lands.

"Take me home," she told the red gryphon.

He'd walked over to me one last time, the small limp from his first injury as a baby still evident. He pushed his head into my palm, purring.

I'd wanted him to stay. But he'd already saved my life twice, and I'd only saved his once. It was time... I owed him his freedom, a chance to return home.

Well, I did tell Artem I'd set him free. At least I kept my word on that.

All I had left was the piece of rope he'd torn from our escape, and one feather I'd found. Red. The color used to make me feel something. Reminded me of something. Of someone. But that had been so long ago. It was so hard to remember what it was like to feel. I wasn't sure I was surviving. My body was exercised, cleaned, fed, and rested each day, but I had once been more than this body. I had once felt...thought...desired...

Even as I cared for myself, I felt nothing, wanted nothing.

I was numb.

AKADIM WERE SIGHTED CLOSE. Too close. It drew the local soturi to my hiding spot. I was forced to leave. I found a new cave. The snow had melted. Winter was nearly over. I knew I needed to head south where it was safer, but there was another reason I needed to go there. I just wished I remembered why...

~

I WOULD HAVE DONE anything to stop my dreams. Does that count as wanting? I moved again.

~

MY BIRTHDAY. End of winter. I turned twenty-two. I didn't celebrate. Someone had once told me they'd stopped celebrating their birthday. I forgot who.... It felt like it was a dream. Now, I was the same.

~

IT WAS SPRING. I'd gone even farther south. A new cave. It didn't matter much. I was where I was. Akadim should have been less. They didn't like this season, the warmth, the lengthening daylight. They didn't like the south. But I'd seen just as many here as I ever had up north.

~

I AWOKE to a sinister growl in the middle of the night. Immediately on alert, I sat up, seeing the fire had nearly smoked out. My heart raced, but my dagger was under the pile of blankets I'd used as a pillow. My sword was my only bed companion.

I stood, pulling my cloak above my head, and made my way to the wall. There, I crept along, not sure if I was being hunted or had become the hunter. At the very least, with the wall behind me, I knew whatever had growled couldn't attack me from behind. During all these months living in exile, I'd come upon more akadim than I'd have liked, but I still hadn't made a kill. I'd come close, I'd injured, I'd maimed. But akadim were simple. They wanted easy prey. The moment they saw I'd put up a fight, they retreated.

Another growl sounded, this one from a few feet away. I shifted, my fingers tightening around my sword. There were footsteps. Two sets of them.

"Smell him," one growled. Male.

"Close," came the animalistic response.

Fuck. I bit the inner corner of my cheek to still my breathing. I'd sunk my body into the cave's pool that morning, but I'd heard people talking and raced to my clothes quicker than usual. I was hoping I didn't smell strong enough that I couldn't sneak up on them.

I neared the corner of the rocky wall and made the split decision of showing myself. I'd go on the offense; I wouldn't wait for them to come to me. I wouldn't allow myself to show weakness to these beasts.

Counting down in my head, my heart thundering, I made my move, my sword piercing the belly of the akadim before me. He roared, his putrid breath smelling of decay, as he pulled the sword from his flesh, his red eyes staring me down.

I kept my hands tight on the hilt, refusing to let go, to let this monster intimidate me. He wasn't human, he had no soul.

Then, the second akadim came up behind him.

I couldn't make out his face in the dim light, but something in his red eyes felt familiar. There was a tug on my stomach, some old memory of my power, of my vorakh, long bound and asleep now for months.

I gritted my teeth, prepared to slash again when suddenly my back burst into flames. The scar... the old scar... the blood oath from Garrett was burning and piercing me. I could feel his blade again as if I'd gone back to that night outside Seathorne, the air warm, the akadim attacking.

With a yell, I struck, fighting past the pain. My blade collided with the akadim's arm. A hit, but not enough. He stepped closer, his clawed hands reaching for me. The akadim behind him stepped closer as well. That sensation of familiarity washed through me, and again, my back flared with pain from an oath that was dormant, an oath I'd fulfilled.

Then, I saw the second akadim's hair. Blonde and wavy.

My breath caught, my body freezing.

The akadim roared, his face turning gruesome and foreign.

This wasn't Garrett. I'd killed Garrett. This was just a nightmare, a nightmare mixing with my waking life.

I pulled my gaze back to the first akadim, both hands on my sword now. I needed to aim for his belly, hit him in the same spot, and deepen the wound. But before I could make my move, there was a shout. The blonde akadim vanished into the shadows, leaving me alone with the first.

The distraction had been fast but deadly.

The akadim's claws reached for my waist. His nails pierced my armor, and my feet lifted off the ground.

"No!" I shouted. Then, I was on the floor. The claws were no longer cutting into me.

I scrambled to my feet, reaching for the sword I'd dropped in surprise. Its clang echoed against the cavernous walls, but I didn't need it.

The akadim's head rolled off his neck, landing with a gruesome wet plunk on the floor. A second later, his body fell forward on top of it as blood splashed across my already grimy boots.

"Are you al–?" The soturion standing behind the corpse froze, his blade clanging against the floor. Brown curls with just a hint of gray at the temples sat atop his head. His forest green eyes widened, filling with tears as he looked me up and down.

He uttered a sound somewhere between a strangled cry and a gasp. "Rhyan?" His gaze deepened, taking in my current appearance: hair too long after months without cutting it, the scar that sliced through my face. He stepped forward, his mouth open, light stubble reaching for his neck. "Gods! Rhyan!"

I fell to my knees. My mouth opened and closed in shock.

"Rhyan," he cried out.

Uncle Sean had killed the beast.

Uncle Sean was here.

CHAPTER
TWENTY-FIVE

"By the Gods," Sean cried. He ran past the lifeless akadim, fell to his knees before me, and wrapped his arms around my back. He pulled me in, his grip suffocating, as I was hauled to his chest in a hug. "I found you," he gasped. "Gods, finally! I found you."

I sat frozen on my knees, letting him hold me, unable to hug him back. My arms were stiff at my sides, and my hands felt useless.

No one had touched me in months. Not nicely. No one had truly spoken to me in weeks. I'd gone unseen, hiding from others' perceptions and ideas. I'd forgotten how to interact. I'd forgotten who I was. I'd been hiding in the dark, and I'd been alone for so long.

As much as I loved and had missed Sean, I wasn't sure I'd wanted to be found. I didn't know what to do with him, how to feel. I wasn't sure I wanted to feel.

"Are you injured?" he asked. His Glemarian accent was thick, reminiscent of home, my old life, the old me... my mother. It reminded me of memories I'd tried to forget, dreams

I was desperate to erase, nightmares that haunted me each night. "Rhyan! Rhyan," he cried, hugging me tighter. "Fuck, I've been so worried. I've been searching for you for months. Ever since I—"

"I'm fine, Sean," I said, my voice numb. This had been my first full sentence in...days? Weeks?

He pulled back, his eyes boring into mine, and I watched as he took in the scar. He reached a tentative hand out to gently trace it from my forehead to my left cheek. I flinched at his touch, and my eyes cast down at the lifeless akadim.

"Does it hurt?" he asked.

I let my hair, far too long, fall over my face, trying to hide the monstrous scar. "Only when I remember it exists." I closed my eyes, leaning back into the shadows, feeling tears begin to well, feeling emotion trickling back to my heart. Fuck. This was why I'd stayed hidden.

"It's okay," he said. "It's okay. I've got you now. You'll be all right. I'm here. I'm going to take care of you. We're going to get this sorted out."

I pushed him off me. "Sorted out? There's nothing to sort. I'm forsworn. I'm fine. I'm alive. Surviving." I spat the word. "You can go home. Back to your wife. Don't waste your time out here on me."

"I'm not going anywhere." He took hold of my chin, pulling my gaze back to his. His touch was so gentle, I was shaking. "Rhyan, you're a lot of things to me, but you have never been and never will be a waste of time. And you're right, I can go home now. Because you're coming with me."

I stood, shaking my head. "We need to dispose of the body. I..." I swallowed. "It can't...can't...because I...I live here." I gestured helplessly around me, turning away. "I live here," I said again, my voice rising.

"Rhyan," he said, coming to stand before me. "I know

342

you've been exiled. I've heard his stories." His voice rose, his aura full of such palpable anger, and I stepped back. "I can only imagine what he did to you. I've heard the accusations. The rumors. And I'm almost positive I know what actually happened."

"I killed her. My mother," I said, my voice void of emotion. "Killed Garrett, too. Two other soturi on my way out. All with these hands." I stared at them in front of me, turning my palms up and down. The itching had gotten so bad my palms were nearly scratched raw.

Sean was opening the pouch on his belt, pulling out fresh sun leaves. "Here, for your hands."

I put them down. "No."

He frowned but replaced the leaves in his belt. "When you're ready then."

"Didn't you hear me?" I asked. "I'm a killer. Forsworn."

"I don't believe for a second that—"

"Believe it!" I snarled. "I did kill them. All of them."

Sean threw up his hands. "Fine. You killed them. Is that what you want to hear? What you need from me? You're a killer. You've done some terrible things. Satisfied?" His nostrils flared, and he pressed his hand to my shoulder. "How about this then? I don't care. You're my nephew. You always were, and you always will be, no matter what you do. And now you're coming home with me. You're coming to Bamaria."

"No, I'm not. Look, I need to burn the body."

"The smell," Sean said. "You won't be able to stay here with it."

"The smell is awful," I agreed. "So, after I burn it, I'll go to another cave. From there, another, or I'll come back here. It doesn't really matter. Doesn't matter what I do. Or where I am. As long as I survive." I laughed, hysterical. My hands trembled at my sides, and my entire body shook. "The only oath I can keep." I kept laughing. "Survive."

"Oh, Rhyan," Sean said. "It's okay."

Then, the tears came, turning into violent sobs. And hours later, they hadn't stopped.

I OPENED MY EYES. They were raw and puffy. My head ached, and there was light, so much light, blasting against my face. I tried to hide, throwing my arms over my eyes. I sat up, my heart pounding. I wasn't wearing my armor. My weapons were gone. And I... I wasn't in the cave. I was surrounded by four walls. And there was a bed next to mine, with real pillows and blankets. It was already made.

"Morning," Sean said. He was sitting in an armchair across from my bed, one leg crossed over the other. Beside him was a round table with a silver tray holding two mugs and a steaming carafe of coffee.

"Where am I?" I asked. "What is this?"

"It's an inn," he said. "Auriel's Flame. I got us a room." He raised his eyebrows. "You don't remember?"

I shook my head.

"You, um, after you...well, you—oh, fuck it." He groaned. "I don't know how to dance around all this, and I don't want to speak in niceties. We're too close for that. So, I think we can be honest with each other, yes?"

I watched him for a long moment, still unused to being around people, to being seen. I bit down on the inside of my cheek. "Okay."

Sean nodded, looking relieved. "After you finished crying, you collapsed. I'm guessing too much emotion hit. I don't think," his nostrils flared in anger, "I don't think you've been feeling everything, or anything, for quite some time. I picked you up and carried you to my ashvan. Brought you here. I told you when you seemed conscious, asked you about coming here with me, but I think you might have been a little too far gone. It was almost morning when we arrived. That was yesterday. You slept through the whole day and night."

I threw the covers off my legs and stood, panic rising in my stomach. "I can't be here. Sean, I'm forsworn. I'm exiled. He's looking for me. I can't—"

"Hey, hey," he said, his voice soothing. "Yes, you can."

"Who knows I'm here? They'll turn me in. They'll tell him."

"They will do no such thing," Sean said fiercely. "They're Branwyn's family. The owners are her grandparents."

Branwyn. Sean's wife. His wife's family owned the inn. But she lived in Bamaria. I had been north when Sean had found me. There was no way we were...

I glanced out the window. "Where are we?"

"Cretanya," Sean said. "In the city of Thene. I promise you, you're safe here. Cal, Branwyn's grandfather, he won't say a word." Sean poured coffee into the mugs, and I watched, transfixed, as steam rose in swirls. The scent was slowly permeating the room, intoxicating.

My stomach growled. I hadn't eaten in over a day. And I'd never wanted coffee this badly before; I hadn't had any for months.

"Come and sit," he said. "I'll get you breakfast, too. Whatever you want. As much as you want. We can order the whole menu."

Gods. I could eat a whole menu. I'd been hunting small animals, rabbits mainly, picking berries, and snatching eggs from local farms, and stealing bread when I dared venture into the villages. I'd gotten rather efficient at feeding myself the basics, feeding myself to stay alive, to keep up my strength. A full meal... that felt like something from too long ago to remember.

After months of flavorless bread and hard-boiled eggs, I started to think about savory breakfast stews, omelets, cooked sausages, pancakes, bread that was hot, bread that wasn't stale, that had flavor and was dipped in oil...and still soft.

My stomach tightened painfully.

"I had Cal include all the spices you like for your coffee," Sean said with a wink, pushing a few bottles forward. There was black pepper, red pepper, turmeric, ginger, sticks of cinnamon, and vanilla, alongside a silver jug of cream.

Tentatively, I sat down at the table, ravenous, as Sean pushed the steaming mug my way. "Go easy," he said. "Your stomach's empty."

I nodded and added each of the spices to my mug as if in a trance, watching the colors shift and blend. I added the cream last before stirring. The routine was so familiar, it conjured up an old life, an old me. I'd been making my coffee this way for as long as I could remember—liking the taste and having learned from a mage the benefits of the spices for someone training— someone injured often. I was just about to take a sip, inhaling deeply through my nose, when there was a knock at the door.

I tensed, setting the mug down, immediately searching the room for my sword, my dagger. I was in only my tunic and riding pants. I wore no armor, no cuffs, and felt naked without them. I hadn't slept without being fully armed since I'd left Glemaria.

Sean grabbed my hand. "Just Cal. And his wife probably. I, uh," Sean smiled sheepishly, "I might have already ordered the whole menu."

Sean stood and opened the door, and an elderly man burst into the center of the room. He looked at each corner, his tongue pressed to the corner of his mouth as if assessing. His hair was white and stringy, standing up all over his head, and he wore blue mage robes over a faded gray tunic. When he spotted me, he grinned widely. "Good morning! Glad to see you're awake. I hope you're hungry."

He gestured back to the door with his stave. A table, large enough to sit six people and so long it stretched from wall to wall in the room, floated inside. Cal, I assumed, moved out of its way, standing at the foot of the bed before lowering his stave. The table legs settled carefully onto the carpet. An elderly woman with white curls piled messily on top of her head peeked around the doorway.

"It fits!" she said happily. She waved her stave over the table. It was full of silver plates and covered trays. "The food is still warm," she said. Steam rose off the platters in heavy swirls, and the scents of every food I'd thought of, in addition to foods I hadn't, wafted toward me. "Everything is nice and fresh. We have some of Cretanya's best cooks at Auriel's Flame." When she saw me, she smiled as warmly as her husband had, as if she were genuinely happy to see me.

I shrank back, fearful she'd recognized me, that she'd see my eye and scar and run.

She smiled wider. "I hope you enjoy yourself. And if you want anything else, or if you want more, you just come right down to tell me. I'll have the kitchen whip up anything you want."

"Marisol, Cal, thank you so much," Sean said. "This is amazing."

"Our pleasure." Marisol leaned over the table, her eyes on me again, and I felt my face warm.

She was seeing the scar. She knew I was a monster. Exiled. Forsworn. A killer. She'd start screaming, tell me to leave. Or worse, call the soturi who patrolled Thene. Have me arrested, dragged back to Glemaria, to my father.

"You have the most amazing eyes, the green," she said.

I could only stare back, stunned.

"It's so lovely to meet you, Rhyan. Sean just adores you. And we adore Sean. I'd come to shake your hand," she said brightly, "but this table here is just too long, and I'm just a little too old to crawl under it."

Cal laughed. "You might be, but I'm not."

"Oh, you!" Marisol laughed.

"I think we'll let the lad enjoy his meal. Come say hello downstairs whenever you're ready. We'll be at the front desk."

"Thank you," Sean said again, turning and eyeing me carefully.

"Oh," Cal said, "almost forgot." He reached back for his stave.

I gasped, pressing my body to the wall, waiting for the ropes to come, for the trick to be revealed.

But the faint blue glow only reached the table, swiftly lifting every lid to reveal the food underneath. "Catch, Marisol," he said, slinging each lid out the door.

She giggled, her own stave lifted, and created a floating pile of tray lids that she balanced in the air.

Satisfied, Cal retreated with another warm smile. "Enjoy your meal, Rhyan. Sean."

The door closed.

With a laugh, Sean said, "Have you ever seen two people who enjoy their work more than they do?"

I swallowed, my throat dry, my face hot.

"Rhyan?"

I couldn't move. I was just staring at the food. There was so much of it. I hadn't seen this much food so nicely tabled, so warm, and all at once since...

Since I'd been Heir Apparent. Since the night before the tournament. My last true meal. A lifetime ago.

Sean squeezed in between the tables and chairs to reach my side. "Too much?" he asked.

I shrugged; my chest was heaving. "I...I don't know."

Frowning, Sean shook his head. "I do know. And it's not enough," he said. "You deserve more. You deserve everything. But we'll start with this." He leaned over to the small table we'd occupied and picked up my coffee mug. Sean put it between my hands, and I inhaled, feeling the warmth spread from my palms down my arms. "Go on," he said. "Drink."

I did. It was the best thing I'd tasted in months.

And I started to cry again. Sean let me. He didn't say a word, just drank his own mug of coffee and fixed me a plate, and then another. I was barely able to see my food through my tears as I ate. When I was too full to continue, he led me back to the bed, and tucked me in like I was a child. I slept the rest of the day, and for the first time in what felt like forever, I slept soundly, with a full belly.

I didn't leave the room at the inn for three days, not even to venture into the hall. I didn't even really talk to Sean. It was too much. I just ate and slept. In all that time, Sean never pushed me. He never demanded I talk or go outside. He just let me be.

I hadn't known how much I'd needed that.

On the fourth day, I asked, "How long are you going to stay here with me?"

"As long as it takes."

I finished my plate of food. Each day, I'd been eating a little more. I'd been training and working out every day for months by myself, running in the mornings before dawn when akadim were in retreat and soturi were in their final shift. It had paid off; I was still strong. But I hadn't realized that I wasn't filling out my armor or that my pants had been loose, and I'd only noticed I was putting weight back on again when I had to move my belt back to the notch I'd worn in Glemaria.

"As long as what takes?" I asked.

"Until you're ready to come to Bamaria."

"I'm not sure I'll ever be ready."

"I'll keep waiting."

I didn't speak to Sean at all on the fifth day. I woke up angry with him for pulling me out of hiding, for forcing me to be in a place where people could see me, a place where I could see myself. Every time I went to the bathing room where the mirror was, I entered without any light, leaving the candles in the main room or blowing the bathing room lights out if Sean lit them.

I didn't need light. My eyes had grown accustomed to the dark.

On the seventh day at the inn, Sean sat me down. "Rhyan," he said. "I need you to tell me what happened."

I stared at my hands. "Why does it matter?"

"Because you're carrying the weight of it with you, and it's too heavy. Give some to me. Let me take it. Let me at least carry it for a while, some of it. Let me know what's been in your nightmares."

My mouth was dry. I'd been screaming, waking to Sean sitting at the edge of my bed and rubbing my forehead until I went back to sleep. "I don't know if I can."

"Try," he said.

"I can't…" I hadn't spoken it out loud to anyone. Hadn't tried to tell anyone what had happened—not since the disaster at Blackthorn.

"Pretend," he said, "as if you're telling me a story. Like you used to."

I scoffed. I used to tell Sean the same stories my mother had told me. I'd loved repeating them back to him whenever I was allowed to see him. Which, thanks to his disagreements with my father, wasn't as often as I'd wanted.

"I can't do that," I said. "Can't just tell you a story."

"Why not?"

"Because!" I slammed my fist on the table, surprised at my own outburst.

"Rhyan." Sean's hands were out, his voice quiet, like he was trying to gentle a wild animal.

"Sean, just stop. Please. My life isn't a story. It's not some neat little fairy tale my mother used to tell me. That's sure as fuck not what happened! That's not what this is. It's real. You think I can turn this into a story? Into a fucking fantasy where good defeats evil and love conquers all? The heroes in my life aren't rewarded, they're punished. And the villains? They win. The ending isn't happy, no matter how hard I try to make it be. I can't tell you a story because that's not what this is. It's my life, and it's pathetic, and it's brutal. It's hard, and it fucking sucks. Even this. Even being here in this inn, in a bed, and having food and shelter—even being with you, it's gryphon shit!"

Sean nodded slowly. "I know that's how you're feeling."

"No, you don't know! You don't know how I feel! You don't know what it's like. You haven't been through this! You don't understand."

"Then, help me to understand. Rhyan, tell me. Please. I want to know."

"Bringing me to an inn and feeding me... it doesn't fix anything. Doesn't change what happened. It can't bring my mother back. Or Garrett... or Bowen. It won't make my friends stop hating me. Undo everything and everyone I failed."

"It's not supposed to undo anything."

"Then what! What's the point."

"You. You are the point."

I shook my head, feeling nauseous. "You think you can fix

me, Sean? You think you can save me? Save this? Well, you can't! You can't fucking fix me."

"What if I told you I didn't think you were broken?"

"Then, you understand less than I thought."

"How so?"

"Because! I'm a monster. I broke my oath. I killed my friend. Everyone who ever tried to protect me, help me, love me... they're hurt, or dead, because of me. Either by my hand or fucking close enough. I've seen what it's like. I see how it's going to be. And this is it! This is it for me. And you might as well go! I'm not a good person, not someone to be around. People die because of me. People lose because of me."

"I'm not leaving you. And I don't believe any of that—not for a second."

"Fuck, Sean! Gods! Don't you fucking see? You're not like me. You're not going to get it. You don't understand," my voice cracked, "that at some point, you start to realize that life isn't fair. That you can be good and try and do the right thing, and it still doesn't matter. And after enough times of trying, and pushing, and giving it your fucking everything, you realize that not everybody has a happy ending. And I think... I think it's long past the time that I admit to myself that I'm one of those people. Admit that my happy ending doesn't exist."

"Your life doesn't have to be a fairy tale. Nor perfect. Not even close. Just because you think there isn't a happy ending doesn't mean there won't be. You're not done yet. You don't know the end. How could you? You're still in the middle."

"Only because," I sobbed. "Because I...because..." I was now choking on my tears. Barely able to speak. "I'm only here because I swore to—" I bit my lip, hot tears blurring my vision.

"Swore what?" His eyes searched mine. "Swore what? Rhyan?" he asked more gently.

My shoulders slumped forward. "To survive," I said, defeated like it was a big secret. A weakness.

"And you did. And you are." He brushed my hair off my forehead, long and wild now with matted curls. "But what if you could do more? What if we could start writing the rest of your story today? Take back some of your life, some control. Be your own author," Sean said.

"No." I wrung my hands together. "I make a gryphon-shit storyteller."

"I doubt that. You've never been gryphon-shit at anything you set your mind to. Quite the opposite, actually. Even with this."

"This? This what?"

"This!" he yelled, gesturing wildly at me. "I don't know what actually happened, not in detail, but it doesn't matter. Because I know you, better than you know yourself right now. I know that even if mistakes were made, even if you somehow made the wrong choice, I know you did your best, made the best decision you could under the circumstances. I've never known anyone who pushed themselves more or tried harder than you. No one! You put your mind to something—anything and you do it! Don't you get it? You're so good at succeeding, at setting your mind to your goals, that you even succeeded in giving yourself the most punishing exile you could manage."

"Shut up!"

"No." Sean stood. "I've been patient. I haven't asked you for anything, haven't pressured you, not for days. I've spent a whole week locked up in this Godsdamned inn. Much as I enjoy Cal and Marisol's hospitality, you know that we can't stay here forever. This isn't real life, and neither was whatever you were doing in that cave where I found you." He pushed his fingers through his hair and sighed. "Look, Rhyan, I don't expect you to change today or even in a month. You've been through shit no one at any age should have gone through. What happened wasn't your fault, you didn't deserve any of it. So, I know this is going to take time. But you're going to listen to what I have to Godsdamned say. I think I've earned that much from you."

My fists clenched, and my teeth were grinding together.

"Well?" Sean asked. His anger was rising, pulsing in his aura.

"Fine," I snapped. "I'll listen. But that's it."

Sean sat back at the table, his aura calming. He took a deep breath, and met my eyes.

"I think you have more power over your life than you want to admit, but you're scared. Because your father spent years of his life trying to convince you otherwise, that he was in control, that he had the power, and that he was the one who was going to tell your story. Well, guess what? He did. He sang his little song about you all over the Empire. And because you've been quiet, his voice has been the loudest. Your father is in charge of the story because everyone lets him be. But that doesn't have to be how it is! You escaped. This is your life. Right now, it's messy and confusing. And it hurts. But it's yours. I know you think you failed; I know you carry the weight of Lumeria on your shoulders. And yes, there's a lot you *can* control. But there's a lot you can't. You lost sight of which is which. Your father's power...it's ruined the balance. But you can still decide how you'll react, still decide to move forward."

Unable to meet his eyes, I turned away, my gaze falling out the window, to the life and business of people in the city, people I'd been terrified to see, people I'd longed to be amongst.

"You've come this far, haven't you?" Sean asked. "You escaped an Imperator, have evaded his reach for months. You escaped Glemarian prison, survived akadim, and being alone on the road with forsworn and Afeya and Gods know what else. That takes strength and will, things you have more than you know what to do with. I don't think you're destined for an unhappy ending. Truly. I don't." He paused, one eyebrow raised.

"But?" I said.

"But it's not just going to be handed to you either. Just like every other victory you've won, you're going to have to earn it. Claim it. And the first step is getting back your story. You need to stop hiding. Stop stalling. Let everyone know your side, too. Stop letting your father be your voice."

"How?"

"Come out of here. Come back to the real world, to your life. Even if it looks different than before, even if it doesn't have the same titles, there's a life out there for you. A purpose. People who need you. People who will love you."

I shook my head. "I can't. It... It hurts too much."

"I know. I know it does. The first step will hurt the most. But it won't always hurt like this. You won't always feel this scared. This sad."

It was so like what Bowen had promised me. And I thought back to what I'd promised him. I wasn't just supposed to survive. I was supposed to make his sacrifice—and my mother's and Garrett's and Kenna's—worth it. But I hadn't been doing any of that. I'd been living like my father was in the cave with me, making sure I suffered every day, making sure I was punished enough.

I'd been keeping the wrong oath. His. Not the ones I'd made to the people who loved me. The ones who'd fought for me. The ones still fighting.

"There's a chance I can't ever go back to life in public. At least in the Empire. I'm forsworn."

Sean took my hand. "Public opinion of you isn't the same

in the South as it is in the North. You made a positive impression on the Bamarian Arkturion and Arkasva in the past. And I can vouch for you. You're strong, and they'd be honored to have you join the fight. Akadim are spreading, their numbers growing like never before, and they're moving south. Agreeing to hunt, that's how I got leave to search for you. You've proven you're more than capable of handling yourself with them. Once you have the Arkasva's protection, your father won't be able to touch you. You'll have his backing and a different Imperator standing between you. A shit one, but a different one. I swear, if you come to Bamaria, you will be safe." He released me and pressed a fist to his heart twice before flattening his palm across his chest. *"Me sha, me ka.* There's a road forward for you. You just need to take the next step."

Living with Sean in Bamaria was what I'd wanted when I'd first crossed the border. "Do you really think I can do this?"

"I've only been waiting for you to realize it."

I wiped at my eyes, a wave of exhaustion washing over me, weighing me down. "I think I need to rest."

"Of course." Sean stood and pulled back the covers of my bed, holding them until my head reached the pillow. A minute later, I was out.

A scroll arrived for Sean the next day. He read it quickly, his eyes full of worry. But when I asked what it was, he only ripped it up and said it was work and not to worry.

The day after, another came, and then another. We were nearing a week and half at the inn.

"Your leave's up," I guessed. "Arkturion Aemon wants you back."

Sean ripped up the scroll as he'd done all the others. "My leave was up a long time ago. And so was my pay."

"Sean!"

He shrugged. "It's okay. Branwyn and I have plenty of savings."

"But you're disobeying your arkturion. Won't you be lashed?"

He was thoughtful, sucking on his lower lip. "Aye." He shrugged. "Worth it though."

I held Sean's gaze. "I want to come back with you."

"Good." He stood up. "Pack up. Let's go."

"But I can't...yet. I'm not ready. I just," I groaned, trying to find the right words, "I know I couldn't have saved Garrett, or my mother. But I keep feeling like I should have. And I know neither would want this for me. But I just...I don't know. It feels like I keep fucking fighting. Like I'll always be fighting. Fighting and getting nowhere, winning nothing."

"I know. You're tired."

"I am."

"It's okay. Be tired. Accept it. Rest. As long as you want. As long as you get back up. As long as you don't stop fighting in the end."

"Sean, what am I fighting for?" Everyone I tried to protect, I failed. Even when I tried to protect myself, it had gone terribly wrong.

"You're fighting for you. Because you're worth fighting for."

I ran my hands through my hair. "What if that's not enough?"

His eyes softened. "What about love?" He smiled. "I wasn't the only one who lost my heart in Bamaria."

Hazel eyes, pink, pouty lips, golden skin, and dark hair that turned to fire in the sun. A warm summer breeze. Scrolls from the library. Lemon cake. Batavia red. "You knew?" I asked.

He smiled. "I saw the way you looked at her at the solstice celebration. Saw the way that she looked at you. I knew."

"She's promised to another."

"So was Branwyn." He sighed. "I have half a mind to knock you out, tie you up, and carry you back to Bamaria myself. But I know now this has to come from you. Not me. You have to be the one to decide. So, here's what's going to happen. I'm going to leave. Give you some time. You'll be able to stay here as long as you want. We have the room reserved indefinitely. Rest longer, maybe venture out into the city when you're up to it. And then, when you're ready, Branwyn and I will be waiting for you in your new home. You'll be able to stay as long as you want. You can finish your studies there, become a soturion. You can have peace, until you're ready to fight back. Until you're ready to get your revenge. And I'll be right behind you."

CHAPTER
TWENTY-SIX

I didn't move for the first day after Sean left. I felt once more like I had when he'd found me. Alone. Lost. I'd heard his words. Repeated them in my head over and over, trying to remember it was different this time. I wasn't where I was before. I'd made progress. Had taken steps to being alive again, to doing more than fulfilling my oath to merely survive.

I knew even just being in this room was a big deal for me. Being in a city, near people. Sleeping in a bed. Not the floor. Not in the wild. These weren't things I'd planned to experience again. Not in Lumeria.

But Sean's absence still hit harder than I'd expected.

He'd given me so much—more than anyone had in a long time. It was hard to accept it all.

Hard to process, hard to take in.

But mainly, I just missed him.

Cal and Marisol checked on me a few times that first day, bringing me meals, and still acting so happy to see me each time. I was a wretch. A right gryphon-shit asshole. I wasn't sure how they could stand me. But I at least managed to say thank you, when they came to the room at the end of the day. It was a start.

The following morning, I got up. My body ached—not in the way I was used to it aching. Not from hard work. Not from exhaustion or brutality. But for once, from too much stillness. I needed to stretch. To move. To run. This was the longest I'd gone without exercise since my imprisonment.

Cal knocked on my door once I'd dressed. I'd tentatively opened the curtains, letting the morning sun stream inside. I'd even cracked the window open, feeling the spring air enter on a cool breeze. It was warmly spiced with the scents of the city, mixed with flowers, and blooms from the nearby park and woods.

"Heading out today, Rhyan?" Cal looked hopeful.

I bit my lip. "I'm going to try."

"That's wonderful," he said with a clap. Then, he eyed the food he had floating on a silver tray between us. Smoke billowed in waves from a small opening on the platter's lid. "I'm sorry, I assumed you'd eat up here as usual. Would you prefer to take your breakfast in the dining hall? It's no trouble at all."

I shook my head, my throat already dry. I was going to go outside of Auriel's Flame. But socializing with anyone besides Cal and Marisol... that was still too much.

Still too dangerous. As it was, I'd need to keep my hood up, and drawn close. I had to remain invisible.

He nodded, his stave directing the tray to one of the room's small tables. "You need anything at all, let me know. And Marisol knows every place in the city worth visiting if you need recommendations. Museums. Libraries."

I stared at my boots. "No... I–I'm just going to take a walk,"

I'd been here before, with my father on a state visit to

Arkasva Zarine. I'd spent hours exploring Thene with Bowen...
well, with Bowen walking sourly behind me. I remembered
he'd been in a particularly grumpy mood. My mother had been
meant to accompany us that day to visit the temple and art
galleries. She loved art. But my father had demanded she stay
behind to attend Court. Apparently Arkasva Zarine found her
attractive. We had no choice but to leave her at the fortress.

Cal smiled, running his fingers through his white hair.
"Enjoy then," he said. "You'll be all right."

"Thanks for the offer," I said, and Cal left the room.

But my stomach was already twisting. Guilt wracked
through me. How was I supposed to just walk around when
Bowen would never trail behind me again? When he and my
mother would never steal an extra secret glance at one
another? When Garrett... Garrett would never even get to see
Thene?

I stared at the room in disgust, at my hot platter of breakfast so carefully made, at the bed with its soft mattress and
warm blankets, at the door that gave me safety and privacy. I
didn't deserve this, living here for free. Being served like I was
—like I was noble. Like an Heir Apparent.

I was no longer a noble. I wasn't an heir. Not anymore.

I was not *Lord Rhyan Hart*. Just Rhyan now.

Nothing else.

I braced myself for a new wave of grief, but it didn't come.
The thought didn't plague me as it had before. I realized, for
the first time, that I didn't actually miss it. I didn't want my
title. I didn't want anything he'd given to me. Not when it tied
me right back to him, to being his son, his likeness. His
property.

I took a deep breath, sat down, and forced myself to eat.

Then, I wrapped myself in my cloak, careful to keep it
folded over my Glemarian armor. I put my hood up, concealing

my face. My stomach churned, and my heart thundered violently as I crossed the threshold. And then, for the first time in days—I left my room. With tears in my eyes, I left the inn.

The sun was warm on the small area of my face I kept exposed. I made my way through Thene, slowly remembering what it was to be part of the world, to be someone.

To be alive.

There were conversations happening all around me. Soturi on patrol discussing their schedules, their annoyances with the turi who were in command, as well as hushed talks of recent akadim sightings. Mages gossiped while on holiday. Scandals amongst the nobility, petty disputes, or simply comments on the weather were exchanged everywhere I went. Vendors were set up around the street selling their wares, calling out to anyone who passed. Jewelry and charms took up most of the tables. But I also found knives and daggers for sale, stylized sheaths for staves, followed by endless rows of food.

I didn't shop. Didn't interact. If I saw someone approaching, I moved out of their way, crossing the street to avoid crowds. But after a while, the smells of the food I'd been admiring suddenly turned my stomach. The conversations caused my head to pound, and the gentle spring sun was suddenly too bright, the air too hot. I started to retrace my steps and went to a small park near Auriel's Flame to sit down. With grass beneath my feet, and trees hiding the buildings of the city, it was the closest to Glemaria I'd felt in months.

A pair of soturi marched through, both wearing Cretanyan armor.

I stilled, and stood slowly, stepping behind the bench to the walking path between the trees, attempting to vanish into my cloak.

One paused, looking me up and down. I felt his eyes linger

on the way I wore my cloak to conceal my armor, the drawn hood that shielded my face. I tensed.

I thought the search for me had died down. No one had seen or heard from me for months... I wasn't as exciting as I'd been when everything happened. And I wasn't recognizable here, at least not by my actual face. But my armor, and my scar...

The soturion's eyes darkened as he took a step toward me.

"Ashten, did you hear me?" His companion grabbed his shoulder with a teasing shove. "Are you listening?"

The soturion's eyes slid past me, back to his friend. "I heard you. Paid for her own drinks. Flexible."

"Bend in half flexible."

They erupted in laughter and I was forgotten.

Barely breathing, I stepped back, sinking deeper into the shadows, letting myself blend in. The trees behind me grew thicker and darker, the pathway coming to a dead-end. A strange sense of foreboding wound its way down my belly. I turned, goosebumps forming across my arms.

Something...or someone was in there. Watching me.

For a moment, I feared betrayal. That Marisol and Cal had been compromised. That someone had looked too closely, had recognized me.

I waited for the soturi to pass, their patrol taking them back to the city streets. I immediately returned to my room.

I didn't even say hello to Cal and Marisol as I returned. I just locked the door, my back sliding against it until I hit the floor, taking deep breaths.

I was okay... I was okay... I told myself that over and over, the mantra repeating for hours. My heart was pounding as if I'd just completed a habibellum, and my hands shook, even as I tried to focus on my surroundings. Small details. A random loose thread of my bed cover. A faint scent of a coffee stain on the carpet. The crackle of the torchlights in each corner.

I threw my cloak to the ground and stripped off my armor. Underneath my tunic was soaked in sweat.

Eventually, I made my way to the bathing room, to shower. And as I laid in bed that night replaying the events of the day, I remembered the warm sun, and the soft grass under my feet, the smell of freshly baked food and spices... the comfort of people chatting around me. Laughing. Smiling.

It was worth it.

For a full week, I ventured out each day. Staying out longer and becoming braver. I knew I couldn't speak to anyone. Couldn't risk a report of Rhyan Hart, the forsworn murderer, being spotted in Thene. I couldn't risk being reported to the Imperator.

I knew I needed to be in the South, outside of his jurisdiction. It was the only way to buy myself time to figure out what to do next. But this wasn't going to last forever. I was playing with fire, attempting to heal as I exposed myself each day. I needed an arkasva to vouch for me, to offer their protection. And it needed to be Arkasva Batavia. I needed to go to Bamaria. Where Lyr was. I just needed the courage to go.

When I returned to the inn at the end of the day, I finally found some courage for another thing I'd been avoiding. I entered the bathing room with the torches lit and looked at myself in the mirror.

My eyes were red as I stared at my reflection.

I looked...not like myself.

But less strange than I'd imagined.

My hair was too long—nearly at my shoulders. I had a full beard—something I'd never had before.

I'd been expecting those changes.

What had scared me was the scar. The blood oath. The

constant reminder that my mother was dead. That it was my fault.

It was shiny and red, running through my left eyebrow and over the skin around my eye, the edge tapering off at my cheek.

Now the outside matches what's within.

When I looked in the pool of the cave that night, it was all I saw. The mark of a murderer. A forsworn. A failure. I'd felt like all I was had vanished, had been eaten by the wound. No face. No me. Just the scar.

I splashed cold water on my skin and looked again. It was still prominent, still noticeable, but... now it seemed just a part of my face. It was no longer the only feature.

Still, I pushed my hair back over it, fingers curling.

I'd never be rid of it. Rid of his touch, rid of the reminder.

That wasn't a choice I'd get to make.

But everything else...

I opened my belt bag, searching for the razor I'd used to shave.

Instead, I found a torn piece of rope. The piece that had been tied to the red gryphon. The piece he'd torn the night we escaped.

I clutched it in my hand.

It was time. Time to tear my own rope apart.

I wasn't Lord Rhyan anymore.

But I was still a soturion.

As I replaced the rope, a small, rolled parchment poked out.

Rhyan,

You're going to be all right. I promise. And it's okay to take your time. As long as you keep your word and make your way to me. As I told you, the room is yours indefinitely. Marisol and Cal are more than happy to keep you safe, and keep you fed. Please keep eating!

I can't wait to see you. I know Branwyn is looking forward to meeting you. But until you're ready, I want you to find some comfort. Some joy.

I know nothing's been easy for you. I am sorry for that.

So, until you're ready to meet me in Bamaria, I left some money for you. Check the back of the desk drawer. Use it however you want. Get yourself something that will make you feel better. Even if it seems silly. Don't feel guilty about it. I want you to have it. I want you to have whatever you need. There should be plenty. Use it when you're ready for safe lodging, and for food every day as you make your way south.

I'll be waiting in Bamaria. We'll go to the arkasva together. We'll make this okay. We will find a way.

I love you,

Sean

My heart was pounding as I went to check the drawer, pulled out the carefully tied linen bag, and opened it.

The money wasn't just enough to get me comfortably to Bamaria. It looked like an entire year's worth of soturion pay.

"Sean," I whispered, taking a fistful of gold coins in my hand. Almost immediately, I realized what I'd do with the money. What I'd needed to do before I could go.

I took a few nights to walk the city, quietly hiding in the shadows, slipping into bars, listening to talk. I frequented the shadier parts of Thene, the parts where those who had something to hide would go. I found who I wanted—a mage that specialized in permanent glamours and body modifications— one who operated quietly, changing the appearance of criminals. A lot of highly skilled mages could have done what I needed—but I needed silence.

I waited until midnight, and I marched into her shop, a small rectangular room off an alleyway. There was no sign. No way to know she was there. Not unless you'd listened for days like I had.

The mage had raven hair that flowed freely down her back as she lounged on a chaise, reading a scroll. A small bell rang, but she continued reading. There were no items in her shop. No décor. Just her chaise, and a small table.

"Can you clear the skin of scars?" I asked.

Setting aside the scroll at last, she stood up. Violet eyes assessed me slowly as torches crackled in each corner of the shop. She sauntered forward in a blue dress that hung off her shoulders. "Can you pay?"

I held out a bag full of gold. Enough to house and feed her for a season.

One dark eyebrow lifted. "Up front." She nodded. "Always appreciated." She reached for the gold.

I pulled my hand back. "Terms first."

"You have no aura. Bound?"

I nodded.

"I can remove your binds. I can replenish your skin. Heal scars." She placed her hand on her hip, her head tilted. "Only physically though. Can't touch what's happening up there." She pointed to her forehead. Right where my scar lay.

"I understand."

Stepping forward, her eyes lingered on mine, and she made a clucking sound. "Can't touch broken oaths."

"No...didn't expect you could."

"You're not supposed to survive them." Her mouth thinned.

"They're not supposed to be forced from you either."

She shrugged. "I suppose not."

"Discretion," I said, "Is also—"

"Don't insult me," she snapped. "I know who you are. Why else would you come here? Why else do you think I'm so expensive?" Her violet eyes held mine. "Hope you don't expect me to curtsey."

"You have no reason to," I said stiffly.

"Good. Show me, before I agree."

I turned away, unbuckling my armor, and pulling them off my shoulders. I tossed the leather to the ground along with the cloak I wore underneath. Nerves crawled up my spine, sweat beading at the nape of my neck as feelings of being exposed, of being vulnerable rose to the surface. I remembered hiding my scars, mentally mapping each wound, lash, and injury. I exhaled sharply, standing tall, my back bare and on display. "Can you take care of these?"

I felt her step in toward me, a small shiver as her finger touched between my shoulder blades. I flinched, my hands balling into fists, but I forced myself to remain still.

My body had always healed quickly. But there'd been so many injuries upon wounds that were still raw when they were received, the process had slowed down. And the healing of scars had stopped completely when I was bound.

The bindings Connal had put on me... they'd been digging into my body for half a year now, unrelenting, keeping me from my power.

The mage clucked her tongue again, a flash of blue light glowing behind me. It cast its light onto the wall before it went out. There was a small rustling sound as she slipped her stave back into her sheath.

"Who bound you?" she asked. There was a small note of horror in her voice—as if one in even her profession didn't come across Connal's type of work often.

"Does it matter?" I turned around to face her.

The mage shrugged. "I'm nosy. Those binds are deep... nearly embedded into your skin." She scrunched up her face in disgust. "How have they not been making you farther than Lethea?"

I glared. "They have."

"I'll remove the binds first. Then, I can clear the scars. But only on your back... and arms." Her eyes dipped low. "Any other parts?"

"No."

"It'll cost double to clear you, and remove these bindings, considering how deep they are."

I'd been expecting that. Plenty of experienced mages could have removed the binds... but between how severe they were... and my true identity... I couldn't just go to anyone. I reached back into my belt pouch and produced a second bag.

"You'll be tired after," she said. "Sore. Are you staying far from here? Might not make it home without a friend to help." Her lip curled. "You could stay here after if you want—"

"No. I'll be fine."

"It hurts," she warned.

I forced myself not to roll my eyes. I didn't doubt her. But I also knew my own tolerance. I wasn't scared. Pain couldn't hurt me. Not anymore.

"Do it."

She gestured to the table by the chaise. "Lie down."

Hours passed as I lay on my stomach. Every rope she took off felt like a weight lifted, like my body was scratching an itch it had been dying to reach for months. Like my skin could breathe.

She paused on my lower back, the warmth of her stave hovering above my spine.

"A second blood oath," she hissed.

"Yes," I gritted through my teeth. "Can you remove it?"

"No."

"It's not broken," I said.

"It's still active," she said.

"That's impossible," I said. Garrett was gone.

She ignored my protest, moving past it to other scars.

I closed my eyes, trying not to think about it as she continued working.

After what felt like hours, she helped me stand, and I walked before a three-way mirror. For the first time, I saw my back.

Bare. Muscled. Pale. Sweating.

But the skin was pristine. Healed. Every touch of my father, of Kane, of Connal...gone.

She looked away as my eyes reddened, the shop silent save the crackling flames, slowly dying. I stretched, reaching my hand back, feeling how soft, how smooth I was.

Except for Garrett's blood oath. It was invisible as always. Only the skin was still raised.

But then, I felt a surge of strength. Of energy. Energy like I hadn't felt in months. I felt like I could run forever. The power that had been beneath my skin was radiating through me. My aura was awakened, and I blasted myself with its cold, drying my sweat. Even just lifting my arms felt easier than it had in months. And a smile spread across my face.

Then, just as rapidly, I fell from the high. Like I'd called on *kashonim* and had burned out.

She narrowed her eyebrows, understanding. But before she could make another proposal for me to stay, I dressed and stumbled from her shop.

I took one step into the shadows of the blackened alleyway, my hood pulled tight over my face, my heart pounding. I had just enough energy left for one more thing. The one thing I'd wanted—needed to access. The one thing that would always remain a secret. My stomach tugged.

I was back in my room at the inn a second later. I laughed, almost uncontrollably through my tears. And then. I flopped onto the bed, my chest heaving—half terrified of what I'd done, half relieved. And I passed out.

I remained in bed all of the next day as I recovered.

Over the next few weeks, I slowly began to come out of my shell. I started helping Cal and Marisol with chores around the inn, assisting with furniture repairs, and picking up food deliveries. They didn't really need my help. Not with their skill and years of perfecting their routines. But I was happy to offer it—to show some small piece of gratitude for their kindness, for letting me stay. For giving me shelter as I came back to life.

And in between assisting them, I used half of what remained in my fortune from Sean to see a tattoo artist. Maybe I wasn't ready yet to tell my story to the Empire, to drown out my father's voice. But I was ready to be the one in charge of my body—to have the final say in its modification.

Every day she added more details, drawing out the red gryphon on my back, the mountains of Glemaria, the talons. The torn rope. All in intricate, exquisite detail. The kind of art that was reminiscent of the Temple of Wind.

The kind of art my mother would have loved.

On the last day, she inked my shoulders and my collarbone with gryphon wings. So I would remember. So I would never forget.

I'd never be tied down. Never bound. Never caged.

Next time I was going to remember. I had to tear the rope apart.

And at the end of the day, my skin itchy and sore from healing, I fell onto my bed. I was careful to not disturb the ink healing on my shoulders and chest. But my back seemed to burn... burn in a way that it hadn't in months. Something niggled in the deepest corners of my mind, but I was too tired to catch the thought. I reached blindly onto my nightstand, found a jar of moon tree oil. I gathered as much as I could on my fingers, sat up and slapped it onto my back. Then, I passed out.

~

Waves crashed against my face, *cold and salty as my body rocked back and forth. Panic fluttered in my belly, until I opened my eyes.*

I lay on a raft, floating in the center of the ocean. There was nothing but endless miles of blue water, and darkening blue skies. I sucked in a breath, terrified at how isolated I was. How far from civilization. How alone.

Violent waves rose in the distance, rising higher and higher, stretching farther into the sky than I could see. These were the kinds of waves that could swallow a city. Drown a continent. Change the face of the world.

"They can't hurt you," Lyriana said. Her voice sounded distant, but she lay on the raft beside me, her hand holding mine, thumb rubbing soothing circles over my palm. Her hair fell in loose waves, flaming red beneath the sun.

She wore a red dress. Batavia red.

And for a second, she seemed to glow. Stars shimmered above her head. Her skin shined golden with firelight. There was no more ocean, no more sky, no blue. All I could see was Lyriana.

All I could see was red.

My heart thundered.

"Lyr," I breathed. "You drowned."

"I know," she said, her voice like the rush of the waves. "It's okay. I came back." She shook her head. "Don't worry. It's not like last time."

"Last time?"

She smiled sadly. "You don't remember yet. You will."

I blinked, not understanding. "Are you okay?"

Her hazel eyes held mine, blinking slowly. "I found you a raft."

"But what about you?"

"I'll lay on yours."

"But I'm lost. I don't know how to get us out of here." I swal-

lowed, my throat tightening as I glanced around at our surround-
ings. At the endless expanse of ocean. The waves were still rising.
Violent. High. But above us the sky was blue, the clouds calm. It felt
like we were on the precipice of disaster.

Lyr's eyes held mine. A soft brown, full of flecks of green and
gold. "You're not lost. You never were. You just forgot."

"What did I forget?" I asked.

"Who you were."

I frowned. "And who am I?" I'd lost my title. My home. I still
wasn't even sure I could call myself a soturion anymore.

"Ani janam ra." Her lips curved. "I know you."

She rolled onto her side, propping her head up with one hand,
the other still holding mine. She brought it to her heart, pressing it
against the soft bare skin of her chest. My fingers curled against the
curve of her breast.

I stiffened. Everywhere. A sensation I'd lost suddenly returned,
with full force. I coughed, trying to shift.

"It's okay," she said, shifting closer, her body pressing against
mine. Everywhere I was hard, she was soft, and warm, and
welcoming.

"Lyr," I slipped my hand from hers, fingers dancing to her
collarbone, up the smooth skin of her neck, until I cupped her
chin.

The raft began to rock harder, and I tightened my hold on her,
afraid she'd slip away.

"We need to get out of here," I said.

She nodded.

"I don't know what to do."

"You know. But you're not done," she said. "Not yet."

"What do you mean?"

"Rhyan, you have to wake up."

I shook my head. "It's a dream. And you're here. I don't want to
wake up."

"Rhyan, you must. You have to wake up now." Her voice had grown in urgency, the clouds darkened above.

"Please," I begged.

"Wake up!"

My palm cupped her cheek, and she pressed her hand to mine, her thumb rubbing over my fingers.

Her hazel eyes vanished, replaced with blue eyes. Blue eyes I knew. Blue eyes I'd watched close forever.

And then the blue vanished, leaving behind eyes that were red.

"Wake up!"

A bell rang. Louder, and louder the sound pounding in my ears, vibrating in my chest.

Lyr screamed.

I opened my eyes, sitting right up, as my blanket fell to the floor. Warning bells were ringing through Thene.

And downstairs, Marisol screamed in terror.

"Akadim! Help!"

I flew from the bed, throwing on my boots, and armor. I grabbed my sword, and with a tug on my belly, I was down the stairs.

A beast twice the height of Marisol and Cal had cornered them in the lobby of Auriel's Flame. Marisol was holding Cal up, there was a slash to his stomach, his tunic torn open.

The monster wore a soturion cloak, ratted and caked with dirt. Its armor was gone—wouldn't have survived the transition–but a leather soturion belt was strapped to its back.

"Hey!" I screamed, running forward with my sword raised.

I wasn't thinking. I wasn't afraid. I only saw a demon trying to hurt my people. Cal and Marisol were mine. In the past few weeks, they became my family.

I wasn't *Lord Rhyan* anymore.

But was I still a soturion.

Only three words were in my mind.

Stop the threat.

The akadim froze when it heard me and growled low. But rather than turning and fighting, it raced for the door, running into the night. And I was right behind it.

Stop the threat. Stop the threat. The words repeated, growing louder and louder. *Stop the threat.*

My back burned like I'd irritated some old wound, but I ignored it. It didn't matter. I was going to kill this beast.

I wasn't going to let one more akadim live. Not on my watch. Not when it targeted the people I cared about. I couldn't save Garrett. Couldn't kill the monster who'd turned him. But I swore to the Gods, I would kill this one.

It ran across the street, into the park, its body nearing the woods. Soturi shouted in the distance, calling out. But they were too far away. It was up to me to take it down.

I retrieved my dagger, my fingers curling around the familiar hilt, and I threw it, using all my strength. The akadim swerved, the dagger just missing its body. But the blade sliced through its belt, and the bag it wore crashed to the ground.

I ran faster, the speed I'd spent years building up suddenly returning. Months of training and practice while bound now allowed me to move faster than I'd ever dreamed. The muscles in my calves burned. I was nearly on the akadim.

And then it stopped suddenly and turned. I froze, watching in horror as it pulled its hood off, red eyes boring into me. Sharpened fangs protruded from its lips.

Sharp pain shot through my back; it was on fire like it never had been before. I cried out.

"How does it feel?" the akadim asked, its voice low, gravelly. Monstrous. And yet there was an undertone I knew. Something familiar in the tenor. In its accent. "Your broken promises?"

My eyes widened, taking in the blonde waves, the familiar

shape of its eyes, the face that I'd loved, now enlarged, grotesque, a demon's.

And then I saw it. Truly saw.

This wasn't just any akadim.

"Stop the threat," Garrett hissed, mocking me. Mocking us.

My stomach twisted. All the lies I'd been told in prison.

My father had never had him killed. He'd allowed him to turn akadim—allowed Garrett to become exactly what he feared, what he hated, what he'd fought against. I'd sacrificed everything to prevent it from happening. But it had. And he'd escaped.

I held up my sword using both hands, understanding now why my scar still hurt. Why the mage said the oath was still active. I'd thought I'd seen him in the cave before Sean rescued me. It had been him. All this time... I hadn't known because I'd been bound. Because I'd been hiding.

It wasn't over yet.

Garrett laughed. "Aren't we forsworn now?"

And then he was gone.

I turned, raising my sword, expecting to see him behind me. But there was nothing. Akadim were fast...but not that fast. There was only one way Garret could've escaped so quickly.

He'd traveled.

I thought back to the night of the blood oath. Of the way the akadim had hunted us, singled us out over the easier prey. How we'd feared they were hunting vorakh, how we'd theorized how catastrophic a monster with vorakh would be. It was why it had been so urgent that Garrett not become one.

I fought the urge to throw up, looking into the empty park. I needed to move. I needed to do something. Warn someone. Check on Cal and Marisol, all the guests of Auriel's Flame. But all I could think was we had been right. And now there was an akadim on the loose, one who was strong and trained in combat, who was already deadly alive. One who could travel.

I noticed the discarded belt bag again, lying a few yards away from me. I picked it up and opened it. Trash fell out. My stomach churned. It was proof of what Garrett had become. Proof I'd failed him.

There was mainly dirt inside and ripped papers. But there were also odd trinkets, a man's wedding ring, and a broken compass. Trophies. Trophies of victims he'd killed.

Gods. Garrett.

And then something that looked like a string of rope fell out. I picked it up to examine it, and my throat went dry. It wasn't rope. It was banners, banners of sigils of the ruling Kavim, all tied together. I recognized the colors right away though the banners were filthy, covered in dirt. And blood. Each one had been rolled up so tightly it was as if the movement had been obsessive. I could almost imagine Garrett as an akadim, sitting in the dark, twisting and twisting until the banners were hardened.

I unraveled the edge. Silver gryphon wings. A golden sun. A green background. Glemaria. Ka Hart.

And then the next one...the banner showed the sigil for Ka Lumerin in Aravia. The golden Valalumir of Emperor Theotis in Numeria was next. And then the sigil for Ka Zarine in Cretanya...

My heart pounded. The banners were in geographical order, the northernmost Kavim at the top. It wasn't just a regular akadim trophy. It was a clue to where he was going. Garrett had been turned in Glemaria. And he'd been in Aravia. That was where I'd first seen him. And now Cretanya. I could lay the banners down on a map, and create a near-perfect southern route across the Empire.

Only two countries remained to complete the path.

Elyria and Bamaria.

He was heading south. Did he know that was where I was going? Or did he have his own reasons for going there?

I gripped the banners in my hands, my fingers tightening painfully around the material as it all came together.

This wasn't normal akadim behavior. But nothing about this was normal.

Garrett was more than just an akadim. He'd become the weapon we fought against, and he'd been deadly in life. Worse. He was now an immortal with vorakh. And he was killing his way south.

Killing his way to Lyriana.

CHAPTER
TWENTY-SEVEN

D espite Marisol and Cal's protests, I was determined to leave first thing in the morning. Garrett could move quickly. Too quickly. I couldn't risk falling behind. I needed to get close enough to track him. Plus...it was time. I was unbound, I was stronger than ever. I couldn't hide at the inn any longer.

With my room cleared, and my few belongings packed and ready to go, I heard Cal's knock on the door. They'd already given me a huge breakfast. And coffee strong enough to keep me on edge for days.

I let him and Marisol inside. She'd been in good spirits despite facing akadim in the middle of the night. She was tougher than she looked. But just then, there were tears in her eyes.

Cal placed an arm around her as she tugged on a golden charm around her neck. It was a carving of Auriel. She squeezed it in her fist, and stared up at me, almost adoringly. They were the grandparents I'd never had.

"What's your plan, Rhyan?" Cal asked.

I shrugged. "Track the akadim. I know he's headed south. Then, go to Sean and Branwyn." I'd left out the part that the akadim was Garrett, that he'd been my best friend. That I'd sworn an oath to him. I left out that I had any other reason for traveling to Bamaria.

"Do you know where you're going to stay?" Marisol asked anxiously.

Cal eyed her, his face grim.

"Wherever I can." I hadn't thought that part through. I was going to use my vorakh when possible, but I still needed a place to sleep each night. I would need to enter each establishment with my hood up, find places where they didn't ask too many questions.

"Rhyan," Cal said, his voice low. He lifted both eyebrows. "Listen. Some advice? Stick to the brothels."

My mouth fell open, and I chanced an embarrassed look at Marisol, but she was nodding enthusiastically.

"Um," I said. "I'm not..." I sighed. "Not really...looking for that?"

Cal laughed. "Oh! *Oh*! No. Not for that."

"Not that there's anything wrong with it," Marisol said.

"Of course, not," Cal agreed.

"Right," I said. "I just, I'm not...um..." I looked back to Cal. "Why brothels?"

"They're not just for sex. They're for secrets." He gave me a pointed look.

For forsworn. For criminals. I should have thought of that myself. I'd found every other seedy place in Thene. But that... that part of me had been asleep for so long, I'd almost forgotten.

"There's one in Elyria, I can recommend," Cal said. "Not for sex," he added quickly, but Marisol didn't look phased in the least. "Right near the Bamarian border. When you arrive, tell them Cal sent you, tell them 'purple sun.' They'll give you a room. And they'll keep your secrets—as long as you keep theirs."

"Purple sun," I said. "Got it."

"And if you ever need anything, you need a place to stay, to hide...you come back here, okay?" Marisol said.

"I promise, thank you." I bit the inside of my cheek and shook my head. "I can never repay you for this."

Cal grinned. "You did...you'll understand one day." He removed his own Auriel pendant, letting the chain it was hooked on slide through his fingers and rest against his tunic.

I reached forward, giving them both hugs. But before I could say goodbye, Marisol handed me a small pastry box.

"What's this?" I asked, untying the golden ribbon.

"Wanted you to have something sweet for the road. They're still baking downstairs for lunch and dinner, so none of our desserts are ready yet. But I couldn't let you go without something." Marisol said. "It's from a local bakery."

I flipped open the lid.

It was lemon cake.

I bit my lip to keep it from shaking, and hugged them both again.

"You like it?" Cal asked.

"It's my favorite," I said.

They walked me out the door, my hood up, and I headed out of the city, to the park, and into the woods. And when I was deep enough, away from civilization, from any eyes... I jumped.

TWO MONTHS PASSED since I'd begun hunting Garrett. My back burned every day. It was nearly unbearable—like it had been when I'd first been bound. The only upside was that the hotter it burned, the closer I was. My blood oath was my compass, helping me track his progress south, letting me know whenever I caught his trail.

In every town, in every village he came to, I stayed in the shadows, watching, waiting. I listened for stories and gossip. For any hints of where akadim had been spotted. If anyone had been reported missing, if any bodies had been found. Every time the bells rang to announce the hour, I winced, preparing to hear a different kind of sound—the warning bells. But they never came. Garrett was like a ghost. Always just out of my reach.

I was tempted to camp outside—to avoid being seen and avoid interacting with anyone. Leaving Cretanya I was reminded of the danger I faced. And until I went to Bamaria— until Arkasva Batavia offered me legal and political protection, I still had to worry about my father's men.

I trusted Cal and Marisol with my life after my stay. But I would never expect, nor want them to be harmed in exchange for information about me. If someone eventually came looking, and they reached the right corners of Lumeria, if the mage in Cretanya, or the tattoo artist were ever approached, ever offered enough money... I'd be given up. I could be given up at any moment.

This left me living rougher in some ways than I had been when I lived in the caves, when I'd been completely isolated, only fighting off random gangs of forsworn, or beating back akadim.

But after a few nights, I'd followed Cal and Marisol's advice, and brothels became my main place of refuge. They asked less questions, and they expected shorter stays. Which was good—because Garrett was on the move.

Every time I swore I found him, every time I uncovered a nest, uncovered a gathering spot for akadim, or a place to store their treasures... or their victims... the activity would suddenly die down. Reports of akadim would stop.

Garrett knew I was after him. I couldn't decide if he was trying to lure me toward him, or not. Why tie the banners together? Akadim kept trophies, but why those? And why had he been willing to leave them behind?

Was there some small part of Garrett's soul that clung to his body? That wanted me to find him? Wanted me to fulfill my oath? Or had the monster simply come out to play, knowing that targeting me would torture me further—torture me in a way that only a soulless beast could delight in?

The former kept me going. I remembered hearing Garrett's voice in my head when I escaped Glemaria.

Stop the threat.

I tried to imagine if the roles were reversed. The mere thought sickened me. The idea of harming people. Killing. Or... worse. Dying by akadim wasn't the most horrific fate in the world. I'd seen enough evidence in the nests to know this truth. Naked bodies, some used, some torn to pieces haunted my nightmares. And the closer I got to Bamaria, the more I found.

Garrett would have wanted nothing to do with this life— would have been horrified with the harm he was causing.

So, I kept pushing forward, pushing past my doubts, and exhaustion. I had to find Garrett. For his sake. For my friends, for everyone who loved him.

And I had to make sure he never stepped foot in Bamaria.

Two weeks earlier, I'd arrived at the brothel that Cal and Marisol had told me about. It had been my favorite so far.

The brothel was made up of several tiny buildings—each room had its own hut. It offered privacy—privacy intended for a very different kind of purpose—but one I needed all the same. It kept me from being seen, being noticed. And it kept my identity hidden when Imperator Kormac and his warlord, the Bastardmaker, stopped by. Despite the privacy provisions in place, I was more than aware of their whereabouts, and just how long they stayed. And unfortunately, I was aware of how many companions they'd requested.

We were approaching Auriel's Feast Day again. The day. The anniversary. Jules's arrest. *Her* birthday.

I tried not to think about it. To think about her. Not when my focus was on Garrett. Not when I had a mission that I absolutely had to complete.

Imperator Kormac and his men had finally abandoned the brothel. I'd been keeping to my room more often, only leaving at night under my cloak. The Imperator knew me, even with the scar, he'd recognize my face.

He wouldn't turn me over to my father. I suspected I provided too much leverage for that. Someone like him would never miss the opportunity to use me. Horribly. And if I was indebted to him, or under his sole control...I wouldn't be able to help Lyriana. Wouldn't be able to complete my mission. I hadn't come this far, or come this close to finding my freedom, just to be bound to another heartless monster. Another Imperator.

Despite being nowhere near the Korterian border and the Imperator gone, I still saw the wolves, saw flashes of the silver armor of Ka Kormac, every day. They frequented the brothel far more than the soturi of Ka Batavia or Ka Elys. I remembered when I'd last been here, it had been Ka Kormac's soturi that greeted us. Something I'd never seen in any other country. It was one thing to have an alliance, to share soturi when protection was needed. But watching the way they marched towards the border after partaking at the brothel, it felt like an invasion.

After dinner, just before sundown, I stepped out of my hut, making my weekly trip to the main building for payment. They wouldn't accept advance stays longer, so this was my new tradition. I was praying it'd be the last time. That'd I'd finally find Garrett. Finally end this.

The front desk was empty, so I headed for the dining hall. The owner, as far as I could tell, lived there with everyone else who worked for her. Courtesans, maids, and cooks. This was also the building where they made all of their meals. And despite the secretive nature of the place, I still preferred eating alone in my room. I wasn't too fond of the company who frequented the hall—too many soturi of Ka Kormac.

I pulled open the door and stepped inside, annoyed I'd have to see more people. But it was surprisingly empty that night of visitors, at least the Ka Kormac kind.

And I didn't recognize any of the courtesans either. It was mostly women with typical Elyrian features—the trademark dark curly hair and tanned skin.

Quietly, I approached the table where the brothel's owner sat. I couldn't call out to her. Even after weeks I didn't know her name. No names were ever used here—although I was more than positive that she knew mine.

"I believe one lives," came a hushed whisper.

"You're farther than Lethea," said another.

"I am not. I have shown my evidence."

"Sorry to interrupt," I said, with a cough.

"Shut your mouth," hissed the second voice. She pushed her hand over the other woman's.

The owner rushed to stand. "You ate in your room." Her voice was accusatory, and I felt everyone's eyes on me.

I nodded. "Just wanted to pay for another week."

Then I realized, no one was eating. I'd walked in on some clandestine meeting. A meeting of regular Elyrian women. I could only imagine they'd met here because they assumed no one they deemed reputable would see them.

One mage carefully folded a flag into her lap, her dark eyes on me, glaring. Daring me to speak. I could almost feel the moment her gaze ran across my scar. The moment her face said, *I know who you are. And if we are betrayed, so are you.*

I nodded. The flag was gone. But it had shown me what secret was being kept deep inside the brothel.

The flag had been embroidered with an old sigil—one that had been banished by the Empire. A sigil that represented a Ka no living person was allowed to hold allegiance to. One that no living person could claim ancestry from. Because every last member of Ka Azria had been murdered by the Emperor. Murdered for hiding vorakh.

The purple Valalumir over a golden sun wouldn't be seen anywhere else.

Except in secret meetings in a brothel on the Elyrian border to Bamaria.

'Purple sun' had been the code word for me to gain their trust.

There was a secret rebellion happening in Elyria.

The brothel's owner played with a golden ashvan charm around her neck—a symbol of Ka Elys, of the ruling Ka she was supposed to be loyal to. She jerked her chin toward the door, walking briskly and I followed her back out to the front desk.

I made my payment, and she seemed to soften. I couldn't tell if she liked having me—liked knowing I was a guaranteed source of income. Or if she was annoyed that I never paid for additional services.

I tried not to think about it. I just knew that Cal and Marisol had told me the right thing to say. And that as long as I kept their secret, they would keep mine.

Once the sun set, I sheathed my blades. And when the path was clear, I snuck out, moving in the shadows past the huts, moving as the sounds of pleasure—sounds that had been lost to me for ages, grew in increasing volume. I took a deep breath, leaving behind the safety of the brothel, their torches and light, and I moved into the woods.

Within an hour, I found a nest.

Empty of akadim. But it contained a trove of random objects. A ripped soturion cloak. A broken sword sheath but no sword. And a trail of blood. One that led to a body. A young soturion. He'd been raped. Mutilated. A black mark over his heart.

Forsaken. He'd be akadim the following night.

I said a prayer and chopped off his head.

My back was on fire, but there was no sign of Garrett, except for one message.

It had been painted onto the wall of the cave. In blood.

You can't stop the threat.

I hunted until the day broke, then I returned to my room, my eyes shutting as the sun rose.

I repeated the process the following night, and the next night after. I'd started traveling lightly around Elyria. Careful not to jump too far. Whatever distance I crossed would equal how exhausted I was when I arrived. I needed to move quickly, to cover as much ground as possible. But I couldn't lose my strength. Couldn't risk being too tired when I faced Garrett. When my back burned, when the pain of the scar increased, I knew I was close. And when the pain lessened, I redirected myself.

And then, exactly one week until Auriel's Feast Day, I was on patrol. It was early in the night. The sun had just set, but the heat clung to the air. And my back was on fire. I was moving south, moving toward Bamaria.

Something felt different. Odd. With every step I took, my stomach churned, the pain so bad I was nauseated.

Bamarian sun trees surrounded me with their familiar

shape. The shape of the leaf I'd held in my hand for weeks traveling across the Empire. The leaf I'd kept hidden for a year, until I burned it.

That felt like a lifetime ago.

The forest around me grew quiet. No birds. No seraphim flying overhead. I stopped moving, stopped breathing. And I waited. But there was nothing. I continued on, making tiny jumps to avoid the sound of my footsteps, my stomach tugging, my boots hitting the soft forest ground, again and again. Every time I traveled, my eyes widened, searching the area, my breath held as I listened.

The bells rang. The hour was called. Almost immediately dozens of blue lights lit up the sky. Ashvan on patrol.

I was so close to Bamaria. To her.

I stared, my heart fluttering. We'd watched ashvan that night together, hidden in the trees. I'd forgotten that detail. Forgotten how beautiful they were. How sure they were of their steps. Knowing that every time they needed support— the magic appeared. A blue light formed and allowed these animals without wings to take to the sky and fly.

For a moment, the forest faded away. I was back in time.

And then a branch cracked behind me. I shifted my gaze, my heart pounding. Another cracked. Louder. But this one sounded like it was in front of me.

I tensed. Two akadim?

We were right at the border... I could jump. I could jump and alert the first soturion I found of the danger.

But as I remained still, my hood pulled close, my body camouflaged and hardly visible in the night, I heard nothing else behind me. Only in front. The akadim was on the border.

Sweat was pouring down my forehead as I sucked in a breath and took a step. The blue lights still made the sky glow, casting shadows around me. The bells continued to ring. But they would stop at any moment. The lights would fade. I'd return to darkness and have seconds to determine what threat I was facing.

"Rhyan," the akadim sang. The same voice I'd heard before, deep, and gravelly. Monstrous. Taunting.

Garrett's voice. But not.

My stomach churned. I didn't answer. If he knew I was here, then he knew where I was.

"Assessing the threat?" he teased. "Trying to stop it?"

I barely dared to breathe. The bells stopped ringing. The lights went out, and my eyes readjusted to the darkness.

"Figure out how many?" Garrett asked. But now his voice was behind me.

Had that been him before? Was he moving?

"Don't worry." His voice was now far away. He was jumping, trying to provoke me by traveling...refusing to give me my bearings. "I wouldn't come with more. Too easy. You're weak. You never killed one."

My fingers tensed, and I imagined the feeling of my swords becoming part of my arms, natural extensions of my strength.

Stop the threat.

Become the weapon.

"Couldn't do it," he said. "Every single time. Never you. It was me. I'm the strong one."

"You died," I said, trying not to feel, trying to squash the emotion that rose up like bile in my throat at those words.

"Killed two. Killed the one that killed me. You couldn't do it. Couldn't help. Couldn't save your friend. All those promises, oaths sworn," he crooned. His voice was even more monstrous as he tried to feign sympathy. "You did nothing. Cried. Snapped my neck."

"I didn't know akadim spoke in full sentences."

"Old ones don't. We're improved. Can't say the same for you."

"It's not going to work. This isn't you," I seethed. I knew akadim kept their memories... but that didn't mean this was Garrett now. Garrett would have never said anything like that to me. Garrett was my best friend. He had wanted to live, and he had loved so deeply. He was a hero who'd die to protect anyone in trouble. He loved his friends. He loved Aiden. He loved his family. He wasn't this. He was nothing like this.

A monster without a soul. A demon who'd left a trail of death in his wake.

"That's where you're wrong." His voice was behind me again.

I squeezed my eyes shut, trying to catch my breath. He could come at me from any direction at any moment. Catch me unawares.

But he was also going to tire himself out like this. Akadim had energy stores, too. If I could keep him talking, keep him thinking he was getting to me, he might wear himself out. But he was making small jumps...the equivalent of circling around me. I didn't know when he'd last eaten... Gods... I couldn't think about that. Garrett feeding. Garrett killing. Garrett... raping. No...no. I just needed to be patient, even if it took all night.

"How am I wrong?" I jumped, vanishing and reappearing before a larger sun tree. I pushed my back against it, so at least he couldn't reach me from behind.

"Because this is me. I'm not different. Only stronger." He sounded closer.

My scar heated, and my heart pounded. "I doubt it."

"Oooh," he crooned, suddenly right behind me. "Finally had your binds removed? I was wondering when you'd travel again."

I tried to keep my breath even as I vanished. My stomach hooked and my boots touched down a few feet away. The dizzying sensation lasted barely a second. "Is that really what you were wondering?" I asked.

"Now you're playing. Good."

"Depends," I said. "What's the game?"

"No game. Just me killing you."

My stomach twisted. "I don't believe you. You could have killed me by now. Instead, you're jumping around like a child."

"Rhyan, that's not going to work. Don't think you can use your father's insults for you, on me."

More sweat ran down my neck. Garrett knew? He knew the things he'd said to me. My stomach twisted.

"Really," I said. "You say you don't want to play games, but that's all you're doing. Maybe you're afraid of me."

Garrett laughed. The sound was demonic and cruel. "You're right where I wanted you," he snarled. "You fell right into the trap."

"What do you mean where you wanted me?" I'd been tracking him for some time and he knew it... so if he'd chosen to reveal himself now...there was a reason. But why here? Why Bamaria? Why had he come here at all? If he wanted to hurt me, really torture me, why not lead me back north? Why not lead me to the place that he knew mattered? Why hadn't he gone where the people I'd sworn to protect lived? He could have gone after Kenna. Aiden. Dario. It made no sense. He had no connection to the South.

"I've been leading you. Here."

"To Bamaria?" I shook my head. "For what reason? What does it mean to you?"

Garrett reappeared in front of me, and I balked, barely stopping myself from pissing right on the spot. His lips curled, and his fangs were glistening. Up close he was so much taller than I'd remembered. I took in his features, his eyes. There was nothing left of my friend. Only a monster who'd pirated his memories.

"It's not what it means to me," he teased. "It's what it means to you."

Sean. Lyriana. Love. Hope. But Garrett didn't know any of that. I never spoke of what happened here. Never once discussed Bamaria. Never once told them of my friendship with Jules, or where my heart had lived the last three years. Sean had all but moved to Bamaria when Garrett and I became friends. As far as he knew, I was still falling in love with Kenna.

"What does it mean to me?" I asked.

He struck out and I ducked, barely avoiding a slash from his claws. With a growl, Garrett raised his arm, his hands clapping. "You know akadim can hear twenty times that of a man? I could hear you. Even with the windows closed."

I paled.

"Hear your blubbering, your cries in Cretanya. I heard everything. How pathetic you are. How weak. *You think you can fix me, Sean?*" he cried, his voice now a cruel impersonation of mine, of my accent. "*You think you can save me? Well, you can't! You can't fucking fix me.*" He laughed. "I guess you were right. Sean can't save you." He looked to the left, and the right, his movements exaggerated. "He's not here."

I thrust my sword forward, but as expected, he dodged. The movement was so eerily how he moved in habibellums.

"You spent months holed up in a cave. Pathetic. Hiding. Wasting your life away. Crying. Starving." He lunged forward, and I jumped, my stomach tugging. I reappeared behind him. "Because you thought you deserved it. Because you knew that was all you were worth."

My nostrils flared.

Garrett was gone the next second. Then, a claw stabbed my

head from behind. I jumped, my body vanishing. I landed in a clearing several feet away.

Myself to Moriel. This was like a twisted game of hide and seek. I needed to end this—or he'd travel further away at some point. Into Bamaria. He could reach Cresthaven. Sean. Or Lyr. I'd be too late.

"Are you just going to hide from me? Wait for Sean to come save you?"

"He's not coming to save me," I said, widening my stance.

"You're right, you'll be dead by then. Unless you want to join me. We could hunt, like we used to."

"We never hunted," I snarled. "We protected. And I didn't think akadim had friends."

"It's more organized than you know. Not like it used to be."

"Like searching for akadim with vorakh?"

"Part of it," he growled.

"Why Bamaria," I asked again. He could have destroyed me in Cretanya. Forced me to become like him. There was something else, something more. And I needed answers. "Why here?"

Garrett stalked toward me, the golden glint of the sun leaves lighting his eyes on fire.

"There's something of importance. Long suppressed. Some great power. The master wants it. Wants to unleash it."

The master?

You've made a huge mistake. That girl has the potential to unleash more power and destruction than anyone in the Empire ever has. You will rue the day we did not control it.

My father's words, spoken here, three years ago, came back to me.

My father had let Garrett turn. Let Garrett go. Let the akadim in.

Fuck. Fuck! This was about Lyriana. This was always about Lyriana.

"Did my father send you?" I seethed.

Garrett laughed. "A mere Imperator?"

"The Afeya?" I asked. "Mercurial?"

Garrett laughed even harder. "We are more powerful than them."

"I doubt it."

"Why? You think you're going to kill me now? I thought you wanted to play? Catch up? Ask me a million questions. Questions you'll never get answers to. Because you'll be dead."

"Or you will," I shouted.

And then he was on me, claws wrapping around my waist, lifting me into the air.

I vanished, reappearing behind him. And I slashed. My blade barely cut through his back.

He whirled around to face me as I rushed backward.

"Interesting spot to cut me," he growled. "Right where your blood oath is. Right where you'll be reminded for the rest of your life that you failed."

"I didn't fail," I said, my eyes burning. "I'm just not finished yet." My back was on fire, no longer directing me, but warning me that as long as Garrett walked, my oath remained unfulfilled.

"Think so? Think you can defeat me? You've already failed three times."

I lunged, my blade and dagger striking. I slashed his stomach. His blood fell. But not enough. The cut needed to be deeper.

He growled, and grabbed me again, his jaw snapping, nearly biting my nose. This time his claws pierced below my armor, into my skin. I couldn't travel. Couldn't escape. Not without risking greater injury.

And with a roar, Garrett's breath, hot and putrid, blasted across my face. He punched me and my head fell back, as his claws dug in. I heard the drip of my blood falling onto the forest floor.

The metallic sound of a clasp unbuckling rang in my ear, the snap of it unlatching, my armor coming off. It dropped to the ground.

My vision was blurring. I couldn't see straight. Couldn't think. Panic was fluttering in my stomach and my back only continued to scald me—reminding me of my failure. Of how I let Garrett down. And my mother. Bowen. Dario. Aiden. Kenna.

Sean.

Lyriana...

My eyes snapped open. Garrett ripped my tunic down its center. The warm air of the summer night hit my skin just as he threw me to the ground. I rolled onto my knees. Garrett laughed.

"A gryphon! And a torn rope!" He laughed even harder. "You think that's what you are? You think you're as strong as a gryphon? A gryphon who tore the rope, a gryphon who broke free?"

"I know I am," I said, my face heating.

This wasn't Garrett. This wasn't Garrett.

I rose to my feet, readjusting my hold on the hilts of my weapons, trying to recenter. To ground myself. Stop the threat. Become the weapon. Follow the chain of command.

But there was no command. It was just me.

I was the chain.

"You are no gryphon. You're a weakling who hid in the caves. Who needed their uncle to carry them while they cried like a baby. A weakling who killed your best friend, and your mother."

I rushed at him. And this time, both blades sank into his

stomach. It still wasn't enough. I needed to aim for his heart—or cut off his head.

I traveled, jumping back until my boots hit a tree at the edge of the clearing. I used it to push off, and I ran, leaping into the air.

In my mind, I saw Garrett up close—right where I wanted to be. I saw a rope. Saw myself tearing it. My stomach tugged, and I landed on his chest, my legs wrapped around him, my dagger plunging. But he shifted and I missed the heart.

He roared in pain, and for a second, my chest tightened. I felt sorry for him. Sorry, he was suffering. Sorry once again, I was in this position and sorry that he was, too—even if he wasn't really here. Because it wasn't right. It wasn't fair.

A slash to my bare back, and I fell hard. The air knocked from my lungs as I met the ground.

Garrett laughed. Fucking bastard. He was using my sympathy against me. Using the love I still had for my friend, to throw me off.

"I knew you couldn't do it." He vanished. The air whooshed from my lungs as his body crushed mine. He pressed me into the ground, his claw stroking my face, the sharp edge running against my scar.

"You're not the gryphon. You're this. Forsworn. Weak. Oath-breaker." His hand wrapped around my neck, and suddenly we were standing, my feet dangling in the air as he choked me. "And soon...dead."

Air was leaving me quickly. But I still had my sword in my hand. If I could just get my other hand around the hilt... I kicked, trying to move my body into position.

But I couldn't breathe. I couldn't...

I grabbed the hilt of my sword.

Garrett's eyes were on my chest. I could feel the heat there now. My stomach churned violently; a burning sensation danced over my heart. He was going to eat my soul. He was going to turn me forsaken.

But I was faster.

I was out of breath, but I still screamed, lifting my arms, my muscles burning as I used everything I had inside of me. I swung up. The blade sliced through his wrist, severing it in half. He let go of me, and the moment my feet hit the floor, I jumped.

My stomach tugged. I swung again, harder. The rest of his hand fell off.

He stumbled back, and then he lunged, his remaining hand scratching down my chest, pushing me onto my back. "Now die," he growled.

The bells began to ring. The warning bells of Bamaria. Someone knew. Someone had seen us, seen the threat.

It was enough of a distraction for me to regrip my sword.

Garrett looked around. "Still...no one is coming to save you."

I struck him, the blade sinking right into his heart. My muscles burned as I pushed and pushed with a grunt. His red eyes widened. And then he fell back, pulling me with him, my sword still lodged in his chest.

Tears welled up in my eyes, as I scrambled to my knees and pulled the blade out, his body twitching. One more hit, one more strike.

"Stop the threat," I whispered.

And then I did what I'd been trying to do for months. Not just stop a threat, or keep an oath.

I was going to do what I should have done ages ago.

I was going to save myself.

I plunged my sword through his heart, feeling the sickening sensation of it piercing through his body, pushing past muscle as blood spilled onto the forest floor.

His eyes closed. His body stilled. It was over. My oath was fulfilled.

Lyriana, and the rest of Bamaria were safe. For now.

A strangled sob came from my mouth as I stumbled backward, falling to my knees.

A light flashed above the trees, one I thought I'd seen before...before I'd fallen from the gryphon at the *Alissedari*. A rustling came from the bushes behind me. And a soturion ran, out of breath, into the clearing.

Dark shadows swept toward me, an aura with a force so strong, so deadly in feeling, it nearly blew me back.

And then a golden glimmer from the sun tree hit his cloak.

Red.

"You killed the akadim," said a deep voice.

I was at a loss for words. It wasn't just an akadim. It was all that remained of my friend. Still, I nodded in response, and took the hand extended to me, accepting help from the man bringing me to my feet.

And then, I met the eyes of the Ready.

CHAPTER
TWENTY-EIGHT

H is dark eyes were penetrating as he carefully looked me up and down. "Rhyan?" He frowned.

"Arkturion Aemon," I said, my throat dry.

His lips quirked, and he lowered his head, almost a bow, but not. "You greeted me at the border of your country, I suppose it's only fair I greet you at mine."

I tried to nod, but tremors darted through my body. My hands were shaking at my sides. The adrenaline of the fight was starting to wear off, and the reality of what I'd done, what I'd accomplished—what I'd lost—was all sinking in. Garrett was finally gone. Finally at peace...if those who became akadim ever found any.

"Was that your first kill?" he asked, both eyebrows narrowed. "First akadim kill," he amended.

My heart sank. "First akadim kill." Second time killing Garrett.

He stepped around me, examining the body, his hands fisting at his sides as his dark energy swirled around me. He removed a vadati from his belt. "Harren." The stone clouded with white mist before it glowed blue.

"Aemon," came the rushed voice of Arkasva Batavia. Of Lyr's father.

"Your Grace, the threat is over. I'm with the soturion who killed it." Aemon nodded at me once more.

"By the Gods," said Harren. "I'll alert Eathan."

"I'll tell Dairen."

"Very good. Bring me the soturion," Arkasva Batavia said. "I'd like to thank them myself."

Aemon's eyes narrowed on me, a calculated look on his face.

Throat tightening, I waited for him to tell Arkasva Batavia who I was. A forsworn. A criminal. A murderer. For Arkasva Batavia to change his mind. To demand my arrest instead. To bring me back to the Shadow Stronghold and keep me prisoner until my father arrived.

Instead, Aemon said, "Of course. I'm at the border, but I shall see you within the hour."

I felt overly aware of Garrett's body. Of my torn tunic, my scar, my long hair...of the vorakh thrumming just beneath my skin. Had Aemon seen me travel?

The stone turned white and Aemon tucked it away.

"Take a breath," he said, gathering my discarded cloak and armor from the forest floor. "An akadim kill can bring forth a lot of emotion." He looked uneasy, almost mournful at the body. "Especially if you knew him." His aura darkened, shadows pushing against me.

"It was Garrett," I said shakily.

Aemon nodded. "I know. I understand what happened."

My chest heaved, I felt like I was going to panic. Like I was going to travel or faint. Maybe all three.

"I killed him."

Aemon clapped his hand on my shoulder. "Then, you did what you were supposed to do."

"I'm forsworn," I said.

"I knew that, too."

"So," I said helplessly. "Will I be arrested?"

"You just defended all of Bamaria from a monster. Any arkasva would thank you for that alone. And as a forsworn, you are legally allowed to enter the country and request protection. I believe you have a very good chance of earning sanctuary here. Your uncle recently returned to Bamaria. He can vouch for you. And you have me as a witness."

"You saw me kill him?" I asked, my heart thundering. How much had he seen? I needed to know. The warning bells had gone off before he'd arrived...but who had seen us?

"As soon as I realized what was happening, I sounded the alarm. When I got to you, I saw you make the final blow. I am sorry I didn't get here sooner. But it seems like you had everything under control."

My stomach twisted. The timeline didn't feel like it made sense. Then again... nothing did anymore.

"Come," Aemon said. "I have an ashvan waiting a mile down the road. We'll ride to Cresthaven together and make your case. I assume you still want to be part of the Empire?"

My chest tightened. "I don't..." I thought of my father. Of the horrible things he'd done. To me. To my mother. To all of Glemaria. The North. Being part of the Empire meant still being a part of that in some small way. And though I knew Arkasva Batavia was nothing like my father, the thought of being bound to another ruler made my stomach turn.

Aemon arched an eyebrow. "You don't?"

My thoughts jumped to Kenna. To Sean. To Dario and Aiden. To Lyriana. Always, always to Lyriana. "I don't want to...not be part of it."

The corner of Aemon's mouth twitched. "And in this Empire, you don't want to not be a part of, do you still want to be a soturion?"

My chest heaved. "I am a soturion. I know nothing else."

Aemon slapped my cloak and armor against my chest. "Then dress yourself, Soturion, and follow me."

My ASHVAN TOUCHED down inside the walls of Cresthaven. Soturi stood on guard, still as statues.

Aemon signaled to the guards, jumping from the back of his horse.

I followed suit, my boots stepping once again on the waterway leading to the Bamarian fortress. The ocean rolled in gentle waves against the shore in the distance, the sound soothing. Familiar. It brought me back to three years ago.

To when I was still Lord Rhyan Hart. To the moment when I'd see Lyriana Batavia for the first time since we were kids. To the moment when I'd fallen in love.

But that wasn't going to happen again. It was well after midnight. I expected all three heirs would be in their rooms under careful guard, following protocol for a threat.

And I had to remind myself, Jules wouldn't be here...

The moonlight reflected in the running water beneath my feet. We had fewer of these in Glemaria. The mountains made them difficult to lay down. For a second, I felt dizzy watching the stream pass beneath me.

Aemon strolled ahead; his walk purposeful as he approached two men on guard before the double entrance doors.

"Evening Euston." Aemon nodded. "Rhodes."

Both soturi nodded.

"Arkturion," Euston said, as he opened the door behind him.

"And?" Rhodes asked, looking me over, his eyes falling on the snags in my cloak, the dirt caked on my boots.

Aemon lifted his eyebrows, clearly waiting for me to answer. For me to state not only who I was, but to own it.

"Soturion Rhyan," I said.

Our names were shouted in the Great Hall, and I stepped inside, seeing the grand staircase again. The columns that depicted the arkasvim of the past. Lyriana's ancestors.

I took a deep breath. Last time I'd been here, my father had dragged me inside after weeks of being trapped in his litter. He'd tried to humiliate me, weaken me on this very floor.

But I realized with a lightness in my chest and shoulders, he wasn't here now. After tonight, I didn't need to fear him the way I had. I'd be free from his reach.

And when I was announced into the Seating Room, it would only be my name shared. Not my title. Not the long, extended name he'd given me. I was no longer his to control. No longer his property.

Aemon continued walking briskly. The fortress was nearly empty. Almost eerily so. Last time, servants had been busy, rushing around the halls even in the middle of the night.

Considering the hour of the akadim attack, the nobility would have been home, tucked into their expensive villas and beds. It would have been deemed too dangerous for them to leave to come here for protocol. But even so, there was still a stark, almost ghostly feel to the hall that left me on edge. Something was wrong. Despite my circumstances coming here, more people should be around, running about Cresthaven, completing all those silent tasks rarely seen by nobility.

Aemon paused before me, and I recognized the door to the

Seating Room. This time when the herald asked for my name, I offered it proudly.

"Soturion Rhyan Hart." My heart still pounded as I stepped inside. Arkasva Batavia could still say no.

The room was beautiful, ancient, and elegant. Far warmer in appearance than ours ever could be. And it was calm. The Arkasva here didn't push his aura out, didn't make it difficult to walk. Red silk tapestries lay elegantly against the walls as warm incense burned in the corners. It left an ache in my chest. After all these months, I was homesick. Strange that a home that was the opposite of mine in every way had evoked these feelings. I felt a wistfulness for Seathorne and Glemaria, but not for how it was. How it could have been. If my mother had ruled. If Bowen had...

My throat felt dry, and my face tightened.

I longed for a life that had felt like this all along. One that had been less harsh. A childhood where I'd met my friends as children, laughing as we ran through the halls together. Less years of my life alone. A life where my days hadn't been filled with fear.

I wasn't naive. The horrors of the Empire were present here, too. They were in every corner of Lumeria. Bamaria wasn't perfect. Ka Kormac was far too powerful and invasive. But I knew in my soul as I approached Arkasva Batavia on his golden Seat, his laurel shining against his dark hair, that the horrors I'd experienced at home weren't here.

And more than anything, I knew I didn't want to be alone anymore.

I had a sudden, urgent desire for Bamaria to be my home. And at the same time, for Glemaria to have been everything it could have been. Everything it wasn't.

Maybe that's how it always would be. Yearning for a place that didn't exist. For friends, I couldn't reach.

For a lover, I could never touch.

Arkasva Batavia hobbled from the raised dais down the aisle, the limp in his leg as prominent as ever. He looked older than last time, still somewhat severe, but honest. And, as far as arkasvim went, kind.

I fell to my knees, my heart pounding. Fear coursed through me. I'd wanted to come here for safety, because it made sense. Because of Sean. Because of her.

But now—now I felt like I needed to be here. Every inch of my body felt like it was pulsing with the need to be accepted, the need to finally be told yes, you can stay. To hear yes, we want you here. I didn't know what I would do if he rejected my plea.

"Soturion Rhyan," he said, sounding uncertain, as if he wanted to make sure he had my title right. He shared a quick look with Aemon who nodded and then to me, he said, "Welcome back to Bamaria. It has been a few years."

"Arkasva Batavia, Your Grace. It has." My voice shook. "And this time, I come to you, humbly, begging for shelter. I wish to request sanctuary in Bamaria, Your Grace."

His golden sandals were before me, and suddenly two lightly tanned hands reached for mine, helping me to stand.

Auriel's bane. Please. Let me stay.

He shook his head, and my heart stopped.

"It is I who should be kneeling before you."

I let out a shaky breath.

"You have kept Bamaria safe. Protected my family and Ka. I am in your debt, Soturion Rhyan." His eyes lingered on my scar, and I fought the urge to pull my hands from his, to brush my hair over the mark. But then his gaze flicked back to mine, and he smiled.

No arkasva had smiled at me for as long as I could remember. Arkasva Taria had mocked me. The others in the

North had always deferred to my father to determine my treatment.

I'd forgotten a ruler didn't have to be cruel. Didn't have to insult to maintain his ego.

"Come. Join me at the Seat." He turned, his sandals slapping against the floor as he limped, his black arkasva cloak floating behind him. There was no golden border. A reminder that he didn't have full jurisdiction over the South. It was both a blessing and a curse. For Imperator Kormac had the power. Still, he wasn't my father. I was beyond his reach.

Back on the dais and seated, Arkasva Batavia requested water be brought to me and Aemon. He also sent for a plate of fruit, flatbread, and hummus. He waited patiently for me to drink, asking if I was hungry for anything else.

I could barely believe it. Not only had I not been tied up this time, but I was being fed. Being cared for.

"I hear your title is... no longer in use," he said cordially when I finished drinking.

"Yes, Your Grace. It was taken by his highness."

Arkasva Batavia frowned. "I've heard many things in the past year. Many rumors. Some highly unsettling stories, most of them about you."

I exhaled sharply and stared back. "I would imagine you have."

"Imperator Hart is a formidable man. I cannot dispute the claims of another arkasva for an issue I was not present to observe. You understand?"

"I understand," I said, my heart sinking. Maybe this was just a thanks. A small moment of kindness before he rejected my plea and sent me on my way. "His power has far reach, as does his voice."

The Arkasva nodded. "I can do very little for a soturion not sworn to me or my country," he said carefully. "However, I can offer you sanctuary, and my full protection." He paused. "If you were to become a Bamarian."

My pulse quickened. He wasn't rejecting me, he wasn't going to cast me out just because of who I was. He was trying to work out the legalities of protecting me.

"I would have to swear my oath to you?" I asked.

He nodded.

My stomach twisted.

As much as I wanted this, I could still see my father standing over me, demanding my oath, ordering my complete and total obedience. I could see Bowen's wrists, his blood oaths, and the line he always had to walk between them. I could see Garrett, holding out his dagger, the fear in his eyes, after he'd traveled with me away from the akadim. And I knew no matter how desperately I wanted sanctuary, wanted to stop hiding, wanted to be part of the world again, I couldn't give my oath to Arkasva Batavia.

I was done handing my life over to powerful men. Even if they were far kinder than the others. Garrett had died because of my father's rule. Kenna was tortured for the same reason. I understood now that Bowen had died, not just to save me, but so I could save all of Glemaria. Sean had known one day I'd want my revenge. And I knew it, too. Somehow, I would find a way to save my people.

I couldn't do that by letting go of where I'd come from—or forgetting the duty I still had to everyone left behind.

"I'm sorry, your grace. I cannot become a Bamarian." I bit the inside of my cheek, barely able to believe I'd said that after everything I had gone through to get here. But in my gut, I knew it was right.

Arkasva Batavia frowned. "That will complicate things. May I ask why not?"

"You may not be free to speak against my father." I took a

deep breath. "But I am. I am already forsworn. And I am guilty of many crimes. I regret many things. But I am not guilty of what he's said. And yet, his lies about me are nowhere near the worst things he's done. Not to me. Not to my Ka or my country. He is not fit to rule. I intend to be there the day he loses power. I cannot do that if I swear my allegiance to another."

I waited for the anger to come, for Arkasva Batavia to yell and scream. Instead, he sighed deeply.

"You understand that in refusing me, I cannot offer the level of protection you may require should he demand your return. I may refuse his initial request. But should he decide to challenge me, I may have no choice. My people will not be pleased to see another foreign armed soldier in our country. They would rebel if I entered into conflict in your name."

My stomach twisted.

Aemon stepped forward. "That is all true. But I believe there is a way for him to be accepted."

Arkasva Batavia nodded.

Aemon continued. "I believe we need him. Tonight alone proves the reports I've made to you are accurate. Akadim are growing in alarming numbers. They are becoming stronger, more cunning. They're more organized. And while I have faith in our soturi, I would feel much better knowing an akadim killer is in our service. Perhaps he is not here as a Bamarian sworn to you. Perhaps he is here offering a service as a private citizen—one we have a sudden and desperate need for. One that our Council can stand behind."

"And if Imperator Hart demands his return?"

"We are under no obligation to the North. We can refuse on account of the service Rhyan is providing. It would be Imperator Kormac's obligation to make the final call. If the people see Rhyan as a protector of Bamaria, even if he is not Bamarian, then we can protect him from any summons to Glemaria."

Arkasva Batavia considered, looking me up and down. "We would need Imperator Kormac's cooperation. He would need to publicly declare it." He frowned. "Refresh my memory, Rhyan. Your last visit was three years ago, correct? You hadn't begun your soturion studies yet."

"You are correct. I should be an apprentice now, taking on my own novice."

"Do you wish to complete your studies?"

That pang returned to my heart. The homesickness, and longing for something that never existed, and in some ways never would. But I wanted to train, to fight, to run. Gods, I wanted to study, and read. To share what I knew with others. To become even stronger than I was. To make sure not a single akadim entered Bamaria.

To keep everyone else I could from Garrett's fate. And to free any of his victims that were now roaming the South without souls.

"Yes," I said.

"Your strength is certainly impressive," he continued. "And we are in your debt. Rumors of the North do reach our shores, yet you are not so ill-thought of that we cannot make this work. But you must be aware, right now, Bamaria is simmering with distrust. It is no secret that my rule has been contentious for many. Many still feel I am illegitimate." He gestured at his foot.

"Keep his identity secret until Auriel's Feast Day," Aemon said. "It is tradition to present a forsworn for forgiveness. We can do that and at the same moment announce he is the hero who slayed the beast."

Arkasva Batavia's face was thoughtful. "Imperator Kormac would be present. He'd have no choice but to agree." He stroked his chin, a small, but nervous smile on his face.

"But that means you must remain hidden until then. No

one may yet know you are here." He frowned. "You will need a relative to vouch for you."

"My uncle, Sean, is a soturion in your service. He'll speak for me."

Arkasva Batavia nodded again.

"And finally, you must also submit to a Bound Five," Aemon said, a sudden darkness in his aura.

I stiffened. "What?"

"It's traditional," Aemon said, his shadows retracting. "If you're not willing to offer your oath, this shows you are willing to submit to our laws. Then, we can swear to Imperator Kormac, and anyone else who might question your presence, that you have done so. It will serve in place of your oath to Bamaria."

My hands felt clammy. The idea of being bound again so soon made me ill. But if this is what it took? "I'll submit."

Arkasva Batavia looked pointedly at my armor. "I have no wish for you to deny your roots, or hide where you've come from—you are too well known. But, would you be willing to accept new armor, with a new sigil? Something that is honest about who you are, but also where your loyalties lie?"

"Can the new armor still be styled the same way?" I couldn't imagine fighting in anything other than my style of leathers.

"That can be arranged," Arkasva Batavia said carefully.

"Then yes."

Arkasva Batavia nodded. "That should satisfy all possible complaints, and believe me, I must satisfy them. It is... a rather tense time for the Council. Understand, this will require me to fight some battles on your behalf."

"I will forever be in your debt."

"You will," Arkasva Batavia said slowly. "I am willing to do this because I do know something of Imperators."

I could sense there was more. That he was leading up to some new demand or condition for my sanctuary.

There was a cunning look in his eyes, and my stomach twisted. He may not have been my father, nor Arkasva Taria. But he was still an arkasva.

"I shall require your sword in my personal service. I have Arkturion Aemon monitoring the threats beyond Bamaria. But my concern right now is for those inside. Whispers of rebellion have grown louder. I have been targeted my entire rule. But now I have heard word of threats made to my daughters."

I stiffened, immediately on alert. "What threats?"

"Hopefully empty ones. But despite her distance from the Seat, I have become increasingly concerned for the safety of my youngest. Lady Lyriana."

My heart pounded just from hearing her name.

"You met her on your last visit."

I nodded slowly. He had no idea the extent.

"Your father was interested in a marriage contract between her and his warlord. I did not desire the match, and when your father retracted his offer... I always suspected you had something to do with it."

"I did not desire the match either," I said carefully.

"That interest has not died down, nor has it been relegated to just Glemaria, despite her well-known courtship. And now with rebellions being whispered, I...I worry for her. Lately, she has been revolting against her constraints. Threats are coming from too many directions, some outright, some sinister in their secrecy. In exchange for my protection, I would trust you to keep her safe."

I shook my head. "What exactly do you want me to do?"

"I want you to be her bodyguard, join her escort team. Protect her."

The words spilled from my mouth before I could think. "I would be honored, Your Grace."

His dark eyes were piercing, looking me up and down as he decided to believe me, to trust me. He clapped his hands together, a symbol of finality and authority. It was done.

"Then kneel, Soturion Rhyan Hart."

I knelt before him.

"You will swear your sword to me. You will attend the Academy and complete your studies. You will help us hunt akadim and make sure my daughter remains safe. You remain a member of Ka Hart, a citizen of Glemaria, and shall be granted the freedom to return to Glemaria for whatever purpose you choose. While you remain inside our borders, you will be given the protections all Bamarians are afforded. Do you accept these terms?"

"I accept," I said.

"Rise, Soturion Rhyan. You shall submit to the Bound Five at once. If you survive, you will be under my protection and rule."

My heart thundered so loudly I could hardly hear as Aemon summoned select Council members from their beds to enter the Seating Room. To witness my submissions.

He called on five soturi as well.

Only three Council Members came to witness. But with Arkasva Batavia and Aemon, they had five.

I remembered the arkasva's Second, a quiet unassuming man with a kind face and graying hair. Lady Shavo, the spymaster arrived next. She wore a cloak that made her nearly invisible. And then finally, my heart paused for a moment as a striking woman with red hair entered the room. Lyriana's aunt, Arianna. Her hair was paler than Lyr's in the sun, and though her face showed signs of age, her likeness to Lyr was startling.

Lyr. I was going to be her bodyguard. Gods... I'd be close. Watching her. Protecting her.

But never touching her.

They're together now. Officially.

She was still with Lord Tristan. But with this agreement... even if that weren't the case, despite what hope Sean had tried to give me, I knew the truth. As her bodyguard, I could never be with her. And if I refused to be her bodyguard, her father had little reason to continue offering protection.

I listened silently as Arkasva Batavia made his case for me, and Lady Arianna created a silver ring around us. My opponents spread out, surrounding me.

"Now for the binding," Arianna said.

I bit down on the inside of my cheek, bracing myself. Sweat formed at the nape of my neck. I felt caged, panicked...my stomach turning as if I was about to travel. Suddenly, it was all too much. What I'd agreed to, what I'd given up, what I had suffered just to be here.

But as she pointed her stave at me, it wasn't black glittering rope that sprung forth. Not the burning binds I'd suffered for years.

I exhaled, blinking rapidly, and almost laughed in relief.

It was just rope. Just a simple piece of rope. Like something we'd use on our gryphons back home

I knew exactly what to do with it.

Arkasva Batavia clapped his hands. "Begin."

413

CHAPTER
TWENTY-NINE

The whole sky seemed to light up in gold as the sun rose. I'd broken free of my binds within the first minute. Taken out all of my opponents while barely breaking a sweat.

Arkturion Aemon had brought me to the guest house attached to the arkturion's home within the fortress. But I couldn't sleep. I laid awake, staring out my window, listening to the waves crashing against the beach. I watched Cresthaven grow lighter as dawn came. Watched the blue mosaic tiles come to life, making the fortress appear as if it were rising from beneath the waters.

I was all too aware of the fact that Lyriana was in there. In her bed. Asleep.

And in danger.

If I was going to protect her with everything I had, then I needed to be strong and steady. I couldn't shut myself off from all my emotions again. But I knew beyond a shadow of a doubt my feelings for her had to be locked away. I had to finally let go. And as much as the thought of doing it hurt, if it kept her safe I would do it. Her safety would be enough for me. Enough for now.

Aemon had left early for duty but had a servant bring me breakfast. I was given instructions to remain unseen and visit the Katurium. There I'd been given keys to my apartment at the Soturion Academy—a private room in a building with the other apprentices.

I shouldn't have been given my own apartment. Not in my disgraced status. But because I was protecting Lyr, they thought it necessary. I was meant to be a silent bodyguard. One Lyriana was not aware of—one no one else was aware of either. Especially not before Auriel's Feast Day.

I did as I was told, leaving the fortress quietly. I wrote a letter to the brothel requesting my things be sent. I also sent a letter to Cal and Marisol, letting them know I'd made it. And after checking that my key worked, I headed for Sean's.

A beautiful mage with tan skin and brown curls opened the door, looking me up and down.

"Rhyan?" she asked.

I nodded. "Branwyn?"

She grinned and pulled me into a hug. "He'll be so happy." She closed the door and yelled, "Sean!"

He rushed into the front hall, took one look at me, and burst into tears.

I spent the next few days charged with learning Bamaria inside and out. And I had to do it unseen. My agreement with the Arkasva was dependent on my remaining invisible for the week. If I were caught before I could be publicly declared, I was fucked.

Luckily, I'd mastered becoming invisible in Cretanya, and though my cloak had clearly been through better days, despite some mending from Branwyn, it still allowed me to nearly vanish into crowds if I wore the hood up. Something that was easier said than done in the Bamarian heat.

But I endured, silently stalking the shadows of the city streets, treading the beaches, and quietly moving through every aisle of all three libraries, memorizing their layouts and doorways.

Aemon provided me with a list of places Lyriana frequented. Places she liked to visit. Urtavia. Scholar's Harbor. The Grey Villa.

Every day I adjusted a little more to the heat, as the sounds of drums and water dancers echoed through the streets, reminding me of her. I worked on hardening my heart, on strengthening my will. I started training in the Katurium each morning. Running off my lingering feelings. Running as soon as I woke up, exercising out my nerves and desire.

When Auriel's Feast Day arrived, I sat up in my bed, my body covered in sweat. The day was already hotter than anything I'd ever experienced. And today I was to begin my duty as Lyriana's bodyguard. On her birthday. And tonight, at the Revelation Ceremony, my sanctuary request would be complete.

I took a seraphim to Cresthaven. I couldn't go inside, but remained beyond the wall, apart from the other guards. I spent the morning standing beneath the boiling sun hiding in the shadows. Part of me hoped she'd stay inside all day, because despite my days spent haunting her routes and favorite places, I hadn't actually laid eyes on her yet.

Something I desperately wanted, wanted so badly I shook with the need. And yet, I feared seeing her. I was terrified I couldn't handle it.

Another hour passed and a seraphim flew overhead. Its golden wings spread, its body tilted in its descent. Warmth blasted toward me, blowing my cloak off my head. I rushed back, narrowly avoiding being seen by the guards at the wall.

The seraphim landed. Imperator Kormac emerged. Followed by the Bastardmaker.

My stomach churned as I recalled the night they'd arrived unexpectedly. The way everyone at Cresthaven had panicked on solstice. The way Jules had been terrified as I reached for her hand. I watched in disgust as Imperator Kormac's cloak blew behind him. The golden border of the Imperator left my heart thundering.

Not long after I recentered and resumed my position in hiding, a second seraphim landed. This time I was ready, keeping my hand on my hood to prevent it from blowing off. Two mages exited the carriage wearing blue robes closed with silver sashes.

Lord Tristan Grey emerged. His brown hair shined in the sun.

Light footsteps sounded on the waterway a few minutes later. Sandals. I couldn't bring myself to look. Fuck. I was her bodyguard, but I couldn't even bring myself to look at her. I wasn't ready.

I settled for pressing closer to the wall, slowing my breathing as I listened.

"There's my birthday girl. I was about to storm the fortress to find you." Lord Tristan Grey spoke like a true noble. Dramatic. Entitled. Self-righteous.

Bastard.

A moment passed, and there was no response. I wasn't sure if she was still walking toward him, or if they were embracing. My stomach turned at the thought. Gods...at some point, I'd have to witness them together.

"Sorry, I was late."

I squeezed my eyes shut. Her voice. Her utterly beautiful voice. My heart thundered.

"No escort today?" Tristan asked.

That grabbed my attention. How could she be without an escort? Didn't she know the dangers? I strained, listening harder. But their conversation was muffled. I could still hear their voices, but no specific words. I suspected his mages were behind it—making sure their conversation remained private.

Minutes passed, and then a gust of wind blew from the fortress. Tristan's seraphim took off.

I vanished, reappearing on the other side of the wall, deep in the bushes.

No wonder her father had asked me to be a bodyguard, if she was able to lose her escort this easily.

I reached for the vadati at my waist to alert Aemon, then stopped. She was already gone. Without an escort. I needed to act. I had to keep her safe, and prove I was capable.

It was Auriel's Feast Day...and her birthday. Where could she possibly be going?

The answer came at once. I remembered from Jules's letters that it was tradition for them to go into the city on their birthdays.

The absolute last fucking place she should be today.

All week I'd heard the murmurs, the talk. The akadim attack had been on everyone's mind. I'd heard it discussed in every corner of the country.

The Bamarians were furious.

That anger needed to be directed somewhere. Or at someone.

I closed my eyes, picturing the map of Bamaria in my mind. Since she was flying by seraphim, she'd land at the Urtavian seraphim port.

I had to beat her there.

But I couldn't simply travel. Too many people would see. I searched the map in my mind. There was a park south of the seraphim port. I knew a cluster of trees I could risk.

My stomach tugged, and I was gone. My boots landed on soft grass, trees overhead offering me shade as I stumbled into a tree, my chest heaving. That was my farthest jump in ages, and the distance I'd crossed caught me all at once. My muscles burned like I'd just finished a full day of training.

In the distance, the timekeeper rang the bells. Lyr would be arriving in just over a quarter of an hour, with nothing but Lord Tristan's mages as her guard.

Ignoring the pain in my body, I ran.

Sweat was pouring down my face as I arrived at the port. I'd reached it just a minute before she landed. My heart stopped as she emerged from the carriage.

But Lyriana kept her hood up, concealing her hair, and her face. Tristan's escort returned to their side with a litter for them. He closed the curtains as soon as they were inside. White with silver moons.

Of fucking course. Ka Grey had to have silver everything.

It reminded me of being stifled behind my father's curtains as our litter made its way here.

But then a slender hand with a golden cuff tore the curtains open.

I couldn't hide my smile.

I trailed behind, keeping a safe distance as they moved down the street, balanced over the shoulders of the mages keeping them afloat. It was more crowded than I'd ever seen it. People from all over the Empire had flocked here for the occasion. Most notably, Ka Kormac had arrived in full force. I spotted their silver armor in every corner, lurking down every alley. All around, people's auras were on edge.

Following the litter, I picked up as many pieces of conversation as I could, listening for anything that could be a threat. The locals were annoyed at the crowds. The visitors were agitated by the heat. And everyone was still on edge after the akadim attack.

The timekeeper rang the bells, shouting noon. Suddenly every hidden wolf of Ka Kormac stood forward for the changing of the guard, their armor instantly giving them away. The auras around me seemed to explode in anger as people began to yell.

"Go home!"

"Back to Korteria, wolf-shit!"

The insults grew angrier, more impassioned.

Then, a new voice spoke. "Fuck Harren Batavia!"

The mood of the crowd shifted immediately. I felt auras spike with fear at the message, but also in anger. Anger towards the arkasva, not the person who'd yelled. I remembered he'd been attacked in the city. He'd been right to be concerned for Lyr.

I picked up my pace, trailing closer to the litter, but not too close. Tristan's escorts were also on high alert. But what would they do if there was actually a threat?

"*Shekar arkasva,*" someone shouted.

False arkasva.

I'd heard a lot of insults hurled toward Lyr's father in the past week. But this gave me pause. The mage who'd spoken waved a flag with what appeared to be a bastardized sigil of Ka Batavia. The iconic gold wings had been painted black.

It wasn't just a message. It was a signal.

But the litter moved ahead. I had a bad feeling. Lyr's father had told me there were whispers of rebellion. This was shouting.

I kept pace as they turned, hoping they would recognize the danger and return immediately to the seraphim port.

Instead, they stopped at what were clearly rows of vendors for the nobility. Lyriana stepped out, her hood still up, her identity hidden. Though it was clear from her gold jewelry and the fineness of her dress underneath that she was noble.

Tristan held her hand possessively, and my pulse spiked as she learned toward him, kissing him quickly. I clenched my jaw, but they'd separated, heading in opposite directions. A woman with red hair stood outside a tent adorned with silk scarves. I recognized her as one of the librarians from the Afeyan Library.

A shopkeeper started yelling before Lyriana walked into the librarian's tent.

I glared at the man, most likely disgruntled he'd lost a potential customer, then blended into the crowd of shoppers. Pretending to shop, my eyes remained fixed on the tent, waiting for Lyr to come outside.

It wasn't long before Lyr exited the tent slowly and weaved her way through the tables. One of Tristan's mages kept close behind her, forcing me to maintain my distance. She finally paused before a vendor. A mage with a black curling mustache stood before a table, gesturing grandly at his products. But Lyr seemed uninterested. Tristan joined her a moment later and they returned to their litter.

Based on the direction the litter mages faced, I decided to run ahead, to scout out what they'd be walking into, rather than what remained behind.

I quickly hit a crowd of people, their bodies pressing together, as auras full of fear and anxiety burst toward me.

Something was wrong. Something I didn't want Lyr to run into. I pushed my way forward.

A few people were singing a song about vorakh, cursing them all to drown. Within seconds, more voices joined, the song quickly turning from a taunt to a death chant. I pulled my hood forward and made my way closer.

The crowd had surrounded a troupe of water dancers—the same one the litter had paused in front of earlier for a performance. But none of the girls were dancing now. They'd all huddled protectively around one of the performers. She was shaking, her eyes widening with fear.

A wave of cold swept toward me, leaving shivers down my spine. The sensation was new, yet there was something familiar about it.

I rarely felt cold like this in the South.

The dancer started thrashing, yelling in fear at something only she could see.

"Vorakh! Vorakh!" came the jeers.

She was having a vision.

I pushed forward, my instinct to go to her, to help her. To pick her up and carry her to safety.

Nausea roiled through my belly. I could feel her distress, her terror. And instead of getting help, she was being mocked and attacked.

Garrett's fears about Aiden discovering his secret rushed through my mind.

I wanted to scream. And I didn't even know this girl.

Had this been what it was like? Was this what Lyr had seen?

Had Bamaria sung this song at Jules? I felt sick.

I took another step forward, then stopped myself as Lyr's litter moved closer. Tristan leapt out, his stave unsheathed as he parted the crowd, racing for the dancer with death in his aura.

I slipped further into the crowd, watching helplessly. I couldn't save her. Couldn't help her. Not without risking my life, being seen. Risking being able to protect Lyriana.

"I am Lord Tristan Grey." His aura exploded, anger and hatred bubbling to the surface. "You have been accused of possessing vorakh in the first order, the power of visions. I will bind you and hand you over to the Soturi of Ka Batavia, where you will be arrested and sentenced by his Highness, the Imperator."

Fuck. I'd spent the last two years so consumed with my jealousy of Tristan, I'd forgotten he hunted vorakh.

Forgotten he would hunt me if given the chance.

I couldn't watch, couldn't bear to see the girl in pain, afraid.

Like I imagined Jules had been.

Suddenly she rushed forward, sensing the danger in front of her. Sensing Tristan. Her nails were like claws as she threw herself into the attack. But she never stood a chance.

Black ropes glowing red shot from his stave, violently wrapping around the girl like snakes squeezing their prey.

My face heated, and my stomach turned. I stared down at my hands as panic rose inside of me.

No ropes. No ropes.

The girl screamed. And then she stopped. Tristan hauled her bound and limp body over his shoulder.

And the danger I still faced became more apparent than ever. I would be under the nose of one of the Empire's most vicious vorakh hunters.

I took a deep breath, trying to focus on small details. My hands were clear. A coffee shop was brewing a fresh batch of beans down the street. A drum had played rhythmically behind me. The water streaming beneath my feet shimmered under the sunlight.

"Glemaria?" a soturion asked, breaking my concentration. I looked up to see that his gaze had gone right to my armor, the gryphon wings and sun marked into the black leather.

Fuck. Fuck! I wasn't supposed to be seen yet.

I rolled my shoulders back, pushed my fear down. "What's it to you?" He wore the silver of Ka Kormac. A fucking wolf. Of course.

"Heard the Glemarian heir's been on the run. Bet his daddy would give a nice prize if I brought him back."

"Hmmm," I said disinterestedly. I carefully took a step back, pretending to look for someone, all while keeping Lyr's litter in my periphery. The crowd was cheering for Tristan now. Every clap made me want to flinch.

"Heard he's got a nasty scar 'cross his face. Looks like a monster," the soturion continued.

"Really? Sounds horrific." I took another step back, mentally marking the possible exits. An alleyway to my right. A shop with a back door behind me.

"Why don't you show me your face?" he snarled.

"Why don't you breathe through your nose?"

"What?" he asked.

His moment of confusion was all I needed. I slipped through the crowd, walking away from him as fast as I could without drawing more attention.

"I know it's you," he shouted. "Forsworn bastard."

I kept walking, watching as Tristan climbed back into the litter.

"Forsworn!" came another shout.

Fuck. The wolf had a friend. My pulse quickened. I needed to lose them before they formed a pack. I'd seen Ka Kormac fight before. They relied on their brute strength and sticking together, intimidating through numbers. I didn't doubt I could fight them. I didn't doubt I could defeat them. Easily.

But no one was supposed to know I was here.

If I was recognized, and word reached any local Glemarian

representative...I could be snatched back north before night-fall. Bound and helpless.

And now that I could see the dangers lurking beneath the surface in Bamaria—there was no way in hell I was leaving. Not until the rebellion calmed down. If it ever did.

I swerved in and out of the crowd, sneaking into an alley-way. My heart thundered so loudly; I was sure the whole city could hear. Everything felt so loud, and bright.

Backing further into the shadows, I spotted an abandoned alley across the waterway, closed my eyes, and felt my feet leave the ground.

I slammed into a wall, resting my forehead against the cool stone for a moment before I straightened and emerged back into the crowd, the pack of wolves now in front of me.

That had been close. Too close.

Lyr's litter paused ahead of me, allowing her and Tristan to enter a restaurant. I retreated into the maze of pop-up bazaars, pretending to shop the wares for sale. The wolves were nowhere to be seen.

After some time, the restaurant door opened. Her face remained concealed in the shadows of her hood. I walked around a particularly long table, my eyes on her as Tristan placed his hand on her back, helping her into her seat. My hands fisted at my sides, an ache coming to life in my chest.

Someone grabbed me from behind.

Before I could react, a thick arm wrapped around my neck as the Ka Kormac soturion from earlier rushed before me. He pushed my hood back, his eyes slowly moving down my scar. A sinister smile curved his lips as he snarled. "Told you it was you."

I was surrounded. Wolves. Bamarians. Lyr's litter wasn't far away.

A thousand opportunities for me to be caught, to be

exposed. To be exiled.

I bit the inside of my cheek, fear tightening to a coil in my stomach.

I just had to stay calm. I could fight these fuckers. Disappear. I just needed to survive a few more hours. And then everyone would know I'd slain an akadim. Know I'd been rewarded with the Arkasva's protection.

Swallowing roughly, I glared at the wolf. "Congratulations. I am in fact me. Your parents must be so proud. Now kindly, fuck off."

"I don't think so. Plan to get a prize."

"Plan again." I thrust my arms up and elbowed the soturion behind me. I could hear the crash as he fell into the table. The shopkeeper cursed wildly.

I kicked the soturion still in front of me. And then I ran.

There were people everywhere. Traveling wasn't a possibility. It was too risky—I'd land where someone would see. But the crowd barely allowed me to move. I started pushing people aside until I lost track of the soturi again.

And Lyriana.

Fuck. If something happened to her...

I whirled around, trying to find the litter. Instead, the soturion found me. This time he had friends. Two grabbed my arms, dragging me backward, my heels sliding against the smooth glass of the waterway. The crowd shifted, clearing the space for our fight. A five.

The shouts and cheers grew as more people came to watch.

Did they know? Did they know who I was? Or did they just see a beat-down soturion?

The wolf who'd recognized me approached first; his fists ready. I blocked his first punch, dodged and missed the second, but that only put me face to face with a new wolf, as blonde and beady-eyed as the first.

Descendants of the Bastardmaker.

He used the same move, as another came from behind.

They were sloppy, their form lacking. I dodged another hit, and another, turning and fighting each one as they came. My elbow jabbed behind me as I broke out of their hold. And I debated, ending it now. Taking them all out.

But the attention I'd receive from doing so would be more than I could afford. They'd all know who I was, and word would spread. Fast. Too fast.

I let myself falter. Mis-stepped on purpose. The soturion to my left knocked me to the ground.

He grabbed the back of my head, smashing my face into the waterway. I cursed, preparing to roll out of his hold and kick as the crowd's jeers grew louder, bolder.

And then, somehow, rising above it all, there was only one voice. A voice that had haunted my dreams for years. A voice that had whispered to me in my sleep. A voice that was no longer muffled behind a fortress wall.

"Stop! Release him at once." Lyriana. Lyriana had left the safety of her litter. Had come to break up the fight. *No. No.* What was she doing? She wasn't supposed to be in the middle of the mob. She wasn't supposed to see me.

"Under whose orders, girl?" asked the soturion to my right.

"Under mine," she said, her voice clear and full of authority. There was a certain power that I knew came from being an heir. But the sheer power in her voice? The force of will? That? That was all her. "You stand in the streets of Urtavia, Bamaria, ruled by Arkasva Batavia. Ka Kormac has no authority here. Now cease and let him go. I command you."

Laughter followed her demand. But she'd created enough of a spectacle to draw the attention of the crowd, to keep my attackers from realizing I was back on my feet, slowly standing, unable to take my eyes off of her. I was transfixed, hypnotized by her presence.

Even beneath her cloak, her face still partially concealed, I could see what my heart had feared. She'd grown only more beautiful, and devastating. There was a fire in those hazel eyes, the same defiance she'd had in my dreams as she looked me up and down. Her mouth opened, her perfectly pink lips forming an O as a hint of her perfume made its way to me. Vanilla. Musk. Just the slightest hint of lemon.

I could feel the moment she recognized me, feel a pull in my soul.

And just like that, my resolve was gone. I'd been a fool. My will wasn't stronger than my heart. My heart was beating so hard I thought it would burst.

I was lost. I forgot the crowd. I forgot Tristan was standing behind her. I forgot it had been three years, forgot I'd broken her heart when I left.

Forgot that mine was still in pieces.

It was solstice and the air was warm, and she was in my arms and the lover's song was playing and we were dancing, and the night was beautiful and everything felt right. Felt like home, like destiny. And I never wanted to let her go. Never wanted to leave her side. I remembered wanting to drop to my knees, wanting to ask her to spend her life with me.

Remembered wanting to live in that moment forever.

Because the wind was soft and I had her pressed against the tree, stars in her eyes, her breath on my lips, her body against mine. The memory seared into my flesh. Into my soul.

I'd been lying to myself for years. Because my memories of Lyr, and my dreams, no matter how vivid, couldn't compare to the Lyriana standing before me. She looked as fierce as a queen. As powerful as a goddess. The most beautiful girl I'd ever seen.

And I loved her. I loved her with everything I was. Everything I had.

I couldn't turn it off. Couldn't stop. Not if my life depended on it. And though I knew every oath I had sworn, every promise I'd made to myself that I could handle this, that this *would* be enough, that being alive and being near her and knowing she was safe was enough...

It wasn't.

My blood was pulsing and she was saying yes when I asked to kiss her and it wasn't enough. It was never ever going to be enough.

The shouts from the mob grew louder, and the wolves of Ka Kormac snarled, and those who would unseat her father, who would come for Lyr's blood and plotted against her, closed in on us.

She was in danger, and I had to protect her.

I made my choice.

This had to be enough. Had to be it. Because I swore, I would keep her safe. And if I was going to do this, if I was going to do this right, I had to remember my place. I was forsworn. I was her bodyguard.

Not *Lord Rhyan Hart.*

Just a soturion. Just a bastard now. No one else.

I stared into her eyes, and my heart surged. And I let it. Just for a beat. Just once.

I felt everything. My entire body came alive, my blood was pounding.

And then I pushed my feelings down. Forced my heart to still.

To stop beating. To stop feeling. To forget.

And then I smiled.

"Hello, lover."

WARRIOR OF THE DROWNED EMPIRE

THE STORY CONTINUES IN THE DROWNED EMPIRE
SERIES, #4

BASTARD OF THE DROWNED EMPIRE

RHYAN'S JOURNEY CONTINUES IN THE DROWNED
EMPIRE SERIES #2.5

GLOSSARY

Names:

Aemon Melvik (Ae-mon Mel-vik): Warlord of Bamaria, Arkturion on the Council of Bamaria, also known as the Ready.

Afeya (Ah-fay-ah): Immortal Lumerians who survived the Drowning. Prior to, Afeya were non-distinguishable from other Lumerians in Lumeria Matavia. They were descended from the Gods and Goddesses, trapped in the mortal coil. But they refused the request to join the war efforts. Some sources believe they allied with Moriel's forces and the akadim. When the Valalumir shattered, they were cursed to live forever, unable to return to their home, be relieved of life, or touch or perform magic—unless asked to by another.

Asherah (A-sher-ah): Original Guardian of the Valalumir in Heaven. She was banished to Earth as a mortal after her affair with Auriel was discovered.

Aiden DeKassas (Ai-dan Deh-cah-sus): Nephew of the Master of Finance, a noble mage in Rhyan's inner circle.

Auriel (Or-ree-el): Original Guardian of the Valalumir in

435

Heaven, stole the light to bring to Earth where it turned into a crystal before shattering at the time of the Drowning.

Avery Kormac (Ae-very Core-mac): Nephew to the Emperor, as Imperator, he rules over the six southern countries of the Empire, as well as ruling Korteria as the Arkasva.

Dario DeTerria (Dar-ree-yo Deh-tair-ree-yah): Son of the Master of Peace, a noble soturion in Rhyan's inner circle.

Efraim Aravain (Eh-fry-yeem Ar-rah-vain): Turion, Second to Arkturion Kane, Garrett's father.

Garrett Aravain (Ger-ret Ar-rah-vain): Son of Glemaria's Turion, a soturion in Rhyan's inner circle.

Kane Gadayyan (Cain Gaw-die-yan): Arkturion and Warlord of Glemaria.

Kenna Gaddayan (Ken-nah Gaw-die-yan): Eldest daughter of Glemaria's warlord, mage in Rhyan's inner circle.

Lyriana Batavia (Leer-ree-ana Ba-tah-via): Third in line to the Seat of Power in Bamaria.

Mercurial (Mer-cure-ree-el): An immortal Afeya, First Messenger of her Highness Queen Ishtara, High Lady of the Night Lands.

Moriel (Mor-ree-el): Original Guardian of the Valalumir in Heaven. He reported Auriel and Asherah's affair to the Council of 44 leading to Asherah's banishment, Auriel's theft of the light, and its subsequent destruction. He was banished to Earth where he allied with the akadim in the war that led to the Drowning.

Rhyan Hart (Ry-an Hart): Forsworn and exiled from Glemaria. Previously was in first in line to the Seat of Power (Heir Apparent).

Ronan DeTerria (Row-nan Deh-tair-ree-yah): Master of Peace in Glemaria.

Shakina Hart (Shah-kee-nah Hart): Noblewoman of Glemaria, wife to the Imperator and Arkasva, mother to Rhyan.

Theotis (Thee-otis): Current Emperor of Lumeria Nutavia. Theotis was previously from Korteria, and a noble of Ka Kormac. His nephew, Avery Kormac, is the current Imperator to the Southern hemisphere of the Empire, and Arkasva to Korteria.

Thorin Oryyan (Thor-in Or-ree-yan): Apprentice soturion assigned to train Rhyan, and part of his kashonim. Nephew to the Senator of Glemaria.

Places:

Aravia (Ar-ray-vee-ah): Northern country bordering Glemaria.

Bamaria (Ba-mar-ria): Southernmost country of the Lumerian Empire, home of the South's most prestigious University and the Great Library. Ruled by Ka Batavia.

Cretanya (Creh-tawn-yah): Northernmost country of the south, ruled by Ka Zarine. Its main city is Thene, and is a popular tourist spot for Lumerians.

Damara (Da-mar-ra): A Southern country known for strong warriors, ruled by Ka Daquataine.

Elyria (El-leer-ria): Historically ruled by Ka Azria, rulership has now passed to Ka Elys, originally nobility from Bamaria.

Glemaria (Gleh-mar-ria): Northernmost country of the Empire, ruled by Ka Hart. Imperator Devon Hart is the Arkasva and Imperator to the North. Rhyan Hart was previously first in line to the Seat.

Hartavia (Har-tay-vee-yah): Northern country of origin for Imperator Hart, ruled by Ka Taria.

Korteria (Kor-ter-ria): Westernmost country in the Empire. Magic is least effective in their mountains, but

Korteria does have access to Starfire for Lumerian weapons. Ruled by Ka Kormac.

Lethea (Lee-thee-a): The only part of the Empire located in the Lumerian Ocean. Ruled by Ka Maras, this is the country where criminals stripped of powers, or accused of vorakh are sent for imprisonment. The expression "Farther than Lethea" comes from the fact that there is nothing but ocean beyond the island. Due to the Drowning, the idea of going past the island is akin to losing one's mind.

Lumeria (Lu-mair-ria): The name of continent where Gods and Goddesses first incarnated until it sank into the Lumerian Ocean in the Drowning.

Matavia (Ma-tah-via): Motherland. When used with Lumeria, it refers to the continent that sank.

Nutavia (New-tah-via): New land. When used with Lumeria, it refers to the Empire forged after the Drowning by those who survived and made it to Bamaria—previously Dobra.

Prominent Creatures of the Old World Known to Have Survived the Drowning:

Seraphim (Ser-a-feem): Birds with wings of gold, they resemble a cross between an eagle and a dove. Seraphim are peaceful creatures, sacred in Bamaria, and most often used for transport across the Lumerian Empire. Though delicate in appearance, they are extremely strong and can carry loads of up ten people over short distances. Seraphim all prefer warmer climates and are rarely found in the northernmost part of the Empire.

Ashvan: Flying horses. These are the only sky creatures that do not possess wings. Their flight comes from magic contained in their hooves. Once an ashvan picks up speed, their magic will create small temporary pathways to run upon. Technically, ashvan cannot fly, but are running on magic pathways that appear and vanish once stepped upon. Residue of the magic is left behind, creating streaks behind them, but these fade within seconds.

Nahashim: Snakes with the ability to grow and shrink at will, able to fit into any size space for the purposes of seeking. Anything lost or desired can almost always be found by a nahashim. Their scales remain almost burning hot and they prefer to live near the water. Most nahashim are bred on Lethea, the country furthest out into the ocean, closest to the original location of Lumeria Matavia.

Gryphon (Grif-in): Sky creatures that are half eagle, half lion. Extremely large, these animals can be taken into battle, preferring mountains and colder climates. They replace seraphim and ashvan in the northernmost parts of the Lumerian Empire. They may carry far heavier loads than seraphim.

Akadim (A-ka-deem): The most feared of all creatures, literally bodies without souls. Akadim kill by eating the soul of their victims. The demonic creatures were previously Lumerians transformed. Akadim grow to be twice the size of a Lumerian and gain five times the strength of a soturion. Immortal as long as they continue to feed on souls, these creatures are impervious to Lumerian magic. Akadim are weakened by the sun and tend to live in the Northern Hemisphere.

Water Dragon: Dragons with blue scales that live deep in the Lumerian Ocean. Previously spending their time equally between land and water, all water dragons have taken to the Lumerian Ocean and are usually spotted closer to Lethea.

Agnavim (Ahg-naw-veem): Rarely sighted in Lumerian lands. These red birds with wings made of pure flame favor the lands occupied by the Afeyan Star Court. Lumerians have been unable to tame them since the Drowning.

Terms/Items:

Alissedari (All-is-a-dar-ree): An ancient soturion tournament fought on gryphon back. Previously fought in honor of kings and queens. Ends with the first death, or last gryphon rider standing.

Birth Bind/Binding: Unlike a traditional bind which includes a spell that ties a rope around a Lumerian to keep them from touching their power, or restricting their physical ability to move a Birth Bind leaves no mark. A Binding is temporary, and can have more or less strength and heat depending on the mage casting the spell. A Birth Bind is given to all Lumerians in their first year of life, a spell that will keep them from accessing their magic power whenever it develops. All Lumerians develop their magic along with puberty. The Birth Bind may only be removed after the Lumerian has turned nineteen, the age of adulthood.

Dagger: Ceremonial weapon given to soturi. The dagger has no special power on its own as the magic of a soturion is transmuted through their body.

Ka (Kah): Soul. A Ka is a soul tribe or family.

Kashonim (Ka-show-neem): Ancestral lineage and link of power. Calling on Kashonim allows you to absorb the power of your lineage, but depending on the situation, usage can be dangerous. For one, it can be an overwhelming amount of power that leaves you unconscious if you come from a long lineage, or a particularly powerful one. Two, it has the potential to weaken the mages or soturi the caller is drawing from. It is also illegal to use against fellow students.

Kavim (Ka-veem): Plural of Ka. A Ka can be likened to a soul tribe or family. When marriages occur, either member of the union may take on the name of their significant other's Ka. Typically, the Ka with more prestige or nobility will be used thus ensuring the most powerful Kavim continue to grow.

Laurel of the Arkasva (Lor-el of the Ar-kas-va): A golden circlet like a crown worn by the Arkasva. The Arkasva replaced the title of King and Queen in Lumeria Matavia, and the Laurel replaced the crown though they are held in the same high esteem.

Mekarim (Mee-kah-reem): Soulmates

Mekara (Mee-kah-rah): Term of endearment, translates to "My soul is yours."

Seat of Power: Akin to a throne. Thrones were replaced by Seats in Lumeria Nutavia, as many members of royalty were blamed by the citizens of Lumeria for the Drowning. Much as a monarch may have a throne room, the Arkasvim have a Seating Room. The Arkasva typically has a Seat of Power in their Seating Room in their Ka's fortress, and another in their temple.

Stave: Made of twisted moon and sun wood, the stave transmutes magic created by mages. A stave is not needed to perform magic, but greatly focuses and strengthens it. More magic being transmuted may require a larger stave.

Vadati (Va-dah-tee): Stones that allow Lumerians to hear and speak to each other over vast distances. Most of these stones were lost in the Drowning. The Empire now keeps a strict registry of each known stone.

Valalumir (Val-la-loo-meer): The sacred light of Heaven that began the Celestial War which began in Heaven and ended with the Drowning. The light was guarded by seven Gods and Goddesses until Asherah and Auriel's affair. Asherah was banished to become mortal, and Auriel fell to bring her the light. Part of the light went into Asherah before it crystalized. When the war ended, the Valalumir shattered in seven pieces —all lost in the Drowning.

Valya (Val-yah): The sacred text of recounting the history of the Lumerian people up until the Drowning. There are multiple valyas recorded, each with slight variations, but the Mar Valya is the standard. Another popular translation is the Tavia Valya which is believed to have been better preserved than the Mar Valya after the Drowning, but was never made into the standard for copying. Slight changes or possible effects of water damage offer different insights into Auriel's initial meeting with Asherah.

Vorakh (Vor-rock): Taboo, forbidden powers. Three magical abilities that faded after the Drowning are considered illegal: visions, mind-reading, and traveling by mind. Vorakh can be translated as "gift from the Gods" in High Lumerian, but is now translated as "curse from the Gods."

THE EMPIRE OF LUMERIA

There are twelve countries united under the Lumerian Empire. The 12 Ruling Kavim of Lumeria Nutavia. Each country is ruled by an Arkasva, the High Lord or Lady of the ruling Ka.

All twelve countries submit to the rule and law of the Emperor. Each Arkasva also answers to an Imperator, one Arkasva with jurisdiction over each country in either the Northern or Southern hemispheres of the Empire.

In addition to the Emperor's rule, twelve senators, one from each country (may not be a member of the ruling Ka) fill the twelve seats of the Senate. The roles of Imperator and Emperor are lifelong appointments. They may not be passed onto family members. Imperators and Emperors must be elected by the ruling Kavim. Kavim may not submit a candidate for either role if the previous Imperator or Emperor belonged to their Ka.

Imperators may keep their ties to their Ka and rule in their country. An Emperor will lose their Ka upon anointing and must be like a father or mother to all Lumerians.

EMPIRIC CHAIN OF COMMAND
EMPEROR THEOTIS, HIGH LORD OF LUMERIA NUTAVIA

The Emperor rules over the entire Empire, from its capitol, Numeria. The Emperor oversees the running of the Senate, and the twelve countries united under the Empire.

Devon Hart, Imperator to the North
The Imperator of the North if an Arkasva who rules not only their country, but oversees rule of the remaining five countries belonging to the North. His rule includes the following countries currently by the following Kavim:

Glemaria, Ka Hart
Payunmar, Ka Valyan
Hartavia, Ka Taria
Ereztia, Ka Sephiron
Aravia, Ka Lumerin
Sindhuvine, Ka Kether

Avery Kormac, Imperator to the South
The Imperator of the South is an Arkasva who rules not only their country, but oversees rule of the remaining five

countries belonging to the North. The sitting Imperator is also nephew to the Emperor. His rule includes the following countries currently being ruled by the following Kavim:

Bamaria, Ka Batavia

Korteria, Ka Kormac

Elyria, Ka Elys (previously Ka Azria)

Damara, Ka Daquataine

Lethea, Ka Maras

Cretanya, Ka Zarine

The Immortal Afeyan Courts*

The Sun Court: El Zandria, ruled by King RaKanam

The Moon Court: Khemet, ruled by Queen Ma'Nia

The Star Court: Night Lands, ruled by Queen Ishtara

Afeyan Courts are not considered part of the Lumerian Empire, nor do they submit to the Emperor, however, history, prior treaties, and trade agreements have kept the courts at peace, and working together. They are the only two groups to have shared life on the continent of Lumeria Matavia.

TITLES AND FORMS OF ADDRESS

Apprentice: The term used to describe a soturion or mage who has passed their first three years of training. As an apprentice their time is divided between their own studies and teaching the novice they are bound to. This is done to strengthen the power of Kashonim, and because of the Bamarian philosophy that teaching a subject is the best way to learn and master a subject.

Arkasva (Ark-kas-va): Ruler of the country, literally translates as the "will of the highest soul."

Arkasvim (Ark-kas-veem): Plural of Arkasva

Arkturion (Ark-tor-ree-an): Warlord for the country, general of their soturi/army.

Emperor: Ruler of all twelve countries in the Lumerian Empire. The Emperor is elected by the ruling arkasvim. They are appointed for life. Once an Emperor or Empress dies, the Kavim must elect a new ruler. The Emperor must renounce their Ka when anointed, but no Ka may produce an Emperor/Empress twice in a row.

Forsworn: Derogatory term for a Lumerian who has

broken an oath. May be an oath breaker, or someone considered criminal. It is also used for those facing exile from their countries.

Heir Apparent: Title given to the eldest child or heir of the Arkasva. The next in line to the Seat of Power or First from the Seat.

Imperator: A miniature Emperor. The Empire always has two Imperators, one for the Northern Hemisphere, one for the South. The Imperator will also be the arkasva of their country, they have jurisdiction over their hemisphere but also act as a voice and direct messenger between each Arkasva and the Emperor.

Lady: Formal address for a female, or female-identifying member of the nobility.

Lord: Formal address for a male, or male-identifying member of the nobility.

Mage: A Lumerian who transmutes magic through spells. A stave is used to focus their magic. The more focus one has, the less a stave is needed, but the more magic one can use, the larger the stave may need to be. Arkmages (the high mages) tend to have staves as tall as them.

Novice: The term used to describe a soturion or mage who is in the beginning of their learning to become an anointed mage or soturion.

Soturion: Soldier, magically enhanced warrior. A Lumerian who can transmute magic through their body. May be used as a form of address for a non-noble.

Soturi: Plural of soturion. May refer to multiple soldiers or an army

Turion: Commander, may lead legions of soturi, must answer to their Arkturion.

Turi: Plural of turion

Your Grace: Formal address for any member of the ruling

Ka. Anyone who is in line to the Seat of Power must be addressed so, including the Arkasva. A noble may only be addressed as "your grace" if they are in line to the Seat.

Your Highness: Reserved as formal address only for the member of Lumerian nobility serving as imperator. The term of address has also been adopted by the Afeyan Star Court.

Your Majesty: Used only for the Emperor or Empress. Previously used for the kings and queens of Lumeria Matavia. This can also be applied to the King and Queen of the Afeyan Sun and Moon Courts.

ACKNOWLEDGMENTS

I feel like I wrote Son in a fever dream. Time was moving very quickly and yet very slowly at the same time. It always felt like the book was never going to be finished, like I just started it, until suddenly it was finished, and much much longer than I'd anticipated. This was such a treat to write after Lady. I loved going back into Rhyan's mind, even though it hurts sometimes. But I love writing him, love filling in and deepening the gaps of knowledge we had, and I'm so grateful to every reader who was excited for more of his POV.

And a huge, huge thank you to the growing team and collaborators for Seven Queens Press!

Sara DeSabato, holy crap! You came in clutch with those developmental edits and seriously helped Son become what it was meant to be. Very few people on the planet know me and this world well enough to be able to extract things from my brain in their mushy form, and make them understandable and pretty. You always knew what I was trying to say, or do, and helped me execute it beautifully and I cannot thank you enough!!! Who knew after all these years, we'd be here, but it's literally perfect and you deserve every editing award there is! Also thank you for yelling at me to finish my edits, lol.

To the members of Corporate, I love our meetings and team calls. I love that reality has nothing to do with our organization. And I am forever grateful to you both for keeping me grounded, and sane, and calling me in, and making me breathe, and sometimes forcing me to do annoying things like relax and take vacations. Also I'm never going to the Seaport again. Except I probably will (just never at 4PM). Whatever. Thank you!

Marcella Haddad, the constant mind resetting is something I can never thank you enough for, even though you really tried to distract me this time! It's okay though, I did it! Thank you forever for your support.

Asha Venkataraman, thank you for literally holding my hair back (you know when) and for always being an enthusiastic beta reader. Your support really helped me to keep going.

Danielle Dyal, amazing, fast copy edits as always! Thank you!

Heather Creeden, so happy to have you join the team! I'm still in awe of how quickly and thoroughly you worked, and your video reactions were absolutely as amazing as your notes! Thank you!

Stefanie Saw, this cover is so magical, you have no idea! I love working with you.

Saint Jupiter, you just elevated everything to a place I could only dream of with your design! The gasp is still gasping.

Morgan Madden, thank you for coming in and organizing the hundreds of tabs I used to have open in my brain. I was able to focus so much more on writing and I am so grateful to you.

Donna Kuzma, just thank you for existing! We're going to do so much more!

Steve Kuzma, the stress I'd have trying to maintain what you do...thank you for being the one to do it!

Dylan, Blake, Hannah, Dani—I love you!

Drowned Empire ARC Team, you're rockstars. I'm so grateful for you, and happy you're on this crazy journey with me! You really are the reason we're here today.

And Team Forsworn Mayhem, I love you all! I am grateful for everything you do! Thank you, thank you!

And finally, as always, thank YOU for reading!

Love,

Frankie

Also by the Author

ABOUT FRANKIE DIANE MALLIS

Frankie Diane Mallis is the bestselling author of the fantasy romance Drowned Empire series. The books became #1 bestsellers on Amazon in Greek and Roman Myth and Historical Fantasy. Daughter of the Drowned Empire was also named an indie top pick by Barnes and Noble. She lives outside of Philadelphia where she practices yoga and belly dance, and can usually be found baking gluten free desserts. To learn more, visit www.frankiedianemallis.com, and join the newsletter. Follow Frankie on Instagram @frankiediane, and on TikTok @frankiedianebooks.